ANGEL BETRAYED

ANGEL
BETRAYED

CYNTHIA
EDEN

KENSINGTON BOOKS
www.kensingtonbooks.com

KENSINGTON BOOKS are published by

Kensington Publishing Corp.
119 West 40th Street
New York, NY 10018

All Kensington titles, imprints and distributed lines are available at special quantity discounts for bulk purchases for sales promotion, premiums, fund-raising, educational or institutional use. Special book excerpts or customized printings can also be created to fit specific needs. For details, write or phone the office of the Kensington Special Sales Manager: Kensington Publishing Corp., 119 West 40th Street, New York, NY 10018. Attn. Special Sales Department. Phone: 1-800-221-2647.

Kensington and the K logo Reg. U.S. Pat. & TM Off.

ISBN-13: 978-0-7582-6762-7
ISBN-10: 0-7582-6762-2
First Kensington Trade Edition: July 2012
First Kensington Mass Market Edition: July 2016

eISBN-13: 978-0-7582-7852-4
eISBN-10: 0-7582-7852-7
First Kensington Electronic Edition: July 2012

10 9 8 7 6 5 4 3 2

Printed in the United States of America

For Brad.

Sometimes, heroes can be good guys, too.

PROLOGUE

Death could be kind or he could be cruel. Tonight, he felt damn cruel.

Sammael's dark wings flapped behind him as he watched his prey. The stench of blood and sweat clung to the men. They'd fought hard and long that day. They'd killed so many—men, women, and children. Sammael had taken the souls from the broken bodies. They'd seen him coming—only those slipping from the mortal world ever saw an Angel of Death—and their eyes had filled with terror.

So many dead in such a short time. He'd watched their slaughter. Stood back while they begged and screamed.

His job was only to take the souls. He gave them peace after their suffering. He served. He didn't question.

Until now.

There was no reason for him to be in this forest. No reason for him to watch these men. They weren't on the list for death, not tonight anyway.

They were laughing and drinking. They didn't sense him. No one ever did—not until it was too late.

Blood still stained their hands.

Watch and wait and take the souls when it is time.
That was his job, and it was the job he'd done for centuries.

Angels didn't feel emotion. They didn't feel lust or love or rage.

No, angels weren't *supposed* to feel. But he'd never fit into that perfect mold. Lately, he'd been feeling too much, and he just couldn't shut off the fury.

Sammael dropped to the ground. His wings closed in behind him. To kill, to take a soul, he only needed one touch. Just one.

He smiled at the men. Some were stiffening and glancing around, as if they sensed him.

They only see when death is at hand.

Sammael reached for the first man. *Death is at hand for you.*

One touch and the human fell to the ground with an expression of twisted agony contorting his face. The laughter stopped then, and the scent of fear teased Sammael's nose.

His black wings spread behind him, powerful and strong. When the others began to run and scream, his smile stretched.

No more watching.

Another touch and another body hit the ground. Again and again. The laughter that filled the air was his now. He had the power, and he didn't feel like being *kind* to the mortals around him.

Shouts of "devil" and "monster" filled the air. The shouts were almost insulting, but he didn't really expect these fools to recognize an angel.

They saw him now because he'd changed their fate. *Marked by Death now.* Death was closing in, and they couldn't fight him. There would be no escape.

When they ran, he just flew after them. He caught

the men, lifted them up into the air, and then tossed their dead bodies back to the ground.

"Please . . . *mercy!*" One man's desperate cry.

He had no mercy.

He touched and he killed . . . until no one was left.

When the haze of rage cleared from his eyes, the dead circled him.

The smile still lifted his lips when the wind began to whip against Sammael's body. The wind howled, screaming like the dead men, no, like those women had screamed earlier that day when they'd been slaughtered. Like the children had screamed when he'd just stood there and watched the bastards attack.

No more watching.

He had the power. He'd take it, and he'd kill anyone he wanted.

Sammael's body jerked into the air. He flew, high, higher, way past the clouds and back to the domain of the angels. But he didn't return to heaven on his own accord. They yanked him back.

"*Sammael.*" His brother's voice boomed as Sammael dropped onto the marble floor. "What have you done?"

Sammael rose slowly and let his wings stretch behind him. His shoulders rolled as he stared at Azrael. He didn't have to answer to the other angel. When it came to the hierarchy of the Death Angels, Sammael was at the top. Everyone else should bow to him. They should all learn that lesson. "Don't dare to question me." He *was* the power. It was past time that he started to use that strength.

But his brother just shook his blond head. "You took them. It wasn't their time."

"I made it their time." No apology. His gaze swept the room. Heavy with thick, white columns. Walls adorned with gold. Perfect. Opulent.

Prison.

Sammael turned away and headed for the gold-plated doors.

Az appeared in his path and blocked his way. The other angel had always been fast.

I'm faster.

"We don't judge," Az said, voice flat. "We deliver those that are charged to us. We are not to interfere in the lives of humans. You *know* this." Ah, his brother had better be careful. It almost sounded like some emotion had slipped into his voice.

"I know we have the power to kill," Sammael told him. "So I killed." And for the first time, it had felt . . . good. *Want more.*

"No, you punished."

Perhaps. But those men had deserved a good punishment. An eye for an eye, and a death for a death.

"There are others who dole out punishment," Az continued, his bright blue stare seeming to blaze right at Sammael. "Uriel is—"

"I just served them up to Uriel early." Uriel and the band of punishment angels that served under his wings. Wrath. Destruction. Annihilation.

Oh, how he envied them.

Envy. One of the seven deadly sins. Angels weren't supposed to sin. Only men could sin and be forgiven. Angels weren't allowed that luxury.

They can torture, they can kill.

What about me?

"They would have found their way to Uriel's hands sooner or later," Sammael said with a dismissive wave. He didn't back away from his brother. He never would. "I just sped up the process."

Az shook his head, and his hair brushed his shoulders. "You disobeyed."

Sammael was tired of pretending. *Not perfect.* "And

I'll do it again." He let the grim smile tilt his lips once more. "Humans don't have the power. We do. *I do.*" He'd be using his power from now on. Humans would learn they should be afraid.

"That is not the way!"

"It is for me." He shoved his brother aside. "The rules are changing. The ones who get in my way . . . they will fear, and they will die." Because he wasn't going to *watch* anything, not anymore.

"Brother . . ." Az sighed after him. "Do you know what you've done?"

The golden doors wouldn't open. Sammael grabbed them and pushed as hard as he could, but they wouldn't budge. The wind was howling again and that painful screech filled his ears.

Angels don't feel pain. But that wind—the noise hurt.

The wind caught Sammael's body and carried him into the air. He hung suspended, his wings flapping helplessly and his body straining, as Az slowly walked around him.

"There's still time," Az murmured, brows pulling together. "Ask forgiveness, brother. Change your ways and you can—"

Watch for an eternity. Hear the screams and do nothing. See the blood and only know the smell of death.

Sammael kept the smile on his face. "I ask for nothing. From now on, I take." Lives. Souls. *Everything*.

Az's eyes narrowed. "Then you die."

With those words, he fell. The elaborate room vanished as Sammael plummeted from the sky. Wind whipped around him, biting into his flesh as he fell, faster, faster, and—

Agony ripped through his body. A white-hot fire consumed him, burning . . . *"Az!"*

But his brother wasn't helping him. No one helped

him. He fell, and he burned. His wings—always the most sensitive part of his body—burned the longest, the hottest.

He screamed and screamed and seemed to fall forever.

When he hit, he expected death. Az had promised death.

But Sammael wasn't dead. Broken, bloody, and burned, but not dead.

Not yet.

And that was just the start of the hell to come.

CHAPTER ONE

The devil owed her a favor, and it was time that Seline O'Shaw called in that debt.

"Well, well . . ." Sammael—*Sam* because he'd long ago dropped the more formal version of his name—raked her with his bright blue stare as she made her way across the crowded New Orleans club and to his side. "Come back for another dance, have you?" His deep voice cut easily through the laughter and whispers that floated in the air.

Dance. Seline's eyes narrowed. "Not tonight." No, tonight she was waiting tables at Sunrise and wearing one of those skimpy black dresses that all the waitresses were forced to squeeze into before each shift. Thankfully, she wasn't scheduled to go onstage again. *Too dangerous.* She'd only danced twice, and she didn't plan to hop up there again. Seline risked a quick glance over her shoulder. "I need to talk with you," she said as her voice dropped.

Sam wasn't alone. But then, he was the big, bad-ass *Other* in the city so he usually had company. Not guards exactly. Why would he need guards? If the stories were true, Sam could kill with a touch. The man wasn't human, not even close.

So, no, the demons weren't around to guard him, but she knew they were there to pretty much jump when he so much as whispered an order. Demon attack dogs.

"Go ahead," he invited softly, his voice low and rumbling, "talk."

Right. Like she was going to bare her soul with his two demon goons right next to him. And Seline knew the guys on either side of Sam were demons. Most folks probably would have thought they were humans— very dangerous looking humans—but *not* demons.

Seline wasn't most folks, and she damn well knew a demon when she saw one. After all, she'd been born with the special curse of being able to see right past a demon's glamour. She didn't have the luxury of pretending that monsters weren't real. She saw monsters every day.

And every time I look into the mirror.

"Alone." She cleared her throat because the word came out way too husky. She really had to watch that. She wasn't trying to seduce Sam, not yet anyway. "I need to talk to you . . ." She let her gaze dart to the goons. *"Alone."*

Sam waved his right hand, and the demons rose. They disappeared into the crowd like good little flunkies even as Sam edged away from the table and closed in on her.

She didn't back down. Seline tilted her head so she could meet his blue stare. The guy was big—had to be at least six feet three, maybe six feet four—muscled, and too sexy by far.

He was also the deadliest man she'd ever met. *Don't forget that. Remember who he is, what he is.*

Death.

Strange. She'd never thought Death would be particularly sexy. He was.

His eyes were the brightest blue she'd ever seen. His cheeks were high, his jaw hard and strong, and his lips—sensual, but with an edge of cruelty she couldn't miss.

Sam took her hand. "Come with me."

A shiver slipped over her at his touch. She hadn't expected her reaction to Sam. The first time she'd seen him, she'd . . . wanted him and that wasn't the way things were supposed to work in her world. She was the one desired. The one wanted. That was the way she'd been made. She might not like the life she'd been given, but screw the bitching and moaning routine. Seline couldn't control what she was, but she could use her power.

Sam led her through the crowd and to a small door on the side of the club. The private room. Yeah, she knew the place. She'd been working at Sunrise for a while now, and she'd learned the rules. This room was for the VIPs. A place for them to have quick sex, to run a business deal, or to party the night away. All without having to worry about any prying eyes watching.

Unless you *wanted* to be watched, because she knew some folks in Sunrise liked that, too.

The bouncer at the door immediately let Sam inside. Figured he'd get instant access because right then, she knew Sam was the most important VIP in the place.

Fear had a way of making certain people very, very important.

The door closed behind her with a soft click. *No watching*. Seline's heart did a too-fast kick when Sam turned around and locked his stare on her. "Better now?" he asked with a twist of his lips. *Sexy lips*. "I'm all yours." He crossed his arms over his chest and watched her with a gaze that always saw too much.

Oh, damn. She swallowed. *Play the game.* "I-I . . . you owe me, Sam."

His dark brows—black to match his midnight mane of hair—rose. "Do I?" His voice was careless, but she saw the intensity in his eyes.

Seline nodded quickly. "I helped you before. I told you—told you when the shifter wanted you dead." Who *didn't* want him dead? But a few weeks ago, she'd tipped Sam off about the very dangerous coyote shifter who'd been hunting him. That tip-off should give her the bargaining power she needed right now.

His head inclined. "So you did." His gaze raked her body, and that hot blue stare lingered a bit too long on her breasts and her thighs.

The top of her "uniform" plunged right between her breasts, and the skirt barely skimmed the tops of her thighs. She shifted slightly beneath his stare but quickly caught herself. "You owe me now, Sam," she reminded him.

That brought his eyes back to hers. His face, that perfect face that didn't belong on someone so dangerous, tilted to study her. Sam might have the reputation of the devil, but the man's face and body were pure perfection. All the better to tempt.

Sometimes she felt like everything about the man was a lie. But, fair enough, she was pretty good at deceiving, too.

She pressed, "You pay your debts, right?" He'd better.

"Depends on the debt."

That wasn't the answer she wanted.

Sam lowered his arms and stalked closer until only a foot of space separated their bodies. The door was closed behind her, and when he leaned in, Sam slapped both of his palms against the wooden frame and caged her with his arms. "What do you need, Seline?"

She wasn't surprised that he knew her name. He'd watched her often enough in the last two months. First, he'd watched her at Temptation. Going in as a dancer had been the only way she knew to get close to Sam—and she *had* to get close.

But when some assholes had torched the joint, she'd had to come up with a real fast plan B. Since she knew Sam spent a lot of time here, she'd taken a waitressing job at Sunrise. *All to stay close to him.*

It had only been later that she'd learned Sam actually owned Sunrise, too.

"Seline?" His breath feathered lightly over her cheek. "What do you want from me?"

Her chin lifted but she kept her hands at her sides. *Don't touch him.* "Protection."

His brows rose.

"I won't lie to you, Sam." Yes, actually, she would. A lot. "I haven't exactly been living the pure and innocent life." Okay, that line was one hundred percent true. "I . . . made a mistake a while back, and now there are some people out there that want me dead."

"Why?"

The door was shut. They were totally alone. She could confess to him. "Because I killed a man." The words seemed to fall into the thick silence of the room. "I didn't plan to do it. It-it was an accident—"

"Was it?"

Her hands clenched into fists. *Ah, caught me.* "No, it wasn't." Again, this part was true. The lies would only come later. "He was an asshole who got off on hurting women. He used his fists any chance he had, and I wasn't gonna be the next body he put in a box." She wouldn't be any man's punching bag.

His eyes studied her. "You're afraid."

Only of a few things in this world.

"Is that why," he continued quietly, "you're always armed?"

He knew?

"With a gun close by, tucked in your purse or . . ." His fingers slid up her thigh. Up, up, stroking over her flesh until he found the sheath of her knife, tucked right on the interior of her thigh. "Or why you keep a knife strapped to your thigh?"

"You can't be too careful," she whispered, her body tight because he was still touching her—and she liked it. *Can't. Too dangerous.* Wanting Sam could make her weak, and lust was a weakness she couldn't afford right then.

Unfortunately for her kind, lust was like kryptonite. The closer the temptation, the stronger the weakness.

"So you need protection." His stare narrowed on her. "What, exactly, does that mean?" He paused. "Do you need a guard? Someone to watch over you? Or . . ." His left hand rose. His fingers curved under her cheek and his thumb brushed over her lips. Her breath caught, and her heart raced in her chest. "Do you want me to kill someone for you, Seline?"

Killing would be easy for him. Sometimes, she worried it might become too easy for her. "I-I don't know what to do. I've been hiding, and I thought I was safe, but they found me."

"They?" His right hand still cradled her thigh and seemed to scorch her flesh.

"His friends. They know what I did, and they aren't the kind of men you can just walk away from." She let fear seep into her voice. The better to sound weak. Men liked it when women were needy, right? *Help me.* "They're dangerous, Sam, and they've got a lot of power."

His gaze searched hers. Then his mouth dipped

close to hers. Seline stopped breathing. He was going to kiss her and her hormones would go wild. *Control.* She had to stay in—

He didn't kiss her. He smiled. And dammit, she'd actually been pressing up on her toes to get closer to him.

Heat stained her cheeks. *I don't blush.* But she was—or rather, she'd started blushing since she met Sam. He made her too uncomfortable.

"What makes you think I'm the kind of man who offers protection?"

She didn't think he'd give her protection. She wasn't a fool. He wasn't the protecting kind.

He was the killing kind.

She wet her lips and felt the tension mount in his body. "I know what you are." Half-truth. She knew what he *wasn't*. She was still working on the rest. Out of a thousand possibilities, she'd narrowed down the choices to a top five list—and nothing on that list was good.

"And what's that?"

Now this was the dangerous part. If she'd calculated wrong, he could attack her. Good thing she wasn't very easy to kill. "You're not human." This she knew with absolute certainty. Demons didn't play guard bitch to humans. The food chain didn't work that way.

No change of expression crossed his face. But his head came closer to hers and his lips—*why would that cruel edge be sexy?*—pressed against her mouth. She expected the kiss to be hard and rough. What else? But when his mouth took hers, it was just . . . a taste.

His tongue licked her lips and stroked inside her mouth. Slow. Easy. As if he were sampling her.

Her tongue slipped to meet his. To taste. To want. *Sam.*

When he pulled back, she had to fight to keep her

hands off him. Or rather, she had to fight not to yank the guy back and take a lot more from him. *Dangerous*.

His gaze studied her a moment, and she barely dared to breathe. "I'm not human," he finally agreed, his voice a deep rumble. "But neither are you, sweetheart. *Neither are you*."

True enough. Now this was the dicey part. Time for some half-truth, half-lies. "You know I'm a demon." Yeah, and good for her, she could admit that truth without flinching in shame anymore.

"Like to like," he murmured. "That's the way, right?"

Right. In the *Other* world, paranormals could recognize their own kind. Maybe it was Mother Nature's way of making sure the *Other* didn't vanish into the mist. If you recognized your own kind, it sure made mating within the same subset easier. Demons could see right through the magic glamour that shielded their kind from human attention. The easiest tip-off that you were dealing with a fellow demon? *Go for the eyes*.

A demon's real eyes were pitch-black. The lens, the sclera—everything was black. But thanks to the glamour that even the least powerful of demons could manage, humans never saw that telling stare. Well, not unless the demons wanted them to see. In that case . . . *good-bye, human*. Because when you saw that darkness, death was coming.

Seline cloaked her black stare with glamour, twenty-four/seven. For her, it was as natural as breathing. When humans looked into her eyes, they saw a warm brown gaze, not that chilling black.

But Sam . . . his eyes were different. She'd caught the slip of his eye color once. Just once—when Temptation had burst into flames, and she'd been trapped in the fire. His bright blue stare had faded to black then. She'd almost missed that change because of the *freaking fire* all around her.

One slip had shown her his true nature. But the problem was that she should have *always* been able to see the black of his eyes. He shouldn't have been able to maintain a shield against her.

Sam wasn't your average demon. Actually, she wasn't even convinced he *was* a demon because there was something else rather unusual about him. When she looked at him hard enough, long enough, Seline could see the dark, shadowy image of . . . wings on his back.

Demons didn't have wings.

Sure, she'd heard of some really, really old demons who had tails and one guy with cloven feet, but wings? Not so much a demon thing.

I know what you are. So that was lie number one for her. When it came to Sam, she didn't know. Not that knowing truly mattered.

"So the people after you . . ." He dropped his hold and stepped back. Seline didn't like that calculating stare he swept over her. "Are they demons?"

"No. They're humans."

He grunted. "Then you should have no problem taking them out." Cold and flat and exactly what she'd expected.

"I'm low level," she admitted, and lowered her eyes because most demons could be ashamed to admit this. *I'm not most.* "Barely a four on the power scale." That wicked demon power scale that had screwed up most of her life. Demon power ranked from a one, barely more than a human in terms of psychic power, to a ten. A ten would be the powerhouse capable of leveling a city block.

She was not such a bad-ass. If only. Her strengths lay in other areas.

Her hands balled into fists. "They'll take me out. I've been running from them for nearly a year, but they keep finding me. They want payback, and they won't stop until they get it."

He sighed. "Seline . . ."

He spoke her name the way a man would say it in bed. Seductive and—

"What in the hell," he continued in that same seductive tone that had her nearly aching, "makes you think I give a damn?"

She blinked. "But . . . but I helped you!" *So not the way I'd imagined this going down.*

He shook his head. "I didn't need your help with the shifter. No coyote will ever be able to take me down."

"If you don't help me, they'll *kill* me." Had he missed that part? She'd thought she emphasized it dramatically well. Maybe she should think about shedding a tear or two.

"I'm not here to save the world," he told her, and then he reached for her again. Wait—the jerk was *moving* her out of his way, not trying to embrace her. Then he yanked open the door and told her, "Sweetheart, I'm just here to watch it burn."

And Sam left her there, with her mouth open. The jerk actually *left* her.

Shit. Time for plan B—and plan B was gonna hurt.

She watched Sam disappear into the crowd. His goons closed back around him, and he whispered to them. Her eyes slit. Oh, she'd make him pay. Was he really so heartless that he wouldn't help a freaking damsel in distress? Hadn't she looked distressed enough to him? Her eyes were actually watering now—she was sure he'd seen that bit. And what about that breathy moan she'd given when he kissed her? That moan had only been half-faked!

Fine. Seline took a deep breath. One, then another, and she let the tears build up. She might have been a low-level demon, but she was also a semi-talented actress. In order to fit in with the humans, she'd had to be.

Her shoulders shook as she pushed her way through the crowd. Seline made sure to rush past Sam and his demons as she sobbed, the better to lay the groundwork for her next plan.

Her hand slammed against the club's back door, and she burst outside. The hot air hit her like a fist as she hurried forward. She lifted her hand and signaled for the man she knew would be waiting.

She'd tried to do this the easy way, but Sam hadn't cooperated. Pity. A real crying shame.

"You're gonna have to use the knife," she said, glancing back over her shoulder. Sam might not even come out after her. He sure didn't seem to be racing to her rescue. But maybe when she started screaming, he'd come play white knight.

The man in the black ski mask nodded once.

Seline exhaled. *So be it.*

She wasn't just going to walk away from Sam. She had a job to do, and she *always* got the job done. Even if she had to bleed to earn her pay.

And she would be bleeding because that knife was about to slice her . . .

The first cut of the blade was always the worst.

Sam stared at the closed exit door. "Seline has a problem," he said to the demons—Marcus and Cole—beside him. *Why do I care? I shouldn't give a damn.* "Check it out. If it's legit, then make sure her problem is eliminated."

Cole nodded. "Someone's bothering her?" Cole's voice held a tight edge. The demon never liked it when someone bothered the women at Sunrise. Definitely a guy with a soft spot for the ladies, even the dangerous ones.

"Seems she's got a past that won't stay dead." Perhaps he would have talked more with Seline, offered her protection in exchange for a few moments in the dark, but he had another agenda then.

His own past wasn't staying dead. His brother was back, and if Sam had his way, he'd be putting the bastard into the ground very, very soon.

A war is coming. Sam could feel the storm clouds gathering.

As delectable as Seline was, he didn't have time for distractions. Azrael had finally gotten his lily-white ass kicked out of heaven, and it was time for a showdown.

Or Armageddon. Whatever came first. Sam didn't have a preference.

Too many angels are falling. The demons are getting restless. A power play is coming.

And, of course, he was getting caught right in the middle of hell.

"Find out who's bothering her," he ordered because he hadn't asked specifics from her. If he'd found out anymore—hell, he would have killed the bastards himself, and that just couldn't happen. He had an angel's ass to kick first. Pleasure kills would have to wait for later. "Make sure she doesn't have to worry again."

Then his debt would be paid because he *did* owe Seline. No one had ever tried to save him before. Mostly because he didn't need saving. But she'd tried, in her way.

So despite his words, he'd help her and maybe one day when the blood washed away, he'd look her up and let sexy Seline thank him properly.

Cole nodded and eased back into the crowd. The demon was probably off to talk to some of the other waitresses so he could get a fix on Seline and her trouble.

Sam waved off Marcus and headed for the exit. He'd

already given Marcus orders earlier. If the guy caught so much as a whisper about Azrael, Sam would know.

He shoved open the club's back door and inhaled the lingering scent of jasmine in the air. Seline's scent. His cock tightened as he remembered the soft silk of her lips beneath his. She hadn't tasted like innocence. No, Seline, the woman who'd stripped and danced on his stage at Temptation, revealing and then instantly concealing her body, was no innocent.

She'd tasted like sin, and sin sure was an aphrodisiac to him.

"Help me!"

The cry had his head whipping to the left, and Sam saw the flash of Seline's long legs as she ran down the alley. Seline wasn't alone. A man in a black ski mask was hauling ass after her, and the bastard had a knife.

The knife lifted and the glinting blade plunged toward Seline's back.

No.

Sam moved in an instant, using the preternatural speed of his kind. He rushed across the pavement, and his body slammed into Seline's. The knife drove into his shoulder even as he and Seline tumbled onto the ground.

Kill. Destroy.

Sam shoved up and barely felt the pain from his wound. He turned for the attacker, ready to rip the man's soul right out of his body.

"Sam!" Seline grabbed him and held tight. Footsteps thudded as the attacker raced away, but Sam's eyes were on Seline. She stared up at him. Her brown eyes swam with tears. "How did you . . . *you're bleeding!*"

Blood ran down his arm in deep rivulets. The jackass had left the knife in Sam's shoulder.

The guy was also *gone*. The squeal of tires grated in

Sam's ears. Fuck. Clenching his teeth, Sam reached up and yanked the knife out of his flesh. The blade had sunk straight into the bone.

You'll pay for that.

Blood spattered around him as he yanked at the knife, and Seline yelled, "No, don't, you'll make it worse!"

Doubtful. She didn't understand who she was dealing with. "The wound will heal." In a few moments, the blood flow would stop, and the skin would mend on its own.

He tossed the knife to the ground and glanced down at her. Seline's thick blond hair tumbled over her shoulders. Her face was pale, too pale, and fear filled her dark eyes.

Definitely pay.

He brushed her hair back, careful not to get any blood on her.

"I thought . . ." She wet her lips with a quick swipe of her pink tongue and whispered, "I thought you didn't care."

You don't want to make me care.

Seline wasn't a classically beautiful woman. Not porcelain perfect.

But she was sexy. *Damn* sexy. She had full, pouting lips and her deep, dark bedroom eyes were surrounded by thick lashes. A sweet little mole rested near the corner of her mouth—he wanted to lick that spot. Her cheeks were high and her chin a little sharp, giving her a slightly exotic look.

And the woman's body . . . when he'd seen her on the stage at Temptation, he hadn't been able to look away. Her legs stretched for miles and her breasts were high, round, and perfect. The woman's body was built for sin, and she could probably make a man beg.

If he were the begging type.

Sam never had been.

"Come on." He grabbed her hand and hoisted Seline to her feet.

"No, your arm—"

He closed his fingers around her shoulders. "I want a name, Seline."

She blinked those sexy eyes at him.

"Tell me who that bastard was, and he's dead." Simple fact. The jerkoff had attacked her *and* left a knife in Sam's flesh. The guy wouldn't be among the breathing for long. Sam would make sure of that fact. He'd also make sure the man's final moments hurt. The days of Death being kind were long gone. Only cruelty remained.

"I-I don't know, I didn't see his face—"

Right. He'd noticed the mask. Sam sucked in a deep breath. "You didn't have to see his face. You knew someone was coming for you. And you know who sent the guy."

She shivered and hunched her shoulders. She stood tall, probably an inch or two under six feet, but despite her curves, her bones had a delicate feel. "I just want it to end."

"It will," he promised. Death was his business, and his business was booming.

She looked at him from beneath the thick veil of her lashes. "You said you wouldn't help me." Her breath hitched a bit, and his hands tightened on her.

"I lied." Like it had been the first time.

She swallowed, and her lips began to curl.

"The name."

Seline threw her arms around him and held on tight. Her body shook against his, and her breasts crushed into his chest.

The scent of jasmine rose over the stench in the alley and filled his nose.

"Thank you." She whispered the words against his neck. Her lips brushed over his skin, and Sam was pretty sure he felt the quick lick of her tongue against him. His body stiffened with sensual tension. When she'd moved, his hand had shifted automatically. His palms now rested on the curve of her ass. What a sweet ass it was.

But now wasn't the time for sex. It was killing time, and he could kill a man as easily as he could caress a lover.

After all, death only needed one touch.

"Please, Sam, get me out of here." Fear had her voice shaking. "I'll tell you everything." She eased back and tilted her head up as she gazed at him. "Just take me to your place. *Get me out of here.*"

Not what he wanted. The thirst for blood and vengeance was too strong then, but he didn't know what kind of attack to expect. The sooner he got her secured, the sooner he'd have his fun. Sam nodded and felt the tightening in his shoulder. The wound was already closing. The attacker would have to do much better next time. He wasn't easy prey.

"Come on." Sam kept her hand in his as he pulled her to the edge of the alley. He was careful to keep his body positioned in front of hers. If another attack came, he'd be ready.

"How did you move so fast?" Her quiet question whispered out after a pause. "You were so far away . . ."

Speed was only one of his many gifts. "I'm not your average demon." He opened the door of his black Jag and waited for her to crawl inside.

"No," her soft voice answered him, "you're not."

Sam slammed the door as his gaze swept the street. Down the road and to the left, a black van waited in the shadows.

He stared at that van; then he grinned.

Come and get me, bastards. He almost crooked his finger in invitation.

Because he wasn't a dumbass demon, and he could smell a fucking setup a mile away. Even when the setup was wrapped in the scent of jasmine and wore a pretty smile.

Not that easy to get to me.

He climbed in the car and gunned the engine.

Time for the real games to begin.

With a flick of his fingers, he locked the door and sealed Seline inside with him.

"He took the bait," Alex Graham said as he yanked the ski mask off his face. "The blind fool fell for her just like all the others have done."

So it would seem.

Rogziel eased back in the seat and watched the Jag's red taillights disappear around the corner. The growl of the engine echoed down the street. He had waited so long for this moment, and now, finally, Sammael's punishment was at hand.

It only seemed fitting that a demon would be the one to send the Fallen to hell.

Sammael had always had a weakness for women and for sin. By the time Seline was done with him, there'd be nothing left of his old friend.

Good.

Ready to burn again, Sam?

Because the fire was sure ready for him. Those flames had been waiting, and it was time for Sammael to face his punishment.

Hell.

CHAPTER TWO

Seline knew where Sam lived. She'd staked out his place shortly after arriving in New Orleans. So when he drove right past the exit leading to the Quarter, her palms began to sweat.

"You never told me the guy's name." Sam's voice was quiet, but held an edge that had her tensing in the leather seat.

"J-John Moorecroft." She thought the stutter in her voice was a good addition. Because a woman who'd nearly been stabbed would be stuttering and trembling, right?

He glanced her way. "John Moorecroft is in prison. His drug ring was busted up six months ago, and the guy is rotting in a cell because he took out a cop during the bust."

All true, and all facts that had made the New Orleans news. Yet there were details that hadn't made the papers . . . "He might be in jail, but he's still got plenty of power." She licked her lips. "He took out a hit on me from his jail cell. Even inside, he still has men ready to jump for him." For the right price. "You don't cross him and get away clean."

They were on the interstate now, and he was driving too fast. Everything passed her in a blur.

"I don't know any other names," she admitted, keeping her voice low. "I don't know who came after me tonight. Probably just some guy looking to cash in on the bounty that's on my head. I-I just want it all to end." Her breath expelled in a rush. "How do you think the cops knew to make that bust? I was the one who tipped them off."

"So you killed John's friend, and turned him in?" He gave a low whistle. "Now he's jonesing for your death."

Not like it was the first time. "I was . . . working at a bar." The cover always worked. It was easy enough for her to get hired at places like that and to work the owners and staff. "I met a guy, his name was Philip Drew. Philip was—"

Insane. The madness had pushed to the surface so easily when he drank. She cleared her throat. "He and John grew up together. They were friends."

The city lurked behind them now, a glittering trail of hazy lights reflected in the water. She swiped her hand along the door handle. "Where are we going?"

He glanced her way, and a faint smile curved his lips. "Don't worry. I'm just taking you someplace safe."

She tried a weak smile in return because his words should have been reassuring.

They weren't.

His gaze returned to the road before them. "Do you trust me, Seline?"

No. Not even for an instant.

"I mean, you came to me, a man you don't really know and you asked me to kill for you."

She swallowed to ease the dryness in her throat. "I asked for your help."

"Because I'm such a fucking helper."

Not exactly. "Because I didn't have anyone else to turn to."

Sam pulled off the interstate, and the car began to rush down the twisting, snaking highway that led into the swamps. There was no light here. Just darkness and predators waiting.

Uneasiness skated down her spine. The plan had worked just as she'd planned, but . . .

Something's wrong.

His low laughter filled the car. "Do you think I'm an idiot?"

No, she didn't, and that was why she was trying to play the game so carefully.

They were off the main highway now. The car bumped along a thin dirt road. The headlights cut a path through the black night.

Finally, finally, a light appeared up ahead. The hunched trees parted and a graveled drive waited. "I'm going to run a check on everything you told me," Sam said. The Jag braked in front of a faded antebellum home. Weathered, but still strong against the swamp. And what the hell was that place doing out there, with its lights shining? It looked creepy. Like something out of a horror movie. Being what she was, Seline should love horror movies.

She couldn't stand them. There were enough monsters in her real life. She didn't want to sit and watch them terrorize people in a movie theater.

"Run the check," she said, her voice too soft.

He killed the engine, and she immediately became aware of the chirping of what sounded like a hundred insects. She knew gators and snakes waited in the shadows. Those were the predators she *didn't* fear, well, not as much as the *Others* that could wait in the night.

Sam turned his head toward her. She could only see

darkness when she looked at his eyes. "If I find out you're lying to me, if this is all some kind of setup . . ."

She didn't flinch. "I need your help. There's a death warrant on me."

His fingers trailed up her arm. "I'm not a good enemy to have."

Neither am I. She tried not to shiver at his touch, but his fingers were slightly rough, and she liked that hint of danger and strength. She had a dark side, too, one that he seemed to arouse too easily. "I don't want you for an enemy. I only want to get my life back."

"If you're telling the truth, I'll give you that life"— he paused—"for a price."

Because everything had a price. She'd never gotten anything for free in this world. Even her birth had been at the price of her mother's life. "What do you want?" she asked. "Sex?" Taking her would be his mistake. Sex would simply give her power and give him a fast trip to hell.

"Eventually." His fingers were still on her arm, and the interior of the car seemed small and tight. The scent of leather and man permeated the air. "But for now, I'll start with a simple trade."

Nothing was ever simple. She had to bite back "Am I the one who looks like an idiot now?" Seline wanted out of that car. He seemed too big and strong, and right then, he had her at a serious disadvantage. Her power was low, and she needed a serious recharge—a recharge she planned to get from him at the earliest opportunity. "When I first asked for help, you—you said no."

His head inclined.

"You were going to let me die." Heartless bastard. Or he would have been, if her story had been true. Since she hadn't actually been in danger of an immediate death . . .

"I'm not here to save the fucking world."

Very true. "But you saved me in the alley."

"Did I?" he murmured. "Guess that is how it appears."

This wasn't going the way she'd planned *at all*. Usually, her plans worked so well. He should have taken her back to his place—that nice apartment in the Quarter—where they would've been under surveillance, and she should have been well on her way to seducing him.

Not. Good.

"I'll get rid of this problem for you, Seline, but when the time comes, I'll need you to do a favor for me."

Offering a deal—wasn't that the way the devil worked?

"What kind of favor?" Not that she'd ever have to hold up her end of the bargain, but . . .

"Does it matter?"

She reached for the door handle. *Locked*. "It does. I'm not trading in one psycho for another."

He laughed, and her head whipped around at the deep, dark rumble. Wonderful. Even his laugh was sexy. The job got worse every minute.

"I know you're not what you pretend to be," Sam said as he leaned toward her. "You're not a stripper, even though you came into Temptation to dance for me."

For me. She'd danced twice. *Twice*. There'd been no choice. She'd worked at Temptation for two weeks as a waitress, and the guy hadn't even glanced her way. She'd needed his attention, and the stage had been her only option at the time.

Seline hadn't realized what a bonus she'd get from the stage. She'd known just how to shield her body and to tempt, a rather inborn trait for a demon like her. But when the crowd had focused all of their energy on her . . .

Power. The rush of energy she'd stolen had been incredible.

And she'd finally caught her mark's attention. Talk about a two-for-one hit.

But Seline hadn't gone back on the stage. Not because she was modest. Modesty was something she'd long ago sacrificed. She hadn't gone back on that wooden stage with the bright lights because she was afraid that she'd steal too much energy from the humans. If she did that, then Sam might start suspecting the truth about her.

"Does it really matter what I am?" she asked him, her fingers still on the door handle.

There was a soft snick of sound as he released the lock. "Everything matters."

She hurried out of the car. Yeah, fine. She jumped and nearly fell. So what? Only a sprinkling of stars lit the dark sky so maybe he hadn't seen that less-than-graceful exit.

"The black van didn't follow us."

Crap. "Wh-what van? Someone was following us? Why didn't you say—"

He slammed his car door shut and shook his head. "You really have to do better than that." Then he started walking toward the house. Gravel crunched beneath his feet. Seline stood there a moment and figured there was no option other than giving chase.

"I don't know what you're talking about." She grabbed his arm, forcing him to stop. "What van?"

He moved in a blur, just like he'd done in the alley. Rushing too fast for her to see the full motions of his body. One instant, they stood a few feet from the car, and in the next second, he had her on the steps of the house, with her back pressed against the wall and his fingers holding tight to her arms. "The black van that was watching us, sweetheart. The one I know you saw, too. Now if you want to keep lying to me . . ."

His breath blew against her cheek.

"You're really gonna piss me off."

She shoved back against him. He didn't move, and she'd even used a bit of her enhanced strength. Fine, if he wanted to play rough, she'd show him rough soon enough. "I'm not trying to piss you off," she gritted out as she kept her chin up. "I'm trying to stay alive. I came to you for help, but you told me to get my ass out of your bar and to take care of myself."

The moonlight showed her his slow blink.

"I got out of Sunrise, and I was jumped in the alley." She pushed against him again. This time, he eased back a bit. "You're the one who came charging out of the club. You didn't have to save me."

"No, I didn't."

If she hadn't already been hired to kill the guy, she really would have thought about doing it for free right then. *Jerk.* "Then why did you?"

He shrugged. *Shrugged.* Time for some payback. "It's been a really long night for me." Seline let her voice tremble. "Please, I just want to go inside and get some sleep." Dawn would come within a few hours.

Perhaps only one of them would make it to see that sun come up.

His hands dropped. "Go to the top of the stairs. You can take the first room to the left."

"Is this your place?" The surprise in her words was real. No one had scoped out this location. Big mistake on their part. Someone on the team had been sloppy.

"It belongs to a friend."

He had friends? Doubtful.

"He owed me, and this place was part of the payment."

Sam turned away and opened the door. "Get inside, Seline. My men will check your story tonight, and if I find out that you're lying, if you're trying to set me up . . ."

"Does that happen a lot?" Seline asked as she brushed by him. "Are people always lying to you?"

"Yes."

Her chin lifted as more lights flooded on inside the house. "Then that's sad. You should be able to trust someone in this world. I mean, don't you even have any family that—"

Oh, yeah. Wrong thing to say. She glanced back and saw his face harden as he slammed the door shut behind them. "Get upstairs."

Wow. That was a barely human growl.

"You know, you really should work on *trying* to be polite. Try asking instead of snapping at people all the time. Charm can work, honestly it can." She shook her head and headed for the stairs.

"Seline."

She didn't stop. Her hand curled around the smooth wood of the banister.

"My brother wants me dead." His rumbling voice followed her. "And the feeling is more than mutual."

Okay, now that made her stop. Seline darted a fast glance back at him, frowning.

"It's a race," he muttered. "We'll see who gets shoved into the ground first."

What was she supposed to say to that? "I'm sorry."

He smiled at her, and the sight wasn't reassuring. "Don't be. It's long past time I ripped Az apart. The world will be a whole lot better once he's gone."

"Why?" She shouldn't ask, but she did anyway. "What's he done? Why would you turn on your own family?" His words hit too close to home for her.

Turn on your own family. She'd been there, done that, and had the scars to prove it.

"Az sent me to hell," he said, voice flat.

She laughed at that, a nervous, rough sound. "Ah, you mean it felt like he did—"

"*No.* The bastard actually sent me to hell."

All the moisture in her mouth dried away.

Sam stared at her. "What? You don't think it's real?" His lips tightened. "News flash. Heaven's there, so is hell."

Her heart slammed too fast and too hard into her chest. "With the devil guarding the gates." She tried to make the words sound flippant.

"Not quite. Not anymore. He's been out of hell for a while now." His head tilted toward her. "But you'll find out the truth soon enough. In the end, we all do." He held her stare a moment longer, then eased out a slow breath. "Get some sleep. Tomorrow, we take care of the bastard after you."

She stared at his dark head. *Tomorrow.*

Seline hurried up the stairs and found the empty room on the left. She hurriedly pushed the door closed behind her and even flipped the lock.

The bastard actually sent me to hell.

This job wasn't turning out like she'd thought. Not at all. But there was no going back now. *Your brother isn't the only one who wants you dead, Sam.* She strode to the bed and stripped off her clothes. *If he wants you, then he can just get in line.*

Because Sammael was a wanted man, and when it came to the killers on his trail—well, she was the one he needed to worry about the most. He'd let her get close, and that was an error that could prove fatal for him.

She climbed into the bed, naked, and closed her

eyes. Sooner or later, Sam would have to find a bed for himself. Even an all-powerful bad-ass had to sleep sometime. She'd know when he slept, she'd feel it. And the instant his eyes closed . . .

You're mine, Sam.

"Cole, how much have you turned up on Seline O'Shaw?" Sam held the phone to his ear as he glanced up the curving staircase. No sound came from Seline's room, and the silence seemed to press onto him.

Sexy. Close.

Dangerous.

"She came to town about six months ago, boss. She went to work at Temptation . . ." Cole's voice floated easily on the line. The guy wasn't telling him a single thing he didn't know. "She's got an apartment in the Quarter, and her neighbors say she never has any visitors."

Okay, that stopped him. "No men?" A woman as sexy as her would have lovers, probably lots of them. Men willing to kill for a taste of her.

Or maybe that's just me.

"Not a single one."

Odd, but good, because he wasn't the sharing sort, and that meant he wouldn't have to kick ass as he cleared territory. Yet . . . *something's off.* "She said that she's on the run from John Moorecroft."

A soft whistle carried over the line as Cole made the connection. "The drug dealer?" Even though he was human, Moorecroft had been able to make some of the *Other* nervous. "What'd she do to piss him off?"

She killed his best friend and turned Moorecroft over to the cops. Set him up and walked away. If her story was true, Seline didn't play nice. Fair enough. Neither did he. Nice didn't usually enter his vocabulary. "Find out, and see if any hits have been put on her." In this city, a strong demon could make anyone talk. Cole was strong and very good at his job. "Pass the word that I'm the one looking for the information." The *Other* world was all about exchanging favors, and a lot of people owed him.

I'll collect from them all. He always did, sooner or later. "Write this down," Sam ordered, and he rattled off the license plate number of the black van he'd spotted. "I want to know who owns this van, and I want to know before the sun comes up."

"Boss, just what the hell is happening?"

His gaze was still on the staircase. "I'm trying to decide if I've got a victim in my house." Victim or . . .

Predator.

"I'll call you back by dawn." Cole's voice was abrupt, and Sam didn't doubt the demon's word. Cole was still busting ass as he tried to prove just how useful he could be.

Demons. Always out to prove themselves. When would they get it? It didn't matter how "good" they pretended to be, they'd always be hated. Always.

Monsters were always feared.

And they were sure as hell not trusted.

Sam ended the call and slowly climbed the stairs. He had another room ready across the hall from Seline's. The better to keep an eye on her. She wouldn't move without him hearing. If she decided to pay him a little late-night visit, he'd be ready—whether that visit was for sex or something far less pleasurable and far more sinister.

Don't trust her.

He knew better than to trust any demon, especially an unknown quantity like her. Maybe he should have just let her die in that alley, but—

Not her.

He'd seen enough women on the ground, with

blood spreading like wings beneath them. When he'd heard her scream, the rage had burst inside of him, and he'd been at Seline's side before he even realized what he was doing.

He'd taken the knife for her. Bled for her. What would she do for him? He'd find out.

Sam hesitated near her door. He could hear no sounds from inside her room. She hadn't balked at being brought into the middle of nowhere, but then, if her story was true, she was hiding from a killer. Maybe being tucked away in the middle of a swamp was just where she wanted to be.

Maybe not.

His fingers curled around the doorknob. He twisted lightly. *Locked.* Sam almost smiled. Like a locked door would keep him out. If he wanted in her bed, nothing would keep him away.

But though he *did* want Seline, now wasn't the time for fucking. Screwing a demon with unknown powers would be a great way for him to get killed. No, better wait until he knew more.

Just a few hours until dawn. He went into his room, stripped, and hit the bed. Maybe he'd get lucky and catch two hours of sleep. Maybe three. Then a new day would start, and the hunting would begin—hunting for the man after Seline and—more important—for his brother.

Because Sam knew Az was close. After centuries, Az had finally gotten his lily-white ass kicked out of heaven. *How does it feel to fall?* Payback was going to be hell. He'd make sure of that.

Sam closed his eyes. He took a deep breath and tried to shove the past away. For once, he'd like to dream of something other than death and fire. Was that so much to ask? Just one time.

His breath eased out. As he drifted into sleep, the fire came.

As always, it burned, searing his wings away and charring his flesh as he fell from the sky.

With her eyes still closed, Seline smiled as she felt Sam drift into sleep.

Time to take a walk into his dreams. Unlike others of her kind, proximity mattered to her. The closer her prey, the easier it was for her to slip into his dreams.

Her heartbeat slowed. Her being centered completely on him. *Sam.* Then, slowly, he came into focus in her mind.

Sweat dotted his skin—naked, strong flesh—and he twisted against the dark covers on his bed. Faint lines appeared between his brows and a growl broke from his lips.

It looked like he was in pain. Poor killer. *Not having a nice dream, huh, Sam?*

"I can make the pain stop," she whispered.

His eyes opened. Flames danced around her for a moment. She could actually feel the heat on her flesh. Her kind always had such powerful, incredibly vivid dreams. This time, the dream wasn't really hers. Not really his, either.

Ours.

Yet she had the ultimate power here. The things she saw now, the things they did—they would all be from her command.

She climbed onto his bed. The mattress dipped beneath her, and everything *felt* real. Because in a dreamwalk, it was real to the spirit.

"Seline?" Sam's voice came out as a deep, sexy rumble. "What the hell—"

She put her finger against his lips. "It's just a

dream." Perhaps saying the lie would make what was to come easier. She forced a smile as she leaned closer to him. The rich scent of man and the harsher scent of fire filled her nose. "Nothing can hurt you when you dream."

"*Bullshit.*" Then he did something a man had never done before in a dream-walk. He ripped control away from her. He grabbed her arms and rolled fast, so that in a second's time, she was beneath him and trapped beneath his powerful body.

Seline's heart nearly stopped. No, *no.*

"Dreams can kill you," Sam muttered. He stared down at her with eyes that were far too aware. "But this is a much better way to go than the fire." Sam crushed his lips to hers.

CHAPTER THREE

She felt real. Far too real for a dream. Seline's body was soft and sensuous beneath his, and the fire was gone. No, the burn was *within* him now, burning from the inside as the lust flared higher.

Want her.

Sam was used to taking what he wanted. One look at Seline's body on that stage in Temptation, and he'd craved. But he hadn't just wanted a small taste of her. He wasn't into sampling. Sam was into taking.

Claiming.

If his asshole killer of a brother hadn't been roaming the streets, Seline would have already been his. He tore his lips from Seline's and pressed his mouth to the delicate column of her throat. She shivered.

"I can be yours now." Her voice whispered to him, and shock had his body stiffening. She'd heard his thoughts. Heard and—

Too real. His fingers tightened on her flesh. Her breasts pressed against his chest, her thighs shifted beneath his legs, and the scent of jasmine surrounded him.

There should be no jasmine now. Just ash. Smoke.

He only dreamed of fire and death. Not sex and pleasure and silken flesh.

But her fingers were sliding around his shoulders and skimming down his back. He knew she'd feel the scars soon. The thick, long scars crossed his shoulder blades. When he'd fallen, his wings had burned off, and he'd been left with only the jagged reminder of what he'd once been.

Her breath hissed out when Seline touched the scars and . . . pleasure knifed through him, a pleasure so intense it was almost pain. An angel's wings were the most sensitive part of his body, and even the ghostly remnants of his wings felt her touch.

More.

His head lifted. Her taste was in his mouth—sweet sin—and he wanted so much more. Seline's lips were even darker, even redder, from the crush of his lips on hers.

And her skin looked almost luminous, as if it were glowing. Had he really thought that she wasn't classically beautiful before? The woman was fucking perfect. So gorgeous that staring at her nearly hurt.

Her lips curved a bit. "You won't have bad dreams tonight. You'll know only pleasure."

His cock was full and aching. Her legs were spread, and paradise waited just inches away. She was wet and arching her hips toward him.

Pleasure. When he'd first fallen, he'd gotten drunk on pleasure. Angels didn't feel as a rule, but once he'd hit earth, the sensations had overwhelmed him, and he'd gone more than a little mad on them. Pleasure and pain were his favorite sensations. They made him react the most, and they made him feel alive.

When he'd spent centuries only feeling death.

Besides, he'd learned he was very good at doling out

pain, and when he wanted, he knew just how to give pleasure to his lovers.

When I want . . .

His hands rose between their bodies as he levered his chest up. Her breasts were amazing to see. Full and plump with tight pink nipples. Sam bent his head and licked one nipple. Seline moaned softly as her fingers curled around his scars.

Sam's cock jerked as the rush of pleasure pounded through him.

She arched her back and pressed her breast more fully against his mouth. He sucked her flesh and found that the taste of her nipples was just as addictive as her mouth. Sweet, like strawberries. She was so soft. He let his teeth lightly score her flesh.

"*Sam . . .*" Her whisper filled his ears.

For an instant, his eyes closed. The temptation was right there. He could take her, take his pleasure, and damn the world.

But . . .

He caught her hands and pulled them from his body even as he forced his mouth from her breast. Then he caged her hands against the mattress, pinning her with an unbreakable grip on each wrist.

She stared up at him with dazed eyes. "Don't you want me?"

Hell, yes, but he knew a trap when he felt one, and even sexy bait wasn't going to push him over the edge. Well, *maybe* not over, just pretty close.

"I want you," she told him. Her eyes promised so much pleasure.

He held tight to his control even as his instincts de-manded that he thrust hard and deep inside her flesh. "For five hundred years, I've dreamed of hell." The gritted admission came from deep within him.

Seline's lips parted. Sexy fuck-me lips. His hips pressed a bit closer to her. *Take her.*

"But tonight . . . tonight I dream of you?" he asked. Bullshit. Did he look like a fool?

She blinked as if confused, but her skin kept that luminous glow. A glow that a human or even a low-level demon should never have.

He brought his lips close to her ear and again felt the light tremble that raked her body. "I can't kill you in a dream," he whispered, the words soft and tender like a lover's even as the rage in him began to burn hell-hot.

She stiffened beneath him. Ah, so she realized this little scene wasn't going according to plan.

"But . . ." Sam continued, letting his tongue just touch the tip of her ear, "I'm guessing you can kill me here, right, sweetheart?"

He heard the catch of her breath and had his answer. Sam's lips pressed lightly against her neck, then harder as he sucked the skin. He'd mark her, if only in their dream.

When she pressed closer to him and didn't try to slip away, he knew Seline was in danger of losing her own control—something that happened a lot with her kind.

"A succubus." He'd suspected from the way she captivated every man in Temptation. He rose above her but kept her chained with his hands. The control and the caging were just an illusion. In a dream, a succubus would be the one with the real power. He was just along for the ride. "Here to seduce me and kill me, Seline?"

No mortal weapon could kill a Fallen. They were too powerful. But a succubus wouldn't use a weapon to kill. She'd simply use seduction until she drained her prey dry.

Sam shook his head, a little regretful. The ride would have been incredible, no doubt. "Won't work."

"I-I don't know what you're talking—"

"Your game probably worked on a dozen other fools"—and he wouldn't think about those jerks right then—"but I'm stronger." Though screwing her just might have been worth the risk. He smiled and knew it wasn't a pretty sight. "You've just made one dangerous mistake. And as soon as I wake up"—because she couldn't keep him trapped in the dream world forever—"your ass really will be mine." In the real world, *he* was the one with the power, and she was prey.

She stared into his eyes and let her mask drop. No longer was she the terrified woman he'd seen in the club earlier that night. Instead, she was sex personified, a temptation so seductive his whole body tightened with lust, and the confidence streaming from her eyes had his control cracking.

Then she smiled. "Promises, promises, Sammael . . ." She thrust him back with a strength he hadn't anticipated. He flew through the air and slammed into the wall, his body shuddering.

Growling, he straightened and charged for the bed. Sam's hands reached out for her—

But Seline vanished.

He blinked and found himself in bed and tangled in the covers. The scent of jasmine hung in the air, and his cock pulsed with arousal.

A grin tilted his lips as he tossed the covers aside. *That ass is mine.*

Oh, hell. Seline's eyelids flew open, and she jumped from the bed. She had her clothes on in less than two seconds. As she lunged for the window, she sent a line of fire skirting toward the closed door. Not that the fire would keep Sam out for long.

"*Seline!*" His shout erupted from the hallway.

The freaking window wouldn't open. Her sweaty

hands couldn't lift the thing up. Screw it. Seline smashed out with her right fist and shattered the glass. Blood dripped from her fingers, but she didn't even hesitate as she climbed out onto the ledge.

Fire crackled behind her, but she still heard the crash of the door as the wood splintered.

Then the fire stopped crackling. Or rather, someone a lot stronger than she was stopped the fire. Seline didn't look back. She kept her eyes on the ground—*just a second-story fall, even if I break a leg, I'll heal*—and then she dropped.

She just didn't drop fast enough. A hard, strong hand caught her right wrist, and her shoulder wrenched as she was gripped tight.

"Going somewhere?" Sam asked, his voice a mocking drawl in the dark.

It was so not her night. Seline tried to send a burst of fire up at him. Controlling fire had never been her strong suit, but she could usually make it burn to life easily enough.

As the fire neared him, it just sputtered away in light plumes of smoke. The bastard laughed as the smoke drifted by him. *Laughed.*

Then he started lifting her back up. The broken windowpane bit into his arm, and blood streaked down his flesh.

She tried to yank away from him—she would have preferred a few shattered bones to what was coming—but Sam's grip was unbreakable. Her heart thudded into her chest. "Does it matter . . ." she asked as he raised her higher and her legs kicked uselessly ". . . that I didn't have a choice in taking this job?" Another truth for him. Not that he'd believe her.

"Doesn't matter at all." Sam hauled her through the window. Oddly enough, the guy made sure she didn't get another cut on her flesh. Probably saving all the blood and gore for his own personal delivery.

Oh, damn.

Then he dropped her onto the floor. When she shoved the hair back from her eyes, Seline glared up at him. His eyes weren't blue any longer. They were demon black. Behind him, she saw the shadowy image of wide wings that shouldn't be there.

I felt his scars.

Demons didn't have wings, yet he had a demon's eyes.

"What are you?" she whispered. *Down to five choices . . . and right then her top choice was not good at all.*

He smiled.

"Fuck." Alex lowered his binoculars and turned to the man beside him. "Did you just see that shit?"

The other hunter, face pale and eyes wide, nodded. *Sammael had caught Seline mid-drop and dragged her back inside the second-story window.*

"He's going to kill her," Alex said, huffing out a breath. They'd parked far enough away that Sammael wouldn't see them, but close enough so that they could keep tabs on Seline.

"Probably," the guy next to him grunted.

Seline had been their best hope of eliminating Sammael. When bullets and knives didn't work, you had to be real freaking creative about taking out the trash.

Rogziel wasn't gonna like this. The boss had been so sure that Seline could handle this job.

"Do we go in after her?" the other hunter asked.

Alex lifted his binoculars one more time. All he could see was broken glass and the dark interior of the house. He didn't hear any screams, not yet anyway. He'd figured Seline for the screaming type.

Maybe Seline would be able to work some of her magic.

Maybe not.

He couldn't say that he particularly cared either way. *One less demon in the world.* "No, she's on her own." He nodded toward the driver. "Now get us the hell out of here before Sammael comes looking for us." Because Seline would talk. She'd beg for her life. For mercy. Everyone always did.

Even the strong broke under the right pressure, and Alex knew that in spite of Seline's demon powers, she wasn't particularly strong. Using sex . . . how much weaker could you get?

Besides, he'd bet that Sammael knew all about applying the right pressure and pain.

I hope it's quick, Seline. Because while Alex hadn't liked what Seline was, he hadn't hated her, either. She'd tried to fight her instincts, and she'd done her duty on the jobs they'd worked together.

The van pulled away and left the faded antebellum house behind in the thick swamp.

Alex knew he'd never see Seline O'Shaw again. Another assassin would be sent after Sammael. Maybe this one would have better luck than the last three. Sammael was just a tough bastard to kill.

But everyone dies sometime.

Sooner or later, Sam would see hell again.

Then he'd be the one screaming.

Sam was naked. And aroused. Seline tried to yank her eyes away from the swollen length of his cock, but when she stared up at his furious features, um—that view wasn't exactly good.

"Who sent you." Not a question, a furious demand.

She blinked and tried to look innocent. Right, like she'd ever been able to manage that feat. Thanks to her incubus father, playing innocent had always been a stretch of her acting abilities. "Look, Sam, I don't know what you—"

"I know what you are." He stalked closer. She scrambled to her feet because she wasn't just going to kneel on the floor and wait for him to kill her. She wasn't easy pickings. "Your skin is still glowing, your cheeks are flushed, and the room is nearly crackling with your power." His eyes narrowed to chips of black fire. "Did you really think I wouldn't know when a succubus was dream-walking with me?"

Well, she'd hoped he wouldn't know. The others hadn't. Most guys just thought they were in the middle of one awesome dream. Just a dream that folks didn't exactly wake up from.

"Seline!"

Her hands clenched. "I'm not a succubus." Her voice came out strong and clear—a very good thing. She was rather proud of that tone. But her heart still raced hard enough to shake her chest, and her gaze wanted to dip down the broad expanse of his chest.

Focus. Why did she have to possess such a weakness? Fear should be her only concern then, not lingering lust. Again, *thanks, Dad*. Wonder if he heard her thoughts in hell? Probably not, but it never hurt to send out bad vibes.

"Liar," Sam tossed out, and the back of his hand skimmed down her cheek. "I suspected the first time I saw you on stage. The humans got weak while you just seemed to shine."

Shine. Yes, that was one of the effects. When she absorbed enough energy, her skin took on a faint glow. The glow was relative to the amount of power she stored. The more power, the greater that glow.

Sam had been a wonderful source of power. All that sensual energy just waiting for her. Now she was lit up like a human sparkler.

His head leaned toward her, and his lips brushed lightly over hers. Seline refused to back down. Instead, she just stole more of his energy. *His mistake.* He should really stop underestimating her.

"Did you know," he began, his mouth hovering over hers, "I can kill you as easily as I kiss you?"

Seline swallowed. *And I can kill you with a kiss.*

His tongue whispered over her lips. "Succubus."

Only a half-breed one. That's why she had to be physically close in order to dream-walk with him. Her lashes lifted, and she gazed into his eyes. Scary, dark eyes that she still found strangely compelling. Then she voiced the suspicion that had fueled her heart as she said, "Angel." The wings . . .

"Not anymore. These days, I'm Fallen."

For an instant, her world seemed to stop as fear froze her blood. Fallen—just like her mother. An angel for a mother and a demon incubus for a father. Oh, yeah, she'd been screwed up from birth, and since her parents had wound up killing each other before she could even walk . . .

Seline knocked his hands away. "I didn't want this job."

"Oh?" One black brow rose. "So you're done playing the innocent victim in need of help?"

"I've never been innocent." Time to drop the act. Partially, anyway.

"Neither have I." His grin was wicked.

Fallen. Damn. She hadn't counted on that, but now it made sense. No wonder Rogziel had been so determined to get Sam. Who better for her boss to take down than Sam? He'd been hot to send Sam to hell, and now she truly understood why.

His knowing smile soon slipped away. "Moorecroft was just bullshit. A sob story to get close to me."

"No." She shook her head. "He truly wants me dead. I *did* kill his friend, but I promise the bastard deserved what he had coming."

"Like I deserve death?"

Rogziel thinks so. "Don't you?" she threw right back. This was her job. Nothing easy, nothing pretty. Just death. *Punishment.* Someone had to stop the monsters out there, and she was the perfect aberration to do the job.

But this is my last assignment. I'm getting out. Going to vanish. Because she couldn't wash the blood off her hands anymore.

She'd tried to atone for the sins of the past by killing monsters, but their blood stained as dark as anyone else's.

Sam stepped back, dropping his hand. He exhaled on a rough sigh. "Someone sent you to die."

Possibly. She held her ground. "You really think you can kill me?"

That wicked grin flashed again, and her breath caught. "I'm Sammael, sweetheart, I can kill *anyone.*" He lifted his hand and stared at his fingers. "I'm the Angel of Death. All it takes is a touch . . ." He glanced her way. "And I can rip your soul right from your body."

Angel of Death. The room seemed to dim. Unlike most *Other,* she knew quite a bit about angels. Not so much *Fallen,* because who would want to fall from Paradise? *Other than my mother.* But she knew the angel lore. There were so many angels in heaven, thousands of them flying around.

There were punishment angels, messenger angels, guardians, and . . . the most powerful, the angels of death.

An Angel of Death could truly kill with a touch. Just a touch. Rogziel had sent her after Sammael, and he'd neglected to tell her that real vital bit of information.

She wet her lips. "Wh-why did you fall?" Most people might not actually believe an angel could fall, but she wasn't like everyone else. Her mother had fallen because she'd been tempted by an incubus. Erina had been weak, and she'd paid for her crime.

And I've been paying, too. Paying her entire life for sins she'd never committed.

"I got a taste for the killing." His gaze flashed back to that deceptive blue, and this time, she did feel like the words held the whisper of a lie. "So I started to kill whoever the hell I wanted." His gaze raked her. "Want to guess who is next on my list?"

No, she didn't want to guess at all. Seline swallowed. The odds of her survival were looking real slim. "Can you—can you at least put on clothes before you kill me?"

He blinked and frowned a bit. "A succubus cares about modesty?"

Her back teeth clenched. "I told you . . ."

"Yes, but nearly every word you say is a lie. So why should I believe anything you say?"

Her bare feet pressed into the hardwood floor. Her dripping blood—maybe his?—had already stained the floor. "Because you need me."

He laughed like that line was hilarious. Jerk.

"You need me," she snapped out, raising her voice to be heard over his laughter, and then she played her trump card. "If you want to find your brother."

That stopped his laughter. "Seline . . ." Her name was a warning. "You don't want to make me angrier than I am."

Oh, was that possible? She hadn't realized. She al-

most rolled her eyes. "If you want your brother—"
Hell, what had been the guy's name? Azik? Azra? She
couldn't remember for sure because she'd just heard
Alex say it once. *Better shorten it to be safe.* "If you
want to see Az, then you'll back off." She flashed him
what she knew was her own wicked grin. "Or you'll
never get the vengeance you want."

The lines around his eyes tightened, but Sam made
no move to touch her. Good. She didn't trust his touch.

Seline didn't lower her guard. She knew better than
to relax when a snake was close to striking. "I didn't
come in alone. You were right. Earlier, we were being
watched." The guys in the van were her backup.

If Sam's eyes narrowed anymore, she figured that
they'd be slits.

"We need to get out of here," she told him. "If we
don't, then they'll blow this house up with us inside."
She wasn't lying then. As soon as Rogziel realized she
hadn't been successful . . .

Burn, baby, burn. Folks in the city would see the
flames from this house as they lit up the night.

Sam waved his hand, and just that easy, he was
dressed. Huh. Interesting trick that she'd never been
able to manage.

He still didn't touch her. Sam just stared at her with
enough heat in his gaze to singe her flesh. "Take me to
Az."

She nodded, more than ready to deal. But first . . .
"Promise that if I do, you'll let me walk away."

He grabbed her arm and they flew through the window. *Flew.* More glass shattered around them. Seline
clamped her mouth closed, refusing to cry out. *Won't
let him hear the fear.* Some monsters liked fear too
much—another lesson she'd learned the hard way. She
plummeted straight down and choked back a scream.

But her body didn't slam into the unforgiving earth. Sam wrapped his arms around her and when they hit the ground, he cushioned her.

Seline blinked. "Why did you—"

He twisted and dragged her to her feet. Then they were running. Not toward his car, but toward the waiting darkness of the swamp.

Smart. If anyone actually was still watching, their eyes would lock on the Jag. Not on the gator-infested swamp. The insects chirped around her, but Seline refused to tense. *Hate bugs. Hate snakes. The Fallen will pay for this.* Once she figured out how to make him pay.

A weathered dock waited up ahead. A small motorboat was tethered close by. Sam jumped in the boat and glanced back at her.

The wooden dock trembled beneath her feet. "You didn't give me your promise," she reminded him stubbornly as her hands clenched into fists.

"What do you actually think a promise from me is worth?" He started the motor with a quick yank that flexed his muscles. The black water lapped at the boat.

"You don't trust me," she whispered. "And I can't risk trusting you." But she wanted to. Her life was hell, and she was on a kill mission that she didn't want. If Sam could just get her out of this mess . . .

He's strong enough. He can give me freedom.

Or she could take him out and earn her own freedom. Provided, of course, that Sam didn't kill her first.

He turned slowly and fixed his intent stare on her. "Who sent you after me?"

"Does it matter? I'm sure that I'm not the first assassin put on your trail."

"Not the first," he agreed as the motor hummed and water spit out behind the boat. "But you're the only one I let live." His body was a big, strong shadow. His voice seemed to make the water shudder.

"I wasn't going to kill you tonight." She felt obliged to point that fact out. Not that she expected it to earn her any points—

"Because you *couldn't.*"

No, he didn't realize how strong she really was. She'd held back with him because she needed him.

But for a few moments there, she'd been afraid her grand plan had blown up in her face. *Your ass is mine.*

"I'll take you to your brother," Seline said, "but you have to promise to help me once you have him." Couldn't the man see the benefit to her offer? She'd thought to seduce her way into getting his aid. Put the guy under, get him hooked—and then she'd been sure he'd do anything for her.

Even kill.

But it looked like that plan wasn't working so well. *Time for the back-up plan.*

Sam moved again in that blur that he seemed to do so well and snagged her wrist. "Still making deals? Don't you know better than to bargain with the devil?"

Her laughter was bitter and weak. "I do. The bargain with him is what got me into this mess." She let her glamour fall away, and she knew that her eyes would be as black as the water that surrounded them. "I want to be free, and you—you're the only one who can help me." Now that she knew what he was, Seline was even more certain that Sam was her ticket to freedom.

Freedom just had a hefty price tag these days.

"Another desperate appeal for my help?" he mocked.

She considered slugging the guy. Right. Like a hit would hurt him. She'd probably break her hand, and he wouldn't even flinch. "A deal this time. You help me to walk away, and I let you live." He should jump at this chance.

But Sam shook his head. "No dice, sweetheart. You take me to my brother." He tugged her into the boat. "You get me to him or you—"

Seline kissed him. She pressed her lips tight against his and crushed her body to Sam's. The kiss was hot, deep, wild, and when their tongues met, the lust exploded inside her.

And inside him because she could feel Sam's need blooming in the air. Getting deeper, stronger. Hotter. Wilder.

Seline took that need, absorbing it greedily even as she rubbed her body against his. Oh, but the man had power. So much wonderful, tempting power.

Power that is mine now.

Taking that power, absorbing it—the energy gave her the boost she needed. She didn't have to be inside a dream in order to take control from him. She could beat the guy right here in reality.

But she let the kiss linger. Just a moment longer. One minute. Two. Sam knew how to kiss, and his body promised such raw pleasure.

Next time.

She planted her hands against his chest. *Should have seen this coming, Sam*. Seline shoved him back just as she'd done in the dream-walk. Only this time, her throw packed one hell of a lot more punch.

He landed in the water with a splash. *Gator bait.* She grabbed the throttle and rammed it home. The boat lurched forward.

Sam would chase her. She knew it. Shaking him wouldn't be an easy task.

Of course, she didn't actually want to shake him. She just wanted to bring him in closer to base.

Whether Sam liked it or not, they were going to be partners. He could hate her, he could distrust her, but in the end, he'd need her.

Just as she needed him.

Seline swiped a hand over her mouth. *I can still taste him.* The man's taste was incredible. Better than that fancy wine she'd grown to crave.

"Seline!" His roar sent birds and insects scattering into the air.

She smiled. Sam was turning out to be exactly what she'd expected. Killing him would have been a crying shame. Some monsters needed to be put down, true, but others . . .

Others just needed to be let out of their cages so they could attack the real bastards out there. *Watch out, Rogziel. This time, you're my target.*

The angel would never know what hit him.

Time for him to be punished.

CHAPTER FOUR

Darkness still cloaked the city. Seline walked slowly down the street as the scent of the river teased her nose. Sam hadn't followed her. She'd looked back—too many times to count—but she'd only seen the dark water.

She hunched her shoulders as she hurried forward. Just because he hadn't followed her *then* sure didn't mean she wouldn't be seeing her Fallen again soon.

A rush of wind blew against her face, and her hair flew up, momentarily blocking her vision. Her hand rose to brush it back, but her fingers tangled with—

His.

"Hello, Seline."

Her body tightened at that husky rumble.

Half of Sam's mouth kicked up in a reckless smile. "Didn't think I'd let you get away that easily, did you?"

"No." Her hand fell. "I was sure you wouldn't." But shoving him into that icy water had felt good. She offered him her own smile. "Enjoy your swim?" Not that she could tell he'd even been in the water. His clothes were perfectly dry; he was breathing easily and not looking at all like he'd just raced out of the swamp to meet her in the New Orleans warehouse district.

His hand brushed back her hair. His touch was gentle, lover-like, but his gaze blazed with a banked fury. Hmmm . . . maybe not so banked.

"Tell me where my brother is."

She ignored the ball of fear swirling in her gut. "I asked for a deal, remember? So either you agree . . ." She knocked his hand aside and walked around him. *Keep walking, don't look back. Act like you've got this.* "Or we're done," she threw out as she stared straight ahead.

Silence.

Her lips pressed together, but her steps continued. Four A.M. The city was dead. Well, mostly. The rest of it was *undead*.

"I could *make* you tell me." And he was in front of her. Just like that. One blink, and bam, hello, Fallen.

She shook her head. "You could try." Now her laughter came, but it had a hard edge. "Do you really think you're the first bad-ass I've come across? I'm not easy to break." Bruise, yes, break, no.

Sam tilted his head to the right as he studied her. "Who tried to break you?" Anger hummed in the words.

You're just like him. He's burning, and you'll burn, too. Only I can save you. Rogziel's words pounded in her mind. How many times had he told her the same thing? *Evil. Hell. Burn.*

She'd been trapped with him for as long as she could remember. "I just want to be free," she whispered, and this time, she was telling Sam the absolute truth.

His eyes narrowed.

"I was supposed to kill you." She could give him that much, here in the darkness, alone on the street. "But I didn't."

He lifted his hand, stared at it, then looked back at her. "You truly don't know what I can do." Then he leaned closer. "Do you know how many angels there are?"

Hundreds. Thousands. She'd greedily absorbed every bit of angel lore and gossip that she'd ever heard over the years.

His hand slid down her arm, and a shiver skated over her skin. She was hypersensitive to him. So aware of his touch, his body.

Damn succubus blood. Sometimes, it just made her weak.

"I was an Angel of Death."

She didn't move. "You told me that already." She'd never met another Angel of Death. Most people hadn't. You only saw an Angel of Death when it was your time to die. The last visit was with the AOD.

"One touch . . ." The back of his hand slid over her skin. "And I kill." His head lowered toward her, but he didn't make the mistake of kissing her.

One kiss and I can kill.

"You sure you want to push me?" His question was barely more than a growl.

Don't let him see the fear. She lifted her chin. "You won't kill me." He'd had too many chances. "You need me. Right now, I'm your best bet for finding your brother." She let another laugh roll free as she stared into his eyes. "So give me your word, Fallen, and let's get this show on the road."

His jaw hardened. "You'll take me to Az?"

She nodded. "And when the time comes, you'll owe me—so you do *exactly* what I say." Having an Angel of Death at her command would be perfect. She'd love to see someone try to take down that guard dog.

"Fine," he gritted out.

Her gaze dropped to his lips. "Want to seal the deal

with a kiss?" He was touching her, and she wasn't running in fear. Surely the big, bad demon could handle one more kiss from her.

His hands closed around her shoulders, and he lifted her up onto her toes. His mouth took hers with heat and lust and wild need, and oh, it was exactly what she needed. A spike of power fueled her blood. *More.* She wanted to touch his flesh. Wanted to sink onto him and let the pleasure take her.

It had been far too long since she'd let go with her lover. When lust could kill, you always had to keep your control in bed.

Even when you wanted to let it shatter.

Sam's dark head lifted. She saw the same lust she felt reflected in his eyes.

But then his gaze left her as his stare swept the street. "Where is he?"

Right. Business before pleasure. "Close." She started walking, and Sam fell in right beside her. Rogziel had a containment center set up in the middle of the warehouse district. A low-profile place on the outside, but one that was well secured and perfect on the inside for the type of work Rogziel preferred.

Good thing she knew just how to get inside that warehouse.

They moved closer to the hulking shadows made by the buildings. They advanced in silence as the path twisted and turned. Ten minutes. Fifteen.

When Warehouse 609 appeared before them, Seline stopped. She put her hand on Sam's chest. "This is as far as you go." Her voice was a breath of sound.

"The hell it is." He rocked forward, and his muscles tensed beneath her palm. "Is he in there, is he—"

Her hand fisted in his shirt-front and she jerked. The fabric tore. He blinked at her. "You don't go in," she said, this time making her words an order. Her gaze swept the front of the warehouse. It looked like two guards were stationed outside.

It wasn't those two that they had to worry about. If Rogziel was inside . . . *hello, hell.*

"My boss could be in there—him and a dozen other guards that we don't want to piss off right now." Sometimes, you had to pick your moments. Going up against Rogziel when he had his little army at his beck and call wasn't a good idea. "Let me go in and scout the scene. Your brother *was* here, but they could have moved him to a new site already." *Or they could have killed him, and just where would that leave me?*

Sam glared down at her.

"We have a deal," she snapped at him, running a not-quite-steady hand through her hair as she tried to smooth it back. "I don't want to go in with guns blazing, okay?" Because she did have a few friends who should be in that warehouse. Well, semi-friends. Humans didn't usually like to get too close to her. "Let's try to keep the body count to a minimum."

"Why do you care?" He seemed genuinely confused.

Well, crap. What? Did he think a succubus couldn't *feel?* She felt too much. "Because I don't want any more blood on my hands. I've already got enough." She took a deep breath. "Look, I can get inside instantly, I can search the warehouse, and if your brother is still there"—okay, this was the dicey part—"I'll serve him up to you on a silver platter." *As long as you remember that you owe me.*

He stared at her. Time slipped away in silence.

She shifted her weight to her right foot. "Jeez, look, we don't have all—"

"Go in." His shoulders rolled. "But if you try to cross me, it'll be the worst mistake you make. I promise you that."

* * *

Sam crossed his arms and watched Seline slip away. He didn't trust her, not for a moment, but . . .

I want her.

Even though he knew better than to want a succubus. Talk about a lethal package.

She approached the guards. They must have recognized her because they opened the double doors and led her right inside the building.

Is Az in there? His back teeth were clenched. To be so close to his vengeance now. *So close.*

Don't betray me, Seline. If she did, if this was just a setup . . .

She'd learn just how painful his touch could be.

"Seline? What the hell?"

She turned at the call and found Alex Graham striding toward her. He wore all black, and a holster circled his shoulders.

A human, one who made it his mission to hunt monsters.

And one who *should* have been her backup for the night.

She let her face harden with anger because she had a role to play. "Did you forget that you were supposed to be watching my ass?" she demanded.

His eyes swept over her, lingering just a bit on the cuts that still sliced across her wrist and forearm. He shrugged, the move far too careless for her taste. "I thought you were dead. I saw that guy grab you and pull you back inside the house."

Oh, so he *had* been watching. Then when things got hot, he'd turned tail and run. *Way to leave a woman behind.* "You didn't think about coming to my aid?" That's what a team was supposed to be for.

"That wasn't my job."

She took the hit and kept her chin up.

"I was supposed to watch. You were supposed to . . . well . . ." His lips twisted, and she caught the flash of disgust on his face. "Do your thing."

Her *thing*. Like she hadn't risked her life for this group over and over again.

"Is he dead?" Alex wanted to know as he came close. Not too close. He never got too close. Like being a demon was some kind of virus he didn't want to catch.

She'd never liked the man. Seline worked with him because she had to—Rogziel wouldn't let her do anything else.

This is all you have, Seline. Rogziel's voice whispered through her mind. *You want redemption, then you fight for it. You kill for it. You earn it.*

The price for redemption was too high. She just wanted freedom.

"Sammael's not dead." Now she could mix truth and lie for this part. "I took some of his . . . power and managed to slip away." She exhaled and shook her head. "He's stronger than we thought. Much stronger. I need to talk to Rogziel—"

"He's not here." A brief pause, then Alex said, "He's out hunting."

Well, perfect. Then she could get the Az guy and slip right away. Because other than a few guards, the place was deserted.

"He wants us to relocate to a more secure site," Alex continued.

Ah, that explained the lack of personnel.

"We'll be transferring out the last prisoner soon."

"The last one?" *Oh, come on, be Az, be . . .*

Alex turned away. "He's a real piece of work. A

Fallen." He shook his head and kept walking. "Can you believe an angel would be dumb enough to fall from heaven?"

"I've seen dumber things." *Like you, just walking away from me now after you admitted you left me to die.* Seline grabbed the nearest object she could find—a metal chair that she lifted easily—and she slammed it into the back of Alex's head.

He went down, and she leaned over him. "Maybe that will teach you to stop looking at me like I'm a piece of dog shit stuck on your shoe." She'd seen the look in his eyes, in most of the eyes of the humans who were under Rogziel's thumb, and she was tired of being trash. Seline yanked the keys off his belt. Alex always had the keys to the cages. As Rogziel's first in command, he was the one given top access all the time.

She jumped up and hurried down the hall on the left. There wouldn't be much time before someone found his body.

So she'd better haul ass.

She turned a quick left, a hard right, and still she didn't see any other guards or personnel. She knew that the most dangerous *Other* were always kept in containment until Rogziel issued his judgment on them. This area of the warehouse had been reinforced for their containment. *Other*-proofed, so to speak. Silver cages for the shifters, magic blocks for the witches, and—

There. She pressed in a fast key code and the door for containment room 107 slid open. She slipped inside and saw—*him*.

The man's muscled chest was bare. His head sagged forward, his blond hair concealing his face. Thick chains bound his arms, holding him securely, even as blood dripped from the cuts that slashed open his arms.

The guy barely seemed to be breathing. Maybe she was already too late, dammit. Now how was she supposed to bargain with Sam? He wouldn't pay for a dead body.

She stepped forward, and her shoes slid over the hard floor.

His head whipped up. *"Help . . . me."* A desperate plea that was echoed by the haunted look in his blue gaze.

She pushed the door closed behind her and gripped the keys in her hand. "That's why I'm here." *Liar, liar . . . You're my ticket to freedom.*

So *this* was Az. Now that his hair had slid back, she could get a much better view of him. Perfect face. High cheekbones, straight blade of a nose, hard jaw. Golden skin. Bright blue eyes. Mouth that looked like it *should* be smiling. Instead, lines of pain bracketed his lips.

Yeah, she could buy him being an angel. Whereas Sam just looked more like the devil.

"Who . . ." his voice rasped out, "are . . . you?"

"My name's Seline." Giving him her name didn't matter and maybe it would earn her the trust she needed to make the escape work. She just had to get him out of those cuffs and then slip him out of the warehouse.

Sam could take over the game then.

His brow furrowed. "Don't . . . know you . . ." He shook his head. "Don't know . . ."

She hesitated just a few feet from him.

He sucked in a deep breath. *"Who am I?"* Confusion roughened the words.

She blinked. "Uh . . . run that by me again?" She sure hadn't been expecting that kind of response from him.

His gaze darted around the room. "Why . . . am I here?" That bright stare came back to her. "Did I do . . . something wrong? Did I . . . hurt someone?" He yanked at the chains.

Seline kept her distance. If he was truly Sam's brother, then the guy before her might be able to kill with a touch, too. *Which makes getting him out of here even harder.*

His jaw clenched. "Please," he grated, *"help me."*

There was torment in his voice. And fear. The keys dug into her hand. "Your name is Az."

He didn't blink.

Okay, no recognition there. *Is this the right guy?* She walked a bit to the left and tried to peer over his shoulder. She couldn't see the flesh on his back, not with the way he was chained, so in order to find out if he carried the same scars as Sam did, she'd have to touch him. Seline sucked in a deep breath. "I will help you," she told him, "but you have to trust me." She lifted her left hand to show that she wasn't armed. "I need to touch you."

His stare bored into her and a faint line appeared between his brows.

"I have to make certain you're the man I think you are." Because these days, she didn't trust a thing Rogziel told her. Not after what she'd seen him do on the last case.

Sam wasn't the first angel she'd met. No, the first angel she could remember was Rogziel. But he wasn't an Angel of Death like Sam. Instead, Rogziel was on earth to punish. Punishment angels were fueled by wrath.

Only she knew that Rogziel had a twisted idea of what constituted guilt. Sometimes, just having demon blood was enough of a justification for punishment in his mind.

He doesn't kill quickly. He enjoys the pain too much.

The *only* time Rogziel ever seemed to feel anything was when he was doling out his justice. Then he smiled.

His smile chilled her to the bone.

Swallowing, Seline lifted her arm and let her fingers trail over Az's back.

He pulled in a sharp breath at her touch, but he didn't move. Her fingers skimmed up his flesh and found the thick, rough scars near his shoulder blades.

Her head tilted back, and she looked deeper into his eyes. His pupils flared as she gazed at him. "You fell." It was hard to mistake those marks. Once you knew what they were, the scars were an instant indicator. She'd only touched Sam's scars in the dream-walk, but she'd never forget them. *He'd had wings, once upon a time.* So had Az.

Once upon a time . . . until the fire came, and he fell to earth. Seline cleared her throat and said, "You fell, and your wings burned away."

Not a flicker of recognition filled his gaze. He just looked . . . lost.

"Fell from where?" he asked blankly as he blinked and shook his head.

She pulled away, hurrying back a step. Getting out of touching range. "I'll get you out of here, but you have to—"

"I woke up in a . . . graveyard. I was on a broken tomb, naked, I was—"

Voices shouted in the hallway. Oh, hell. No more time.

She grabbed the chain on his right wrist and shoved the key into the lock. "Doesn't matter."

"It does." He caught her hand the instant the cuff popped open. Now it was Seline's turn to freeze. *One touch.*

But his fingers just smoothed over her skin. "You're . . ." He broke off and the blue of his eyes seemed to fade a bit. "Danger."

Oh, yeah, she was dangerous to him, but she wasn't about to confess to that bit now.

His hold tightened. "Be careful. Evil . . . it's at the door."

What? Chill bumps rose on her arms.

Then the scent of smoke reached her, burning her nose, and Seline's head whipped around. She could see thick, dark smoke sliding beneath the bottom of the containment room's door.

Smoke and then—the door exploded inward as a ball of flames swept into the room. Seline screamed, and Az laughed.

Laughed.

Her gaze flew back to him, and she saw that he was smiling. Oh, hell. That smile reminded her far too much of Rogziel—it was the same smile he wore right before Rogziel got ready to punish some bastard.

Playing with the big boys . . . Had she really thought Az wouldn't be as dangerous as Sam?

The fire licked her arm, and she screamed again.

When the scent of smoke drifted to him on the wind, Sam stiffened. Then the armed men ran out of the warehouse, one of the guys carrying an unconscious man over his shoulder. They were running away.

Seline, where the hell are you?

The smoke thickened, and the flames began to crackle.

Sam raced for the warehouse. A retreating guard saw him and fumbled for his weapon. "Wait, stop! You can't—"

Sam flew forward and knocked the guy aside. Sam blasted the warehouse door open with a stray thought and rushed inside. The flames swelled, growing higher and higher. His power pushed out, and he should have been able to instantly quench the fire, but the flames didn't so much as flicker.

Az. Only another angel could have enough power to stir the fire like this.

Time to find his brother and give him some payback—payback that had been centuries in coming.

Another scream ripped the air. This one echoed with pain.

"Seline!" He rushed after that fading scream, never feeling the touch of fire on his skin as he leapt right through the flames.

And then he saw her. On the ground. Rolling as she tried to put out the fire that burned her flesh. He roared her name and lunged for her.

"Sam . . ." Her hoarse whisper and there were tears—*fucking tears*—sliding down her cheeks. He held her close against his chest, and, through the flames, his gaze locked on his brother.

Azrael. The second Angel of Death created. One without feelings. One who existed only to kill.

One who'd finally fallen.

The fire rose higher, hotter, and those flames seemed to come right after Seline.

Holding her, cradling her carefully, Sam stepped back.

Az was smiling.

"Bastard!" Sam yelled even as he retreated a few more steps from that fire. The fire wouldn't hurt him, but Seline was a different story. She was shaking in his arms, and he could feel the waves of her fear.

A manacle dropped from Az's wrist. Still smiling, Az stepped forward.

"I'm going to kill you," Sam promised him.

Az's brows rose. "No . . . you won't." Az lifted his

hands. The restraints were at his feet, and Sam knew his brother's power was ready to burst free again. "Not now." And Az vanished. In less than a second's time, he simply disappeared.

Holding tight to Seline, Sam sent out a wave of his power and blew out the wall on the right. He ran forward, holding her as tightly as he dared.

The shrill scream of sirens reached his ears. He caught the flash of red lights. A fire truck was racing to the scene, leading a line of police cruisers and an ambulance. Sam hesitated.

"No." Seline's rough whisper. "Humans . . . don't let them see me. They . . . can't help."

He risked a glance down at her. The tear tracks were still on her cheeks, and angry red blisters covered her arm.

Az, run . . . run fucking fast. His brother had just earned more pain before his death.

"Please," she said, holding his stare, "get me out . . . of here." More tears slid from her eyes.

"You're hurt. You need—"

"I'm a succubus." Her eyes closed even as a flash of pain had her face tightening. "Medicine won't heal me."

No, not medicine.

He turned away from the cops. He kept his hold on her, and he knew just how to help Seline.

Medicine couldn't take away a succubus's pain, but pleasure could.

Rogziel watched as the warehouse burned. His guards had escaped, and Alex waited behind him, swearing and muttering because he had a bruise on the back of his head.

Humans could be so dramatic.

"You're sure Seline was the one who hit you?" Rogziel asked again, because he had to be certain.

"*Yes!* She hit me, and she took the freaking keys. She went after that Fallen . . ." Alex stalked forward and pointed to the blazing building. "And they did *that*."

Burned their way to freedom?

Maybe.

Or maybe Azrael had just burned Seline and sent her to hell.

His gaze slid over the fire. He'd expected the betrayal from Seline. He'd hoped that she'd stay true to him, but, deep inside, he'd known. It had been just a matter of time.

Blood always tells. Poor Seline had the blood of the wicked coursing through her veins. He'd tried to warn her, but there had been no changing fate. There never was.

"We'll wait until the authorities secure the scene." He'd learned how to keep a low profile over the centuries. So he'd let the cops do their work. Let the firefighters fight the blaze that was already cooling, and once the smoke cleared, he'd see if any bodies were recovered.

If Seline had somehow slipped away, then he'd find her. Seline was his, and he wouldn't let her get away. He'd see her dead long before he turned her loose on the world.

Because he knew just how dangerous she truly was. The pretty face was a lie. Inside, Seline was a monster, one that he'd been fighting to control since the day he'd found her.

Tossed away in an alley.

Trash.

Evil.

And the evil ones in this world had to be punished.

* * *

Sam took Seline to one of his safe houses. Acquiring a car wasn't hard; he just took the first one he saw and drove as fast as he could. Within minutes, he had Seline at his place, locked inside, and on his bed.

Carefully, using a gentleness he hadn't even realized he possessed, Sam removed her charred and ash-stained clothing, and he wiped away her tears.

"You couldn't . . ." His fingers hovered over her injured arm. The burns pissed him off and made him want to rip Az apart. "You couldn't control the fire at all." Odd. A demon usually had some ability to manipulate the flames.

Her lashes slowly lifted. "I'm not . . . I'm a hybrid."

Hybrid. Half-demon. Half . . . what?

"I can make some fire like I did in the swamp, but I can't control someone else's. Not . . . strong enough." The last sounded like an embarrassed confession.

He stared down at her, lost, angry. She *hurt,* and her pain made him furious.

"You know"—her voice was husky, and her eyes so dark—"what I need to heal."

He knew how to heal a succubus, yes, but . . .

"Kiss me?" she whispered.

Bracing his arms on either side of her head, he brushed his lips across hers. Light. Soft.

"No." Her growl. "I need . . . more."

His lips pressed against hers again. Her mouth parted for him, and his tongue swept inside to meet hers. Wet. Warm. She moaned and he stilled, afraid it was a cry of pain. He began to pull back.

Then her hips lifted and pushed against his. She caught his bottom lip between her teeth and gave him a light bite.

His cock hardened. *Want her. Need . . .*

"I'm not human," she whispered, and already her

voice sounded stronger. *Just from a kiss?* "*This* is what I need." A pause. "You're what I need." Stark.

Sam didn't have to be told twice. He kissed her again. Her breasts pushed against his chest, and he could feel the tight press of her nipples. He hadn't removed her sexy black bra, but he wanted the lace gone. He wanted her nipple in his mouth, and he wanted to know that her moans were from pleasure.

But he put a stranglehold on his lust, and instead of stripping her, he took his time with her mouth. Sam stroked with his tongue and his lips, savoring her taste. Her hips arched more, her hands rose to clutch him, and she kissed him back with a raw hunger that had the lust blazing hotter. Her body was soft temptation beneath him, and the need within him deepened with every moment that passed.

Then her fingers pushed between them, easing along his chest. *Both* of her hands. But her right arm had been burned . . .

He pulled back instantly.

Her skin had taken on the faintest of glows. Her eyes were pitch-black, her lips plump and wet.

"Seline, your arm . . ." He glanced down. The blisters were already gone. The skin still appeared a dark red, but the flesh looked unblemished now.

"I'm a fast healer," she told him quietly, "with the right power." Her gaze met his. "And you," she told him, licking her lips as if she were still tasting him, "you've got more power than any *Other* I've ever met."

Because he was far more dangerous than any *Other* she'd met.

But he kept his hands light and easy on her as he stroked her body. "Do you want me to stop?" She'd be all right now. Even without more power from him, she wasn't in danger any longer. He'd given her enough power to heal.

Sam knew his control wouldn't last much longer, not with her body pressed so intimately to his and her taste on his tongue.

She shook her head, and the heavy mass of her hair brushed back over her shoulders. "No . . ." Her fingers seemed to burn through his shirt. "I want more."

Those words were all he needed to hear. In an instant, his clothes were gone and her fingers were pressing against his bare skin. Lust pumped through him as he kissed her and touched her. He'd learn every inch of her body and have one fucking fine time as he did.

He tossed her bra away and glimpsed her dark pink nipples. She'd stripped on the stage of Temptation, but she'd been so careful, hiding her body just as she revealed a sliver of flesh. He hadn't seen her breasts then, just the sweet curve of her stomach and the long length of her legs.

Want her. Take her.

He'd been furious that others had been around that night in Temptation. Normally, he couldn't care less who saw the dancers, but Seline was different.

Then she'd danced again . . . He actually had knocked out two demons and a shifter that second night. They'd gotten too close to the stage—no, too close to her. And if anyone had been going to touch her . . .

It would have been me.

Not some dumbasses who were still probably nursing the bruises he'd given them.

"Sam?"

Take. He liked the way she said his name. A whisper of sex in the darkness.

Now there was no one else to watch. Rage and hunger twisted within him, and Sam took the woman he wanted enough to walk through flames.

His mouth became harder on hers. Her breath

came faster, and the frantic thunder of her heart raced against him.

Want more. Sam kissed a trail down her throat. Over her collarbone. His lips closed over her nipple. *Sweet*. So very sweet. He licked and he sucked and he enjoyed the quick rise of her hips against his.

As he tasted her, his fingers slipped between her legs. Her thighs were parted, but a thin scrap of silk covered her sex. He stroked her through her panties, and the soft fabric quickly dampened with her arousal.

Her skin had taken on a light glow, and Sam knew she was absorbing the sensual energy he generated. Yet he didn't feel any kind of drain.

Instead, he just felt . . . hungrier, for her.

Her nails scored down his chest, and he growled low in his throat.

"You don't have to be careful with me," she whispered. "Not now."

Good because his control was fading, fast.

So he slid down her body. Shoved her thighs farther apart and ripped her panties away. Then Sam put his mouth on her.

She gasped out his name and pushed her hips harder against him even as her fingers sank into his hair. He worked his tongue against her clit, loving the richer taste of her and the way her body shuddered against his.

When the first orgasm hit her, he felt the ripple against his mouth.

And he kept tasting her.

When the second orgasm built, rising quickly and tensing her body, he rose above her. He guided his cock to her wet entrance, pushed inside—

Her legs wrapped around him. Long, smooth. Her gaze met his—so black but burning with need.

His cock rested just inside her body, her heat and

cream coating the head of his aroused flesh. The glow had deepened on her skin, and she looked so beautiful that it almost hurt to stare at her.

Her tongue swiped over her lips, and he plunged balls-deep inside her.

The bed creaked beneath him as he thrust. Deeper, harder. She met him with eager lifts of her body. Fighting with him as they raced for the climax.

Their mouths met. She took his breath. Gave him hers, even as her sex clamped around him.

She came with a fast release that rippled along his cock. He drove into her again, lifting her legs so that he could go even deeper into her tight sex.

Her nails dug into the sheets. He heard fabric tear.

The air seemed to crackle with energy. Still he thrust. Wanting more of her. Wanting to take and take . . .

Bodies met. Flesh to flesh. The scent of sex drifted in the air. Her power, his, filled the room.

Sam thrust hard once more, felt the silken caress of her flesh, and exploded. The climax wiped through him, seeming to burn his body from the inside out, but this time, the fire felt *good*.

Better than good.

Pleasure blasted through him, and he held on to Seline tighter than he'd ever held on to anyone or anything in his life.

And he knew . . .

More. For him and Seline, this would be just the beginning of the pleasure to come.

Sam began to thrust again.

The flames were out. The warehouse smoldered but the fire no longer lit the sky. Rogziel stared at those drifting plumes of smoke.

Seline hadn't perished in the fire.

Pity. It would have made things easier on him.

But she'd escaped and so had that bastard Fallen, Azrael.

"I know she took the keys from me," Alex snapped behind him. The human, always so impatient and so certain of what he *knew*.

In reality, humans knew very little in this world.

And Alex knew only what Rogziel told him. Rogziel glanced at his guard dog, because that's all Alex was. A dog that he used to hunt his prey.

Humans did have some uses. Pity they weren't more durable.

"She hit me," Alex said, rubbing the back of his neck. Was he still complaining about that bump? The guy acted like he'd never known pain.

When pain could be such a wonderful companion.

"She hit me," Alex said again, his face hardening, "and then she took my keys. She helped that freak escape!"

Angels weren't freaks. The faintest hum of what *could* have been anger moved beneath Rogziel's flesh, but then the feeling faded. Feelings always faded for him.

Angels weren't supposed to experience emotions. They only had duties, no desires.

His duty was to punish the wicked.

Azrael was wicked. Sammael had sinned too many times to count, and little Seline . . .

Now you've betrayed me.

And after all he'd done for her. Years spent—wasted—trying to save her immortal soul, only to have her give in the first time she was tempted by a Fallen.

He'd expected her to hold out a bit longer. Her mother hadn't caved in so easily.

No matter. The choices had been made. Now he'd have to punish her, too.

"Seline's gone." Alex's voice roughed with the fury Rogziel knew humans carried so often. "And the watchers you put on Sunrise can't find a trace of Sammael."

Now Rogziel's eyebrows lifted. "You think Seline was working with him?"

"I think Sammael saw a chance to bust out one of his brethren, and he took it."

But Alex didn't understand. Sammael wouldn't have wanted to free Azrael. Based on what Rogziel knew, Sammael would want to kill his brother. Perhaps torture him, *then* kill him, but not help Azrael. Never that. Sammael wasn't the forgiving sort.

Another sin to lay at his feet.

But Rogziel began to understand as his gaze drifted back to the warehouse ruins. *Sam, did you underestimate your brother again?*

Azrael wasn't easy pickings, even if he was still a fresh Fallen.

Azrael—Az—they'd once been friends, as close as angels could be to friends, but Rogziel still planned to punish the Fallen. He always did his duty.

Az's time would come, *after* Rogziel took care of Sam. Sam had been on his list for centuries, but he was so strong that getting to him hadn't been easy. Luckily, the situation had now changed.

Good thing I have the right bait.

Sam wouldn't even realize what was happening, not until it was too late.

No one could escape hell. Not Az, not Seline, and not Sam—and not any *Other* who thought they could escape him.

Rogziel would make certain of it.

Time for them to pay. Judgment was at hand.

CHAPTER FIVE

Seline's breath choked in her lungs. Her skin was so sensitive that just the touch of the sheet against her had her tensing.

Sam lay beside her, but she could still feel him all along the length of her body. Inside and out.

Oh, boy. She was in trouble. Serious trouble. Her wounds had healed, her power scale was about to rocket through the roof, but she was so scared in that moment that her stomach knotted.

Didn't expect that.

It hadn't been just sex. She'd had sex before. Sex didn't make you so hungry and wild that you just wanted to take and take and take until you could barely breathe, much less move.

That was—*addiction.*

Everyone knew demons had a problem with addiction. Even a half-breed like her understood just how deadly an addiction could be.

Never suspected a Fallen would be my drug of choice. Fate sure liked to play games.

"Why . . ." Her voice came out sounding rather like

a frog's croak. *Way to be a sexy succubus*. She cleared her throat and tried again. "Why did you save me?"

He'd had the chance. If he wanted to attack Az, he could have gone after the Fallen and left her to the flames.

And where the hell had that fire come from? The sprinklers on the ceiling hadn't kicked on, and the flames had actually seemed to be zeroing in on her.

"Because I know what the fire feels like." He turned away from her. Her hands clenched into fists, and her nails bit into her palms as she fought the urge to reach out to him.

She could play this cool, maybe. Not like it was her first after-sex scene. Just her first after-really-awesome-nearly-knock-me-out-sex scene.

He rose from the bed. Naked, strong, those muscles flexing with his movements. What a fine ass. Totally biteable. The scars on his back were dark, still appearing a light red even after all this time, and she had the strangest urge to . . . lick them.

Next time.

"I thought . . ." She sucked in a breath and tasted him. "I thought you said you were here to watch the world burn."

Sam glanced back at her, and his blue eyes glinted. "You're not the world."

No, she was just one half-breed succubus who was in way over her head. She pulled the sheet up to her chest. "Az got away."

"Azrael won't get far." A promise reflected in that deadly tone. "The bastard can run, but I will find him."

She didn't doubt him. *Azrael*. Right, so that was the guy's full name.

His eyes hardened as he stared at her. "But you won't come between us again."

Not like I planned to get in the middle of a fire—or a war between Fallen.

"Stay here as long as you want." Sam waved his hand, dressed in a flash with that magic of his, and headed for the door.

It took three seconds too long for her to realize that the guy was actually leaving her, naked, in his bed. "Wait!"

Yeah, this had never happened to her before. Men didn't usually leave a succubus. Beg for more, check. Offer anything for a chance to have her again. Right, been there, done that a time or two.

But walk away without a backward glance? That was just insulting.

And he truly wasn't even looking back at her. His shoulders were tense, and his hand was on the door-knob.

"Where are you going?" She jumped out of the bed and realized that her knees felt a little wobbly, even as power had her skin flushing.

Sex with Sam had been very, very good for her. But since the guy was hightailing it out of there, maybe it hadn't been so great for him.

Then why had he been so eager for follow-up rounds? Seline kept her chin up even as she secured a sheet around her body, toga-style.

"Hunting." Flat. He wrenched open the door. "And I'm doing it alone."

Not like she'd volunteered to go after the big, bad fire-starting angel with him. But . . . "That's it?" Why did her voice sound so lost? Oh, this was not good. Not the way for a confident succubus to act. *I've never been that confident.* "You're just leaving?" She sucked at after-sex dialogue because she couldn't pull off the whole I'm-a-succubus-and-I-don't-care bit.

Maybe I'm too much like my mother. Her mother had

cared too much. If Erina had cared less, she'd still be alive, and Seline never would have been born.

Her spine straightened. Sam still wasn't looking at her. Screw that. She lunged forward and grabbed his arm. She spun him back around and *made* him look at her. "We have amazing sex and then you—"

"Did you think it would be any other way?"

What?

His lips curved the faintest bit, and his eyes seemed to lighten to an even brighter blue as his hand rose. The back of his fingers brushed over her face. "Just so you know, that was just the start. I *will* have you again."

Her sex clenched. Her body was way too eager for him. *Down, succubus, down.*

"But first, I have to hunt. If I don't take him out, Az will come for me." Sam's white teeth flashed in a full and very lethal grin. "And I've owed him an ass-kicking for centuries."

His hand dropped.

She sucked in a deep breath. "That's it?" *Do not get distracted by sex again.* "Hot sex, then you're gone? While I—what? Hide here?" Seline gave a hard shake of her head. "Hiding wasn't the deal. Look, I took you to Az." She hadn't exactly delivered him, but that wasn't the point. *Hello, fire, my hot friend.* She'd done her best. "I did my bit, and now you have to hold up your end of the bargain."

A muscle flexed along his jaw. "I saved you."

Yes, right, and that did count for big bonus points, but she had another, much more pressing issue right then. "The guy who took Az, he's gonna know . . ." Ah, damn. "The guards saw me go in. I brained one jerk-off with a chair, and while he was out, I stole the keys to Az's chains. I burned my bridges." Unfortunately, those bridges had tried to burn back. She realized that her fingers had a death-grip on the sheet. "When the smoke clears, they'll be coming for me."

He would. Rogziel would take her betrayal very, very personally. For a guy who wasn't supposed to feel, he sure had a vengeful streak.

Hell hath no fury like an angel betrayed.

"Stay here," he told her again, "no one will find you." So confident. So careless.

Then he tried to pull away. No, not happening. With that power boost, her grip was pretty unbreakable. "I'm not hiding here forever! Besides"—her breath expelled on a rush—"you don't know Rogziel."

He seemed to turn to stone beneath her touch. *Uh, oh.* "Sam?" Her stomach twisted. Maybe he *did* know Rogziel. Maybe he knew the guy too well.

In a blink, Sam locked his hands around her arms and dragged her up on her tiptoes. The sheet slipped away and pooled on the floor.

"You worked for *Rogziel?*" he gritted from between clenched teeth.

So much for the post-sex glow and tender moment time. "H-he was the one who found Az. He knew because—"

"Because he's a fucking punishment angel."

"Ah . . . I guess you do know him." The angel world was composed of *thousands,* but it figured that her bad luck would hold and Sam would know Rogziel.

His hands tightened. "I know he's a sick asshole who should have burned long ago."

Yep, definitely sounded like he knew Rogziel. Maybe the angel world was smaller than she realized.

Falling from heaven had hurt like a bitch.

Omayo stared below at the bustle of the streets. He didn't remember how long ago he had actually fallen, because time had lost meaning for him. He didn't know, didn't care.

Humans flocked on the street below. He watched them, had always watched them.

The morning sunlight slipped across the river's surface. Couples walked hand-in-hand. Young lovers stopped to kiss. Tourists snapped photographs. Laughter and voices filled the air.

Emotion.

He could sense it all around him, and, finally, he could *feel*.

Pleasure. Joy. Happiness. No more watching, now he felt everything. Just like humans. No, *more* than the humans. He appreciated each moment more because he knew what it was like to live in a void and feel nothing.

He turned away from the balcony and paced back inside his apartment. His shoulders rolled, and for an instant, he felt the flutter of wings that weren't there.

Small price to pay.

So he'd burned. So there would be no more flying for him. The clouds lost their appeal after centuries anyway.

He'd fallen. He'd fucked. He'd loved. He'd laughed.

Humans were the lucky ones. They had paradise right at their fingertips, and they didn't understand their joy.

He understood.

He'd burned for this joy.

A knock rapped at his door. He frowned but walked forward. He glanced through the peephole—humans had such fun little inventions—and surprise had his jaw slackening.

He jumped back—too late. The door flew inward, and the heavy wood landed on his body.

"Hello, *friend*." The mocking voice grated as

Omayo shoved the wood away from his body. He surged to his feet, more than ready to—

A growl reached his ears. Low, menacing.

He stilled even as terror rose within him, spiking his blood and making his heart shudder.

"I know all about you," that voice he knew too well said.

Omayo saw what waited in the doorway. The building was empty—just his apartment and a vacant garage downstairs. No one could help him.

As if humans could fight *this*. They'd be slaughtered in an instant if they tried. He'd never risked a human life. He wouldn't start now.

"You watched them too long . . ."

Omayo stumbled back and sent a burst of power right at his old *friend*. "Get out!"

But the one he'd known for centuries didn't move.

The blast seemed to have no effect. "You wanted to feel, Omayo . . ."

Was that so wrong? His hands fisted. "Centuries of nothing. *Nothing*. They have it all. I just wanted—"

The attack came at him in an instant. Teeth bit into his neck. Claws raked his body. He tried to scream, but the blood choked him.

Pain ravaged his body. Fury and fear twisted his stomach . . . even as the claws ripped into his gut.

No!

"Hope you enjoy every moment . . ." That damn voice. "Hope you like how it *feels*."

Cold swept over his skin, and Omayo fought. No, no, he hadn't fallen for this. Not the pain, not hell—

The twisted teeth sank into his throat and stole his scream.

"Go to hell, Fallen. See how that feels."

* * *

Sam stared down into Seline's face as a roaring filled his ears. "Rog . . . ziel." He bit the name out from between clenched teeth. His least favorite punishment angel. Rogziel liked the job too much.

Time for a house cleaning upstairs. Rogziel needs to fall, and I need to rip him apart.

"How long have you been with him?" he demanded.

Her lips parted, and he glimpsed her small, pink tongue. Even though he should have been sated—*how many times did I have her?*—his cock didn't get the message. It jerked and rose eagerly toward her and she was naked and—

He dropped his hold and stepped back. His elbow rammed into the door.

"I've been with him for nearly thirty years."

What? "Impossible, you can't—"

"When my mother died, he took me in." Her shoulders straightened. "He raised me, provided me with shelter and food, and in return . . ." A brief hesitation as she drew in a deep breath, then Seline said, "In return, when I was old enough, he wanted me to help him hunt."

He stared at her. Didn't risk touching her again, couldn't. He knew a lie when he heard it, and if he touched her with rage, his control might slip. When his control slipped, people died. "Bullshit." Was she still setting him up? Was this all just some trick to get under his guard?

Sam caught the faint narrowing of her eyes. "It's true," Seline said.

"An angel would never take in a succubus." And sure as sin not one as freaking rule-oriented as Rogziel. Rogziel was old school. Sam had heard his spiel plenty of times. Demons were abominations. Angels shouldn't have sex with humans. Do your duty. Punish the guilty.

Blah, fucking blah.

She grabbed for the sheet, and he missed the view when she covered herself. "For your information, I'm only half-succubus."

Right. Which begged the question . . . "So what's your other half?"

Her lips clamped together.

Fine. It didn't really matter to him. She could be some new breed half-vamp, half-demon miracle, and he wouldn't feel differently. If the little hybrid didn't want to share, he sure wouldn't lose any sleep. "He kept you for thirty years." Now that part actually did piss him off, more than it should, and the rage pumped hotter.

"He didn't *keep* me, okay? I was a baby."

Shit, she was only thirty? Talk about robbing the cradle. A succubus could easily hide her age— or just not age at all. He'd never suspected she was so young.

Seline huffed out a hard breath. "I didn't even know—" she began as red stained her cheeks.

"That Rogziel was a sadist with his own twisted sense of right and wrong?" She'd worked with him. So much time— enough time for Rogziel to twist her. "Tell me, how many men did you kill for him?" *Don't touch her.* He could never touch her with this fury fueling him. "How many did you seduce?"

She spun away and grabbed her clothes. The sheet dropped, he got one fine view of her ass, then she yanked on her clothes. "Screw you!"

He raised a brow. "You already did."

Obviously, that wasn't the right thing to say. A blast of psychic power hit him and tossed him across the room. When Sam picked himself off the floor, he glared at her. The woman was definitely stronger than she'd been before.

But, wait, if she was stronger, then shouldn't that mean he was *weaker*?

Hell. A succubus only got stronger when she took power. He'd been so busy drinking her in that he hadn't even realized what she could have been doing to him.

If she's trying to set me up, I gave her the perfect opportunity.

The fire . . . had it been a trap? A way to get to him? He'd burned and would never forget that pain, so he hadn't been able to just stand there and watch the fire ravage her skin.

Then she'd told him sensual energy was the only way for her to heal . . .

"Why are you looking at me like that?" Seline demanded as she crossed her arms over her chest. "You deserved that shove. You're lucky I didn't slam your head into the wall."

Sex equaled strength for her.

Weakness for him?

He waved his hand.

Seline yelped and her body lifted up into the air. Then wind rushed against Sam as she fought back, but this time, he was ready for her push of power.

In the face of her psychic blast, he didn't move. Interesting. So she hadn't taken enough to weaken him, not yet.

One more reason to leave the pretty succubus behind. Because if he stayed with her, he'd have her again.

He couldn't afford any weakness.

She swore as she bobbed in the air. He skirted around her.

"Sam! Dammit, let me down!" Her feet came close to kicking his face.

"No." He would though, eventually. But right then, he had a bastard brother to hunt, and he couldn't have her slowing him down.

He also couldn't trust her. Not if she'd been working with Rogziel. So she'd stay put, for now.

Sam opened the door.

"No! You can't leave me like this!"

He looked back at her. Seline's face was flushed with fury. Her eyes couldn't have burned darker. "Don't you do it!" She yelled as she thrashed helplessly in the air. "Don't—"

"Sorry, sweetheart, but Az is out there." He'd already lost too much time, but he hadn't been able to turn away from her when she needed him—or when he needed her. "He's still weak from the fall, but he won't stay that way for long." Sam would take any advantage he could get in the battle to come. "But don't worry, I'll send a demon to take care of you."

"What?" Did fear flicker in her eyes? "No, Sam, you—"

He shut the door. Her screams followed him. So did the thud of furniture. The woman must be using her power to wreck the room. If she wasn't careful, she'd wear herself out, or rather, she'd wear her power out.

Good. That was just what he wanted . . . Seline weaker and more controllable. Sam began to whistle.

Hunting time.

He'd left her hanging—literally. Seline twisted and snarled, but she seemed to hang suspended courtesy of invisible hands. The guy wasn't even around, but he still trapped her easily. Talk about a powerhouse.

Just what would happen when a demon came to "take care" of her? She bit back her anger and pulled in her energy. No sense wasting her power now. Okay, yes, she'd already smashed two chairs and a TV set, but she was back in control now. She could *think* past the fury, and she knew she'd better save her power for whoever was unlucky enough to come in that room.

So she waited. *Waited*.

Time seemed to crawl by as she dangled in the air. Then finally the door began to creak open.

Cole's dark head appeared. It figured that Sam would send his right-hand demon flunkie to deal with her. Cole glanced at her, and his brows rose. Then he leaned back against the door frame, crossed his arms, and actually smirked.

Thanks for giving me a reason.

She blasted the jerk.

The fire at the warehouse was out. Now, all that remained was a sodden black mess that reeked of ash. A few firefighters were still at the scene, and Sam saw several cops and a guy he tagged as an arson investigator scanning the area. They were making notes, talking to each other, and looking worried. This was way above their pay scale.

As the sun rose higher into the sky, Sam stood in the shadows of a nearby building and watched. Waited.

Rogziel. He'd wondered if the bastard was lurking around. Sam had been itching to rip that guy's wings off for centuries. Pretentious prick.

And Seline had spent thirty years with him? Her whole life? Talk about a living hell.

Why would a punishment angel even take in a succubus? Didn't make any sense. To stay with her . . . to keep watching her all this time.

Why Rogziel? What made you develop such an interest in Seline? Maybe that other half of hers *did* matter.

Brakes squealed as a familiar black van pulled to the curb near the blackened warehouse. Ah, he'd been wondering when the van would show again. Cole had traced the van back to a fake name and address. Interesting . . . so Rogziel was trying to cover his tracks a bit.

Two men jumped out of the vehicle, one with pale blond hair and one with hair a dark red. They talked to the cops. Gestured to the scene. Looked all angry and pissed.

Human minions.

What happened to the good old days? The days when angels took care of the dirty work themselves, without hiring it out to the humans. Sometimes, you really had to get your lily-white hands dirty in order to get the job done.

His hands curled around the bars of the motorcycle he'd "borrowed" earlier. He watched the two males climb back inside the van, and when they took off, he was right on their trail.

Getting his hands dirty had never been a big problem for him.

"Get me down from here!" Seline screamed.

Cole slowly picked himself off the floor. He rubbed his jaw. She'd been feeling pissy, so she'd let his pretty-boy face slam into the bathroom door. "No can do, ma'am."

Oh, great, and Texas flowed beneath his words.

Seline kicked out into the air. She was flailing like a freaking fish.

"Boss's magic." Cole gave a shrug. One of those I-don't-give-a-fuck shrugs. "I'm just here to make sure you don't hurt yourself."

Fabulous. Sam had actually sicced his guard dog on her. "More likely, I'll hurt you."

A ghost of a smile lifted his lips. "I'm not the one who left you hanging." Now his gaze drifted down her legs. "I don't . . . ah . . . normally leave women like that."

She stilled. No way was the demon Casanova hitting on her. But . . .

She was still riding high on the energy she'd taken from Sam. She'd never gotten a boost like that in her whole life. As far as she knew, she could be emitting some kind of succubus beacon. *Come . . . let's sex it up*.

She lifted her hand. "Get the eyes off my legs or you'll get another hit." As if she didn't have enough to deal with right then. "And get me *down*!"

He crossed his arms again—must be his favorite pose. Then as she glared at him, Cole slowly lifted his eyes and propped his back against the wall. "Only Sam can free you."

"Then call him on the phone and tell him to put me down!" So she could go and kick his ass.

Cole shook his head and managed to look exceedingly unconcerned. How many times had he found floating women in his boss's bedroom? Her jaw clenched so hard that her back teeth ached. *Bastard*. Was this a normal morning routine?

"I can't go calling him now. Sorry, ma'am," he finally drawled. "See . . . Sam doesn't exactly trust you."

Good enough for sex, not good enough for trust. Damn him.

Cole's eyes flashed demon black and his handsome face hardened. "He doesn't trust you, and neither do I."

Well, so much for being a succubus beacon. Right then, the guy looked like he could readily kill her.

The humans didn't lead Sam to Az. They took him to a graveyard instead.

It was still too early for most tourists—he'd noticed they liked to hit the cemeteries in the evening or at night—so the place was deserted. Sam shoved down the kickstand on his motorcycle and waited a beat, then he followed the men past the old, wrought-iron gates.

He'd seen the humans grab a bag before they'd gone inside. He knew he wasn't the only one hunting this day.

The tourists who came to New Orleans would be freaking terrified if they knew what really waited in those crypts. Then they'd stop leaving their offerings for voodoo queens and stop slipping in for "haunted" tours.

He knew what hid inside the coffins, but didn't care enough to be terrified.

He watched as the men pried open a door and then slipped in an old vault. One that had been around since the late 1800s. Sam heard the shuffle of footsteps and then the sudden scream that erupted, a scream that seemed to burst from the crypt.

Sam tensed, but then the redhead came flying out of the crypt. *His* scream. The scream ended abruptly when the guy hit the nearest monument.

Sam guessed the hunters had taken on prey they couldn't handle.

If that "prey" killed the blonde before Sam got a chance to question him . . . *I'll lose valuable time.*

He hated wasting time. Sighing, he rolled his shoulders and stalked forward. He'd just reached the old entrance to the white tomb when the explosion hit him. Fire raced around him—more fucking fire—and the world disappeared in a swirl of red.

Too late, he realized that he'd walked straight into a trap.

Seline fell to the floor. Her hands slapped against the hard wood even as her knees bruised at the jarring impact.

"What the hell?" Cole lunged forward.

Not so fast. She threw up her hand and sent a bolt of power at him. It crackled in the air like electricity, and it arched as it hit him dead center in the chest.

Normally a demon's power didn't work so well against another demon. But then, she wasn't a demon. Not really. Not fully. So those "rules" didn't work when she was playing.

She shoved back up to her feet even as a bad feeling settled in the pit of her stomach. "Why am I free?"

He grunted and rubbed his chest.

Seline lifted her arm. She didn't like the possibilities that were running through her mind. She liked it even less when Cole snapped—

"You're free . . . because Sam's power must have just taken one major hit."

And Cole wasn't coming at her to attack. He'd jumped to his feet, and he was running out of the room, leaving her behind.

The right-hand demon, going to protect his big boss.

But if Sam needed protecting . . .

Then my plans are shot to hell.

Seline raced right after Cole, aware that she should still be pissed with the Fallen. But, instead, she was just worried.

Sam's power must have taken one major hit.

No, dammit, *no.*

She needed him too much to lose him this quickly.

CHAPTER SIX

The smoke led Seline and Cole to the cemetery. It was pretty hard to miss that giant black cloud of smoke and the screams of all the sirens that filled the streets.

They pushed through the crowd of gawking on-lookers, and, oh, hell. It looked like some kind of bomb had gone off. The old mausoleums were savaged. Chunks of marble littered the ground, and yeah, Seline was pretty sure that bones were scattered around the fire.

"Where is he?" she whispered to Cole, keeping close to him. When he'd jumped in his truck, she'd bounded inside with him and rushed to the rescue. Not that she'd given the demon much of a choice in getting her company. She hadn't planned to be left behind.

A body had been covered on the ground. Not one of the cemetery's older residents—no, those poor souls would need to be picked up for days and semi-pieced back together—but from the looks of things, the covered body was a fresh arrival.

Don't be Sam.

She took a step forward.

Cole grabbed her arm. "That's not him."

Then she saw the wisps of red hair sticking out above that dark cover.

She released the breath she hadn't realized that she'd been holding. Her gaze swept the scene. Maybe Sam hadn't been here. Maybe this was just some really screwed-up—

Alex's van.

Seline stiffened when her gaze locked on the vehicle she knew too well. *This isn't good.*

"The place was an inferno when I got here!" A man's raised voice had her eyes flying to him. "And I ain't drunk!" He waved his hands at the cop who stood before him. "I'm tellin' you for the sixth time—a man came out of that fire. He just fuckin' walked right out of it!"

Sam. She finally took a deep breath.

"His clothes were burnin', but he wasn't." The guy, older, wearing a white shirt that had already started to show his sweat, shook his head. "He looked like the damn devil."

Definitely her Sam. No one else fit that description quite like him.

The cop sighed and glanced at another uniform. She caught the raised brows and knew they weren't even close to buying the guy's story.

Didn't matter. She was ready to buy it.

Seline waited until the cops stepped away and went off to interview more witnesses, probably folks they hoped would be more reliable. Then she grabbed Cole and headed for the man who was now making the sign of the cross over his body.

"Uh, excuse me, sir . . ." Seline began.

He turned toward her, with his eyes narrowing.

She tried a smile. "I couldn't help but overhear—"

"I'm not fuckin' crazy!" Sweat trickled down the side of his face.

Firefighters were shooting giant streams of water at the remaining flames.

"No, of course not," she soothed. "But could you tell me . . . the man you saw"—the man she didn't see any place now—"where did he go?"

The witness blinked his light blue eyes. "You believe me?"

She gave a quick nod. *"Where did he go?"*

A sigh heaved out of the guy as he swiped his hand over his forehead. "He chased after the other one."

She kept her expression blank, but it was Cole who demanded, "Other one?"

"That blond guy." He glanced down at the dirt stains on his shirt. "I tried to help him, thought he might have been hurt in the fire, but the guy just shoved me and ran." His gaze tracked to the right and to the alley that snaked behind the cemetery. "Poor dumbass. The devil was followin' him."

"Not the devil," Seline muttered. Not quite.

"Close enough," Cole said instantly.

That just made the witness stare at them with a slack jaw.

Time to leave.

They hurried toward that alley. Blond. Okay, two possibilities for the blond male's identity. Option one . . . Alex. His van was parked close by and the cemetery still burned—had he set a trap for Sam?

Rogziel wouldn't be giving up on his prey so easily, and she'd seen Alex use his come-and-get-me routine before. He lured the prey in, then attacked with everything that he had.

But if Sam had chased after him, *everything* hadn't been enough this time.

Or if it wasn't Alex, then it could be Az. Her option two was a whole lot scarier than a human who thought he was tough.

Seline and Cole followed the snaking alley away from the cemetery and the crowd. The stench of garbage surrounded her as she jumped over things that she really didn't want to think about too hard.

They turned another corner, and she stopped cold when she saw the scene before her.

Alex stood with his back pressed against a dirty brick wall. His hands were up, his eyes wide. Dark ash covered his face and clothes. He was breathing hard, the ragged sounds filling the air, and it sounded like he might be . . . begging?

Sam stood in front of him. No burning clothes. Perfect clothes again. Not so much as a hint of soot or ash on him. Mere inches separated Sam from Alex.

"Seline!" Alex saw her and screamed her name. "Call your dog *off!*"

Not her dog. Sam didn't glance back at her.

"Stay away, Seline," he said.

But Alex's desperate eyes were on her. "He's going to kill me!" he cried as spittle flew from his mouth.

"Only fair." Sam's voice held a taunting edge. "You tried to kill me today."

Seline crept forward. Cole stood back, waiting.

"Here's a tip," Sam said, and as Seline circled around the men, she caught the flash of his grin. "You're not strong enough to kill me. Your weapons aren't strong enough. All you manage to do is piss me off." He lifted his hand. "Guess what happens when I get pissed?"

Alex pressed back even more against the bricks. It looked like the guy was trying to shrivel up.

"I make you hurt." Sam moved in that too-fast blur he did so well.

Alex screamed and grabbed for his left hand. Uh, his hand was facing the wrong direction. The bones had been broken in a blink of time.

She swallowed. "Sam . . ."

He didn't look her way. "You should have stayed at the safe house."

She tensed. Now he was going to talk about that?

"She's in this!" More spittle flew from Alex's mouth as he cradled his injured hand. "She's fucking in this! Do your job, Seline—get this bastard! Drain him like you were supposed to!"

Seline didn't move, not so much as an inch.

Did Sam's shoulders stiffen? Hard to say. No change of expression crossed his face.

"Seline!" Alex bellowed.

She glanced back over her shoulder. Good thing those sirens were still wailing. Otherwise, they'd be having company. But the sirens *were* wailing, and she knew they were covering Alex's cries. "I'm not working for Rogziel anymore."

Alex laughed. "Is that the story you're spinning?" He let his hands fall.

"Yes," she said quietly, and took a deep breath. "Alex, where's Az?"

His lips firmed into a thin line.

"Just tell me—"

"How the hell should I know? You're the one who let him go last night!"

Not quite.

She glanced over her shoulder once more. This whole setup wasn't good. They shouldn't be outside like this. "We need to get out of here." If Sam wanted, he could bring Alex with him, but right then, they needed to split. "We're gonna have company soon." Because Rogziel's teams never worked alone. There was always backup lurking nearby.

And not all the other teams would leave Alex to his fate—*the way he left me*.

"Let them come." Sam shrugged.

Right. Well, if she was an all-powerful Fallen who'd walked through fire without a burn, she might be shrugging, too. And to think, she'd actually raced over on the idea that he might need her help.

Delusions. Apparently, she had them.

But a loud *pop* filled the air, like an exploding firecracker, and Cole cried out in pain. Her gaze flew to him, and Seline saw that he'd grabbed his shoulder. His bleeding shoulder.

Shot. Not firecrackers, nothing nearly so innocent.

More bullets littered the alley. Sam didn't flinch, but Seline ducked for cover even as one bullet flew right by her.

Too close!

Bullets hailed down around them. Sam grabbed her and twisted, protecting her with his body. She glanced up at him. Oh, wait, there he went, being all nice again. But it was probably a trick; he'd probably just leave her dangling in the air again in a few moments once the gunfire stopped.

A rush of wind filled the alley. Alex's footsteps thudded as he raced past them. She heard distant yells, quickly choked off, and knew that Sam had used his power to reach the gunmen.

Guess that backup team wouldn't be coming after all.

"Cole?" Sam snapped out. "You okay?"

The demon was on his knees, bloody, but his head lifted and he gave a wave with his left hand.

Sam stepped back and turned to him.

Alex was getting away. Seline took off after him. Her legs pumped fast and she jumped into the air.

"Seline!" Sam's snarl.

She tackled Alex. "You're not getting away that easily." They crashed onto the pavement.

"Fucking demon bitch. *Traitor.*" He rolled and came up fast. "You're not getting away at all." And the knife he'd gripped in his right hand came at her throat.

Before he could touch her, Sam touched *him*.

Alex's whole body jerked as if he'd just been hit with an electrical charge. His eyes rolled back into his head, and a silent scream contorted his face.

He shuddered, then a moment later he fell to the ground, his body frozen. Dead.

Seline's gaze rose to Sam's. The pounding of her heart seemed far too loud. He'd told her what he could do, she'd known how powerful he was, but *seeing* him, well . . .

He'd just killed with a touch.

Very, very scary.

He offered his hand to her.

She was afraid of him. Sam could all but see her fear. Seline climbed onto Sam's motorcycle, and she tentatively put her arms around his waist. Slow motions, every move so very hesitant, as if she were worried that touching him would be lethal to her.

"Tighter," he ordered as he kicked away from the curb. They had to clear out of there as quickly as they could. Even the human cops wouldn't overlook the thunder of gunshots.

Or the dead body that they'd left behind.

But the moment that the human Seline called Alex had risen with his knife and gone for her throat, the guy had been a dead man.

Alex just had to wait a few precious seconds for Sam's touch to make his heart stop.

Death could be slow. Death could be fast. And when he wanted, Sam could make those last moments *hurt*.

Alex hadn't been given an easy death. The proof had been in the torment that twisted his face.

Seline's hands tightened a bit around Sam. The motorcycle raced forward, and the heavy metal body vibrated beneath him.

Seline still wasn't close enough.

Because of the fucking fear.

Why? She'd known what he was before. He'd told her. She worked for Rogziel. She had to know how dangerous his kind was.

But her eyes had gone so wide when Alex dropped to the ground. Her lips had trembled, and when Sam had reached for her, Seline had pulled back.

She'd begged for his touch just hours before. Now she pulled away from him. *Too scared to touch.*

His hands tightened around the handlebars.

The wind pushed against them as he swept through the streets.

Were more of Rogziel's goons following them? Why did the punisher suddenly have such a hard-on for him?

All these years, and *now* Rogziel decided to focus on him? Right after Az's fall? No way could that be a coincidence. But if Rogziel wanted to play . . .

Come and get me.

He'd love to rip those wings away for old 'Ziel.

Sam took Seline away from the city. He raced across old railroad tracks and slid beneath sagging bridges that looked like time had forgotten them. When they went off the road, Seline gasped and clutched him tighter.

Finally.

He didn't stop until the sounds of the city were no more. Then, when he was sure he could see any hunter coming after him, he killed the engine.

The swamp surrounded him again. Twisting trees, heavy heat.

She immediately pulled away and jumped off the bike. Jaw clenching, he followed her.

Seline put a good five feet between them. "You . . . you . . ." Her hand gestured in the air, and she seemed to struggle for words. He didn't help her. He just watched and waited while the anger grew inside of him.

Afraid to touch me.

"It's true," she finally said, a faint furrow between her brows. "You can really—"

"You're a succubus. You use your body as a lure to drain power from men." He made the words deliberately harsh, and she flinched.

"Dammit, that's not—"

"You work for a punisher who spends his days doling out vengeance. You *knew* I was a Fallen." He stalked toward her. She backed up a step.

His eyes narrowed. Was she trying to piss him off even more? "Everything you know, everything you've seen . . ." he grated. "And what? You thought I was lying?"

She swallowed and shook her head slowly. "N-no." The sun spilled behind her, lighting her hair, making her skin shine and making her look even more gorgeous. "I've never seen . . ." Her voice was husky and stroked right over his groin. "You killed him with just a touch."

And he knew demons who were strong enough to kill with a thought. Evolution had made the *Other* stronger, and for some, too hard to kill. Death could be a challenge some days.

Her chin rose. "Why haven't you killed me?"

He lunged forward, knowing the move would look like a blur to her eyes. A handy Fallen side effect—near super speed. Not that it made up for having his wings burned away as he plummeted, but . . .

Sam caught her arm and pulled her close. Tension held her body taut. More fear. He hated fear in a woman's eyes. "I didn't fall yesterday." No, so many centuries before. "I've learned how to"—he brought his face close to hers—"*control* myself," Sam finished with his lips inches from hers.

The Fall had been brutal. He'd woken, naked, broken with his mind torn open. It had taken weeks for him to remember who—what—he was.

No control. Not then. At first, he'd been like a wounded animal. More than ready to turn on anyone or anything who came too close.

But he'd learned to focus his powers. Slowly, painfully. "I can bring death with my touch." His lips brushed over hers. She didn't flinch. He took that as a sign of progress. "Or I can bring pleasure." It was all a matter of what he wanted.

With her, he wanted pleasure.

"Still scared of me, Seline?" he asked, even as his fingers sank into her hair. He tipped her head back.

"Yes." He knew she spoke the stark truth. He could see it reflected in her eyes. "How do I know"—she licked her lips and he wanted that tongue licking him—"that you won't turn on me?"

Now there was an interesting question. "And how do I know that the next time we fuck, you won't try to kill me?" Because there would be a next time. He'd found something he wanted, and he wasn't planning to let her get away.

He caught the faint flash of black in her eyes. Yes, he was rubbing his body against hers, letting his fingers play with the sensitive spot he'd found just on the back of her neck. A succubus's strength was her passion, but that passion could be used against her.

If her lover knew what he was doing.

I know, sweetheart. He wasn't above manipulation.

"You need to trust me," he said.

She exhaled on a soft breath. "And you'll trust me?"

Not yet. Maybe one day.

"Rogziel will come after you," Sam stated flatly, but didn't let her go. "Do you think you'll be strong enough to stop him?"

"Will you?" she fired right back.

The calculation in her eyes reached him and gave Sam a moment's pause. Well, well. "Is that what you wanted from the beginning?" When she'd been so eager to serve up his brother and abandon her allegiance to Rogziel?

"I want my freedom. That's all I've ever wanted."

But he held her trapped against him then.

"I've always known that Rogziel would never just let me walk away." Her lips twisted into a humorless smile. "He thinks I'm too dangerous to be loose."

Her curves pressed against him. Her plump lips tempted his mouth. So he said, with certainty, "You are."

Seline gave a hard shake of her head. "No, when it comes to the power scale, I'm nothing like you."

His little succubus didn't understand. There were all kinds of power in this world. Some were subtle, but still damn dangerous.

"When you're free of Rogziel," and she'd only be free when that guy was dead, "what are you going to do?"

"Disappear," she said with soft longing. "I'll leave this city. Go somewhere with a white sand beach and crystal blue water. I won't think about death or monsters . . . or anything, but life."

She didn't get it. When you were an *Other*, you didn't get to close your eyes and pretend that the monsters weren't real. Not when the humans in the world thought you were the monster. But he didn't shatter her little dream, not yet.

He needed her. If he told her the dream was bullshit, the woman might tell him to fuck off. "Do you still want our deal to work?"

Her gaze held his. Not black now, but that false brown stare of hers that could look so warm and trusting. "Yes."

"Then you stay with me." Because he'd been telling her the truth. Rogziel would come for her, sooner or later. "I get Az, then I'll make sure you get your freedom from Rogziel."

He could see the hope light her face. Demons had hope? Yes, they did. Sometimes they had more hope than angels.

But then her eyelashes flickered. "I don't know where Az is anymore. I can't help you—"

Ah, honesty. Trust might even be coming soon. "Yes, you can." He released her and stepped back because if he kept touching her, they'd be fucking soon.

Now wasn't the time to fuck, no matter how tempting she was.

Hunt.

"Rogziel caught Az," he said.

"Uh, yeah, I know—"

"How'd he do that? How'd he know where my dear brother would be?" He lifted a brow because he already knew the answer. "Rogziel can always find those on his punishment list, right?" That was supposed to be the way for the punishers. No need to waste time searching for prey; not when you had a built-in homing device for them.

But Seline shook her head. "No, no, we always have to hunt those that Rogziel targets."

Sam didn't let the surprise flicker on his face. *That*

wasn't the way the game worked. Seline wouldn't know that, though, and the humans that Rogziel had on leashes sure wouldn't understand how a punisher's power worked.

"Finding Az was almost an accident."

Sam cocked his head. "Some say there are no accidents. No coincidences. Everything happens the way it was meant to be." If you subscribed to that philosophy, he'd been born to Fall, and to kill.

Seline shrugged, but the move didn't look careless. "Rogziel had another Fallen in his sights, a guy named Omayo."

Sam didn't let his expression alter. "What happened to him?"

"Before we could move to capture Omayo, Az literally fell into our laps. You could say our focus of attack shifted then."

Az's Fall had been recent. He would have still been weak when Rogziel caught him. What a stroke of luck for the punisher. "You want me to help you, then you stay by my side and you give me every bit of information that I want on Rogziel and that group he's got helping him."

Now she slipped back. Fear didn't flicker across her face, but hesitation sure did. "What will you do to them?"

Because she *cared* about some of the humans there?

"Alex was a jerk, don't get me wrong."

A jerk who'd tried to kill her.

"But the others . . . they're just trying to do what's right. They've lost people they love. They know that evil has to be punished and—"

And he was bored. She sounded like some pupil reciting a lesson she'd learned at school—a mantra that Rogziel had no doubt taught her. A nice way to brainwash his recruits into being good little killers.

"Don't worry," he said, lifting his hands and holding them, palm out, to her. "I won't touch them." *Yet.* "Just give me the information you know, help me to find Az, and I'll make sure you get what you want most in this world."

Her stare judged him. One moment. Two. Then she gave a small, grudging nod.

Good.

He didn't let the satisfaction show on his face. Even if she hadn't agreed, he hadn't planned to let her go. The deal wasn't truly about Az or Rogziel.

I just want her.

He turned away, knowing she would follow. He climbed onto the motorcycle and revved the engine. "We need to see Omayo." He'd give the messenger angel a heads-up. After all, Omayo had never done anything to anger him.

Omayo had just lusted too much for humans. Not for their bodies, but for their emotions.

Then he'd fallen and gotten slapped with every feeling he could possibly want.

Giving Omayo a warning that he'd made Rogziel's list only seemed fair. Besides, Sam also knew that Omayo still had an in with a few angels. Messages always had to be exchanged, and even the Fallen could still manage some jobs.

He'd warn Omayo, and in payment, Sam would see if he couldn't get a message sent to someone who would lead him to Az.

Run, brother, run fast—because I'm coming for you.

Seline slid on the motorcycle behind him. Her hesitation was brief, barely a second, but he still felt it, and then her soft hands slowly slid around his waist.

He spun the motorcycle around, kicking up a cloud of dirt, and headed back for the city. As they drove, her hands tightened more around him and her body pressed closer.

He smiled.

The succubus wouldn't realize how she truly fit into his plans, not until it was too late. By then, there'd be no hope of freedom for her.

You can't make a deal with Death.

Seline eased off the bike. She could still feel the vibration in her thighs. Her steps were a bit unsteady as she hurried down the sidewalk.

Omayo's apartment waited less than a block away. "How did you know he was here?" she asked Sam.

He glanced at her, raising a brow. "Omayo found me after he fell." One shoulder rolled in a light shrug. "Let's just say he came to my club looking for Temptation."

Oh, right. She'd been on stakeout duty a few times at Omayo's place. From what she'd seen of him and the ladies, he'd liked his *Temptation* a lot.

They walked in silence for a while, then they eased up on Omayo's place.

With a wave of his hand, Sam sent the front door of Omayo's building flying open. They stepped inside, and Seline's gaze went to the staircase on the right. The bottom level was just an old garage, but she knew they'd find Omayo upstairs. Seline hurried forward.

Sam grabbed her hand. *"No."*

She froze. The place was as quiet as a tomb, and it kinda smelled like one, too. Her nose wrinkled.

His nostrils flared at the same time, and his gaze darkened to midnight black. *"Omayo."*

Then he was gone. No, he hadn't vanished—he'd just run insanely fast, and when she saw him again, he was already at the top of the stairs. Seline rushed after him. "Sam?"

Wood splintered and crashed upstairs, and she heard a bellow from Sam that sent a shiver through her.

Then she was at the top of the landing. Seline ran into the apartment, but after only a few steps, she froze at the sight before her.

Blood—so much blood. *Everywhere*. On the walls. The floor. Even the ceiling.

Sam had bent over the broken body that lay sprawled on the floor. He shifted a bit, and she saw Omayo's face. She wanted to close her eyes and look away because there was so much terror and pain carved onto his frozen features.

Sam's hands fisted and his head turned, very slowly, to meet hers. "Is this what you've been doing for your whole life?"

She barely heard the words. Her gaze was on Omayo's throat. No, what was left of it. His throat had been ripped open. Her own hand rose to cover her mouth as the stench of death and blood nearly choked her. *So much worse than a tomb.*

Sam surged to his feet and stalked toward her. "*He didn't deserve this!* Omayo never hurt anyone or anything. He fucking delivered messages! He delivered his messages, did his job for five thousand years, and the bastard just wanted the chance to *feel*. He got to Fall, and he wasn't hurting anyone."

No, no, Omayo hadn't been hurting anyone. When word had come through that he was a possible Fallen, she'd been sent in for surveillance. Though she'd watched, she'd never gotten very close to him. Everything had been from a careful distance. Hell, she'd never even noticed his wings, or rather, the shadowy image that followed Sam.

After just a few days, it had quickly become clear that—whatever he was—Omayo wasn't in town to hurt or destroy anyone. He'd kept to himself, barely communicated with anyone except the human ladies he seemed to like, and he sure hadn't been looking for trouble.

"Your *team* did this!" Sam stood right in front of her now. His power seemed to surround her, trapping her in place. "Is this—is this the kind of twisted shit that you've done to the *Other*?"

She shook her head as his words finally sank in. *"No!"* She grabbed his arms. "You can't think—"

But his face could have been carved from stone. "It's your job to take out the guilty, right? By any means necessary." He glanced back at Omayo. "Fallen aren't easy to kill. So I guess, sometimes, things get a little . . . messy."

Her nails dug into his skin. "This isn't the way we operate." The kill was fresh. That smell . . . She tried really hard not to inhale. Her gaze flew around the room. Blood had dripped in rivulets down the walls. "This was—"

"A slaughter?"

Yes. She nodded. "The kills are clean and quick, and only for those that Rogziel has—"

"But Omayo was on his list, right? Another Fallen to take down."

"He was only to be watched, not killed! Dammit, not killed!"

"I guess someone didn't get that message."

Sam pulled away from her and yanked out his phone. He punched the screen and lifted the phone to his ear. A pause, then he barked, "Cole, dammit, I need a cleanup crew at Omayo's, and I need the crew *now.*" He ran a hand through his hair. "We aren't leaving him like this."

She turned away, not wanting to look at the body. But the blood was all over the place. So much and—

Her heart slammed into her chest. The blood on the left wall . . . Someone had *written* in that blood.

The letters had dripped, become slanted and twisted, but she could still make out the one word.

Fallen.

"Sam." She said his name too softly. He was still growling into the phone. She spun around. *"Sam!"*

He turned to face her. She lifted her hand and pointed to the wall. "I think we've got a problem."

Sam marched to her side. He stared at the letters on the wall. After a moment, he asked, voice lethally soft, "Did Rogziel have other Fallen Angels that were being watched?"

She swallowed to ease the desert dryness in her throat. "Other than you?" she asked, wanting desperately to be out of that apartment. "Not like he even *told* me you were Fallen." No, he'd just let her walk blindly into that one. "The guy wasn't exactly sharing confidences with me."

Sam's eyes were still on the bloody wall.

She had to get out of there. Seline rushed for the door, nearly running because she couldn't stay in the apartment with the body another moment. She'd done plenty of things that she regretted in her thirty years, but she'd *never* seen anything like that. Sam was right. It was a *slaughter.*

Had Rogziel really gone that far past reason?

She nearly flew back down the stairs. Seline was desperate to get some air that didn't taste like death. She shoved open the building's front door. The light hit her, too bright, but the air was clean. She sucked in deep, gulping breaths and stumbled away.

Oh, crap, had Rogziel done that? She'd tried to put on a front with Sam, but she'd *seen* what Rogziel had done on his last hunt. His attack hadn't been quick and easy, and she wasn't even certain that his prey had been marked for punishment.

That's when I knew I had to get away from him.

She'd wanted her freedom for years, but it hadn't been until that moment that she'd truly realized . . . *if I don't get away, I'm dead.* Her fingers yanked through her hair as she sucked in another desperate gulp of fresh air.

Had he done this . . . and, oh, God, did I help him?

Because she'd been the one to first find Omayo. She'd been the one to keep tabs on him and give those ridiculous punctual reports to Rogziel.

I might as well have just tied him up with a big, red bow for Rogziel.

If . . . *if* Rogziel had been the one to kill him.

Another deep breath. Maybe one more gulp and her hands would stop shaking.

Seline didn't get that breath. A hand slapped over her mouth, blocking the air and choking back the scream that built in her throat.

CHAPTER SEVEN

In the next instant, Seline was shoved back against the side of the building. The bricks bruised her flesh as she stared up at the man who'd attacked her.

Not like she'd ever forget those icy blue eyes.

Azrael stared back at her, and, oh, damn, oh, no—he was covered in blood.

Now *she* was covered in blood. His body smashed into hers, and she could feel the wet stain of blood on her chest. And, *please,* don't let that be blood on his hand, not on the hand covering her mouth. *Don't let it be . . .*

"Angels . . . fall . . ." he whispered. His voice came out sounding a bit distorted and hollow. She tried to wrench her head back and get away from that hand, but there was nowhere for her to go. "They burn," he muttered. "They . . . fall."

The guy wasn't saying anything she didn't already know.

His blue eyes slowly faded to black, and Azrael glanced down at the hand that covered her mouth. "They . . . bleed."

She rammed her knee into his crotch. As hard as she could.

He didn't release her, but his face hardened even more. "I . . . know you." Now that sounded like an accusation.

Her stomach knotted. She couldn't throw her power at him because she was bone dry. Where the hell was Sam? *Hello, come and get your big, bad psycho brother—he's right here!* She punched Azrael. The punch bruised her knuckles but didn't do anything to him. Az frowned, and he caught her fingers in a grip that *hurt* with his left hand.

Hurt but didn't kill. If he could kill with a touch, why was she still breathing? What was he waiting for?

And why had Omayo been savaged? If Az had gone after him, there would have been no need for torture, not when a light touch would do the job.

"*Know* you," he said again, but the words were stronger now. "Erina."

Seline stopped struggling as her blood turned to ice. Erina had been her mother's name, well, at least that was what Rogziel had told her.

"You'll die," Az said, his voice rough and a little sad. "The Fallen . . . they'll all die."

But she wasn't Fallen. She tried to shake her head as she muttered desperately behind his hand. *Sam! Get your ass down here!*

Az's gaze rose to the building behind her. No, to the balcony above her. "One down," he whispered, "but hell wants more." His stare was so dark now. Too dark. "See," he whispered, and leaned forward so that his forehead touched hers.

Pain ripped through her, an agony that tore and twisted and *burned* because flames were suddenly around her. White, red, and dark orange flames that crackled as they burned the skin from her body. The flames were everywhere, and the fire was so hot it blistered her lungs.

Hell. Somehow, this was—

"Seline!"

She screamed and her eyes flew open. She was on the cement, and Sam was crouched over her. His hands were on her arms, and he was shaking her.

"A-Az . . ." Her throat hurt, and she could actually taste ash on her tongue.

Sam's eyes narrowed. "What?"

"H-here . . ." Her eyes wanted to fall shut again, so she let them. Screw it. Sam was there. He could more than handle Az. *Don't want hell.*

"No, sweetheart, no one else is here."

She couldn't open her eyes. In that moment, everything hurt too much. "He . . . said I'd—die. All Fallen . . . gonna die."

His lips pressed to hers. The kiss was hot, hard, and his tongue pushed right inside her mouth. The ash vanished, the memory of flames receded, and Seline just tasted him. Her hands lifted and curled around Sam's shoulders. Her body shuddered against him.

Thank you. She took his power, drinking it in greedily as the fear faded. He kept kissing her, slow, long kisses.

Sam.

After a time, Sam's head lifted. "Okay?"

No, but she was getting there.

"Az was with you," he said. No question.

She nodded anyway and, yeah, she hunched a little closer to him. When a Fallen tried to kill you—*twice*—it made sense to buddy up to the toughest guy in town.

"Is the blood yours?" he demanded as his gaze swept over her.

She looked down. "I don't . . . think so." Seline wanted to strip those bloody clothes off right then.

Sam's eyes narrowed.

"Omayo's," she told him, her voice still hoarse. "I think it's Omayo's."

"Fuck."

Yeah. "Az said . . . Fallen die." And he'd meant it.

The last thing she remembered before the fire was Az touching her forehead. She'd been sure that he just sent her to hell. That fire had been unmistakable. So . . . "Why am I still breathing?" she asked softly, aware that her fingers were trembling.

Sam rose and turned away from her. His gaze swept the street.

Her movements much slower, Seline stood as well. Despite the power infusion he'd give her, Seline's knees wanted to do a little jiggle. She looked to the left, then the right. She didn't see anyone. "There was so much fire."

His head whipped back toward her. "Where?"

She rubbed her forehead. She could almost feel Az's touch still on her skin. "I-I think I was in hell. I couldn't stop burning."

A silver SUV barreled down the street. She tensed. "Sam . . ." Her hands reached for him and clamped around his arm. *Keep him close.*

"Easy." His breath blew against her hair. "It's just Cole."

Another SUV—blue this time—followed. The vehicles slammed to a stop, and the doors flew open.

Cole rushed toward them. You never would've thought he'd been shot earlier that day. The demon was sure a fast healer.

"Get her out of here," Sam ordered.

Cole blinked. The guys behind him—they were all demons; she could see right through their glamour—hesitated.

"But what about—" Cole began.

"Take her to Sunrise and make sure guards stay with her. No one gets in or out of that place without my permission."

Cole reached for her. Wait, this wasn't the way this scene was supposed to go down. "No, Az is here, he wants—"

"He wants me," Sam said, and a muscle flexed in his jaw. "I'm Fallen, and he thinks he's gonna make me burn. You were my message."

So a little bit of torture for her was a way of jerking around Sam? Az was a sadistic asshole.

Cole had his fingers locked around her arm. She glanced back at Sam. Her knees were still shaking, and, this was awkward because that little trip to hell sure had done a number on her. Her energy had plummeted and though Sam had given her a little boost, the kisses hadn't been enough to fully strengthen her.

She needed so much more, but admitting that fact in front of this group of demons wasn't exactly her plan. "Sam . . ." *Never look weak.* Demons fed on weakness.

She did it often enough.

But Sam had turned away. He and a few of the demons were fanning out on the street. Searching for Az.

Others were heading into the building to take care of Omayo. Or what was left of him.

"Sam . . ." She cleared her throat and tried again. "I need . . ."

He still wasn't looking at her. His whole focus was on searching the scene.

Good luck with that. She knew Az was long gone. Again.

Shaking her head, Seline climbed into the silver SUV. Cole slammed the door shut behind her.

And as the vehicle pulled away from the curb, she wondered why her back still hurt—right beneath both of her shoulder blades. Her back burned and ached, and she felt like she'd lost . . . something in the fire.

A fire that had only been in her mind.

When Sam finally made it to Sunrise, two demons were guarding the door. Tension held his body tight, and rage continued to pump through him.

When he closed his eyes, he could still see Omayo. The messenger angel had never hurt anyone. He hadn't deserved to go out like that.

Sam pushed past the guards and hurried inside the club. The place was deserted, of course, that's why he'd ordered Cole to bring Seline there. No one ever actually came to Sunrise when the sun was up. And he didn't worry about any uninvited guests following him inside then. The demons at the front would keep the place secure. They were a whole lot stronger than they looked.

His gaze drifted around the bar. No sign of Seline. Or Cole.

He remembered the pale flash of Seline's face. Her hands had trembled as she'd talked about the fire.

Damn Az. Though he'd tried to show no reaction, Sam knew just what his brother had done. Az had given Seline a taste of hell.

Soon you'll be the one tasting hell, brother.

The faintest murmur of voices reached him. He glanced upstairs. He had a small apartment up there. Just a bedroom and a bath, a place to crash when the nights rolled together.

He headed for the metal stairs. He needed to find out exactly what Az had said to Seline because he already had a dark suspicion, one that didn't bode well for the Fallen in the area.

A few weeks back, Az had tried to kill another Fallen, but Keenan had been too strong for his brother's attack. Well, Keenan and the vampire lover who'd fought so fiercely at her man's side.

If Az had already tried to kill one Fallen, and Omayo's blood had been on his hands . . . *still trying to play God, Az? Even after the Fall? You think you're the one who should send souls to hell?*

He threw open the door to his apartment, and it took the scene before him a bit too long to register.

Seline lounged on the bed, clad in an oversize white robe while Cole bent over her.

What. The. Fuck.

She'd been attacked, weak, so she would have needed power—

I didn't give her enough.

So she'd turned to Cole? A snarl broke from Sam's lips.

What. The. Fuck.

Sam lunged across the room and grabbed for Cole.

Seline saw him. She jumped up and knocked the demon back before Sam could touch him.

"Dammit, Seline, you didn't have to—" Cole broke off when he got a look at Sam's face. Then the demon's eyes darted from Sam to Seline. "Guess you did." A long sigh slipped from his lips. "I am so screwed," he muttered.

Seline's clothes were tossed onto the floor. "Yeah," Sam said very definitely, "you are."

But Seline stepped between them before Sam could make Cole wish for death. "Ease up, Sam. This isn't what you think."

Doubtful. "That so? I'm not staring at a succubus who decided to get a little power surge . . . and a horny-ass demon who is about to learn a whole new meaning to the word *hurt*?"

"*Succubus?*" Cole repeated, and gave a low sigh. "Yep, that would explain some things."

Seline's cheeks flushed. Sam wasn't sure if that was from anger or embarrassment, and, why would a succubus feel either right then?

He hesitated.

"My clothes were covered in blood," she snapped. "*I* was covered in blood. I showered, and I didn't have anything else to wear. I was *not* putting those back on again." She pointed to the bloodstained pile of clothing.

That bit he could buy, but why had Cole been close enough to take a bite out of her? Sam slanted a hard glance the demon's way.

Cole had his hands up. "Easy. There was some blood on her cheek. I was just wiping it away." There was a cloth in his right hand. Cole's chin lifted. "Though I won't say that I wasn't tempted."

Bastard.

As they glared at each other, Cole's eyes narrowed and bled to black. "If you knew she was a succubus, then you knew what she'd *need*. Next time, you'd better take care of her."

Or I will.

Sam clenched his teeth. He could see the message in Cole's gaze. One of the reasons he liked the demon—Cole wasn't the type to scare easily.

He also loved the ladies, too much.

"Don't worry," Sam managed. "I've got her." *And you stay the fuck away from now on.* Sam knew his message would be crystal clear in his gaze, too.

"Uh, excuse me?" Seline interrupted, waving her hands near his face. "You don't have anything." She was still pale, but her body wasn't trembling.

She still needed him.

"Get out, Cole," Sam ordered bluntly.

Cole shrugged. He cast one more look at Seline, and then he headed for the door.

Sam pushed down his—*what the hell? Was it really jealousy eating its way through his stomach?*—and offered Seline his hand. "Let me help you." Kissing her wasn't exactly a hardship.

"You bastard!"

He blinked.

"You come in here, acting like a jerk, ready to attack Cole. And, yeah, I saw your eyes, so I *know* what you were planning. You bust in here, do your Hulk routine, and then you actually think I'm going to jump into your arms!"

That would have been the best scenario for him, yes.

"Just so you know." She belted the robe around her middle even tighter. "I don't need your help. Whatever your brother did, it was temporary. No permanent damage, so don't feel like you have to sacrifice that hot bod of yours for me again."

It hadn't exactly been a sacrifice. Sam stared at her and decided to be honest. She deserved that. "He showed you hell."

Her lips parted. "Uh, come again?"

"You saw fire, right? I'm betting flames of nearly every color, and they were bright and hungry and it seemed like they were feeding on your flesh." Been there, done that, and he'd never forget the trip. "It's a trick some angels can manage. It's an illusion, nothing more, but let's just say it's a tool that's real effective at getting some folks to repent."

She rolled her shoulders. "It sure felt real. I could even taste the ash."

Because Az was so powerful. With a lesser angel or Fallen, the illusion wouldn't have been as consuming.

Sam stepped toward her.

She stiffened. "I said I didn't need any power. I'm fine now."

But he knew she was lying. He could see the faintest

lines of strain around her eyes and mouth. "Maybe this isn't about you. Maybe it's about me."

She blinked and stared up at him. The confusion was plain to see on her face.

He eliminated the last bit of distance between them. His hand rose slowly, and his fingers traced down her cheek. She didn't flinch away from him, but Seline held herself perfectly still as he stroked her.

"I want you." Blunt. But that was just the way he was.

"You had me," she told him. Those sexy, dark eyes of hers narrowed. "Then you walked out, and left me *hanging*."

Rather literally. He managed not to wince, but he figured he could give her some more truths as payment for his crime. "I don't trust many people in this world." Maybe two. Possibly three.

"Neither do I," she shot right back, and he knew she'd given him truth, too.

Her skin was like silk beneath his fingers. "Perhaps it's time we both tried a little harder."

Her husky laughter took him by surprise. "You actually want me to trust you? After you left me?"

"I was trying to protect you." Another truth, one she might not believe. He frowned, then said quietly, "When it comes to trust, do you have a choice? Rogziel knows that you're involved with me. I hate to break it to you, but your name has just been blasted across the news. The cops found Alex's body, and a witness ID'd you as being at the scene of the crime." A witness he was sure worked with Rogziel.

They were making it known to the world that she was to be hunted.

"You already have others on your trail," he told her. "Stay with me, trust me, and I'll get you through this."

Her gaze held his. "And when it's over? You'll let me just walk away?"

"If that's what you want." A nice blend of lie and truth.

Her breath expelled in a soft rush. "But you have to stop acting like a jealous jerk, got me? I'm gonna be around other men."

Right. Succubus. That's what she—

"But I won't have sex with anyone . . . but you."

She nearly had him lunging at her then. Her confession had his already eager cock swelling even more for her. Did the woman realize how sexy she was?

Her fingers trailed down his chest.

Probably.

"The thing is," she confessed as her fingertips skated across his nipples, "I don't want anyone else."

He had on too many clothes. And that robe she wore—*his*—had to go.

But before he could push the robe out of the way, Seline stepped back. Her hands rose, and she slipped off the robe. It dropped to the floor with a soft rustle. She stood before him, completely naked. Skin pale and perfect. Nipples tight and pink. Sex . . . waiting.

"I don't want soft kisses and sweet words," she told him as she straightened her shoulders. "I don't want promises or lies. I just want you. And I want you now."

Could she be more his kind of woman?

He yanked off his shirt. "Sweetheart, I'm yours."

Her smile would have made a lesser man beg. It made Sam lunge for her. A guy could only hold out for so long.

In an instant, they were on the bed. He didn't start with her mouth. Didn't start with those delectable breasts. Instead he spread her beneath him on the bed. Sam took his time letting his hands slide up her thighs, and then when she was parted and ready, he bent his head and took his taste.

Better than wine.

He stroked her with his tongue. He worked her sweet flesh, enjoying every husky moan that broke from her lips. His fingers slipped inside of her. His lips feathered over her clit.

She jerked her hips up. Not to get away, but to get closer to his mouth.

Taste. Take. He did. Again and again, and she came against his mouth as she gasped out his name.

Her nails dug into his shoulders. He felt a push of power, and the room seemed to roll around him. He looked up and realized that *he* was on his back.

Seline smiled down at him; then she bent and took his aroused flesh into her mouth. Hot. Tight. And her tongue . . .

His back teeth clenched as he gritted out her name.

But Seline didn't stop. She took him in deeper, and she swallowed. She sucked. Sweat slickened his skin as he fought to hold on to his control—that desperate control that wanted to crack.

Then she lifted her head and licked her lips.

A growl burst from his throat.

Seline straddled him, and the hot core of her sex pressed over the length of his cock. She leaned forward, positioned the head of his erection at the entrance to her body, and then she rose above him, her breasts too temptingly close to his mouth.

His lips closed around her breast just as she pushed down with her hips. His cock slid deep inside, and her hot, tight sex gripped every inch of him.

Fucking perfect.

She rose again. Slid down.

He licked her breast. Sucked the nipple. Let her feel the score of his teeth.

She pushed down. Rose up.

His control shattered. He grabbed her, wrapping his hands tightly around her waist. He rolled them and knew they were wrecking the bed. His hips drove down, and he thrust as deep into her as he could go.

Harder. Deeper.

The bed shook. Her nails scraped over his back. His hands bit into her waist. His cock plunged inside of her.

Again, again.

Her eyes were closed. No fucking good. "Look at me," he growled.

Her lashes flew up, and pitch-black eyes met his. The darkness had never burned so bright.

Yes.

She came as she stared at him. He saw the flash of pleasure wipe across her face as her inner muscles clamped around his cock. The ripples of her release stroked his length, and he erupted inside of her.

He held her as the tremors shook him. The pleasure burst through him, hot and long.

She held him, too, her grip so strong—almost as if she were afraid he'd pull away. She didn't need to worry. He wasn't about to let her go.

His stare was still on hers, and he wondered just what she'd seen in that wild instant when he'd only known . . . her.

Her skin glowed. Her cheeks flushed a light pink. The black of her eyes faded to warm brown as she stared up at him.

She looked beautiful, sexy, and . . . vulnerable.

A deceptive package.

Slowly, he withdrew from her. The wet glide of flesh on flesh had his cock hardening again.

But as much as he wanted to take her more—over and over—there was danger coming.

He stared down at her body. His. No condom. His gaze rose back to hers. He hadn't used a condom before, either, and . . .

"It's all right," she told him quietly. "I'm safe."

No, she wasn't. Neither of them had to worry about diseases, those didn't spread between the Other, but safe? No, they were a long way from being the *safe* sort.

So they'd "trust" each other, but they'd both keep lying.

When she walked into her house, Anthea Johnson heard the soft rustle of footsteps. She smiled, knowing her husband was already home. She and Ron had planned to sneak away this weekend. They'd head out to the little cabin by the lake that Ron loved so much and enjoy a weekend of nonstop sex. "Ron?" Maybe she'd get lucky and come back pregnant. Oh, that would be—

She saw Ron sitting in the kitchen chair. She hurried forward. "Hi, honey, I'll be ready in five . . ." Her voice trailed off as she realized something was wrong with the angle of Ron's head.

Not his head. His neck.

Very wrong.

Her scream echoed around her and shattered the windowpanes. She lunged forward and grabbed his shirt. "Ron?"

He slumped against her.

And that was when she heard the soft laughter coming from behind her.

Sam had found her clothes to wear. Or rather, Sam had sent Cole to find them. The jeans and T-shirt fit perfectly, and even the boots were the right size.

Never underestimate a demon.

Or an angel.

Dressed and semi-ready to face the world, Seline took a deep breath and said, "Your brother wants me dead." The lust had cooled, and her energy was back, finally. A girl could only bluff so long, and now was the time to lay all her cards on the table.

"He wants me dead, too."

Yes. He did. "Az told me that all the Fallen would die." She was pretty sure that the guy had meant by his hand.

"It's not easy to kill Fallen," Sam murmured. "The Death Touch doesn't work on our own kind."

Well, that was interesting. She filed that little tidbit away in her mind.

Sam had pulled on a pair of jeans, nothing else, and her eyes wanted to stray down the muscled expanse of his chest as she looked at him.

Seline cleared her throat. "But the Fallen *can* die." Just not by any weapon of man, so the legend and rumors claimed. *No mortal weapon.* No Death Touch. Now that sure raised the question . . . how had Az killed Omayo? The guy's throat had looked like an animal ripped it open.

"This isn't the first time Az has gone after a Fallen." Sam's rumbling words had her gaze flying to his face.

"He's attacked someone else?"

Sam's lips curved in a smile that caused goose bumps to rise on her arms. "Before his lily-white ass got kicked out, Az took it upon himself to deliver out justice to the Fallen."

Justice. She did not like where this was going. "He left *me* alive deliberately," Seline said. Not just a great stroke of luck on her part. Az had wanted her to live so that she could deliver his message. "He's going after the Fallen." No wonder he'd written *Fallen* on the wall—the guy had been marking, *claiming* his kill. "I don't think he's going to stop until they're all dead."

His stare measured her.

"Are there more Fallen in the city?" Seline didn't know of any, but maybe Sam did. The guy knew everything about the *Other* in New Orleans. "If there are, I think—I think Az will go after them."

Sam's stare still locked on her, and she realized that, yes, he knew about more Fallen. He just didn't know if he could tell her about them. Anger whipped through her blood. "Dammit, Sam, *trust,* remember? I'm not asking because I want to hurt them! I want to help them. If we can get to the Fallen before Az does, we can stop him." Didn't he see that this was their chance?

"We can kill him."

Seline nodded.

His head tilted to the right as he studied her. "There is one more Fallen in New Orleans."

Her heart started a double-time beat. "Where is he?" But she was already heading for the door as she tossed out the question. "Let's get to him, now."

"Not him," Sam muttered. *"Her."*

Anthea's head lifted slowly, and she stared at the man who walked before her. Her husband was dead. His eyes—green and empty—would haunt her forever.

"Why?" The one question was torn from her. "Ron never hurt anyone. He wasn't meant to die yet, he wasn't—"

"You weren't meant to be with him." Cold, callous, and the words fanned the rage that was slowly splintering her apart.

"He was the only one I was meant to have!" The pain, the burn, the fall . . . everything had been for him.

"You had a duty. Angels serve." His eyes were arctic. "They don't fall."

She had to force her hands away from Ron. *Not*

there anymore. His body remained, but his soul was gone. Ron had been a good man. Loyal. True. He would have paradise waiting for him.

"If angels fall," the bastard continued, "hell waits."

She rose to her feet.

"Was he worth it?" He cast a dismissive glance at Ron. "Everything you could've had—was he truly worth the sacrifice?"

"Yes," she whispered. "He was worth everything." And she attacked.

The low growl reached her ears too late, and Anthea realized that he'd just been baiting her. Setting the trap, distracting her . . .

This time, her scream held as much fear as rage.

The beast leapt for her, and his razor-sharp claws went straight for her heart.

CHAPTER EIGHT

The motorcycle roared down the highway, zipping in and out of the line of cars. Seline's arms curled around Sam, and, with every mile that the bike ate, he cursed beneath his breath.

Anthea hadn't answered her phone. Not her cell. Not her home line.

She was the only other Fallen in the city right then. Keenan, a Fallen that Az had mistakenly tangled with before, had headed to Mexico with his little vamp. To be safe, Sam had put in a fast call to Keenan and warned the guy to watch his ass.

But Keenan always did.

Anthea . . . sweet, gentle . . . she never saw the threats in the world. Not until it was too late.

He spun the bike into the quiet neighborhood that Anthea had used as a refuge. Small flowers waited near the entrance, swaying lightly in the breeze, welcoming the home owners and their guests. He'd been to Anthea's home only once. He'd come to make certain she was safe, but she hadn't wanted his protection.

She'd just wanted the human who was at her side. A

man she called husband, and a man that Sam strongly
suspected had no real clue about his wife's past.

Fell for love.

Anthea hadn't been the first to lose her heart to a
human. She wouldn't be the last.

Her tidy brick home waited at the end of the street.
More flowers surrounded the sides of her house.

And her car waited in the driveway. Her car—and a
black Jeep.

The husband's vehicle.

Sam had done his research before he'd slid out of
Anthea's life. Ron, her husband, had checked out. A
doting human who was crazy for his beautiful wife.

Sam killed the engine and leapt off the motorcycle.
Seline hurried behind him, or tried to. He threw out an
arm to block her. "Let me check first." Because he
knew what he could find, and he didn't want her to
walk inside another blood-soaked room.

"No." Her chin came up. "I can handle this."

She wasn't as heartless as she wanted to pretend.
Blood affected her too much. Strange for a demon.

"Besides, the last time you left me . . ." Seline threw
a quick glance over her shoulder toward the line of
perfect houses on the opposite side of the street. Perfect houses, perfect human world. "Your brother
jumped me. From now on, where you go, I go."

His jaw clenched, but she had a point. Az could be
close by, and Sam wouldn't risk Seline again. He
caught her hand and hurried forward.

The door was locked. He lifted his left fist, ready to
blast it right open.

"No!" Seline frowned at him. "What if they're just
inside, having coffee or something? We can't burst in
there!"

But then he heard a faint sound. Not a moan, more
of a gasp. One filled with pain.

Seline's eyes widened. She'd heard it, too. "Bust that door down!"

The door shattered, and he ran inside. The stench hit him like a punch. Fresh blood and death.

The gasp came again, even weaker now, and he leapt across the room. Blood pooled on the floor, deep and dark, and it spread beneath Anthea's body.

Her chest was open, the blood gushing out. Her dark eyes were wide and filled with pain. Tears leaked down her cheeks even as blood dripped from her mouth.

And her heart was *gone*.

She should have been dead—she *would* be dead, soon. There was no way she could survive. She was in agony, fighting to keep going, able to manage these last moments only because of her angel blood.

"Anthea." He said her name with fury. *Pay. Bastard would pay*.

She didn't look at him. Those wide-open eyes were to the left. Sam followed her stare and saw Ron's body.

"Oh, God," Seline whispered.

God hadn't done this.

He positioned his body between Anthea and Ron, forcing her to see him. He didn't touch her, not yet. "Who did this?"

More tears. More blood.

"Sam, she's suffering!" Seline grabbed him. "Help her."

They both knew there was only one way to help her.

"Why is she still alive?" Seline whispered. "Why won't she let go?"

Anthea's wet lashes dipped a bit. Her gaze seemed to focus on Sam. Seemed to. "Hell . . ."

Her body began to shake. Great, hard shudders that made the blood pump faster. There were gashes on her arms. Her legs. Her neck.

And that hole in her chest . . .

"Was it Az?" he demanded, his hand so close to her cheek.

More shudders. More blood.

"Help her!" Seline screamed.

But there was nothing to do.

Anthea's body stilled. A slow whisper of breath slipped past her lips as she surrendered to death.

His fingers rose and pressed lightly against her eyelids. There wasn't anything else she needed to see in this world.

"Sam?" Seline's hesitant voice.

He stared down at Anthea. The tear tracks and blood looked vile against her light coffee skin. "She fell in love with a human, and she chose to fall." *I know love, Sam. I finally know what it feels like.* He shoved aside the memory of her voice. "All she wanted was to live with him."

Live with him. Die with him.

She had.

Sam gazed at the marks on her body, forcing himself to see past the fury. Those deep gouges and slashes looked somehow . . . familiar. "You didn't deserve this," he whispered to her. Of all the Fallen he had ever met, Anthea had been the kindest.

She'd deserved this death the least. *I will find him. I will make him pay.*

Anthea would be avenged. Death wouldn't come easily to Anthea's killer.

It hadn't come easily to her.

"Sam, the guy's neck is broken. Whoever did this— they made his death quick."

He rose and let the rage build. "Because Ron was just a human." Collateral damage. In order to hurt Anthea, they'd taken her heart . . . not just the one that beat in her chest.

Seline's face was pale as her stare darted around the room. "I swear those marks look like they were made by a shifter."

His shoulders stiffened.

"I was sent after a wolf shifter once." She pushed back her hair and swallowed. "He'd gone Lone. He'd killed about five women. With every attack, he went right for their throats. The guy just . . . tore them open."

His gaze returned to the marks on Anthea's body. Those claw marks were too big to have come from a wolf.

But another shifter . . . perhaps. While no mortal weapon could kill a Fallen, a shifter's claws would sure be able to get the job done.

Except Az wasn't a shifter.

Sam carefully skirted around Anthea's body. When he heard Seline's sharp inhalation, he knew that she'd seen the bloody letters written on the floor.

Fallen.

"Are there more?" Seline asked, rubbing her arms. "Are there more Fallen close by? Dammit, you know this is a pattern of attack. He's taking them out! Any Fallen around here is prey for him."

"I'm Fallen." He took her arm and pulled her toward the door. He wasn't just going to leave Anthea's body sprawled and broken like that. Screw the cleanup team. He'd handle things his way. No one would touch her again.

"Yeah, but you aren't exactly low on power."

No, he wasn't like the two dead messenger angels—Omayo and Anthea had both been messengers. Messengers couldn't touch and kill. They couldn't bind humans. Couldn't punish at will.

They just made sure that orders were carried out. Last requests granted. Peace given to the departed.

As far as Fallen prey was concerned . . . the messengers never had a chance.

His fingers threaded with Seline's. "There's a little rule about Fallen . . ." A rule not many knew.

Seline frowned as they walked slowly outside.

About ten feet away from the entrance to Anthea's place, Sam turned back and stared at the house. The home next to Anthea's was empty. No cars in the drive, no one there to hear Anthea's screams. He knew that she'd screamed. Anthea wouldn't have gone down without a fight.

"What rule?" Seline's worried gaze swept the street.

"If you kill a Fallen, you get his power." A nice little bonus rush that could be quite addictive to some.

Had Az discovered that addiction?

Some vampires were hooked on angel blood because that rush could be tasted. And for those who killed Fallen, there was nothing quite like that psychic blast to amp up your power. The blast hit the person closest to the Fallen at the moment of death.

Whoever had attacked Anthea had been forced to leave before the job was finished. *Because you heard me coming?* Yeah, he bet the asshole was close by, watching him and cursing because Sam was the one with Anthea's power.

Power he didn't want.

He pulled Seline to the edge of the sidewalk. Then he stared at the house.

Good-bye, Anthea.

The house exploded in a ball of flames.

Rogziel perched on top of the brick house, his gaze on the fire trucks and humans who swarmed below. He'd followed the fire trucks and the cop cars. He'd suspected they would take him to his prey.

Not many would dare to light the sky this way. The

smoke from the inferno drifted high, so high, into the sky. Like a giant black fist striking out at heaven.

Careful or heaven will hit back.

The house was gone, burned in flames that were far too hot for a normal fire. Yet despite the heat, the fire didn't spread to any of the other houses.

Because that wasn't the plan.

Rogziel's gaze swept the crowd. *There.* Sam was on his motorcycle, watching the fire, and not caring that the human cops were just feet away from him.

Seline was at his side. She should know better than to get so near to the fire.

As he watched, Seline leaned in even closer to the Fallen. She whispered something in his ear, and Rogziel saw her lips brush against his cheek.

Like mother, like lying daughter.

Seline climbed on the motorcycle behind Sam. After a moment, the bike pulled away from the curve.

The humans—so blind—didn't even glance up. But maybe that was Sam's power at work. He'd been walking the earth for centuries. If anyone could manipulate the humans, it would be him.

Sam should have been the one to burn. He *had* burned, but, somehow, he'd escaped the fire of hell.

Seline's body hugged his as they left the neighborhood.

Rogziel straightened to his full height. Humans wouldn't see him. Not unless he bid them to. His wings stretched behind him, powerful, strong, not burned away to hideous scars like Sam's.

He still had power. Enough to take down the Fallen and the half-blood demon who'd finally shown her true colors.

Which one would die first?

Did it really matter?

He smiled and leapt into the air.

* * *

Sam didn't take them back to New Orleans. Seline curled her body against his and held on. She didn't know where they were going, but as long as they were putting those flames behind them, she wasn't going to question him right then. So she held on, and the miles drifted past. The sun sank and the dark night sky covered them.

They stopped only long enough for gas and for Sam to make some phone calls. Probably alerting his men. And some guy called Keenan.

She fell asleep at some point. Her dreams were restless, filled with blood and fire, and when the motorcycle braked to a stop, Seline's eyes flew open. "Wh-where are we?"

Darkness. Thick and total.

"Laredo."

Wait. "Laredo? As in Laredo, Texas?"

He grunted. "We'll sleep for a few hours, and then we'll cross the border tomorrow."

And hit Mexico.

She saw that there actually was a light up ahead. A small motel flashing a vacancy sign. Sam headed for that sign. She grabbed his arm and realized that her legs were seriously like jelly after that drive. "What's in Mexico?" she demanded.

"More Fallen."

Seline exhaled slowly. They wouldn't be the only ones heading across the border.

"But this time, we're gonna get to the prey first," Sam said.

He caught her arm and pulled her toward the motel. She hoped the guy was right because she was tired of getting to the party only to find that death was waiting.

The desk clerk barely glanced their way as he tossed

them a key. At least he muttered, "honeymoon suite"—
but she knew sarcasm when she heard it. She growled
back at him and realized she probably looked like
warm hell.

They headed back outside—all of the rooms were
accessed from the outside. All twelve of them. They
strode to the last room on the right. Sam opened the
door.

"Honeymoon suite, my ass," she muttered, glancing
around. She was pretty sure that bed was the kind that
did the shaking when a quarter was inserted. One sagging bed, a frayed chair, and—that was all.

But at least the place had a bathroom. She'd kill for
a shower right then. The door hadn't even shut behind
them before she started to strip.

"Wait . . ."

She glanced over her shoulder.

He had a brow up, that one brow that he liked to lift
when he studied her. "As much as I do enjoy it when
your clothes come off, I think you'd better keep them
on for now. We'll be having company soon."

Company, there?

His lips twisted, and it wasn't a smile with a whole
lot of warmth. "I've spent a lot of time in Mexico. A
hell of a lot more than I have in New Orleans."

But he'd been in the city almost constantly for
weeks. She knew—she'd been watching him for most
of that time.

"I have . . . a friend . . . who will be stopping by
when word reaches him that I'm here."

He had friends? Not just minions? Her hands were
on the bottom of her shirt. She let the garment fall
back over her stomach. "How will he know you're
here? If we're only gonna be staying for a few
hours . . ."

"The clerk was a charmer."

She knew he wasn't referring to the guy's social skills. Charmers were *Other* who could psychically communicate with animals. Sort of like very amped-up snake charmers.

They could talk to gators, tigers, and heck, once she'd even met a guy who spent his nights talking to rats.

Of all the paranormals, charmers were usually her favorites. They didn't sprout fangs and claws, so she considered that bonus points for them.

"Benny knows who I am," Sam said, "so he'll make sure only the right people realize I'm in town."

Okay, well, the *right* people sounded better than the wrong ones. "So we don't have to worry about folks gunning for you."

His gaze hardened. "The *Other* in Mexico and along the border know better."

She just bet they did. One touch, game over.

His lips tightened. "You know, I don't always enjoy torture." He strode toward her with slow, deliberate steps. "No matter what your boss may have told you."

She wondered what had shown in her expression. She'd have to keep better guard of her emotions. "I don't believe everything Rogziel told me." Though he had told her some truths over the years. Her father *had* been a lying demon who'd murdered her mother. As for her mother, well, she'd been weak.

That's what happens when you fall for the wrong man.

Seline knew she was staring up at a man who could be very, very wrong for her.

She cleared her throat. "Ah . . . what happens when your friend gets here?" she asked him as the air seemed to grow thicker between them.

He sighed softly. "You won't like it."

The kick in her gut told her this was gonna be bad. What else was new?

"Trust, that's what I asked for, wasn't it?"

She nodded, aware that her heart was racing too fast and that her palms had started to sweat.

"But you see, *my* people are dying. It's not so easy to kill Fallen."

"Az is——"

"Az isn't a shifter."

Uh, no.

"And Az isn't the only one out there who'd like to punish the Fallen."

As his words sank in, her jaw almost dropped. "Wait, hold on, you're saying——"

"I'm saying your Rogziel could be doling out his punishment."

"No, no, that last Fallen wasn't even on his list!"

"Have you ever seen his list? This magic, mythical list that the punishers receive?"

No, she hadn't. Seline shook her head.

"Before I take you to find more Fallen, before I let you get any closer to me . . ."

She was standing less than three inches from him. They'd had sex so intense she could still feel him inside her, and he was worried about her getting close now? *Too late, buddy.*

". . . I'm afraid you're going to have to pass a little test for me, Seline."

She blinked and shook her head. "You're bullshitting me." It was one hell of a time for his warped sense of humor to show itself.

"No, I'm not." His gaze held hers. "The clerk will have already summoned the man I need for this job. Benny knows that when I bring someone here with me, it's because I want the test."

More with *the test*. She'd always sucked at tests.

Sam rubbed the back of his neck. "Two days ago, you came to kill me."

Okay, true, that had been her assignment, but . . .

His fingers slid down her cheek and eased over her neck. "You came into my dreams and you tried to take my power."

Power he'd willingly given to her when his body took hers.

"Now Fallen are dying around us. You say that Rogziel is after you . . ."

"He *is*." Like she'd lie about having a punishment angel on her trail.

"Then why did he let you drive away with me?"

Now she was lost. "What?"

"Rogziel arrived at the scene after the firefighters. He perched on the house across the street from Anthea's place, and he just watched us." His mouth tightened with distaste. "When we left, so did he. No attack, not yet . . . he just followed."

That was fear eating at her heart. "He knows we're here?"

"No."

Her shoulders sagged. Aw, jeez, for a minute there . . .

"I let him follow at first, just to see what the bastard would do, but after we left New Orleans, I cloaked us."

Uh, okay. She didn't really know what he meant by cloaking, but she figured it was another little handy magic trait that he possessed—and just how many of those traits did the guy have? "I didn't know you could do that."

"There's a lot you don't know about me."

She saw the ripple of dark wings over his shoulders. Shadows. *Not there*.

"And there's a lot I don't know about you."

Now he was starting to make her angry. Her eyes narrowed. "Well, I guess that's why they call it *trust*, right?" He'd been the one spouting about trust before, now he wanted—

A rap shook the door.

She didn't like this.

Sam turned away from her. "Don't worry. If you have nothing to hide, this will be over in a few moments."

She grabbed his hand. "What if I do have something to hide?" Because, dammit, she hadn't been straight with him, not entirely.

And she still didn't want to be.

His gaze glittered down at her. "Then I'd say we have a problem."

Yes, they did. *She* did. "Demons can't look into the minds of other demons." In case his master plan was to bring in a level eight or nine demon to rip into her head. It wouldn't work. Her demon blood would keep any psychic mojo out of her mind.

"I'm not pulling in a demon."

Seline tried not to let him see her relief. She could probably handle this. She could usually handle just about anything.

Usually.

"I'm not looking for your past," he told her. "The past is over. It doesn't matter."

Bull. The past made the monsters of today and tomorrow.

Sam's eyes seemed to see too much. "I need to know the future, for both of our sakes."

Oh, no, *no,* he'd better not mean . . .

Sam pulled away from her. He opened the door. Seline wasn't sure what she expected, but it sure wasn't the tall, tattooed guy with the devilish grin.

Not a demon. Then . . . what?

He wore all black, and the guy glided easily into the room. His shaved head inclined toward Sam. There were tribal tattoos sliding over his scalp. He asked, voice rumbling, "Is she the one?"

Crap. The one what?

"*Sí*, Mateo. I need to see what will happen with her."

Sam crossed his arms. The guy, Mateo, pulled out a knife.

Then he came at *her* with that knife.

Oh, hell, *no*.

CHAPTER NINE

When Seline looked like she'd take a swing at Mateo, Sam lunged forward. He grabbed her right wrist, then her left, and held her tight.

She glared up at him. "You are making one huge mistake here."

No, he was just doing what he had to do. He'd been misled by an innocent face before. Once upon a time, he'd even thought he was in love, then the human had found out exactly what he was. Even genteel ladies in 1880 could have a very dark side. Helena had drugged him with laudanum, then lit him on fire while he slept. The fire had burned through his skin. The drug had dulled his power so he couldn't control the flames. He'd just burned, for hours . . .

When Helena saw that he wasn't dying, she'd brought in every man she could find from town. The good preacher had called him a devil, and the men had stabbed him. His muscles had been slashed, bones hacked . . . and he'd still lived.

Torture could come in many forms.

When the drug finally wore off, he'd shown them just how much of a devil he could be.

Helena hadn't been the first, or the last, human to betray him, but these days, he was far more careful.

"Keep that guy and his knife away from me!" Seline said, voice rising.

Not possible. "He needs your blood."

Her eyes widened. "Vampire?" A whisper, one he was sure Mateo heard.

Sam shook his head. "Witch."

She paled even more. Apparently she knew that witches could be far more dangerous than vamps. Good for her.

He glanced over his shoulder but kept his hold on Seline's delicate wrists. Mateo had placed his scrying mirror on the floor. Its black surface gleamed up at them. The witch chanted softly.

It wasn't easy for a witch to look into the future. Many considered it forbidden.

Good thing Sam and Mateo didn't fall into that "forbidden" category.

"Give me the knife," he told Mateo.

Mateo glanced up at him. "You always did like to get your hands dirty."

Seline kicked Sam in the shin. "I don't know what you *think* is about to happen here—"

Mateo rose and closed the distance between them. "I'm going to take a few drops of your blood. Then I'm going to get a little glimpse of the future." Said flatly and with only the faintest hint of his Spanish accent. The guy sounded like he cut women all the time and peered into their futures—because that was exactly what he did.

Just another ordinary night for him.

"One glimpse will show us just where your allegiance lies," Sam said because that part was what mattered. The body count was rising. Az and Rogziel would be closing in soon. Not just one threat—two. When the end came, could he trust her to have his back? Or would she serve him up to his enemies so that she could save herself?

Been there, done that.

"You expect me to bleed for you?" she demanded, voice sharp.

Yes.

Her eyes slit. "Then you will damn well bleed for me, too."

Now he hesitated.

"Uh, boss?" Mateo muttered. "I don't know about taking your—"

"You bleed," she said, baring her teeth in a wicked grin. "I bleed. You want to know what my future holds? Well, I want to know what's gonna happen with you. I want to make sure when the cards are down that you don't turn on me, too."

So trust was truly a lie for them both.

He released her and stepped back. "Fine, but ladies first."

She glared at him. But, after a slight hesitation, she brushed by him and took the knife from Mateo. Mateo touched her lightly on the shoulder, and Sam saw the witch inhale a sharp breath. Mateo's eyes met his.

Succubus. Mateo mouthed the words and grimaced.

Mateo had been burned, quite literally, by a succubus once upon a time.

"How does this work?" The knife glinted in Seline's hand.

Mateo cleared his throat. "I just need a few drops of your blood. Stand over the mirror and let them fall onto the glass."

Seline gave a grim nod. She braced her legs apart and stood just over the mirror. Mateo crouched near the glass and whispered the last of his spell.

"Now," Mateo ordered.

Seline took a deep breath, then she sliced across the tip of her left index finger. "Just a few drops, right?" The blood dripped onto the mirror.

Mateo's body jolted. His eyes went blind as he cried out.

Then he started to shake. Hard tremors rattled his frame. A gust of wind swirled through the room, and a deep crack raced across the ceiling.

Seline looked at Sam with wide eyes. "Is this supposed to happen?"

No.

He took the knife. *Mateo!*

The witch fell back. Mateo sucked in great gulps of air. Sam caught sight of the deep claw marks on his arms and back.

Sometimes, you had to pay a price for seeing the future.

With this job, Mateo's debt to Sam would finally be paid in full.

Sam had killed for the witch. Wiped out four coyote shifters. Now it was Mateo's turn to face the dark.

Sam's left hand wrapped around the witch's shoulder. "What did you see?"

Seline began to sidle toward the door. Sam glanced up and pinned her with a stare. "Going someplace?"

"What?" She shrugged. "Look, whatever he saw, that *couldn't* have been good."

So she was already preparing to run away? "You aren't leaving."

"Yeah? Well, you need to—"

"Az comes for her."

Mateo's gravelly voice had Seline halting.

"He seeks her now," Mateo said, voice weaker as he tried to straighten. "He won't stop until he finds her."

Well, well. "Why?"

Mateo looked up at him. "Death."

"He already promised me that sweet deal," Seline said, sounding very aggravated. "I *told* you this."

"Won't stop," Mateo muttered, his eyes squeezing shut as he rocked back and forth. "Nothing will stop him . . . will come . . . *her*."

Sam's gaze locked on Seline. "Interesting." The word was growled.

Seline swallowed. "Not really. To know that I have a psycho stalker isn't exactly what I'd term *interesting* news. Terrifying, maybe. Not interesting."

"Why her?" Sam demanded, and felt a lick of rage spike his blood.

Mateo's dark eyes opened. "Don't know why. Only know what will be."

"Does he get her?" Sam asked, voice flat.

"Yeah. I'd like to know that one, too." Seline brought her hand to her lips and quickly sucked her bleeding index finger.

Lust jolted Sam.

Blood and sex. Usually, the combination only worked for vampires.

Her mouth—

She lowered her hand. "You said he wouldn't stop. Does that mean—when you looked in that mirror— did you see him kill me?" Fear had her eyes widening.

Sam knew the witch would give Seline the truth, whether she really wanted to hear it or not. "I saw you covered in blood," the witch told her.

"Maybe it was someone else's blood." She sounded flippant, but Sam saw the tremble of her hand. "I can kick ass, too, you know."

Sam took the knife. "You ready?" *She wouldn't die.*

If Mateo had actually seen her death, he would have said that. Mateo wasn't the type to sugarcoat, even for a lady.

Especially for a lady.

She might have been hurt, but in Mateo's vision, she'd still been breathing.

I'll make sure she stays alive.

Unlike Seline, Sam didn't lightly cut his finger. Instead, he sliced his arm, right above the wrist, and the blood splattered onto the mirror.

Mateo took a deep breath. Sam heard him mutter, "I don't want to see this shit."

Too late.

Mateo's body began to spasm. He leaned in close to the glass. Then he screamed.

An instant later, Mateo collapsed on the floor, completely unconscious.

Angels weren't supposed to lust. They weren't supposed to covet. They weren't supposed to want.

They were supposed to guard. To watch. Not interfere.

So many rules.

Tomas had never been particularly good at following the rules.

Guess that's why I fell. He stretched his shoulders and felt the burn of the scars that would never fade.

Tomas strode out of the cantina. Voices followed him, and laughter drifted in his wake. The night waited, dark and deep, with stars glistening overhead.

He didn't look to the heavens much these days. What was the point? He knew who looked back, and those guy upstairs sure wouldn't be granting him any favors anytime soon.

Tomas hurried down the narrow alleyway. He'd

crash at his motel and hit the road come morning. Time for another town. More cantinas. More drinks. More women to try and make him forget . . . *her.*

The softest rustle sounded behind him. Could have been nothing. Could have been a rat. A piece of garbage rolling in the breeze.

But Tomas stopped at the sound, and an icy shiver of awareness skated over him. Since he'd fallen, he'd learned a lot about survival. *Rule number one . . .* never ignore your instincts. When you felt hunted, you probably were.

He glanced back and saw nothing but the shadows. *Rule number two . . .* there's always more to the night than you see.

His nostrils flared as he drank in the scents around him.

Rule number three . . . what you can't see, you can probably smell. Everything had a scent. Right then, he smelled . . . brimstone.

Hell.

When you felt hunted, you probably were.

When the witch fell over, Seline knew that was a very, very bad sign.

But Sam grabbed the guy and hauled him to his feet and held him with a strong grip. Right then, Seline got a look at Mateo's arms and the back of his shirt. Blood soaked the shirt, and deep claw marks ripped the material—and Mateo's flesh.

He hadn't been bleeding when he'd come into the room. She'd seen his back when he put down his mirror. He'd been *fine* then.

She inched away from them.

"*Mateo.*" Sam barked the witch's name. He lifted Mateo's drooping chin. "*Mateo, wake up.*"

The witch's lashes began to flutter. Seline didn't

dare move. So much for a few hours' rest. Her heart was pounding so fast she could barely breathe.

"What happened? Dammit, what did you see?" Sam demanded.

Seline didn't think she wanted to know. She'd never wanted to know about her future. Why would anyone want to know if bad things were just waiting around the corner?

Mateo's hands flew up and grabbed Sam's wrists. "Hell . . . after you."

So not what she'd wanted to hear.

"You can't escape him." Mateo's voice grew stronger. "Not once he has your scent. You can't run. He'll find you. You can't kill him . . . you aren't strong enough."

Um, Sam wasn't strong enough to kill someone? Who could the Angel of Death not destroy?

He has to be strong enough to defeat Rogziel. Sam was the strongest Fallen she knew. Mateo had to be wrong. He'd *better* be wrong.

"Days . . . ," Mateo said, "only days left."

Sam didn't look even a little bit afraid. The smile that twisted his lips was vicious. "I've never been afraid of hell."

She couldn't say the same. She was terrified—that was why she'd stayed with Rogziel. He'd told her she would burn because of what she was, unless she earned redemption.

She'd just gotten blood and death.

Sam's shoulders rolled. "I'm not the running type."

Again, not so much her. Seline was very tempted to flee then.

"He'll come at your throat. You *will* fear," Mateo promised. "You will . . ."

Sam shoved the witch away from him. "This *he* . . . does he have a name?"

"Too many names."

"Great," Seline muttered, dragging her hand through her hair. "We needed the all-seeing Oz, and we got the freaking Riddler." Why couldn't the guy just answer a simple question? "Hey, buddy, over here." She snapped her fingers and pulled Mateo's attention her way. She was *not* going to look at his torn flesh. "Who did you see coming for Sam? His brother? Rogziel?" Some other supernatural that she needed to start worrying about?

"They all come," Mateo said, and the strength vanished from his voice. Now he just looked and sounded beaten. "Time for a reckoning."

Crap. An attack from all sides. *We are so screwed.*

Mateo bent and picked up his mirror. "Are we finished?"

Sam's hands fisted, but he nodded.

Mateo's fingers tightened around the mirror. "Then the debt is paid."

Whoa, wait, the guy had peeked into the future because he owed Sam? Seline rocked back on her heels, and, helplessly, her gaze darted to Mateo's wounds. She could smell his blood and see the pain on his face. She asked, because she had to, "What happened to you? How'd you get those marks?"

"When you look into the world of the spirits . . ." The mirror disappeared into a faded black bag hooked near Mateo's hip. "Those spirits see you, too."

Creepy. "And they—what? Touch you?" More like claw and bite.

"Yes," he said flatly.

So he'd willingly let his body be savaged because he owed Sam. Her stare drifted to her silent Fallen. "What kind of debt was that?" Had to be something big. You didn't agree to use your body as a ghost punching/clawing bag over some piddly deal.

Sam didn't answer.

Mateo did. "He took the heads of four shifters who wanted to rip all the flesh from my body." He inclined his head toward Sam. "A few scratches seemed like equal pay to me." Then he opened the door and walked into the night.

Seline followed and shut the door. Because she didn't want any more surprises, she pushed the lock into place. It clicked softly.

Seline was silent for a moment. Then two moments, because she really wasn't sure what she was supposed to say. Finally, when the silence got too thick, she cleared her throat and asked, "Um, you got any more guests coming tonight that I need to know about?" Was anyone else coming by to spread doom and gloom?

His eyes slowly slid to her. "Not tonight."

She expelled a hard rush of air. "That's something." Okay, first order of business . . . shower. Then sleep. Then hopefully no dreams that involved nightmares about fire and blood.

Right, good luck with that one. Considering the week she was having, Seline was pretty sure that her real life would definitely chase her in her dreams.

She moved to brush by Sam. He blocked her path. "Are you afraid?"

Let's recap. She had a psycho Fallen on her trail, one who apparently wasn't gonna stop chasing her until she was dead. She'd turned her back on Rogziel, and the guy wasn't exactly the forgiving sort. And, bonus, now it looked like Sam was in danger of serious dismemberment. "Damn straight I am."

Because she wasn't sure she'd be surviving the coming week. "It's not like your witch said he saw us living happily ever after behind some picket fence, Sam."

A faint furrow appeared between his brows. "You . . . want to live with me?"

Her lips parted. Her words had come out way wrong. "Look, we *need* to be afraid. Both of us. That guy didn't say that you managed to come away unscathed."

"But he didn't say we died, either."

Um, no. "He also didn't say we lived." Had he missed that point?

Sam shrugged.

She snarled and marched around him. "I am too tired for this crap. I'm showering, I'm hitting the bed, and then," she threw over her shoulder, "when morning comes, we are going to figure how to kick ass . . . and not get our asses kicked."

She grabbed the bathroom doorknob.

"You don't have to worry, I won't let Az hurt you."

Sure. Easy to say. Right then, she could still taste ash. She slammed the bathroom door shut behind her without replying. The room was a matchbox, but it was better than nothing. She took one step forward and yanked on the shower. The water thundered out—at least that worked well enough. She stripped, climbed into the shower, and as the water fell onto her in hot, rough bursts, she wondered what the hell would happen next.

She dreamed of fire and blood. Of falling, faster, faster, plummeting from the sky as her body burned. No, not her body.

Her wings.

Seline tried to scream, but only a whimper escaped from her lips. Her body trembled, and she fell. The ground was coming up fast beneath her, and she knew she'd slam into that unforgiving surface.

Burning and falling.

Her eyelids flew open. "No!"

And she wasn't falling anymore. She was in the

lumpy bed at the motel. The sheets were twisted around her legs, and Sam lay sleeping beside her.

She yanked a hand through her tangled hair. She didn't usually have nightmares, but after the day she'd had, no wonder she'd been dreaming of death.

Sam groaned beside her. Her eyes darted to him. His features were tense, his jaw clenched, and, hold on, was that pain on his face?

He rolled away from her, and with the sunlight streaming through the blinds, she got her first true look at his back.

The thick scars cut right across his shoulder blades. Exactly where wings would have been. No, exactly where they *had* been.

Seline realized what had been happening. The fire and fall hadn't been her dream. It hadn't been his, either, not really.

Because it hadn't been a dream at all.

Memory. A memory Sam was trapped in right then.

Seline's hand reached out to trace the thick marks that cut across his left shoulder blade. Her fingertips lightly touched his warm flesh.

She felt the sudden stillness that tightened his body.

She leaned closer to him, and her lips feathered over the raised flesh.

"Seline . . ." Her name seemed torn from him.

Her breath blew against his skin, and she pressed a series of gentle kisses against the marks. First one scar, then another.

He was so warm beneath her lips. Leashed power, waiting to explode.

Her mouth lingered on his skin, tasting him. He'd endured so much pain . . . to have lost his wings . . . what was worse for an angel? "I'm sorry," she whispered. She didn't know why he'd fallen, but he'd obviously born a terrible price for whatever crime he'd committed.

He'd already been punished. Rogziel should leave him alone.

In an instant, Sam rolled toward her. His eyes were solid black. "I don't need your pity." And in that deep rumble she heard a mix of anger and . . . lust?

He kissed her then, crushing his lips to hers, and, oh, yes, that was lust she tasted on his tongue. This kiss was different from all the ones that had passed before. Wilder, hotter.

Too late, she remembered one more whisper about angels . . . *the wings are the most sensitive part of their bodies.*

Even the scars? Were they—

Sam lifted her over him. One yank, and he tore her panties away. Her knees dug into the mattress on either side of his body even as the broad head of his fully aroused cock pushed at her entrance.

His gaze blazed at her.

Staring right into his eyes, feeling her own arousal heat her blood, Seline pushed down with her hips and took him in as deep as she could.

Not deep enough. His hands clamped on her hips, and he began to move her, harder, faster. Bedsprings broke beneath them. The bed thudded against the wall.

And still he thrust harder.

Power filled the air, that sweet, wild rush of power that she only got from him. Like nothing else . . . *nothing.*

She wanted to take and take. To absorb every bit of his sensual energy and lose herself completely with him.

She'd held on to the edge of her control before. In

the past, she'd always had to hold back with her lovers. If she let go of that control, bad things could happen.

"Seline." This time, her name was a snap. "With *me.*"

He heaved up, and Seline found herself on her back in the tangled covers. His mouth took hers, his tongue thrusting against hers. She wrapped her hands around his shoulders and held on tight, drinking in that wonderful energy. Taking, *taking* as she hadn't dared before.

Her fingers slid down his back and stroked over those scars.

He thrust faster. Even harder. Her hips arched against him. Her sex was wet and so sensitive now that he slid in deep and easy, pushing right over her clit as he thrust into her. Then his fingers were there, pushing between their bodies and rubbing right where she—

Her climax slammed through her, hot, consuming, and so intense that the last thread of her control snapped.

She took all of his sensual strength, pulling it right inside her. The pleasure blasted her, again and again, and she could only whisper his name.

As her sex rippled around his cock, he came. She felt his release, actually *felt* the eruption of pleasure sweep through his body.

The shove of psychic power that pulsed from him was so intense that the room dimmed for a moment. She clung to him, holding on, even as she tried to grab hold of her control. *No, no, can't take too much . . . can't.*

She'd taken too much once before and nearly killed her lover.

Death.

Not Sam! The hands that she'd had holding him so tightly suddenly shoved him back.

But apparently, he wasn't in the mood to be shoved.

Sam's body was like freaking granite. "Look at me, Seline."

She'd squeezed her eyes shut a second before, afraid of what she'd see. Now, breath choking out, Seline slowly lifted her lashes.

Sam stared down at her. His hands held her tight. Seline shook her head and said, "I'm sorry." The apology came because for just an instant, she remembered another time.

Another man.

She hadn't understood her power then. Rogziel hadn't told her how quickly the lust would build inside her and how she'd want to *take*.

No, Rogziel hadn't warned her, not until after he'd found her lover's weak body.

Never lose control. You could have killed him. Rogziel's voice blasted from the past. *Take only a little. You have to survive on tastes. Small sips of pleasure. That's all. No more. Nothing more.*

"You're apologizing again? For what?" Sam demanded. He was still inside her body, and hardening again.

But was his cock swelling because he truly wanted *her*? Or because she'd let too much of her power out and he had no control now?

"You need to let me go," she told him, and hated that her voice came out so husky. He couldn't afford to be weak with all the dangers closing in. How could she have taken such a foolish risk? He had to be at full power, she——

"And you need to tell me why you're afraid to look me in the eye."

Couldn't he feel why? She forced her stare to meet his. "Because I took too much from you." Her energy level was spiking so high she felt like she could fly right through the ceiling. Her fingers slid once more over his scars, almost helplessly.

He shuddered beneath her touch. "You gave."

She blinked.

"When you came . . ." His head bent toward hers and his lips brushed across hers. "Sweetheart, you hit me with one powerful blast of energy. You didn't take."

Yes, she had. Her blood was pumping, and the energy all but crackled in the air.

"You gave me a surge of pure power, and it's the damnedest thing I've ever felt before."

She blinked eyes that had gone blurry. "That's not possible. Rogziel—he said that I couldn't ever transfer power. That if I wasn't careful, I'd take too much from my lovers . . . all I can do is take, and if I take too much . . ." Her voice dropped. "I kill."

Sam pushed his aroused flesh deep into her eager sex. "Angels are good at twisting the truth."

She lost her breath.

"I'm not weak." His gaze almost seemed to burn her. "I won't ever be weak, no matter how much you take."

He wasn't human. Not a sixteen-year-old boy who had fumbled with her in the dark and gotten a near-death experience for his trouble.

"You can't drain me, but, sweetheart, you're not even trying . . . you're . . ."

He withdrew. Thrust deep. Her legs wrapped around his hips as she pushed back against him.

"Giving to me," he gritted, "making me stronger . . ."

He was making her stronger. Every touch. Every kiss.

His lips met hers in an openmouthed kiss. His tongue swept into her mouth.

Tension filled her body once more as they moved together. The thrusts weren't as wild this time. Slow and steady, so deep. Her sex, sensitive from her climax, closed eagerly around his cock.

"Let go," he told her. "Take, give . . . do whatever the fuck you want with me. You *won't* hurt me."

A lover who could handle her. She swallowed and held him tighter.

And took.

When the climax hit them both, the pleasure rushed through her body and flooded her being. She sent that pleasure out, working on instinct, and gave it right back to him.

The release she felt then was so powerful that it stole her breath. Her heart nearly burst from her chest, and she held on to Sam as tightly as she could even as the ripples of climax rocked between them.

When she could suck in a full breath, she tasted power and pleasure.

And knew—as she'd suspected from the beginning— that she'd found an addiction.

Sam.

This time, he held her. He didn't speak, just wrapped his arms around her, and she heard the strong thunder of his heartbeat beneath her ear.

His heart pounded so quickly. A powerful beat. Not like before, with the boy she'd hurt so long ago.

"I'm not human." Sam's voice vibrated beneath her. She didn't look at him, but her hand pressed harder against his flesh. "You know that means the usual rules don't apply to me."

She had to swallow again because her throat felt parched. "Meaning if you were human, I'd hurt you."

Because that was what she did. At sixteen it had been an accident, but as she'd gotten older, Rogziel had deliberately sent her out to lure others.

She hadn't killed by draining them, but she knew that had been a risk.

"Who was he?" Sam's fingers slid down her back, and goose bumps rose at his touch. For someone so dangerous, he could also be incredibly gentle at times.

"He was the first boy I kissed." It was easier to tell the story without looking into Sam's eyes. "And also the first boy I almost killed." The kisses had turned into touches. Need had built within her. So hungry and new. She hadn't even realized that something was wrong with the feelings she'd experienced, not until Patrick had collapsed.

"You're sixteen, you're making out, and then your boyfriend almost stops breathing." Like that wouldn't scar a girl. It had sure messed her up. "Rogziel told me how close I came to killing Patrick. I didn't mean—I didn't even know then that I *could* kill someone that way."

Killing with a kiss. At sixteen, she'd learned just what kind of a monster she was.

Sam was silent, just . . . waiting. So Seline kept talking to fill that void. She'd never liked silence. It made the ghosts that surrounded her seem too loud. "At first, Rogziel was furious. I went to him for help." A sad laugh slipped from her lips. "I didn't have anyone else to turn to."

His hand tangled in her hair. "You do now."

Sam's fierce vow brought her eyes to him. She wanted to believe him, wanted to so badly, especially with his body warming hers, but what would happen when the danger was gone? She wouldn't have him at her side anymore.

No, then she'd have her freedom.

"Tell me the rest," he growled.

She'd never told anyone before, but right then, it just seemed right to tell him. "A few years later, Rogziel realized just how very useful I could be. When he wanted to get close to one of his marks, he let me do the dirty work for him." She hadn't fucked the men. Did that matter? She'd seduced, she'd charmed, but she'd never actually had sex with the marks that were her assignments. She'd never crossed that line.

Until Sam.

"Was the story about Moorecroft real?" No emotion hinted in his voice, and his hand still tangled in her hair.

She nodded and felt the tug against his wrist. "All of it. I killed his friend." *No choice.* The bastard had almost broken her jaw. If she'd been a human, he would've shattered it. "When he has a chance, Moorecroft truly will be coming after me."

"I don't think so," Sam murmured, and slowly released her hair.

She blinked and felt an ache in her chest. *He doesn't believe me.* The first time she'd ever tried to bare her soul, and Sam thought she was playing him. "It's true, I swear! Philip Drew was an asshole who used his fists on women every chance he got. When I wouldn't have sex with him, he started hitting me." And for a mortal, he'd been incredibly strong. Once again, her backup—Alex—hadn't come to her aid. "Philip had me on the ground. He kept hitting my face and kicking me with his steel-toed boots. The bastard broke two of my ribs." She'd been coughing up blood.

"Then it's a good fucking thing he's dead." A lethal softness had entered Sam's voice. "He's dead, and now his buddy Moorecroft has joined him in the grave."

It took a moment for the words to register. "What? Moorecroft is dead? How—"

"Someone stabbed him with a shiv in his cell block." His gaze glinted. "I guess he pissed off the wrong demon."

Or the wrong angel—one who had connections to the demons in Moorecroft's block. She was quickly realizing that the so-called heavenly beings could be more dangerous than any *Other* on earth.

"So don't worry about Moorecroft coming after you. He won't be hurting you, or any other woman, ever again."

Seline couldn't look away from him. There was so much darkness around him. Tonight, she felt that darkness more than ever before. "Do you ever want to go back?" Probably not what she should have said, but the question just slipped out. "Do you want to trade what you've become and just go—"

"I've delivered death my entire life. Moorecroft was just another in a chain for me."

But that just sounded sad and wrong. "Don't you want more than death?" Didn't everyone? She sure did.

His fingers slid down the curve of her shoulder. "We can't always have what we want."

"Sometimes we can."

His hand tightened on her. "I tried for the mortal bit, tried love, once upon a time."

Now why was she feeling that hard spike of jealousy? *Because I want him.* "What happened?"

"When she found out what I truly was, she tried to kill me."

"I'm sorry." The words just seemed trite. And she sure seemed to be saying them a lot. Her lips pressed together.

"When she couldn't kill me, Helena brought in the rest of the town. They spent hours stabbing, slicing, and burning me."

Yeah, she could see where he might be turned off from the whole love thing.

"She'd loved me one day, and the next, she wanted to send me to hell." No expression flickered on his face.

"What did you do when you got free?"

A faint line appeared between his brows. "Do you mean, did I kill her?"

She waited.

"What do you think?" His head came close to hers. "You think I killed the woman I thought of loving? She sure tried hard enough to kill me."

Seline shook her head. "You didn't."

"What makes you so sure?"

She raised her hand, and her fingertips traced over his lips. "Because there is more to you than death."

His lips parted and her finger slipped into his mouth. He sucked her fingertip, and his tongue rasped over her skin.

Seline felt the dark desire begin to rise within her again. With him, it was so easy to want.

One more lick, and he pulled away from her. "Don't be so sure of me. I'm very good at the business of death." His gaze had heated with a fury she hadn't seen before. "Aren't you even going to ask . . . why did I fall?"

"No." She didn't want to know.

Maybe she was afraid to find out.

Because she'd already started to care for Sam. Despite the darkness that cloaked him and the danger that he wore like a shroud, he'd slipped under her guard. When they were together, she was more open with him than she ever had been with anyone else.

He offered her freedom. He offered her hope.

He made her want more.

Love. Life. Wasn't that what normal people had?

"Scared, Seline?"

Her lashes lowered. "How long ago did you fall?"

"Centuries."

Exactly what she'd thought. "And are you the same man now?"

Silence. She glanced up and read the surprise on his face. "Are you?" she pressed.

"No."

Seline nodded. "I didn't think so. We've all done things we regret. The past can't change. Only the present matters." *And you can't think about the future. Don't think about it—and keep that witch away from me!*

It was hard enough to keep going some days without knowing that a fiery future waited.

She pulled Sam down beside her. Seline took his arm and wrapped it around her body. He fit her well. Better than any other man ever had. Within his arms, she felt safe. Finally.

Her breath eased in and out slowly, and the minutes ticked by. Sleep tugged at her, and she began to slip into dreams.

Then she heard his whisper in her ear.

"I don't regret why I fell. If I had to do it again, I'd still kill them all."

Her eyes squeezed shut even harder. "Did they—were they innocents?"

"No, but the women and children they slaughtered were. Trust me, those bastards deserved exactly what they got."

And, wrapped in his embrace, she wondered just what she deserved.

Tomas locked the door of his motel room. Sweat trickled down his back. He was being hunted.

He peeked out of the sagging blinds. The early rays

of sunlight streaked across the sky, making the heavens look blood-red.

Heaven wasn't supposed to bleed. *Bad things are coming.* He understood the omen.

He grabbed the phone off the bedside table. He knew when he was in over his head.

Fucking now.

One ring. Two. There was only one guy who could help him. Provided, of course, that the bastard wasn't just in the mood to stand back and watch him die. After their last encounter—one that had ended in fists and fire—there was really no telling.

But then Sammael answered his phone.

"Sam! I'm in trouble . . ." Not that Sam usually cared about that, not for anyone, but . . .

I'll make a deal with him.

"Tomas?" There was a murmur in the background. Sounded like a woman's voice. It figured the Fallen would be fucking.

I'd be screwing, too, if I didn't have someone aiming for my head.

"Yeah, yeah, it's me . . ." He glanced out of the blinds again. He didn't see anyone, yet. But he probably wouldn't see them coming. Good hunters never showed themselves until they were ready to make the kill. "I've got a problem, and I don't really care how much I have to pay, but I need some help." He sucked in a deep breath. "I-I'm being hunted."

There'd been some coyote shifters who'd gone after Fallen before, or, more specifically, after their angel blood. Because it was so pure, their blood was very, very powerful.

But this was different. He'd caught the scent, and he *knew.* "It's one of our own," he snapped at Sam. "One of our own is gunning for me."

"Where are you?" Sam didn't sound surprised or worried. Nothing new there. Emotions were supposed to hit angels when they fell to earth, but Tomas hadn't noticed that Sam ever felt much of anything—other than boredom.

"Anahuac." He'd been sinning his way through most of Mexico. What was the point of falling if you couldn't enjoy some sin? "At a rundown dump of a motel three miles from the main cantina. Are you in New Orleans? Are you—"

"I'm in Laredo. I can be there to meet you in a few hours."

Something thudded into his door. Something very hard and very big.

His hand clenched around the phone. "I don't think I've got that long."

The door began to splitter apart.

I don't have any time at all. The devil was already at his door.

The line went dead. Sam stared down at his phone. He'd known Tomas was in Mexico, but the Fallen didn't exactly move with the times. Having a cell phone would have been too much to ask of Tomas . . . *Maybe next time you'll buy a phone so I can warn you when a psychotic bastard is picking us off.*

If there was a next time.

He glanced at Seline. "We've got to go."

Seline's delicate face was tense. "Another Fallen?"

Sam nodded. "And Tomas knows that he's being hunted." Which meant they didn't have much time. Judging by the way that call had ended—*not much time at all.*

They dressed and ran for the door. Sam spared only one glance for the heavens above him. Blood-red.

Sailors thought that sign mistakenly meant a storm was coming.

It really meant an angel was dying. You could always see the blood in the sky before it hit the ground.

He jumped on the motorcycle. Seline wrapped her arms around him.

I'm coming, Tomas.

But he was afraid he wouldn't be fast enough.

CHAPTER TEN

More demons met them in Anahuac. One man, one woman—both with matching grim expressions carved on their faces.

Sam pulled into the dusty motel parking lot. The guy seemed to have connections all over Mexico, connections that he used without even the slightest hesitation. The demons had guided them to the motel. It seemed they'd heard screams but had arrived too late.

Too late.

The place appeared deserted, probably not a good sign. No other cars were in the lot, and the door to the motel's main entrance swayed drunkenly in the breeze. It looked like even the desk clerk had cut and run.

Seline walked slowly toward room 12. The door had been busted down. Shards of wood littered the ground. She stepped over the wood and crept just inside the entranceway. The room itself was a total wreck. Furniture smashed. Bed overturned. Mattress slashed.

But no dead Fallen.

No Fallen at all.

"You think he left willingly?" one of the demons asked from behind her.

Seline's gaze darted around the chaos of the room. "Doubtful," she muttered. But this wasn't like the other scenes. The victims hadn't been taken away. They'd been slaughtered where they stood.

Sam had entered the room seconds before her, and now he crouched near the window. His fingers were smoothing over what looked like deep grooves in the floor.

She inched closer to him. *Very* deep grooves. The kind of grooves that were made when something *clawed* the floor.

Just as something had clawed the other victims. "A Fallen couldn't do that," she said.

He looked up at her with a hooded gaze. "No."

"Shifter?" Her best guess.

"Only one with very big claws."

My what big claws you have . . .

The better to rip you wide open.

She took a slow breath. Did folks even realize that the old Red Riding Hood tale was based on truth? A hungry wolf had gone after Red one day. No matter what the stories said, she hadn't made it back to Grandma's house in one piece.

"A bear?" Yeah, bears had big claws. She frowned at those claw marks. They'd sunk deep into the wood, and they were so wide. "A tiger?"

"It'd have to be something bigger."

That wasn't good to hear.

Sam stalked toward the open door. The demons backed up, being sure to give him plenty of room. Smart demons. Sunlight fell on him and threw shadows in his wake. His hands rose to his sides, stretching far out, and he looked for all the world like he was trying to *feel*—

"He hasn't gone far."

The demons glanced at each other. Seline ignored them and crossed to Sam. She touched his shoulder, being careful not to let her fingertips reach his scars. "How do you know?"

He turned his head, and his gaze met hers. "Before he fell, Tomas was a guardian. Guardians always leave a distinct trail in their wake."

A guardian angel—those were supposed to be the nice ones. Pity she'd never had a guardian on her side. "You actually see this trail?" She rose onto her toes and peered over his broad shoulders.

"No, I *feel* it." He caught her hand and pressed a quick kiss to the back of her palm. "And I want you to stay here while I go find him."

"Bad plan," she said immediately with a hard shake of her head. "Where you go, I go, remember?"

He stared back at her, face determined. "I'm not going far, and I don't want you out in the open while I hunt."

Still, *bad*. "But I don't want to be a sitting duck!" Az was after her. What if he decided to pop back in while Sam was gone? He'd already used that separate-and-attack technique before. She didn't want to give him another shot at her.

Sam jerked his thumb toward the demons. "They'll watch your back."

Like she trusted them. Never trust a demon you don't know—her motto. And even then . . . *be careful*. Since she had demon blood, she knew just how tricky her so-called brothers and sisters could be. "I want to come with you. I can—"

"You'll slow me down."

Blunt and pretty brutal. She managed not to flinch, but she was pretty sure her cheeks heated. "I'm not without power, you know."

"But you can't come close to fighting the ones hunting out there."

Did any more of her pride need a hit? Maybe he should just call her useless. Sure, her demon power scale might not be the best, but she could fight in other ways. Like she hadn't spent years fighting *Other*.

Was inept written on her forehead?

He released her hand. "I have to go. Tomas could be out there, hurt, and I need to find him."

Right. She had to suck it up and deal with the situation. *Put on your big-girl panties.* "Go. I-I don't want to slow you down. Help him."

His eyes narrowed a bit, but then his attention shifted away from her as he pointed at the demons. "Guard her with your damn lives—or else I'll make sure you lose them."

Black eyes wide, they nodded quickly.

Then he was gone.

Seline rubbed her palms on her jean-clad thighs. One demon immediately took up a position near the door. Seline eyed the guy. *Please.* She could take him. No kind of protection there. But at least there were three of them in the room. Three against . . . well, whatever might come.

She spun around and let her gaze sweep the room once more. Maybe she'd find a weapon, or some kind of clue. Something.

Her shoes padded over the deep claw marks.

Sam didn't hunt. Or, rather, he didn't leave the motel so that he could go racing across the town after Tomas.

He hadn't lied to Seline, not really. Even Fallen could never truly lie. He'd felt the slight shift in the air that told him a guardian had passed by, but he had no idea where that guardian was now. The trail didn't work like that.

Usually, the only way to tell if an angel was close . . . you had to smell them. Those who hadn't plummeted and burned smelled like damn roses. You could always smell 'em before you saw 'em.

But Tomas didn't carry that scent any longer, and Sam wasn't sure where the guy was or even if Tomas was still living.

The threat was close, he knew that. Tomas might have escaped. He hoped the guy had. But either way, it was time to spring his trap.

So he walked away from Seline. He left her open and vulnerable in that unsecured motel room because he knew Mateo had spoken the truth about what he saw. The witch couldn't lie about the visions that came from his scrying mirror.

Az was fixated on Seline, for whatever reason. Sam wasn't the type to spend his days running, so he wasn't going to grab Seline and race away with her.

His jaw clenched as he waited in the shadows and watched that motel.

He wasn't running, but, dammit, he was going to use Seline as bait . . . because he had what his brother wanted.

So fucking come and get her, Az.

The bait couldn't be more tempting. Now he just had to wait for his bastard brother to make his move.

Then I've got you. And any shifter that had been dumb enough to pair up with his brother in the blood bath.

A twig snapped behind him. Sam smiled . . . *trying to sneak up on me?*

That wasn't going to—

* * *

Seline heard the rumble of thunder in the distance. She was on her knees near the bed. A Bible lay on the floor. An old, worn Bible that looked as if it had been read many times. Her fingers hovered over it as the rumble faded.

Then the attack came.

The male demon flew through the air and thudded into the wall on the right. Seline jumped to her feet as the woman—Rosa—screamed.

And fled.

Seriously? She fled?

Can't trust a demon.

Rosa jumped out of the window and hauled ass. But when Seline got a good look at the man in the broken doorway—tall, blond, strong, and with the shadowy image of black wings stretching from his body—she thought about running, too.

But in the next instant, Az was in front of her, and Seline knew that she wasn't getting away.

Okay, Sam. Now's the time for you to haul that sorry hide of yours out here.

Because she knew a setup when she was shoved into one. She wasn't stupid, and she'd gotten pretty good at reading a Fallen's twisted truth.

She threw up her hands and sent a burst of power right at Az. *"Don't touch me!"*

Her power slammed into him, and he stumbled back. Right. Take that. She truly wasn't weak. If folks wanted to be dumb and think she was . . . *their funeral.*

She blasted him again. Again. He retreated a few clumsy steps. A furrow appeared between his brows, and his arm lifted.

"I said, *don't touch me!"* Another blast of power. Harder. Stronger. Az hit the floor this time.

Her hands were shaking. Sam sure needed to hurry the hell up.

Because Az was already rising again. He stood on his feet, stared right at her, and said, *"Help me."*

She blinked. "What?" Her hands were still up in the air.

"Help . . . me." His blue gaze burned with intensity. His hand lifted, but it was in a beseeching gesture, not one that looked like an attack move.

"You're here to kill me," she whispered, not taking a step toward him. Did she really look gullible?

He shook his head. "Here . . . followed . . . to protect you."

She needed a weapon more powerful than, um, herself. *Hurry, Sam.* Just where was he?

"Woke up . . ." Az rubbed his head. "Didn't know who I was." The words came stronger. "Didn't know where." His hand waited between them, still open to her. "Then you saved me."

Technically, she'd been about to serve him up to Sam, but Seline didn't bother to point out that pesky detail. "You've been killing angels."

Again he shook his head. "I haven't killed anyone."

The crazy thing was that she actually wanted to believe him. Huh. Maybe she wasn't so good at understanding angels and their half-truths.

"I didn't even know my own name," Az told her, "not until you said it." And she remembered the confusion in his eyes.

But she also remembered the fire. "Nice try, jerk. But you *burned* me in that warehouse."

"Not me." He shook his head. "I didn't stir the fire."

"Then who did?"

The thunder rumbled again. Louder. Closer.

"Help me, and I'll give you anything," he whispered.

"Help you? How am I supposed to help you?" The delusional, psychotic angel wanted her help. Figured.

Sometimes, she felt like she had a beacon for crazy. *That would explain Rogziel.*

"My brother is the one killing. Not me. I know because I remember what he's done."

It sure felt like someone kicked her in the gut right then. *Keep him talking.* 'Cause if he was talking, then he wasn't killing her.

She didn't take Az for a multitasker.

She also didn't take Sam for the killer on this one. "I've been with Sam, and he hasn't been killing anyone."

"Have you been with him every moment?"

No, not every but—

"He's slaughtered before. That's what I remembered first. He killed so many." Az's hand fisted. "I have to stop him. *You* can help me."

Help the guy kill Sam. Right.

"Anything—I'll give you *anything* if you help me."

So that was why he'd been following her. He thought she'd be the perfect tool to help eliminate Sam.

Hmm. *Anything* from a powerful Fallen. Tempting.

But, no. "Sorry, bud, I'm not—"

For sale.

Her words were drowned out by Sam's roar. Jeez. Freaking finally.

Then she saw Sam racing toward the broken door. Sam—and his blood-soaked chest. What the hell? He'd been shot, over and over again.

Not thunder. The sound that she'd heard had been gunshots.

And he'd still come back for her. Now that was impressive. Damn straight she wasn't going to turn on him.

"Get away from her," Sam snarled as he advanced on them.

"I'm not here to hurt her," Az said, rolling his shoulders. "I am just here to send you to hell."

Sam smiled, and it wasn't a pretty sight.

Where do you want to be when two Fallens go at it?

Not there. Seline tried to inch toward the open window. She figured Sam would have this. He'd better.

She'd just reached out to touch the windowpane when the room exploded.

Rogziel smiled when room 12 blew up. The explosives had been so carefully placed after Tomas had been contained. The devices had been hidden well, and activated with just a press of a button.

Humans could be very useful and so clever with their toys.

He knew the blast wouldn't kill the Fallen. Just as he knew that the bullets his man had fired into Sam's body wouldn't slow the guy down for long.

Not long, just a few precious moments. That slowdown, that weakness was just what he needed.

Time to take out two sinners.

The smoke billowed, and Rogziel stalked toward the motel. The only humans around worked for him. His team—one that he'd ordered to seek cover in the nearby woods. All the innocents were gone.

Suffer, sinners, suffer.

The blast had blown Sam out of the motel room. He lay in the parking lot, some of his flesh torn away. His clothes burned as he pushed himself to his feet. He stared at the wreckage and screamed, *"Seline!"*

Interesting. Another way to punish.

Rogziel flew forward. "She won't walk away from that." Not weak Seline.

Sam's head whipped toward him. The smoke and fire had covered Rogziel's scent, just as he'd planned, and Sam hadn't even been aware that the true threat was so close. Rogziel saw the fury in the Fallen's eyes, and he said, "She won't walk away, and neither will you."

"Fuck you!" Sam tossed a ball of fire his way.

The ball withered to smoke before it could touch Rogziel's skin.

He expected another attack. Instead, Sam whirled and rushed back toward that burning building.

Rogziel frowned. The Fallen thought to save someone? Now that was surprising. He hadn't anticipated this sacrifice.

Pity it was too late for Sam to atone.

Before Sam could rush straight into the flames, Az appeared in the smoke. His arms cradled a too-still Seline.

How perfect. He should have known that Azrael would kill her.

Sam roared and lunged for his brother.

The Fallen didn't understand that rage made them weak, even as it made his little pet hungry. The beast was close now. Just minutes away. Soon it would burst free and feed.

Seline coughed.

Rogziel stopped smiling.

The smoke was choking her, and the arms around her were way too tight. Seline blinked her streaming eyes. "Ease up, Sam. We're out, it's—"

Sam wasn't holding her. Someone was yelling. Fire crackled, and Az held her in his arms.

"You're safe," he whispered, and she realized that his clothes were smoldering.

In the next instant, she wasn't in his arms any longer. Sam had her. *Yeah, thanks for the too-late rescue.* Sam shoved her behind his body. *"Run,"* he ordered as he faced off against Az.

She glanced around. She hadn't been burned because Az had protected her with his body. *He saved me*. That just didn't jive with the story she'd been given. A crazy psycho wouldn't care about protecting her. "Sam, wait!"

Something was very wrong. Two fire attacks, and she was sure neither had come from Az.

Sam sent a blast of energy at Az, and the Fallen flew back into the fire. Sam spared her a brief glance over his shoulder. "Rogziel is here, and you need to *run*."

She stumbled back. Her gaze swept around the parking lot. She didn't see Rogziel, but since the bastard could fly, he could be anywhere.

Az shot out of the fire and barreled into Sam. Power crackled in the air as they tossed psychic attacks at each other. They rolled on the ground, and a deep crevice appeared beneath them.

Too much power.

Lightning crashed between them.

Not right. "Stop!" She wasn't running. Where would she run to? If she ran, she'd probably rush straight into Rogziel.

Sam and Az didn't hear her. Or if they did, they just ignored her. Sam had his hands around Az's throat, and he lifted his brother up high—then tossed him about twenty feet.

The flames flickered. The scent of smoke burned her nose. Smoke and . . . wait. That wasn't the normal smell of fire. That scent was more like—

Brimstone.

Once you smelled hell, you never forgot it.

She spun around. The lightest scent of flowers tangled with the brimstone. She knew what that light, sweet scent meant. *An angel was close.*

Rogziel had appeared in the middle of the parking lot. His wings, black, strong, and powerful, stretched behind him.

He wasn't alone. At his side, a real-live freaking monster crouched. It wasn't a wolf. It was bigger. Triple the size of any wolf shifter she'd ever seen. Its fur was thick and black and matted. One long streak of white fur cut across its right eye. Its fangs were longer than her hands. Its claws were like thick butcher knives digging into the ground, and its eyes—*eyes locked not on her but on Sam*—were bloodred.

Redder than any fire in hell.

Rogziel *patted* the beast on its back. Then Rogziel lifted one of his bony fingers and pointed right at Sam.

No. *"Sam! Behind you!"*

He whirled around, and she knew he'd caught sight of the creature. His body tensed, and she was pretty sure he said, "Shit," but then Rogziel turned that bony finger toward her. No . . . no, he was targeting her! Telling the weird beast to—

"Attack." Rogziel's screamed command drowned out everything else.

The beast charged at her. It moved so fast that its legs blurred. She turned away and tried to run, but the fire waited in front of her.

She spun to the left. There were woods that way. The ground was actually shaking as the beast pounded after her.

"Seline!" Sam was there. He grabbed her arm and shoved her behind him, using his body as a shield.

Too late.

The beast grabbed him. The animal's thick fangs sank into Sam's arm, then, using that painful grip, the hound tossed Sam away like some kind of rag doll. Blood littered the ground in his wake. "No!" Seline screamed. What the hell was happening? What was that thing?

The beast's attention was on Sam now. Sam rose to

his feet. The gashes on his arm went all the way to the bone.

No mortal weapon can kill a Fallen.

But she wasn't looking at a mortal weapon, and Rogziel was laughing. The punisher had planned too well.

A setup. From the beginning. A setup.

The creature lunged for Sam again. Its teeth were heading straight for Sam's throat.

Sam threw a ball of fire at the beast. The flames hit the animal but just dissolved right into its dark fur.

Then the animal got even *bigger.*

"Fuck, *a hellhound,*" Sam snarled.

Hellhound?

The beast slammed its paws into Sam's chest.

Seline stopped just standing there like a scared scream queen. She grabbed the hound's tail and yanked as hard as she could.

The hound howled and snapped at her, taking those deadly teeth away from Sam's throat.

Rogziel just watched and laughed.

"Leave him alone!" she yelled. Where was Az? She didn't dare look away from the hound, not with those teeth so close to tearing into her.

Sam's hands flew out. He grabbed the hound's neck and snapped. She knew that crack meant the hound's neck had been broken. She jumped back as the heavy body collapsed.

Sam pushed the hound to the ground. "We don't have much time," he told her even as his gaze flew around the lot. She saw his stare lock on something to the right.

She followed his gaze—Az. Rising slowly, frowning.

A low growl rumbled near her feet. Seline looked down. *No way.* The hound had been dead.

"You'll have to do better than that," Rogziel taunted.

Bones snapped back into place. The beast rose slowly, rolling its neck back into position with a crack that chilled her blood.

Can't kill it.

Its claws swiped out and tore open Sam's side.

Then the beast turned that hellfire stare on her.

"You'd better run, Seline," Rogziel called out. "This time, my pet is going after you. Get ready to see your daddy, little demon."

What she saw was her death, burning in the hound's eyes.

She didn't have time to move. The beast leapt up, and its paws slammed into her chest. The hound took her to the ground, trapping her with its huge body. Its fangs snapped toward her throat. She could smell brimstone, ash, and death.

"Hell's waiting, Seline!" Rogziel called out.

In the hound's eyes, she saw that hell.

CHAPTER ELEVEN

Seline shoved her hands against the beast's body. It was heavy and hot and—

It licked her.

Her breath rasped out as she pushed against it. She couldn't get the thing to budge. It was too big. Its breath smelled of death, and she knew the thing was going to rip open her throat at any moment.

The beast licked her again. Then it whined low in its throat.

What?

The hound wasn't attacking. Not ripping and tearing out her throat.

Rogziel's laughter had stopped. Now he was shouting, calling out for the beast to kill, but the hound wasn't hurting her.

Why?

The hound's head rose and it stared down at her. Its breath was horrid. The creature's face was like a nightmare, but it looked up at her like—like it was *her* pet.

Hellhound.

Whispers and half-forgotten stories floated through her mind.

"Get off me," she told the beast quietly. "Be a good, um, hound, and get up."

The beast whined but actually began to shift its body as if it were going to rise.

Her breath expelled. *Maybe I am like my mom.*

The hound flew through the air . . . because Sam had just grabbed the beast by the tail and yanked it away from her.

Maybe not.

Seline pushed to her feet. Sam grabbed her arm.

"Sammael!" Not Rogziel's scream this time. Az's. The Fallen was racing toward them.

Sam pulled her closer. "Don't be afraid."

Way too late for that. She had hellhound saliva on her neck.

Sam started chanting. It sounded like Greek—no, Latin. Then smoke swirled around them, closing tighter, tighter, rising . . .

Seline screamed.

And the world disappeared.

"No!" Rogziel bellowed as Sam and Seline vanished.

The Fallen shouldn't have been able to escape, not without—*magic*. His eyes narrowed. Trust Sammael to be dealing with the witches.

But at least he still had one sinner to punish.

Az stumbled to a stop in the middle of the charred earth. The hound rose to its feet.

Rogziel said, "It's nothing personal, Azrael." He'd known the Fallen for centuries. "But the job has to be done, you understand that."

Az blinked slowly. "Rogziel."

"You knew I'd come for you sooner or later." Not

too long ago, Azrael had been an angel with power. Now he was just another Fallen on the road to hell. Rogziel sighed. "Unfortunately, your death won't be quick. You didn't earn that mercy."

Az straightened his shoulders. No wings. Pity. What did that feel like? To be stripped of everything you were and cast out?

Rogziel pointed to the Fallen. The hellhound's ears perked at the signal. Rogziel nodded and said, "Prey." The hound would understand and attack.

The beast whined.

Rogziel frowned. He glared at the hellhound. *"Prey."*

The hound hurried forward but didn't attack. The beast put its nose against the charred ground and sniffed. Then its body stiffened, and it looked to the right.

Ah, now Rogziel understood. The hound had caught the scent. Sam and Seline hadn't truly vanished. They'd just moved too fast for even his eyes to track, but the hound *would* be able to track them. "Kill *him* first," Rogziel ordered, "then we'll hunt the others." Power flowed in his voice. Hellhounds always obeyed their masters.

The hound turned its head toward Rogziel. The beast's lip curled back to reveal bloody teeth. *Took a good bite out of Sammael. No wonder the beast caught the Fallen's scent so easily.*

But then the hound leapt up—and raced away from the parking lot. Away from Azrael.

Impossible. "No! Come back!" The hound couldn't get too far away or it would—

Vanish. The hound disappeared in a flash of smoke. The hound could only take substance when it was near a punishment angel. Otherwise, it was just a nightmare with no power or form.

The roar of an engine reached Rogziel's ears. He spun back, too late. Az plowed a motorcycle right into him. Rogziel flipped and slammed into the ground. Az drove away, spewing gravel in his wake.

Rage burned in Rogziel's gut, dark and ugly, twisting within him. *They will all suffer . . . they will beg for death, then hell will claim them.*

When the smoke cleared, Seline was still screaming. Sam's ears ached, and nausea rolled in his belly. The next time he bought a transport spell from Mateo, he'd make sure he read all the warning labels.

"It's okay," he told Seline, "you're safe."

She stopped screaming. Her eyes narrowed, and she slugged him.

He took the hit on the chin, figuring he deserved that one.

"You set me up!"

True. He tasted blood in his mouth. "I needed to draw out Az."

"Well, you did, and we both almost died." She yanked away from him. "Where the hell are we?"

Not safe. Not yet. "The spell dropped us about fifty miles away." His lips twisted. "Mateo refers to it as his get-the-fuck-away spell."

Maybe he'd use it again. Maybe. The spell had sure worked at getting them free from Rogziel.

Handy.

"Are you hurt?" he demanded as his gaze swept over her.

"No. It didn't bite me."

He frowned at her. The hound had been so close to her.

She glared right back at him. "Did you say 'spell'? What kind of spell?"

"A transport spell."

Her eyes slit a bit. "I don't like spells."

"Well, you would have liked dying even less." They could bitch and moan all day, or they could get moving.

They were on the side of an old, dusty road. No one was to the left, no one was to the right. No one, nothing.

Seline suddenly stiffened. She glanced over her left shoulder. "Did you hear that?"

He hadn't heard a thing. "What?"

"It sounded like . . ." She sidled a bit closer to him. "A growl."

Fuck. Yes, that would bring them to their next order of business—right after they got out of there. "Come on." He took her hand, threaded his fingers through hers, and started walking. Blood pumped from his wounds, but he could already feel the torn muscle and skin beginning to mend. Since he was away from the hound, he could heal.

Hellhound. Rogziel had certainly pulled out the big guns this time.

Their shoes crunched over the gravel that littered the side of the road. "You . . . left Az back there," she said, her voice hesitant.

He grunted. "I thought he might enjoy tangling with the mutt."

Still no sign of cars.

"But . . ." He heard the soft inhalation of her breath. "That was your chance, right? Your shot to kill him?"

His gaze slanted to her.

"You left me as bait." Spoken without inflection. Her gaze was on the road stretching ahead. "So you could get him."

His stomach knotted. No, that weird twist was just from the healing wounds, and *not* from any kind of guilt. The claws had scraped down his chest and ripped into his stomach. "I was watching you the whole time."

She stopped walking but still didn't look at him. "Well, you sure took your sweet *time* coming to save me!"

"I got shot!" Four times. "I came as soon as I could." As soon as the human died. But the guy had been a sharpshooter, and it had taken a few precious moments to get touching close.

An old pickup truck rattled up the road. Y*es.*

"Az didn't start that fire," Seline said.

Her words pissed him off. "So now you're defending him?" The truck was closing in. Sam stalked to the middle of the road. The better to stop the truck.

"He saved me." Quiet, confused. She didn't follow him, but instead waited on the side, looking a bit lost. "If it hadn't been for him, I would have burned."

His jaw clenched. "The blast threw me out. I didn't— I *didn't* leave you." He'd been ready to race back in and fight the fire for her, but Az had beat him to the punch.

So the bastard had done one good thing. *Now I owe him for that.*

"Why do you hate him so much?"

The rattle of the truck should have drowned out her words. It didn't. He heard her far too clearly.

He heard her, but he just didn't answer her.

The pickup was slowing down. Sam caught sight of the man driving. Older, thinning, gray hair, rounded shoulders.

He could almost smell the fear rolling off the guy. But then, the man's truck was being blocked by a blood-soaked Fallen. Smart folks would be afraid in that situation.

"Az told me what you did." Seline's voice was so

quiet. "He said you just . . . slaughtered. That it was why you fell."

Fury spiked, but Sam lifted his hands and focused on the driver. *Az, dammit, you always twist the truth so well.*

"He said you fell because you killed—you killed and you wouldn't stop."

"I told you the truth already. You believe whoever the fuck you want."

The truck's engine idled. Their voices had been too low for the driver to hear. The driver's side door squeaked as the man rolled down his window. *"No quiero apuro, hombre."*

Sam nodded. The guy was saying he didn't want any trouble. Too bad he'd found some.

The fellow wasn't a demon, and he didn't have the look of a shifter. He just seemed . . . human.

Sam eyed the truck. "I'll give you five hundred American dollars for the truck," he said in Spanish.

"You got the cash on you?" the guy fired right back, in English.

Yes, luckily, he did. One thing he'd learned, money talked in the human world, so Sam always made sure he was well stocked. He pulled out his wallet. The leather stuck a bit, courtesy of the fire. He waved the bills in the air. "Right here."

The guy smiled, then he lifted his right hand—the hand that was holding a weapon. "Then put it down, *cabron,* and walk away with the *puta,* or I'll put more holes in you."

"Are you kidding me?" Seline snapped.

The gun barrel slid to the side and pointed at her.

The man's already small eyes slit even more. "Or maybe I put holes in you . . ."

Sam closed the distance between him and the bastard in less than a second. "Or maybe you *don't.*"

Sam slammed his fist into the man's jaw. Then he grabbed the gun and pointed it right at the old asshole's forehead in a lightning-fast move. "Maybe I keep my money," Sam growled. "Maybe I take your truck, and maybe I leave you with a few holes to remember me by." The dumbass had picked the wrong Fallen to fuck with.

But the idiot just laughed, then he said, "No bullets. Just messin' with you—"

Screw this. Sam head-butted the guy. The asshole fell back onto the vehicle's seat.

"Is he dead?" Seline asked as she crept closer.

Sam climbed in the truck and tossed the gun out behind him. Bullets wouldn't do him any good against Rogziel and his hound. "Despite what Az told you, I don't kill every person I meet." Just most of them. "You're still breathing, aren't you?" He grabbed the guy's body and tossed him into the road. He'd wake up soon. The blow hadn't been that hard.

She opened the passenger door and slid onto the cracked seat. "You're saying that he was wrong?"

Sam gunned the engine. The truck just screeched. As get-away vehicles went, this one sucked. But beggars couldn't be fucking choosy. "No." Because he couldn't lie to her. "I'm saying, sweetheart, that Az isn't lily white when it comes to sin. His hands are dirty."

"Dirtier than yours?"

He didn't answer. *She just had to keep pushing.* If she wasn't careful, he'd push back soon. Yes, he got it—she was furious that he'd used her as bait, but he hadn't been given a lot of options.

The truck lurched forward. Dust spun in the air. Sam glanced in the rearview mirror. The old guy was already standing up, shaking his fists in the air, and screaming.

"I don't think Az set those fires," she told him, and

it was the same verse she'd been singing—one that was royally pissing him off. Why did the woman keep defending his brother? "I think Rogziel did it," she continued in a determined I-Know-The-Truth voice.

Ah, yes, let's not forget the other fun player in their little game. Now just how had Rogziel been able to—

The bed of the truck suddenly sank to the ground, as if something very big had jumped onto the back. The vehicle swerved as Sam fought to control it. Cursing, he risked a glance over his shoulder, but he saw nothing.

But he could swear that, through the broken back window, he felt the hot stench of hell's breath.

"Sam! Sam, what's happening?"

Metal grated. The few bits of glass still on that back windshield broke away. "You tell me," he shouted, but he knew what was happening.

He'd fallen for lying eyes. Innocence that he should have *known* was a trick for a demon. He lunged forward as far as he could and drove the gas pedal down to the ground as he deliberately jerked the steering wheel from the left to the right in an attempt to dislodge their new passenger.

Sam knew a hellhound had hitched a ride with them.

Sonofabitch. A succubus shouldn't be able to summon a hellhound.

Invisible claws ripped into his shoulder, and deep rivulets of blood sprayed into the air.

"*Sam!* What's happening?" Terror and fear seemed to cloak Seline's lying words.

He grabbed her hand and held tight even as he fought to steer with his left hand. "Call it off," he demanded. Because he understood—finally—just what was going on. No wonder the hound hadn't so much as scratched Seline's skin . . . the beast couldn't.

A hellhound could never hurt its master.

He risked a fast glance at her—even as claws raked him again—but he didn't free her hand. *"Call it the fuck off."*

"Call what off?" She didn't try to tug free. Her eyes were wide and scared—and black as night. "There's nothing back there!"

Nothing that could be seen, not yet, but the beast's claws and teeth could sure be felt.

"It's your hound." Why hadn't he seen this before? He'd been so unconcerned with Seline's "other" half. A hybrid . . . hell, he'd been so blind.

The hound hadn't attacked her.

The beast had found them too fast, and there was only one way a hound could track this fast.

The hellhound had honed in on its master.

And the next words had to be said, because that last swipe of the beast's claws had come too close to his neck. "Call it off . . . or you die." If a hound's master wouldn't call the beast back, then the only way to stop a hellhound was to kill that master.

Without the master, the hound went back to hell instantly.

"What?" Her hoarse whisper.

His hold tightened on her. He could hear the beast's snarls now. Hungry growls. The hound wanted a soul to feed on. Too bad. His wasn't on the menu. "Pull the beast back . . . or go to hell with the hound." *Betrayed.* All of it had been a setup, and he'd been too blind to see the truth.

Lust had made him stupid.

The hound's growls kept rumbling in his ears, and he had to dodge more swipes from those claws. The truck pushed forward faster, *faster,* and he felt razor-sharp teeth press into the back of his neck.

"I-I don't know what you're talking about!" Now

Seline was fighting to pull free of his grip. "Sam, you're scaring me!"

She wasn't going to call the beast back. Damn her. "The hellhound . . ." Those teeth clipped his throat. Fire burned along Sam's flesh. "Send the beast back, *now!*" Another fast glance at her.

Her eyes were huge and filmed with the glimmer of tears. *Tears.* He'd never seen her cry. Fear had her face paling, and he knew she understood as she stared at the wounds spreading on his body. Those growls and snarls filled the truck as the hound gained strength from Sam's blood.

"I-I can't." Her confession and she stopped trying to pull away from him. "I'm sorry . . ."

So was he. Power pumped through him. He had to do what was necessary for survival.

The truck thundered faster, its bald tires wobbling.

Faster, faster . . .

Those invisible teeth snapped at him again.

Sam slammed on the brakes. His chest rammed into the steering wheel, but those teeth—those damn sharp teeth—tore free of him. A giant gaping hole appeared in the windshield—a hole that had been made by the hound's body. He could see the ghostly image of the beast struggling to take shape on the dirt road. The beast was bloody, and its hind legs were broken.

Seline slumped beside Sam. Her head had hit the windshield an instant before the beast had gone through and sent glass shattering, but she hadn't been thrown from the truck.

Sam still had his hold on her wrist, and his grip was far more unbreakable than any seat belt ever could be.

Her eyes were closed. Blood trickled from the wound on her head, and he was pretty sure he'd dislocated her shoulder when he'd stopped her from flying out of the vehicle.

The hound's ghostly image began to vanish. With Seline unconscious, the hound couldn't marshal enough energy to focus and attack again.

Sam's fingers curled around Seline's limp hand. He glared at the disappearing beast. "Fuck you," he snarled, and drove the truck right at the hound. Just as the front bumper reached the beast, its image completely melted away.

Her shoulder hurt. Seline felt the throbbing pain push through the cloaking darkness that surrounded her.

"We've got a big problem." Sam's angry voice.

She tensed and wondered why she couldn't open her eyes.

"You're sure she summoned him?" A voice she hadn't heard before. Male. Deep. Not angry like Sam's, more . . . measured.

She tried to lift her lashes. Not happening. *What's wrong with me?* The last thing she remembered was being in that old, beat-up truck with Sam. He'd told her . . .

Call it off . . . or you die.

Then the world had stopped. No, not the world, that crappy pickup truck. Glass had exploded and a hound's roaring cry had filled her ears.

Then, nothing.

"The minute she went out, the hellhound vanished. The beast didn't hurt her, not even once, but it sure tried to take more than its pound of flesh from me." Sam again. She could feel him, knew he was close.

Sam threatened to kill me. The thought had rage building within her. She'd saved his butt, and he'd actually said he'd kill her?

She hadn't even *seen* anything in the back of that pickup. Yeah, something had been there. Once the blood started flowing, there had been no denying that fact. But she hadn't summoned anything. She didn't even know how to do something like that.

As for killing her? *Kiss my ass, Fallen.* The way Seline figured it, their deal was now over.

And the fact that it felt like Sam had ripped her heart out? Well, she'd find a way to deal with that later. She was good at dealing with disappointment.

Shouldn't have trusted him. She knew better than to trust anyone.

Seline tried to talk, but only a moan slipped from her lips.

What happened to me?

"How long are you going to hold her under?" that other male voice asked again. No anger, no judgment. Just mild curiosity.

Then she understood what was happening. Sam had put her out of commission. Damn him. He'd used his powers to trap her inside her own body. A psychic shutdown. She'd heard of this happening before, but Seline had never thought it could happen to her.

Or that he'd be the one to do this to her.

Bastard. Just when she'd started to care, to think that, maybe, she'd found a guy who understood her.

Can't trust anyone in this world. Or the next.

Another weak moan slipped from her.

As soon as she could move again, he'd be hurting.

But the memory of that truck filled her mind. His blood had been everywhere. He'd been attacked, again and again, by something she couldn't see.

Hellhound?

Talk about your living nightmare.

"She . . . looks familiar to me." The other guy again. "Her nose, her cheeks . . ." A sharp inhalation. "I swear I've seen her before."

"This hellhound . . ." And who the hell was talking

now? A woman with a soft voice and the hint of the South drawling below the words. "Will it come back if she wakes up?"

I'm awake now! Awake, but not able to open her eyes. Or talk. Or move at all. Freaking paralyzed.

Why had she thought that she could count on Sam? She knew the stories about him, the mile-long list of enemies that he had. But still she'd gone right in and thought he'd be different with her. Obviously, she was delusional.

"If she's the hound's master, she'll be able to summon it from hell anytime, anywhere." Sam's voice was flat, but his fingertips were on her cheek, gently brushing back her hair. The light touch felt . . . strange. It should have felt wrong, but it didn't. Just . . . *damn him.* "Doesn't matter where or when, she has an attack dog at her beck and call," Sam finished.

"A dog that can kill you and Keenan?" the woman asked, and even Seline heard the fear in the chick's voice, particularly when she said, "Keenan."

"No one's killing me, Nicole," the guy, had to be Keenan, promised.

Something creaked. Probably a floorboard. Which brought up a new question . . . where was she?

"The hound *can* kill you, though?" Nicole pushed. Her voice had risen with fear.

"A hellhound can kill anyone." It was Sam who answered. "It doesn't matter how strong the *Other* is, a hound can still drag 'em down to hell."

"And *she* can summon one of these hounds?" Nicole demanded.

No, I can't. Could she?

"Yes."

"Then why are we wasting time?" That southern accent got a little thicker. "Let's kill her now."

Oh, no, the chick just hadn't said that. *Bad plan.*

"Nicole." Keenan's calm voice.

Yeah, that's right, pull back your guard dog.

"Just *touch* her, and the threat's gone." Nicole was talking fast. Seline really didn't like this woman. "Sam, why haven't you killed her yet? If you know she's this dangerous then why is she still breathing?"

Sam touched Seline's cheek again. She wanted to flinch away yet couldn't move. But his touch didn't kill. Didn't hurt her at all. "Because I'm addicted," he said, the words rumbling, low.

Not exactly a giant declaration of love there.

"She doesn't look like an angel," Nicole muttered.

If she could have, Seline would have laughed. She knew exactly what she looked like. *Sin.* She'd been told that often enough over the years—both by lovers who thought they were seducing her and by humans who thought she should be repenting.

"You said she was a succubus." Now Keenan was talking again. "A succubus can't control a hound."

"She's only half-succubus." From Sam. His fingers trailed down her throat and rested over the pulse that beat at the base of her neck. "As for her other half, well, there's no doubt . . ."

"She's angel," Keenan said.

And there was the shame she'd tried so hard to hide. Mixed-blood daughter of an angel and the incubus who killed her. Abomination. Living sin.

"She's crying." The woman's voice was soft now.

Seline realized a tear had leaked from her eye.

"I thought you put her under," Keenan charged, and for the first time, she heard anger vibrate in his voice.

"I *did.*"

More creaking of floorboards. "She's hearing everything we say." Nicole was the one to state the obvious. "And she sure doesn't like what she hears."

"She's fully aware." Keenan's voice had taken on a definite edge. "Hellhound callers don't have to be able to *speak* to summon their beasts. They're linked psychically. If she's screaming for the beast in her mind . . ."

"Then it'll be at the fucking door," Sam growled. His hand slid under her hair, and he tilted up her head. "*Seline.*"

She felt a push of power, and it was like a curtain lifted from her body. Her eyes opened. She blinked away the teardrops that blurred her vision.

"Tell me you didn't call the hellhound. *Tell me.*"

Her right hand curled into a fist. She licked her lips. She could move everything again. So she moved that fist and swung for him.

But he caught her hand before it could hit him. "I gave you one free hit. No more, sweetheart." He dropped her hand.

Bastard.

Seline leapt from the bed she'd been lying on. She lunged for the door.

Only to find it blocked by a woman with pale skin and black hair. "Not so fast," Nicole told her, and Seline caught the flash of her fangs.

Vampire.

No wonder the woman had been so quick on the whole kill urge. Vamps were made that way.

Seline squared her shoulders and sucked in a deep breath as she prepared to punch and claw her way past the undead girl. But, before she could attack, Sam grabbed her left hand. Pain stole Seline's breath as the agony throbbed down from her shoulder. Jeez . . . what had happened to her shoulder?

Sam forced her to face him. "The hound is coming."

She glared at him, feeling so angry that she expected

her skin to start burning. "I trusted you." She'd been so foolish. "I fought for you!" He'd wanted to kill her.

Silence in the room.

"You're an asshole, Sam." An asshole who'd—*dammit!*—broken her heart. She'd actually thought he was different. A man strong enough to stand beside her, no matter what came.

No one else had even come close to hurting her like this. It seemed as if she were splintering apart on the inside. "I didn't turn on you! I didn't set you up. I *helped* you!"

The others—the female vamp and the deadly-looking male with the shadow of black wings on his back—weren't moving.

"I've never summoned a hellhound in my life. I didn't even know they were real until that thing came out and attacked us. *Us*, okay, not just you. The hound came for me, too!"

"But the beast didn't so much as scratch you."

No, it hadn't. The hound had been ready to rip out her throat. She'd never forget the smell of its breath. Brimstone and death. But it had stopped. She blinked and fought to remember. "It . . . smelled me." Then the beast had licked her.

And it had stopped growling.

Sam frowned at her.

"Why am I not dead?" she asked him. He was touching her. He thought she was some kind of deceitful bitch. And she had been, but not with him. Not since they'd become lovers. "If you think I've been setting you up all along, if you think I've sicced a hellhound on you, why am I still alive?" Screw the two watching. "Because you like to fuck me? Is that why I'm still standing here instead of rotting in the ground?"

A muscle flexed along his jaw.

"You're *addicted*, right?" The word grated in her throat. It was just lust for him, but it had been so much more for her. She'd gotten all weak with him and hoped for an actual chance of happiness.

Ridiculous. When the chips were down, men couldn't be trusted. Humans and *Other* were all the same.

Sam wasn't speaking, and that just made her angrier. Her head throbbed. Her shoulder ached, and her heart hurt. "There's no hound breaking down the door right now." She stated the obvious. "If I was this all-powerful hound master, don't you think I would have called the beast in by now?"

The seconds ticked by.

"It's Rogziel." Couldn't Sam see that? "He wanted you to doubt me. He knew we were working together, and he wanted us to turn on each other. He sent the hound after you."

"Rogziel's a punishment angel." Keenan had moved to stand beside the vamp. Seline glanced his way in time to see him nod. "Only punishment angels can summon the hounds, you know that, Sam."

Seline's heart squeezed tighter at his words. *No. Oh, this was not good.*

"Punishment angels can walk between heaven, earth, and hell," Keenan continued, and his words seemed too loud, echoing in her ears. "And when they enter hell, they can bring anything back to this world with them."

"Seline . . ." Sam's voice pulled her focus right back to him. "Tell me about your parents."

She didn't want to tell him anything right then. She wanted to run away. Why couldn't a girl run once or twice in her life? *Run as if hounds from hell were on my trail.*

But a Fallen and a vampire were blocking the door. And another Fallen had his hands on her.

Addiction.

She wrenched away from him. Fine. "My father was an incubus. I already told you that."

"What was his name?" Keenan wanted to know.

"Brion." So she'd been told. "Not that I ever met him. He died right after I was born."

"Died?" Now Sam was the one pushing.

Whatever. So she'd strip bare what was left of her soul. Maybe then he'd let her walk away, because she sure needed to get out of there. It felt like she was suffocating right then.

"He killed my mother, so, in turn, he was killed. By Rogziel."

She heard Keenan whistle.

"Who was your mother?" Sam's eyes had never looked so dark.

"Don't you mean . . . *what* was she?" Seline laughed then, but no humor filled the hard sound. "She was an angel, one charged with the task of punishing an incubus who'd been seducing human women." The shame was there, just as it always was when she thought of her father—and how like him she truly was.

Addiction.

"But instead of punishing him"—the words came quickly now because she wanted this story over—"she fell for him."

Literally. Her mother had traded heaven for a night in her demon's arms.

"Too bad for her," Seline whispered. "She trusted the wrong man. He killed her."

Just like I trusted the wrong one.

A bit of blue bled back into Sam's eyes.

"Rogziel was sent for Brion then. He succeeded at his job." And he'd kept her alive. All those years . . . Rogziel had always been around. Watching. Monitoring her as she grew up. He'd placed her with a family, the O'Shaws—humans who guarded her but reported directly to him.

Then he'd come for her and begun to train her.

Time to punish. Make your mother proud. Earn redemption.

At first, she'd tried for that sweet promise of redemption. Only later, she'd realized that Rogziel's punishments weren't always just, and she'd wondered how much of her soul he was stealing away with each kill.

She looked at her hands, expecting to see blood. Two months ago—when she'd found the woman he'd "punished"—her blood had dripped onto Seline's hands.

She glanced over at the vampire. Unlike many of Rogziel's flock, Seline didn't think all vamps were evil.

And that poor girl that Rogziel had "contained" . . . she'd barely looked twenty. *H-help me . . .*

The girl had been past the point of help. Seline had only been able to hold her hand as death came.

"So now you know," she told Sam, and forced her chin to rise. "I'm the daughter of an incubus, made for sin, and the child of an angel who fell for her *addiction*." She stepped back. "I'm not controlling a hellhound. I'm not betraying you. All I want, all I've *ever* wanted, was to just get away from Rogziel and my past."

Why was that so much to ask?

She stared into his eyes. "Our partnership"—was that what it had been?—"is over. You think I'm betraying you? That I'm setting you up? Then when I leave, I guess you won't have to worry about that anymore, will you?" Her lips twisted in a smile that she knew wasn't pretty. "Wish I could say it's been fun, but really, I guess it's just been hell."

Then she turned on her heel and walked for the door. The vampire's gaze met hers. Would she have to

fight her way out? It would be hard, especially with the
memory of another vampire weakening her.

But Nicole's head inclined slightly toward her, and
the vampire pushed the one called Keenan aside, clearing Seline's path.

She left, and didn't look back, not even when she
heard Sam whisper her name.

*Yeah, it's been hell, but for a moment there, I was
hoping for heaven.*

She should have known better. Demon half-breeds
didn't get to glimpse heaven. They spent too much
time tasting hell on earth.

CHAPTER TWELVE

Sam lunged forward, only to find his path barred by Keenan. He leveled a glare at the Fallen. Old ties would only bind so long. "You don't want to come between me and Seline."

"She wants to get away from you."

"We don't always get what we want."

The black shadow of Keenan's wings stretched out behind him.

Sam fought for patience, something he'd never really had. "If she goes out there alone, she's just a target. Rogziel will find her, or Az will go after her. Seline needs me."

"Bull," said the pretty little vamp who had a possessive hold on Keenan. "I think you're the one who needs her. She's your *addiction*, right?"

He almost winced. "Bad fucking word choice—"

"If she controls a hound . . ." Keenan rolled right over his snarl. "Then I don't think she needs a Fallen watching her back."

The front door slammed. *Seline was gone.*

He hadn't actually expected her to leave him. And

she was hurt. He'd done his best to repair her shoulder and tend the cut on her head, but she still had to feel weak. She couldn't just prance up and down the town of Monclova without expecting to attract attention. The woman attracted attention *wherever* she went.

"Unless you're using her as bait," Nicole murmured.

His mouth tightened, and that was definitely guilt that bit into him.

"Ah . . ." Keenan nodded. "Already done that, have you? And how'd that work out for you?"

Worse than my nightmares. "Az had to pull her out of a burning motel."

Nicole's eyes raked him. "No wonder she's so eager to get away from you. I would be, too."

But Keenan was frowning. "Az saved her? Az doesn't save anyone."

Enough of this shit. Sam shoved Keenan out of his way. "Not without an ulterior motive, he doesn't." Seline wouldn't have gone far. He was sure she was just pacing outside and cooling down. Seline knew she needed him. She'd said herself there was no way she'd be strong enough to defeat Rogziel.

He kicked open the front door. "Seline, dammit, let's both just—" *Calm down.* She wasn't there. The street looked deserted. No, no damn way could she vanish that quickly.

Then he saw the disappearing taillights at the end of the road. *Sonofabitch.*

A hard hand slammed down on his shoulder. "I've been thinking about this . . ." Keenan began.

He was going to hurt the guy. "Think later. I've got to track Seline." Good thing Keenan had brought him a motorcycle. He'd cut through the narrow streets and alleyways of the town in no time.

You can't leave me.

"I don't think Seline realizes just what she can do."

Keenan's words made Sam pause and glance back.

The Fallen stood in the small doorway, with his vampire right at his side. Figured. Nicole always liked to watch her man's back.

"She said the hound smelled her."

Sam waited, his whole body tensed to attack. No, to hunt.

"Rogziel summoned the beast, but maybe Rogziel wasn't that particular hound's master. Maybe your girl was its true master, and the hound recognized her scent." Keenan shrugged, but his intent gaze belied the casual gesture. "That would explain why the beast didn't try to make a meal of her."

It sure as shit would. If Seline truly hadn't known . . .

I have so screwed this up.

Sam jumped onto the bike and revved the engine.

"Better be careful," Keenan called out to him. "Once a hound gets its master's scent, there's no severing that tie. It'll track her and destroy anything or anyone who tries to hurt her."

Sam spared a glance for the claw marks that still hadn't completely faded on his arm. "I won't hurt her."

"Yes, you will." Nicole's quiet voice was certain. "Maybe you should just let her go."

Not an option. The motorcycle roared forward, and he chased after those disappearing taillights.

Getting a ride had been easy. Too easy. She'd stumbled outside, walked right into the street—and nearly been run over by a Jeep.

Luckily, the driver had stopped in an instant. Then the tall, dark guy with the quick grin had offered her a ride.

His eyes had offered more.

She'd taken the ride. As for the rest . . . even though her power was burning low, she couldn't stand the idea of actually touching anyone right then.

No, there was only one man she wanted. He was an undeserving jerk, and he'd seriously screwed her for others.

"Just drop me off at the nearest bar," she told Javier. Javier Martinez. He spoke perfect English and had a light, rolling Spanish accent. The guy really seemed to fill the interior of the vehicle. She had the impression of raw power and energy and . . . something more. A wild scent clung to him, one that made her a little uneasy.

"Why?" He tossed her another smile. "You won't find anything at a cantina that I can't give to you, *cariño*."

Right. But in a bar, she could just soak up the sexual energy in the air without actually having to touch anyone.

She needed a boost, but she'd be damned if she would seduce in order to get it. The daughter of an angel . . . forced to seduce and tempt in order to survive. Her whole life had been nothing but a sick punishment.

And Captain Horny over there, driving the busted-up Jeep, might think he'd just found a grand old time in her, but he couldn't be more wrong. "Trust me," she muttered, rolling her shoulder to relieve the ache. "You can't handle me."

He spun the Jeep to the left and killed the ignition. She instantly became aware of the thick silence outside . . . and she noticed there were no lights around. No houses. Nothing. Civilization had vanished in an instant.

Her night truly just couldn't get any better.

Claws burst from Javier's fingertips. "Trust me," he

growled right back at her. "I'm not going to have a problem." His canines were stretching, sharpening up, even as his cheeks seemed to hollow out.

Oh, perfect. She'd hitchhiked with a shifter. "Coyote?" she guessed because she'd heard the stories about the coyotes running wild in Mexico. Not pack, not anymore. All free, all fighting for survival of the fittest, and all vicious.

His grin widened. Not a friendly grin anymore, not even close. "I'll be real careful . . ." He leaned forward and his claws slid down her arms. "Not to cut you, too much."

Wasn't that gentlemanly of him? Seline took a deep breath and fought to control her racing heartbeat. She might not like what she was, but she still knew how to use her strength to protect herself.

Instead of trying to push away from him, she let her body relax as she leaned forward. "Do you know what I am?" she whispered, and used the last of her sensual energy to entice him to her.

She saw his eyes widen. He licked his lips and inhaled deeply. "You smell like fucking sin."

Because that's what she was. Seline didn't flinch. "I enjoy men like you," she whispered, and let her fingers rise to his chest. She kept her eyes open and on his— the better to hypnotize. That's what her kind did, kind of like a cobra with its prey. You lock stares and you don't let go—not until you strike. His heart thundered beneath her hand. "Men who are strong and dangerous."

"You're . . . not scared of me?" Surprise roughened his voice as lust burned in his eyes.

"No." This time, she was going to let the beast *she* kept inside out of its cage. How many women had this bastard picked up and then used his claws on? How many? *Punish.* Rogziel had taught her a few things, after all. "But you should be scared of me." Then before he could react to her words, she put her lips on his. She kissed him, and his hands tightened on her. His claws scraped over her skin.

No, coyote, I'm the one in charge. She let her precious control shatter. She took his energy, took and took and took.

Because she truly could kill with a kiss.

The coyote shifter gave her all of his power. Too weak to resist, he slipped right under her spell. When he went limp, she lifted her head and smiled. "That was good, but I'm gonna need more."

It looked like he didn't have more to give.

He fell back, and his head slammed into the steering wheel. The long honk filled the night. Seline shoved him out of the way—right out of the Jeep. His body hit the ground with a thud. She climbed into the driver's seat, yanked the gear shift into reverse, and spun the Jeep around. Gravel and dust kicked into the air.

The shifter didn't move.

"Now to figure out where the hell I am," Seline muttered. Because she knew the shifter wouldn't be the biggest threat she'd face that night. Not even close.

He'd just been her warm-up.

Javier stared after his Jeep. Gravel dug into his palms and knees. He'd been trying to rise, but the *puta* had drained his energy.

With a kiss.

Fucking succubus. He should have known better. But she'd looked so sexy in his headlights. Lost eyes. Trembling lips. Wild tangle of hair. She'd appeared so *human* and weak.

A perfect snack. Or plaything.

Zorra. Slut. He still couldn't rise. His whole body felt weighted down, and moving made his head ache.

He'd find her. If there was one thing he knew how to do, it was track. He'd find her, and he'd make her pay.

A low growl came from the darkness.

Javier tensed. The last thing he needed was an attack right then. He was so weak that his claws wouldn't even come out.

When I find her, I'll cut every inch of skin off her body. She'd beg for death, just like the others had.

Another growl, but this one sure was much closer. "Back the fuck off!" Javier tried to roar, but the words barely rumbled out of his throat. He tilted back his head. No way would he bow before another shifter—

No one was there.

His eyes narrowed. His sight was five times better than any other coyote in the area. But right then, he didn't see a damn thing.

But I smell fire. Ash.

Death.

The ground began to tremble. Fear had his heart racing too fast and his blood chilling in his veins. Javier opened his mouth to beg—

But invisible claws ripped into his throat.

Sam stared at the body on the ground. The blood puddled beneath the man, dark and still so fresh. The scent of death hung heavily in the air.

So did brimstone. Seline and her hound had been at work.

His gaze slid over the dark earth. He'd learned to track long ago when he studied with a Native American hunter who could find anyone, anytime. Sam had followed the Jeep out to that desolate spot and found death.

Not what he expected. *Had the hound been protecting Seline again? Had she summoned the beast?*

He stared at the markings in the dirt. Seline had

turned the vehicle around here, then she'd driven north, toward the lights of the town. His eyes narrowed as he tried to figure out what her next move would be.

If you were a succubus low on energy, where would you go?

To the loudest, raunchiest bar you could find.

Seconds later, the motorcycle hurtled toward those shining lights.

The bouncer didn't make the mistake of trying to keep Sam out of the club. He just wisely stepped to the side, and Sam followed the pounding music inside *El Diablo*. Fitting name. The place was packed with *Other*. Shifters—he caught the flash of their claws. Vamps—two were drinking in the back corner. Demons—so many black eyes filled the room.

Humans mixed with them. Aware? Or just blind? Maybe both.

Dancers twisted in cages that rose above the wooden floor. Lights flashed in a swirling circle. And he didn't see Seline.

Fuck. He'd been so sure she'd come here. A dozen clubs lined the strip. He'd found the abandoned Jeep, so he'd known that she came this way. He just didn't know exactly *which* bar she'd gone into once she'd gotten off the street.

The couple on the right began to claw at each other's clothing.

The man and woman on his left were nearly fucking right in front of him.

Sam stilled. Damn that was sure one whole lot of sexual energy. An unnatural degree, even for the *Other*.

Seline.

He looked up, up again . . . and stared harder at the woman who'd just entered the cage lined with steel bars.

She was alone in the cage. The other dancers had vanished. She wasn't dancing. Her long, blond hair hung loosely around her shoulders. Her arms were up, and she seemed to be pulling energy right from the crowd.

Because she was.

He grabbed the ladder that led to that cage. The music kept pumping behind him, and now he could feel the sensual power in the air. Not normal. Far from it.

Her. Something was different about Seline tonight. He'd never felt this particular rush of power around her. His body was suddenly on edge. His heart raced too fast in his chest.

He leapt into the cage. She didn't whirl to face him. Didn't do anything but stand there with her arms up. This close, he could see that her hips were swaying softly in a sensuous flow that made him ache.

He stepped toward her.

"Leave, Sam." She spoke in a way he'd *never* heard before. Pure sex. Temptation. Sin.

She might have just ordered him to leave, but his body was determined to stay.

"Seline." Her name came out raw and hungry.

The music flared louder.

Slowly, so slowly, she turned to face him. She looked . . . different. Eyes smoky. Lips plumper, redder, skin so translucent that it glowed. He looked at her and wanted.

But that part—well, the want wasn't exactly new for him.

"I'm not playing tonight," she whispered, but he could easily hear her over the crowd. "Tonight I'm taking all the power that I want, and if you come any closer, I will drain you dry."

This wasn't the Seline he knew. "You don't drain people, remember?"

But she smiled, and an evil grin should never have been so sexy. "Why don't you find the shifter who gave me a ride and see what he has to say?"

Sam blinked. "I already found what was left of him." And he hadn't expected that.

"He wanted to cut me open." Her chin lifted. "Coyotes always think blood and sex mix."

Fury spiked his power and sent the cage rocking on the narrow chain that held it secured to the ceiling. "So you cut the bastard open in return?"

She blinked, and some of the glow seemed to dim from her skin. "Cut him? I-I didn't cut him!"

"I found him with his throat torn open."

Shock rippled across her face, and she stumbled back.

She hadn't known. That definitely put a spin on things—and made it look like Keenan had been right.

"I didn't . . ." She shook her head. "I just . . . I kissed him."

A snarl broke from Sam's lips, and in an instant, he was before her. He grabbed her arms and pulled her onto her toes. "Did you fuck him?"

"Didn't have to . . . didn't *want* to. I can drain with a kiss." Then she leaned up and kissed him.

Lust roared through his blood. His head swam with a burst of euphoria. Want, need, pleasure . . . the rush of sensations filled his body, and he kissed her harder, deeper.

She pushed against him, her nipples tight, her body soft. And still she kept kissing him. Hot, openmouthed, drugging kisses.

I can drain with a kiss.

He couldn't hear the music anymore. Couldn't hear the thunder of the crowd. She was the only thing he knew. The only thing he wanted.

Her tongue slid against his.

He wanted her naked. He wanted to drive into her and make her forget anyone that had come before—any man who'd had her before.

There will be no other.

He caught her hips and lifted her up against him. Her legs wrapped around his waist as she rubbed against his erect cock. Not enough. Not even fucking close.

The floor swayed beneath them. Not the floor . . . *cage.*

Seline's lips lifted slowly from his. Sam's eyes opened. Her mouth was wet from his. The darkness of her eyes reflected the same lust that he felt but . . .

Sam saw confusion in her gaze.

She shook her head and said, "You . . . should be weak."

He was so hot that Sam felt close to exploding. His cock was so full that he ached. *Want. Need.* "You're not taking, sweetheart." Didn't she realize what she was doing? "You're pumping me up." With lust, with power.

Her eyes widened as she tried to push against him. "No, no, I'm—"

A succubus didn't always have to take power. He knew that. He also knew that a succubus usually only shared her power with one person . . .

Even a succubus could mate. In fact, if she wanted to have children, a succubus *had* to find a mate—one man she could share her power with over her lifetime. Otherwise, there would be no births for her. Reproduction wasn't just about sex with a succubus—it was about mating. Life, love—forever. Did Seline even know that? Because he was betting Rogziel hadn't shared that information with her.

"Let me go!" She wrenched back, but he held her tight.

"No, you're not running again. We're settling this." Anger and lust battled in his blood. "You're not—"

The screams reached him then. High, full of terror. Breaking glass. Shouts. The thunder of footsteps.

Through the bars, he looked out over the club. Chaos reigned as the humans and *Other* rushed for the exits.

Then he heard the growls. Smelled the brimstone. No wonder the shifters were at the front of the fleeing mass. They would've caught the scent first.

"What's happening?" Seline's stare followed his.

Sam saw the deep claw marks that scraped across the table tops. Fuck, fuck, fuck. "Are you afraid?"

"Yes!" she yelled immediately as she wrestled away from him. Sam let her feet touch the bottom of the cage, but he held tight to her hand. "Something's coming this way!" Seline said.

"Not just something . . . your hound."

She stilled and stared at him with dazed eyes.

"When we were kissing, were you afraid?" he demanded. *"Were you scared of me?"*

She nodded, and it was like a punch to his chest. Fear and desire. They shouldn't have merged for her. For them.

They had, and now hell was coming.

The other cages were falling from the ceilings now. Most of the folks had already fled *El Diablo*. Some stragglers were hiding behind the bar or crouching under tables.

Those claw marks were heading for Sam . . . for the cage that swayed drunkenly on a chain that looked ready to snap at any moment. *Too much power in the air.*

"The hound's protecting you," Sam muttered as he grabbed the nearest steel bar with his left hand and fought to steady them. "That's why it went after the shifter and tore his throat out. That's why it came after me in the truck . . . the hound fucking thinks it's protecting you."

A *whoosh* of wind came at them. Something—*the fucking hound in question*—slammed into the cage. The cage rocked hard to the right, to the left, and then that chain snapped. They fell to the floor with a bone-jarring crash. Sam twisted and tried to cushion Seline's body with his own.

His hands held her tightly to him. He was sure that if he'd been human, his back would have broken when the cage pounded into the floor. As it was, the fall hurt like a bitch.

Then the cage bars started to snap—no, the hound *snapped* them.

Seline stared around with wide, stunned eyes.

Sam hurried to his feet. He still had his hold on her. No way was he letting her go. "You don't know how to send the hound back, do you?"

She shook her head. "I don't even know how the hell it got here!"

She didn't know and only she could send the beast back. Talk about being screwed. Sam took a deep breath and tried to think of a way to survive.

"Are you going to kill me?" she whispered, and that fear flickered in her eyes again.

Sonofabitch. Growling, he pulled her even closer. His lips crushed down on hers. He tasted her, kept his mouth on hers, and drank her in, even as claws raked down his legs. "No," Sam promised, his voice gritty as he lifted his head. "But when we get out of this, I am going to fuck you again."

She blinked. He would have said more, but the hound's teeth sank into his ankle and the beast dragged him away.

The hound's image was slowly coming into focus. It

looked like a beast made of smoke right then. Pale, hazy, but with really big teeth. Sam kicked, but the beast didn't let go.

Fire won't work. Rogziel had been right. Fire only made hellhounds stronger. Bullets wouldn't keep the beast down.

Sam reached out and grabbed one of the cage bars. Metal snapped and popped. He shoved the bar right into the hound's side.

The beast cried out and backed off.

Sam rose to his feet. Seline was behind him. "I'm not hurting her," he said to the beast. Right, like reasoning with a hellhound was the way to go. "She's mine, got it? So you'd better get used to seeing me—"

The hound—still with that pole sticking out of its side—lunged for Sam. The breath of hell came at him.

"Stop!" Seline screamed, and she pushed Sam to the side. Pushed him with that power she'd absorbed from the bar, then put her body in front of his. "*Stop!*"

It figured the woman didn't know you were never supposed to come between a hellhound and its food. Especially not once that hound had gotten a taste of its prey's blood.

The hound snarled and tried to lunge around her. It didn't look so ghostly anymore. The beast's thick, matted fur was a mix of black and blood.

Seline's fingers sank into that fur. "I said, *stop!*" Her voice had risen to a scream. "Don't hurt him!"

The hellhound stopped. Its great body shook, as if holding back were an enormous effort.

Sam stood as frozen as the hound. Even masters couldn't usually call back their hounds once the beasts had had a taste of blood. Nothing stopped them but the prey's death.

Seline caught the hound's great head in her hands.

The beast's teeth were longer than her fingers, and the hound was way too close to her throat.

"Seline . . ." He inched closer to her.

The hound growled. Screw that. Sam kept closing in on her.

"You're so sure I'm its master." Her voice was quiet now, void of any emotion. "Let's find out if you're right."

The woman obviously didn't understand the rules about hellhounds. They had been known to bite *off* the hands that summoned them. They could never be fully controlled.

Which was why they were always sent right back to hell when their job was done. That was the prime rule with the hounds—*always send them back fast*.

The hound's teeth snapped together.

"Easy." Seline didn't look worried then. She was frowning as she stared at the hound. "You're a big, ugly bastard, aren't you?"

The hound blinked.

Her left hand smoothed over its side. "This is gonna hurt," Seline warned. She grabbed the bar and yanked it out. Blood gushed and sprayed into the air.

But almost instantly, the wound began to heal. Seline dropped the bar.

The hound's thick, raspy tongue came out and licked her shoulder.

"Uh . . . let's not do that, again, okay?" Seline said softly. This time, Sam caught the faint tremble in her voice and saw her wince. "But you're welcome."

The hound's head began to lower. Subservience. Acknowledgment that she was its master.

Well, damn.

Seline glanced at Sam. "I don't think it's so bad. Just a big dog—"

Bullshit. Sam reached out to touch Seline's shoulder. In an instant, the "big dog" lunged up and slammed its claws into Sam's chest.

"No!" Seline's snapped order.

The hound froze.

"Tell the beast to go to hell," Sam said. He wished he understood how to send a hound back, but that was one power beyond him.

"Go to hell," Seline told the hound instantly.

The hound didn't vanish. In fact, the beast appeared to be getting bigger, stronger. Not good.

When they weren't in hell, the hounds survived by drinking blood and fear. They weren't some cute freaking pets. They were pit bulls for the devil.

But Seline was *petting* the thing now.

Sam risked a fast glance around the club. The stragglers were rushing for the door. Smart. But even as those folks pushed out, two familiar figures hurried forward.

Keenan and his vampire.

Keenan took one look at the hound and froze. He grabbed Nicole and tried to push her behind his back.

Fuck.

Too late. Over the centuries, hounds had developed a particular taste for vampire blood.

Seline's hound whipped around and leapt into the air. The floor shook as the beast hurtled toward its new treat.

"No!" Seline's shout, but this time, the beast didn't slow. Claws swiped out and cut into Keenan's chest, but the Fallen didn't move.

"Run, Nicole," he choked out, *"run."*

Wrong advice. The hounds liked the chase. Keenan should know that.

Keenan grabbed the hound's paws. Sam rushed to help him, with Seline right by his side.

With a howl, the hound shook off Keenan, and Sam saw that Nicole hadn't run away. She started kicking and clawing at the beast. Her fangs were out, and she was screaming for the hound to get away from her angel.

Before Sam could reach her, the hound tackled her and the beast's teeth went for her throat.

Nicole stopped screaming, but the whole room vibrated with the sudden wild rush of fury that Sam knew came from Keenan.

Sam and Keenan grabbed the hound. They dragged it off Nicole even as the hound snapped and bit.

Then Seline was there. Her hands locked around the hound's body. *"Leave her alone! Leave them all alone!"* Fury hardened her words. "Just get the hell away from us. *Go back to hell!*"

The hound whined. Its head lowered.

Then the beast vanished in a blur of smoke.

About fucking time.

CHAPTER THIRTEEN

Sam hadn't been lying to her. Seline stared at her hands and realized her fingers were stained with ash.

She'd just sent a hellhound back to hell. *She* controlled a hellhound.

Oh, damn.

"Baby, are you okay?"

She glanced up at the voice, so deep with concern. Keenan had his vampire in his arms. Seline could see the blood pouring from the woman's throat. *Okay* sure didn't seem like the right word. More like get-me-to-a-hospital-stat.

"Drink from me," Keenan said, his hands so gentle on the woman.

Nicole's head sagged back weakly, and Seline glimpsed her fangs. Then those fangs sank into Keenan. He shuddered. Not with revulsion, but with what she was pretty sure had to be pleasure.

"She'll be all right." Sam's voice didn't carry any concern. "Angel's blood—even if the angel has fallen—is incredibly strong."

Something to remember.

"How did I send him back?" Her gaze darted to the floor. To the scorch marks and the deep grooves that the hound's claws had left.

"Guess you just had to get mad enough," he said. "Mad enough to let that control of yours crack."

Crack? It had fragmented there in that last terrifying moment. If she hadn't been able to pull the hound back, Nicole would have died in front of her. "I didn't want more blood on my hands." She didn't know Nicole. Just because the woman was a vamp, it didn't mean she deserved hell.

Who did these days?

Sirens screamed in the distance.

"Humans . . . on the way to the rescue." Keenan said this even as Nicole continued to drink from him.

"You've got her?" Sam asked with a nod at Nicole.

"Always." Keenan's answer was immediate.

Sam's lips twisted. "Then get her out of here. Meet up with me at dawn, at Pedro's place."

Keenan's brows rose. "You trust that shifter?"

"More than most."

Keenan nodded and carried his feeding vampire toward the back door.

Seline didn't move. She wasn't sure where to go or what to do. Energy still pumped through her blood. She'd taken too much when she kissed Sam, she knew she had, but he didn't look weak.

If the hound had killed him, Sam's death would have been on her. She straightened her shoulders. "You need to go. Get away from me. What if I accidentally bring the hound back? You just—*go.*"

One dark brow climbed. "And what are you going to do? Stand here and wait for the cops?"

Maybe. Perhaps she deserved to be locked up. "You said the coyote shifter was dead?"

"Not by your hand. The hound killed him."

The sirens were louder. "I meant to kill him. I took as much power from him as I could." It was time for Sam to realize just how dark she was on the inside.

"If he'd still been breathing when I found him," Sam said, "*I* would have killed him."

His admission had her eyes widening.

Sam's stare had dropped to the front of her shirt. "I can see the marks he put on you."

She could feel them. "Just scratches. They'll fade."

Doors slammed outside. She glanced toward the front door. "How will we explain this?" Her gaze came back to him.

"We won't." He still didn't move. "The cops will say the people who talk about a monster attacking them are all just high. *Other* events always have a way of being covered up."

She knew many humans only saw what they wanted to see. "And the dead shifter? What happens when he's found?" The front door rattled. She glanced over and realized that thick tables had been pushed in front of the entrance.

Sam. She hadn't even realized he'd used his power to bar the door.

"There won't be anything left of him by the time he's found."

Again, the way of their world. The real animals would have their turn.

"Come with me." He offered his hand but didn't step closer.

She shook her head.

His face hardened. "We both have too many enemies now. You need me," he said, "and I—"

Seline turned away and headed for the back door. Her steps were fast. *Get away.* "I know, you're addicted to me, right?"

Unfortunately, that addiction burned both ways.

Her father had been addicted, too. So addicted that one night, he hadn't been able to stop taking energy from her mother. He'd taken so much that he'd killed her.

She pushed open the old door. Metal grated, and she glanced to the left, then the right. The cops hadn't made it to the alley yet.

Seline hurried outside.

"It's more than an addiction."

She kept moving.

He followed. The soft pad of his footsteps should have been swallowed by the sirens, but she heard him. She'd always been too conscious of everything about him.

Sam grabbed her arm and spun her back to face him. He crowded her against the side of the narrow alley.

"Don't move," his breath whispered over her ear. "Cops are coming."

And the cops thundered past the mouth of their hiding spot. Heading toward *El Diablo,* and not even noticing the couple in the shadows.

But Sam didn't release her when they were gone. She was too aware of the solid length of his body and the heavy press of his arousal against her.

She wanted Sam. Had from the first moment she'd seen him. But had he ever really wanted *her?* Or had her succubus side just pulled him in, an automatic instinct to acquire that strong psychic blast of power that was his core?

"I'm not going to run from Rogziel," Sam said. "I don't care how many hounds he has at his beck and call." His mouth brushed against her cheek.

Seline swallowed and tried *not* to want him so much. He didn't trust her. He'd threatened to kill her—

"I'm going hunting, Seline." His fingers slid under her jaw. The cops were gone. Probably swarming the empty interior of *El Diablo*. "And I want you by my side."

Her hands came between them and pressed against his chest. She had so much power boiling inside her, if she wanted she could have tossed him into the air and walked way.

The problem was that she didn't want to walk away. She'd found something she wanted more than freedom. "I didn't think I trusted me."

"I'm an asshole most days." She felt the hot lick of his tongue on the edge of her ear.

A shiver trembled over her.

"With you . . . something happens to me."

Great. Still not the declaration she wanted to hear.

"I don't trust *myself* when I'm with you," Sam continued. "I want you too much."

She needed more than *want*. There'd been too many other men who wanted her. *There had to be more*. She pushed him back. Not a toss into the air, just a shove that gave her a few precious inches. "I'm an abomination." She'd been called that before. Heard Rogziel say it when he hadn't realized she'd been around.

But now, she knew Rogziel had been right. The powers of a succubus and an angel, all boiling inside of her. "Only punishment angels can control hell-hounds." Even she knew that much. "I'm no angel." Would never be. The wings and the sweet promise of heaven hadn't been offered to her.

His fingers were still under her chin. "Do you know how the first demons were made?"

She knew the legend. "From the Fallen." From the first angels who'd sinned and been cast out of heaven. "They mated with humans and their offspring were cursed."

He laughed at that. "I'm betting you heard that tale from Rogziel, didn't you?"

Yes.

"It's all in how you look at it," he murmured. "Maybe they weren't cursed, maybe they were blessed . . . given powers no mortal had ever held before."

Now it was her turn to give a rough laugh. "That blessing killed many of them."

"And it turned some of them into kings and queens. They were given the power, and the free will to use it how they saw fit." He closed the distance between them again.

"You're telling me I'm blessed?" More sirens. She wanted out of there. That small alley was making her feel claustrophobic. "I'm not buying it." She pushed away from him and headed toward the darkness that waited for her.

"I'm saying you're a whole lot stronger than you realized, than Rogziel probably realized. But now that he knows just what you're capable of, he's going to come after you with everything that he has at his disposal."

She knew that. She'd taken Rogziel's attack dog away from him. The angel would have viewed that as the ultimate insult.

"You can wait for him to come . . ." Sam's feet tapped on the old stone walkway. "Or you can hunt with me, and we can kick his ass."

That had been the original plan. The darkness thickened as she advanced down the alley. More bars waited. More drunken laughter. More sex on the breeze that tickled her face.

"When you decide I've turned on you again—what then?" Seline asked because she wasn't just going to forget. Some things could never be forgotten. "I saw your eyes in that truck. You were ready to kill me."

"If I'd been ready to kill you, you would've been dead." Flat. Brutal. Truth.

Another club beckoned. She slipped inside, leaving him to the shadows. She just needed some space. Seline went to the bar. Motioned with her hand for a drink. She didn't care what the bartender gave her. She just needed something to take the edge off right then.

The guy on her right immediately sidled closer. The man on the left crowded in against her. Seline looked in the mirror and barely recognized the woman who stared back at her. Blood-red lips. Heavy-lidded eyes. Skin a shade no human's should be.

Her top had torn in the struggle, and her breasts pushed against the fabric. No wonder the men were closing in.

Built for sin.

The guy on the right, an American frat boy who'd wandered into the wrong bar, ran his fingers down her arm. "*Hola,* sexy *señorita,* where have you been all my—"

Sam's image appeared behind her in the mirror. He grabbed the kid's fingers and squeezed. "Want me to break them?" he asked, his voice bland, but she caught the fury flaring in his eyes.

"Shit! Shit, man, no! Ow!"

"Then don't touch her again." Sam shoved the college boy away. He glanced at the other man. "Get the hell out of here."

Both men scrambled for the exit. Seline took her drink and downed it in one gulp. It burned her throat, and she wanted more.

"You can't be out now, Seline." Sam positioned his body too close to hers.

She motioned for another drink. *Daughter of a demon. Daughter of an angel. Made for sin.* She stared at her image. "And why not?"

"Because your powers are cranked too high." He swore, then turned his head to the right. "Back off, assholes, she's with me."

Two more men turned away.

His hand fisted on the bar top. "You're pulling them in, and you don't even realize it."

No, she realized it. There was just nothing she could do to stop the pull.

"I've slept with three men in my life." Her confession seemed too loud even in the noisy bar. "This isn't what I wanted to be." But maybe there had never been a choice. Seduce. Kill.

Had Rogziel been right about her? If he could see her now . . .

He'd laugh, then he'd kill her.

The long, twisting house in the woods had served many purposes over the years. Weapons storage. Hideaway. Lover's retreat.

Tonight, it was a prison.

Rogziel stared down at the Fallen who knelt in the middle of the holding spell. He'd learned over the years that even witches could have their uses, and he'd certainly made sure to use the witch Mateo as much as he could.

Some spells could bind any being, even a Fallen. Not forever, of course. But he didn't need forever. He just needed a few hours. "Ready to talk, Tomas?"

Tomas's dark head lifted. He smiled. "Go fuck yourself, 'Ziel. I don't answer to you."

A growl rumbled from the shadows behind Rogziel. This time, he'd made sure to summon the hound that belonged to him. Using Erina's hound had seemed like such a fitting vengeance before. But obviously, that plan had been a mistake.

He would make no more. "I'm not here to kill you."

His words had Tomas blinking. Dry blood coated the right side of the Fallen's face. "No? You just hunt me down, sic that hound on me, and let it nearly rip my face off . . . but you're not planning to kill me. Of course not. How stupid of me to think that was the end goal."

Slowly, Rogziel stalked around the containment circle. "I know why you fell."

Tomas pushed to his feet, and pain flashed on his face. Those broken bones hadn't healed yet. "Kiss my ass. You aren't going to judge me. Save it for the humans—"

"How about I save it for *your* human?"

Rogziel's heart raced a bit faster when he saw the fear flash on Tomas's face. *Hit.* Rogziel cocked his head as he studied the Fallen. "She was the cause of your fall. She tempted, you succumbed. If anyone needs punishment, then she should be the one to pay."

"Leave Sierra alone! You stay the hell away from her." Tomas lunged forward and slammed into the side of the invisible wall that held him. His nose broke and blood splattered.

So much blood. Not dark. Bright red. Rogziel smiled. "You wanted her, you fell to fuck her. But . . . she's not with you now."

Tomas's hands clenched into fists. "What do you want?"

Rogziel frowned and moved closer. "Why is that?" He really wanted to know. "You burn for her, but you let her go? Or maybe—maybe she didn't want you." Now that would be a nice twist. "Once she found out what you were, did she run away?" Humans were always so afraid of the things they didn't understand, and they didn't understand most things.

"What do you want?"

"So emotional." Rogziel shook his head. "But that's what happens when you fall. You feel too much."

"And you think you don't feel?" Tomas fired right back, but he was careful not to get too close to the white powder that formed a circle around his feet. "I can see it on your face—you *like* hurting people. You've gone bad. You're fucked in the head."

His heart was pounding too hard. "I serve. I do my job. I punish." His lips twisted in disgust. "I have my wings. They didn't burn away because I disobeyed."

"It's not always about disobeying," Tomas muttered, and then *he* smiled. Rogziel didn't like that bloody smile. So close to death, Tomas shouldn't be smiling.

He should be begging.

"How long has it been . . ." Tomas asked, raising one brow, "since you were upstairs?"

Rogziel's eyes narrowed. "I travel between heaven and earth. Earth and hell. I have the power to—"

"Yeah, yeah," Tomas cut in, rolling his eyes. "I've heard the spiel before."

Tomas would die. Soon. Once he was no longer useful.

"Bet you can't remember the last time you were upstairs, can you?" Tomas pressed. "You know why? 'Cause you're *fucked in the head.* You think humans are the only ones who go bad? Angels do, too. I heard about the Fallen who've died. I know it was you. And I know you *liked* killing them."

The thunder of his heartbeat filled his ears. Rogziel became aware of the sweat slowly trickling down his back. "I have my wings. I am favored."

"The hell you are. Try to go back upstairs." Now Tomas laughed. "Bet you'll find out they changed the locks on you. You aren't favored by anyone, and when Sammael gets a hold of you . . . you'll be burning."

For an instant, Rogziel's vision went red. His body trembled with the effort to hold back. He wanted to lunge forward and tear Tomas apart.

This one dared to judge him? For centuries, he'd punished the wicked. He'd seen the worst humanity had to offer. He'd *punished*.

And he would continue to punish. He didn't need assignments anymore. He could smell the wicked. See the sin.

He turned away from Tomas. "I will give Sierra your regards." *When I let her feel the wrath that is her punishment.*

"No!"

Just that quickly, the arrogance and fury were gone from Tomas's voice. But Rogziel didn't look back. Tomas needed a lesson.

Changed the locks . . .

A blood lesson.

"Leave her alone! *Dammit,* just stop, Rogziel!"

But Rogziel had planned this moment. He opened the door to the connecting room and found his prey waiting. Her hands were bound to the chair behind her. A blindfold covered her eyes. Duct tape smothered her screams.

She'd been working on a site in Mexico. An archaeologist, digging into the past.

No wonder Tomas had been in the area. Some sins always drew you in.

He cut through the binds on her wrists, and he knew the blade sliced her flesh when tears leaked from her eyes. He hauled her up, not caring when she immediately shoved back her blindfold.

What did it matter if she saw his face? She wouldn't be escaping alive.

He dragged her into the room with Tomas. Tomas— still yelling. But when he saw Sierra, he froze and his cries died on his lips.

"Now, I think you may be understanding your situation better," Rogziel said. His humans had brought

Sierra to him. Always so eager to please. He'd make sure they were rewarded one day.

In the end, everyone always got the reward they deserved.

Rogziel yanked off the duct tape from the human's mouth. "Recognize him?" he asked her.

Sierra stared at Tomas. Her brow furrowed and her lips quivered. Then, slowly, almost sadly, she shook her head.

Rogziel laughed—deep, bellowing laughter that shook his chest. "You fell . . . you traded your powers . . . and she doesn't even know who you are?"

"Let her go!"

Sierra trembled in his grasp. Her red hair brushed against Rogziel's fingertips. "I'm going to punish her. She made an angel fall."

"You're crazy, buddy!" Sierra twisted against him, but Rogziel wasn't about to let her go. "Crazy! You can't do this! I'm—"

"What do you want?" Tomas asked, voice muted and his eyes on Sierra.

It was the question Tomas had asked twice before, but this time, Rogziel knew Tomas was really saying, *I'll do what you want.*

"I want Sammael." He was the problem. He was the one deserving hell. Sammael had destroyed Seline. He'd flaunted his transgressions for centuries. Sammael was the one who would be punished.

First.

"He thinks you're . . . friends," Rogziel told him. Foolish of Sammael. "He came to save you."

Tomas's head moved in a jerk that was agreement.

"Now you're going to make sure that I kill him." He ran his fingers down Sierra's throat. "Or you'll watch me hurt her. An eye for an eye . . ."

"Get your hands off her!"

"Give me Sammael, and you can have your human."

Sierra stared at him with wide eyes. "You have the wrong woman! Just let me go, okay? Please, let me—"

More laughter tumbled from Rogziel. Tomas was willing to trade his life for a woman who didn't even know him. Priceless.

"You fell for nothing," he told Tomas, and disgust thickened his words. Heaven, for this?"

"No," Tomas said with certainty. "I fell for everything." His eyes blazed at Rogziel. "Get me out of this witch's prison, and I'll give you Sammael. I vow it."

If another man looked at Seline like she was some kind of dessert, Sam was going to erupt. He crowded closer to Seline. "We need to get out of here." She smelled like an aphrodisiac. Silken woman. Sensual heat.

No wonder the guys in the joint were foaming at the mouth.

He grabbed her wrist. "Correction, we're *getting* out of here, now."

She turned her bedroom eyes on him. Sexy, but . . . sad. Because her stare looked a bit lost. The power pumping through her was obvious, but Seline appeared scared.

He wrapped his arm around her waist. "I'll take care of you."

A sad laugh slipped from her lips. "You almost killed me."

The woman wasn't going to let him forget that. He waved his hand and pushed the others back, clearing a path to the door. "I damn well didn't almost kill you. I had to get the hound off my neck." Literally. "Braking the truck so hard was my only option."

"But you said . . ."

He'd said a lot of dumbass things. He didn't always know what to say to her or what to do with her. "I thought you'd lied to me. That you'd set me up from the beginning." So he'd gone a little crazy. But he'd *never* touched her and thought of death.

With Seline, it was always about life. She made him feel more alive than anything or anyone else could.

He led her outside. Three motorcycles were waiting by the curb. So thoughtful of some folks. He jumped on the newest one, had it hot-wired in three seconds, and he told Seline, "Hold on."

They had a meeting at dawn. He was done running. The game was changing, but first . . .

First he needed Seline.

Pedro's place was an inn, of sorts, on the edge of town. Not for humans. They rarely wandered that far off the beaten path. But, over the years, Pedro's had been a safe house of sorts for paranormals. Since Pedro had split town a few weeks ago, Sam knew the place would be perfect for crashing.

They didn't speak as they drove through town. Sam was too conscious of Seline's body pressing against his. Her scent surrounded him and, every breath he took, Sam swore he tasted her.

The old inn came into sight soon enough. He braked and made sure to hide the bike under some bushes.

"Is this place safe?" Seline's voice was like a stroke right over his groin. He wanted to tell her again, *pull it back*. But he knew now that she couldn't. Too much power, burning her from the inside out.

"Safe enough." The two-story building was dark, and Sam sensed no *Other* presence there.

Not yet. Keenan and his vampire would be arriving soon. It was about an hour until dawn.

He caught her hand, but this time, he threaded his fingers through hers. Sam felt her hesitation. "Trust me," he told her, and really wanted her to do just that.

She stared at him with a gaze that was slowly breaking a heart he hadn't even realized he had, not until he'd met her.

Sam took her inside and up the stairs. He wondered if Seline even noticed the old weapons that lined the walls—weapons that could come in handy later. Pedro had been a collector, of sorts.

He didn't mention the weapons. Right then, he only wanted to focus on her. The bedroom on the right had a bed nestled inside. The sheets looked clean. Not perfect. Not good enough for her, but it would have to do.

Seline burned too hot, and he had to help her.

He took her clothes off slowly, skimming his fingers down her body. Perfect breasts. So full and sweet, with dark pink nipples. Her stomach curved gently, her legs stretched for freaking ever, and the soft flesh between her thighs made him burn.

She reached for him, but he caught her hands. "Not this time." This time, he had to show her something different.

Seline's brows furrowed. "I thought—"

"I can do more than take." And she was more than an addiction. He didn't understand what was happening between them yet, not fully, but she was more and he'd prove that to her.

He lifted her onto the bed and spread her out on the mattress. Her legs shifted a bit, exposing more of her sex, and he felt like he'd just taken a punch to the gut.

Control.

He would have it, for her.

His mouth pressed against hers. The lightest of

kisses, then . . . deeper because he had to taste more. His hands cupped her breasts and his thumbs feathered over her nipples. She'd see this time, he wasn't like the others she'd known.

This time, it would all be for her.

He settled his hips between her legs and began to kiss a path down her neck. With every press of his mouth, with every lick of his tongue against her skin, he wanted more.

But he wouldn't take.

The only sound was her breathing, his, coming too fast. He felt the thunder of her heartbeat beneath his hands.

When Sam took her breast into his mouth, she moaned and her hands tunneled into his hair. She pulled him closer. He let her feel the light score of his teeth on her flesh.

He sucked. He licked. He wanted.

He didn't take.

Sam kissed his way down her stomach. She was shaking now. Whispering his name. Her power crackled in the air and brushed right over his skin.

Seline might not realize it, but she was giving, too. Giving all that powerful energy right back to him.

He spread her legs wider and stroked her sex. He slid a finger into her, stretching her lightly. Then another finger. He pushed them inside her, knuckles deep, and her hips arched off the bed.

"*Sam!*" Not need. Demand.

His thumb pushed against her clit, and he thrust his fingers fully inside her. Again. Again. Her hips rose up, trying to make him move faster. Harder.

"*Come . . . inside . . .*" she whispered, and her voice was pure temptation. "I want you."

He wanted her. His whole body shuddered.

Sam withdrew his fingers but only so he could lock

his hands around her hips and hold her exactly where he wanted her.

He tilted her hips up and put his mouth on her.

Seline's taste . . . hot and sweet . . . more, need more . . .

She came almost instantly. A hard explosion that had her gasping and arching beneath him.

He didn't let her pull back. He kept licking her, kissing her, and he thrust his tongue inside her body because he wanted *more of that sweet taste.*

Seline climaxed a second time. Energy hit him, a hard burst of euphoria that he knew came from her.

But he didn't stop. He loved her taste too much. Loved the feel of her pleasure.

Her fingers were in his hair again. Her legs trembled around him.

His cock pushed hard against the front of his jeans. He could feel the zipper shoving against his flesh.

But he wasn't stopping. Not yet. Not until he'd given her all the pleasure that she could handle. *This time . . . for her.*

Her flesh was wet and hot. His fingers slid easily into her even as he bent to press his mouth against her clit. Her body began to tense again. He knew she was close to finding her release once more.

"No!" Seline's choked cry.

He froze, then, slowly, pulled back and glanced up at her.

"With you this time." She swiped her tongue over her lips. *"With . . . you."*

He'd wanted only her pleasure.

Sam slid his hand right over the tight center of her need, and Seline came. This time, she yelled his name.

Her body was limp and so sated Seline really didn't want to move for at least a week.

Her heartbeat slowly stopped its frantic racing. The bed squeaked as Sam pulled her close. *Sam*.

She turned and stared at him. The faintest rays of light were starting to spill through the blinds, but most of the room was still cloaked in darkness "You didn't . . ."

"You're not an addiction." There was no mistaking the rasp of lust in his voice. "You're . . . *mine*."

She didn't know what to say.

Then she'd realized what he'd done. Sex with a succubus. But no pleasure for him. Only her.

She blinked quickly, afraid she'd do something weak and human like cry. "Sam, I *want* you."

She felt the weight of his stare. "You're not an abomination," he told her, and she heard the echoes of anger in his words.

Good thing it was dark. She wasn't sure she wanted him to see her now.

"I don't care who your parents were—or *what* they were," Sam said.

She cared. "My father took too much from my mother. He drained her." Killed her.

"Then Rogziel killed him?"

"Punishment," she whispered, and her hand pressed over Sam's heart.

He swore. "How long has Rogziel been playing God?"

She blinked. "Wh-what?"

He caught her hands. More light spilled through the blinds. Dawn. "You don't know much about your demon side, do you?"

No. Not her demon side or her angel blood.

"A succubus and an incubus can only have a child with a true mate. If they could have kids with just anyone, don't you think the world would be exploding with little incubi and succubi by now?"

Yes. It would be, but there weren't many of her

kind. "You're saying we . . . mate?" Like wolf shifters? Like . . . forever?"

"I'm saying you can only have kids with the person you choose as a life-mate. That's forever. That's bonding." He exhaled. "And a mate wouldn't take enough power to kill. Sure, an incubus could drain others, but it's real unlikely—next to fucking impossible—that he'd drain the one woman he loved."

Her head started to throb. An engine growled outside. "What are you telling me?"

"I'm saying that I think Rogziel fed you a load of bull. Your father didn't kill your mother."

She rose from the bed and dressed with hands that were too steady. They should be shaking. She should be shaking. "Then who did?" All her life, she'd thought her father had destroyed her mother.

"When we get Rogziel, we'll find out."

No, no, this isn't possible. "You're wrong. My father killed her. He lost control, and he *drained*—"

"Mates share power. They don't take."

Seline blinked. She'd shared power with Sam. Fear tightened her belly. Did that mean he was hers?

Footsteps pounded below. Sam was on his feet now and in front of her. He stared into her eyes. "Whatever happens, remember . . . I don't care what shit Rogziel told you, *you aren't an abomination.* You aren't evil." His gaze narrowed. "But, sweetheart, you are damn well mine."

She was very much afraid that he might be hers.

When did this happen? When did I start to fall so hard for him? Had she been trying to bind them from the beginning?

There was so much she didn't know. No, much she hadn't been told because of Rogziel.

"Sam . . ."

But he stiffened and his head jerked toward the

door. She saw the slight flare of his nostrils. "That's not Keenan and his vampire." Anger roughed his voice.

"Sam?"

He lunged forward. Seline rushed right behind him.

And from the top of the stairs, Seline saw who waited for them just inside the inn's doorway. Waited with a grim smile curving his lips.

Az.

CHAPTER FOURTEEN

"Hello, brother," Az called, raising his brows. "Figured I'd find you here."

Sam shoved back the rage and slowly climbed down the stairs. He was too aware of Seline behind him.

"My memory grows stronger every day," Az said, and Sam saw the hardness in his stare. "I remembered how much you liked to hide here. Hide, and hunt."

Sam reached the foot of the stairs. *Attack*. His control was razor thin. "Enjoying your new life? I certainly hope you have been . . . because it will be over soon."

Seline didn't speak, but Sam heard the soft whisper of her steps as she crept down the staircase.

Az's gaze drifted to her. "I came for you."

The guy wanted to die. Slowly. Painfully.

Then Az lifted his hand and said to Seline, "I can offer you safety."

Sam attacked. In an instant, he was across the room. His fist plowed into Az's perfect face. "And I can offer you an ass-kicking."

Az stumbled back, but he didn't fall. His chin lifted.

"You can't kill me. I remember that part. The touch doesn't work on angels, even Fallen."

"That's right . . ." Sam growled, fists ready to attack. "That's why you had to work so hard to try and *kill* me a few months back."

Az's brows lowered.

"Oh, what? Don't remember that part?" Another drive of his fist. Damn but it felt good when Az backed up. *Weakness.* "You teamed up with a coyote shifter so that he could kill me and Keenan. Guess being Fallen was too much of a sin for us."

Az shook his head. Blood dripped from his lip. "Rogziel . . . he said . . . Fallen should burn."

Of course. Fucking Rogziel. "And you were ready and willing to serve your own brother up to him?"

Sam didn't see the blow coming, not until it was too late. And Az didn't pull his punch. Sam tasted blood in his mouth, and he was pretty sure that his brother had broken his nose.

Good thing he was a fast healer.

"You've *killed!*" Az yelled, his face darkening with fury. Ah, yes, fury. Now that he'd fallen, Az would be *feeling*. If he wasn't careful, those feelings could break him apart.

Sam would make sure his brother wasn't careful. *Break.*

"You had your orders . . . you were only supposed to take the souls slated for Death." Once again, Az's gaze darted to Seline. "Do you even know how many he slaughtered?" The question was fired at her.

Sam didn't look at Seline. "They deserved to die."

"Who were you to judge? It was war, they were fighting. We don't get the luxury of picking sides. We follow—"

He grabbed Az and lifted him high into the air. "You weren't there. You didn't see them raping the women and killing the children. You didn't see them just wipe the blood away, as if that took the stain off their hands. Over and fucking over again . . . I had to *watch*."

Az didn't fight. "You think you're the only one who ever saw innocents suffer? We do not punish—"

"No, twisted pricks like Rogziel are supposed to do that, right?" Screw that. "Those men *deserved* to die."

"You didn't make the deaths easy." More censure. What else was new?

"Why should I? They made their victims suffer, so I made them suffer." Fair enough.

Seline's footsteps tapped across the floor.

"And after you fell, you didn't learn to control yourself, did you?" Az was pushing, obviously determined that Seline would learn all of Sam's sins.

His brother didn't understand. There were too many sins for her to ever learn them all. "No, I didn't stop. I hunted those who needed punishment, and I made sure they got it."

Not always with death. Sometimes he'd let his prey live, but with the scars to remember him by.

"You see . . ." Az shoved against him and landed agilely on his feet. "He's really no different from Rogziel. Power mad. Determined to deliver *his* brand of justice." His gaze raked Seline. She stood just a foot away now, her body tense. "He's using you. He saw what you can do with the hound, and he wants to—"

The building trembled around them. "Az . . ." He couldn't use his magic to kill his brother. The powers-that-be had been real specific about the rules of engagement between angels. The death touch wouldn't work—that only worked on humans and most *Other*. And no mortal weapon could kill an angel. Those weapons just weren't strong enough.

He could kick Az's ass easily, but Az would heal from just about anything.

Just about.

"*He* can't kill me," Az said, and Sam saw the shadow of his brother's lost wings shift behind him. "He can't kill Rogziel. But you . . ." He smiled at her, and the sight enraged Sam. "You can kill any angel or Fallen you want. All you have to do is summon your hound."

The puzzle pieces clicked into place for Sam. "You knew her mother, didn't you?" *Sonofabitch.* "You made the connection in New Orleans." That was why Az had been desperate to get Seline. He'd found a weapon to use.

"She looks a lot like Erina," Az said, cocking his head to study her. "Same cheekbones, same nose . . . same eyes."

To hell with his brother. Sam wrapped his fingers around Az's throat. "You're *not* using her."

"But you are?" Az asked, voice snapping. "Stop lying to her, *brother.* You wouldn't have brought her along if you didn't think you could use her. What? Did you think she'd knock out both me and Rogziel for you? Your perfect weapon—and what a nice bonus for someone who likes to sin as much as you do . . . she's a succubus."

Sam tossed his brother through the nearest window. Glass shattered and Az hit the ground outside with a groan. Sam's gaze flew around the room, *to her.*

"Sam . . ." Seline's quiet voice. "He's lying, isn't he?"

"Angels are good at twisting the truth." He forced his stare away from her and, once again, his gaze swept the area. There was a reason he'd chosen this safe house. Pedro had a rather interesting collection of artifacts lining the walls. Weapons. Ancient, new, deadly. Because, sometimes, those seeking a safe haven needed a way to protect themselves.

Sam grabbed the spear that rested over the mantel.

A wooden spear, simple in construction, one that had journeyed all the way from Africa.

But the tip of the spear, that sharp, deadly curve—far sharper than any knife could be—that wasn't so simple. The curving tip was a finely honed dragon's claw, a claw that had been taken from a dragon shifter right before the moment of his death.

No mortal weapon.

Seline grabbed his arm. "What are—"

"I don't need you to kill my enemies," he said, smiling grimly. The whole place was a perfect weapon room. Pedro had taken out more than a few "immortal" enemies over the years. "I can do the job myself."

Then he flew through that broken window.

But Az wasn't alone any longer. Keenan was there, facing off against his brother, as was Nicole, and despite the rising sun, she didn't look particularly weak.

No, she looked fucking furious.

Payback will be a devil.

He lifted the spear, and they all closed in on Az.

Seline started after Sam, her heart racing. Az knew her mother. Oh, jeez, Az *knew* her mother.

This was Sam' big moment. Vengeance. He'd been waiting to attack his brother, and that moment was finally at hand for him. But . . .

My mother. She couldn't let Sam kill Az, not yet. There was too much Az could tell her.

"Sam, stop!" she screamed, and lunged forward.

She didn't make it to the door. A man appeared before her. Tall, dark, with bright blue eyes and a face that could have been carved from stone.

She screamed and kicked out at him. But he just caught her arms and dodged her kicks.

And Sam didn't hear her scream. He was too busy fighting Az.

"I'm sorry," the man before her said. No, not a man. She could see the outline of his shadow wings. *Fallen.* No wonder he'd just appeared in front of her. Angels had that fast movement that she hated. "I don't . . . my plan wasn't to hurt you."

She drove her knee into his groin. *Didn't dodge that!* "Too bad because if you don't let me go, you'll be in a whole world of pain."

His hold didn't break.

Dammit! What kind of Fallen was she dealing with? *Please, not an Angel of Death.* She had too many of those to deal with already.

"The pain will only be for a moment."

Forget that. She let her power out. It swelled, wrapping around them. She'd make him beg, tremble—

He shook his head sadly. "That doesn't work on me, succubus."

And now she was scared. *"Sam!"*

He clamped his hand over her mouth. "You won't die." Sadness flickered in his eyes. "Though he will."

Then he started to chant. Words in Latin that she'd heard before. *"No!"*

Smoke swirled around them.

When the world stopped spinning, Seline found herself on another deserted road. In the middle of freaking nowhere.

The *get-the-fuck-away* spell. "Sam!"

But he wasn't there, and neither was the Fallen who'd just dumped her in the middle of Mexico.

Sam had the spear at his brother's throat. "Any last words?"

Blood trickled down Az's neck.

Sam could see the struggle in his brother's eyes. Rage. Fear.

Regret?

"How does it feel?" Keenan pressed. He stood beside them. "Because you are *feeling* now, aren't you, Az?"

Before Az could answer, Nicole stiffened. "Seline." She glanced back. Stared at the quiet house. "I thought . . . she screamed."

When Sam looked over his shoulder, Az broke free and leapt away.

No, Az wouldn't escape this time. "Check the house," he told Nicole, never taking his eyes off Az.

"No need." The rumbling voice came from the left.

Tomas walked from the brush, his steps slow and his face grim. "Your Seline isn't inside."

Az wasn't moving. Nicole and Keenan were eyeing Tomas with suspicion, and Sam—his guts were twisting. "How the fuck do you know that?"

"Because I'm the one who took her." A shrug. "You shouldn't have trusted Mateo, you know. Once he saw your death, he figured it was time to align with someone stronger."

"You?" From the corner of his eye, Sam saw Nicole run into the house. Checking to see if Seline was still there. No need for that. Angels, even Fallen, couldn't directly lie.

"No." Tomas's lips twisted. "I'm just the errand boy. Guess it was my turn to play messenger."

Sam's blood chilled. "Rogziel did catch you, didn't he?"

A sad, regretful nod of Tomas's head. "You didn't arrive soon enough."

Sam could smell the blood that still coated Tomas. He couldn't see the wounds, but he knew they were there. "Why are you still living?" A brutal question but one that had to be asked.

Nicole appeared again and shook her head. No Seline.

"Rogziel wanted me to trick you—to get you to come in willingly with me."

Sam waited.

Tomas held his stare. "I agreed."

"You traded your life for mine?" And to think, he'd once saved Tomas's sorry ass. A pack of vampires had closed in on the Fallen just days after he'd hit earth. The angel blood was often a lure for the undead—the taste of it made them feel alive again.

I should have let him die.

But he'd been in the mood to kick vampire ass then.

"Something like that," Tomas muttered. He glanced at Keenan. "You need to get out of Mexico, K. *Get out.*" His jaw tightened when he saw Nicole. "And make sure you take her with you."

Tomas hadn't been real keen on vampires since his attack. But then Tomas said, "The last thing you want to do is leave her unprotected."

And Sam understood. What was said . . . and what wasn't. Some angels couldn't even twist the truth that well.

Tomas was such an angel.

"You know Rogziel's crossed the line," Sam said. Az was still there. Not moving. Just watching, waiting. Because he understood what it was like to be Rogziel's captive?

Because he wanted to find out where the bastard was so he could rip him apart first?

No dice. Rogziel's mine.

"Yes, I know . . ." Tomas lifted his shirt, and Sam saw the deep claw marks that crossed his stomach. "He let his pet play with me for a while."

"The hound?" Keenan demanded. "The hound is back?"

"He doesn't just have one hound," Tomas told him, shoving his shirt back down. "He's got two. The second bastard is even bigger than the one I saw at the motel."

That wasn't good to know. Sam took a step toward Tomas. "Where's Seline?"

"Two hounds?" Az muttered. "Two?"

Kill him. The spear was still in Sam's hand. It would be so easy.

"If you want her to live, you'll come with me now."

Angels could twist the truth . . .

"We'll all come," Keenan snarled, and his shadow wings flared.

But Tomas shook his head. "Sorry, that's not how it works."

Then he lunged forward and grabbed Sam. "When it comes to angels, you were always too trusting." Then a familiar chant filled Sam's ears.

Mateo.

Sam didn't fight. He could have broken free. But if he had, then Seline might suffer. In the instant of time that he had, Sam broke the head off the spear and curled his fingers around the claw. The wood fell to the ground.

Az's tense face vanished. Keenan shouted his name.

And the world became a swirling vortex of dark gray smoke.

"Something you should know," Sam grated as wind howled in his ear like demons screaming.

Tomas grunted.

"Mateo knows better than to sell my ass out." He slammed his hand into Tomas's chest. "He's too smart for that."

The wind stopped howling. The smoke vanished. Sam and Tomas slammed into the ground. But in an instant, Sam was back on his feet. On his feet, and with his weapon pressed against Tomas's throat. "Obviously," Sam told the dumbass, "you're not."

Tomas glared up at him. "How the hell did you do that?"

He used his left hand to yank at the charm around his neck—a charm Mateo had given him. "Let's just call it my little get-out-of-jail free card. It's real handy for breaking spells." He let the claw slice Tomas's throat. "You take me to Seline, *now,* or you die."

Seline glared down the long, winding road. The sun was rising slowly in the sky, and she was already baking out there.

No one was on this road. That freaking Fallen had dumped her in the middle of nowhere. No phone. No people. No help.

No Sam.

And, oh, damn, she was worried about him. What if Az killed him? What would she do then?

Her shoulders hunched even as her head tilted back, and she stared helplessly up at that stretching expanse of blue sky.

"Please," she whispered, aware that her voice was thick with emotion that nearly choked her. *Az had known her mother. Sam could be dying.* "Help me."

Because she knew Rogziel had gone after Sam. Despite his strength, Sam couldn't defeat both Az and Rogziel, and if Rogziel brought his hounds with him, there wouldn't even be a chance for Sam to survive.

Her eyes squeezed closed. She was lost, had no clue, and Sam—

"Sam is stronger than you think." A soft laugh floated in the air. "He's stronger than pretty much any angel on earth or above it."

Slowly, Seline opened her eyes. A woman stood before her. Small, delicate, with close-cropped dark hair and a delicate, almost elfin face.

The woman wore all white, a bright contrast to her light brown skin, and strong, powerful black wings spread behind her.

Seline's knees trembled. Rogziel usually kept his wings hidden, an old angel trick. This woman—she wasn't bothering with tricks.

And she also wasn't *standing* in front of Seline. The woman hovered about a foot in the air.

Black wings . . . Rogziel had black wings, too. All punishment angels did. And, because of Sam, she knew that all Angels of Death did, as well. Seline swallowed back her fear. "Are you here to kill me?"

The woman glanced around. "Um, no."

The scent of flowers was strong. Roses. The woman smelled like roses.

"Then you're a punishment angel."

"Um . . ."

That really wasn't an answer.

The woman flew closer. Those wings fluttered behind her. "You look a lot like Erina."

Seline licked her lips. "So I've been told."

The angel's bright stare raked her. "It's a pity you never knew her."

Her throat hurt when she cleared it. "Yeah, it is."

The angel's gaze saw too much. "Why didn't you call sooner?" the woman asked softly. "All these years . . . it sure took you long enough, Seline."

She was missing something. "What?"

The angel pointed toward the blue sky. "If you'd wanted help, you should have asked sooner." A soft sigh slipped from her lips. "As it is, you've almost waited too late now."

"You're kidding me!" A hot spoke of anger burned

in her belly. "You're telling me that to make this night-mare stop, all I had to do was *ask*?" In-freaking-sane.

"Ask and you shall receive," the angel told her with a slight nod. "You asked and now help is here."

"Here to do what?"

The angel's feet touched the ground. Her wings curled in behind her, and a hard, fierce expression crossed her face. "To punish."

"Yeah? Who exactly are you here to punish? Me? Sam? Azrael? Or what about that power-mad Rogziel? Do you *know* what he's been doing?"

"I'm not the one who will give Rogziel his punish-ment," the angel said in a serene, clear voice.

"So you're not going to do anything?" Seline de-manded, her voice closer to a screech. "You're just gonna stand there and watch him kill angels?"

No emotion flickered over the angel's face. "Rogziel is not the same angel he once was."

"No shit! I figured that out the first time I saw him slice open a vampire and *smile*." But how did you get away from someone who had the power of heaven on his side? "I thought you said you'd *help* me."

"I will." The angel's gaze raked her. "You're a very fortunate woman, Seline."

Not so much from where she was standing. Both parents dead. Raised by a psycho angel. Destined to live off the energy of others, like a psychic vamp. Not so great there.

"You can control a hellhound." Was that a trace of admiration in the angel's voice? Yes, a bare whisper. "That means you can be . . . more."

Seline wasn't sure she liked the sound of that. "More what?"

Those black wings stretched out. "All your life, you've never felt as if you truly belonged, did you?"

"Try being a demon half-breed in a world of humans. You won't *belong*, either." A trickle of sweat slid down her back.

"You don't have to dwell with them."

Seline rocked back on her heels. "What are you saying?" Couldn't the angel just spit it out? "I just want to get back to Sam. I want—"

"He can't kill Azrael." Flat, but whispering with the underlying timbre of power.

Seline blinked. "Um, well, then I suggest you use those wings and fly me to them because when I left, it sure looked like it was close to killing time."

"Brother against brother . . ." The angel's brows furrowed. "That way leads to destruction. Azrael *cannot* die by Sam's hand."

"If he does . . ." She had to ask. "What happens?"

"Their blood is bound. They were linked from the beginning of time." The angel's head cocked and she seemed to be looking far away. Into the past? "One cannot live without the other."

The fear in Seline's belly twisted harder. "You're telling me this *now?*"

"They were twins. One light, one dark. Now both are becoming dark. There has to be balance." Those bright eyes bored into Seline. "You have to give them balance."

The wind began to whip behind Seline. She glanced back, expecting to see a car barreling toward her. No one was there.

"*You* seek justice," the angel told her. "You are the instrument."

No, no, no. Seline's head snapped back around. "I thought you said you'd help me!"

"I will . . ." The angel rose into the air. "I'm going to help you come home."

But she didn't have a home. Never had.

"Seline!"

She jumped at Sam's shout. She whirled and found him behind her. Him . . . and the jerk who'd dropped her in the middle of nowhere.

But Sam's eyes weren't on her. They were above her. On the angel. "Delia! Get away from her!"

His rage blasted through Seline.

Afraid now, she glanced over her shoulder. Delia had a sword in her hands. The long blade gleamed. "Stop him," Delia told Seline. "Or I will be sent after him. Balance will be maintained, one way or another."

Then she rose higher into the sky. Her wings stretched, and the angel vanished.

Seline finally took a deep breath.

"You summoned a punishment angel?" It was the dumbass who spoke. Sam had a tight grip on him, and some kind of small blade—looked more like a wicked sharp claw—was at the guy's throat. "You must have one serious death wish."

Seline ignored him. She stared at Sam. "I was—" *Worried. Afraid.*

Sam nodded, and she knew he understood. Then his gaze turned to the Fallen. "Time for you to die, Tomas." He shifted his hand, placing the weapon right against Tomas's jugular. "See you in—"

"No!" Tomas's face flushed. "He'll kill her!"

"No one will kill Seline," Sam roared.

Seline hurried closer to them. *I want to bring you home.* Her fingers pressed against Sam's back, right over his shoulder blades, and she felt the instant tenseness of his body.

"Not her!" Tomas's throat was bleeding. "Sierra. *My* Sierra. The bastard has her. If I don't bring you back—just you—then she's dead."

CHAPTER FIFTEEN

Azrael stared across the clearing at Keenan and his vampire. Blood gushed from Azrael's wounds while Keenan showed no visible signs of weakness. How unfortunate. "You think you're going to finish what my brother started?" He couldn't believe that his brother had actually vanished. Left the battle . . . for a woman.

Sam should know better than to lust for a succubus. They could twist any man, human or *Other,* inside out. A succubus took and took until nothing was left, then she tossed away the husk of the being—the empty shell was all that remained when she was finished.

Azrael laughed and hoped the sound didn't show how weak he was becoming. "The sun's up." Stating the obvious, but perhaps Keenan hadn't realized the full significance of what was happening overhead. "And your vamp is starting to look awful pale."

The sun wouldn't burn a vampire. That was just a mortal misconception. The sun simply made a vampire weak. Human level.

As Az expected, Keenan immediately stepped in front of the vampire as if to shield her.

This time, though, Azrael could see—*and under-stand*—the emotion glittering in Keenan's eyes. "You truly do love her."

Emotions. He'd never tasted them until he burned. Sam . . . he knew his brother had never been like the other angels. Angels weren't supposed to feel. They were just supposed to serve. But he'd seen the flash of rage too many times in Sam's eyes. He'd known the fall was coming, long before Sam slaughtered those men.

My fault. I should have stopped him.

The Fall had initially washed away Az's memories, but every day, he recalled more of his past. When he thought of Sam, the guilt gnawed in his chest.

"You'll never hurt her," Keenan yelled at him.

Az's blood stained the ground. "I don't want to hurt her."

True enough. He didn't, not anymore. But Keenan wouldn't be forgetting just what Az had tried to do to the vampire before. There would be no forgetting—or forgiving—from Keenan.

Keenan blinked, then his eyes narrowed as he studied Az.

Once, he and Keenan had been . . . not friends, but—almost. As close as angels could get to friendship. Then Azrael had tried to kill Keenan's vampire—the little female currently glaring so fiercely at him as she peered over her lover's shoulder.

A mistake. He just hadn't understood how Keenan felt, not then.

Even now, he didn't fully comprehend, but he could still recognize love when he saw it staring back at him.

"I thought returning to heaven was best for you." Az admitted his arrogance. He hadn't seen that arrogance, not while he'd been in heaven, but it had been there, just beneath the surface. When had the emotions begun to slip past his guard? Like a poison, they'd worked under his skin, but, again, he hadn't realized, not until the fire burned his flesh. "I thought I knew how to save you."

"You thought wrong."

The vampire wasn't speaking. He could see the lines of strain on her face. Still new to the undead world, she wouldn't have adapted so well to her daytime weakness.

Her weakness would be Keenan's.

"So I did." Azrael turned away. His battle was not with Keenan or the vampire.

Sammael. A true brother of his blood. When he'd fallen and woken in that cemetery, a witch had found him. She'd tended his wounds, fed him, and told him that hell would come calling.

One brother would die.

He hadn't even known who he was then. She had. *"Hello, Death. I saw you fall."* Her hands had clasped a darkened mirror.

He hadn't trusted the witch, with good reason. She'd been the one to turn him over to Rogziel.

I'll find you again.

He'd be sure that hell called on her one day soon, too.

Az stepped forward and found his path blocked by Keenan. "You're not going anyplace."

He didn't want to hurt Keenan. "I've got a millennium on you. You don't want to get in my way." Blood loss or not, he could still take Keenan out. He didn't have to play by angel rules any longer. He could fight as dirty as he wanted. He *was* leaving. Even if he had to go through Keenan in order to get away. "Rogziel is hunting Fallen." He probably had Sammael right then. "I'm stopping him." *I'm the only one who can kill Sammael.* Rogziel didn't get to end his brother's life.

"You're so full of shit."

Az blinked at the vulgarity. Keenan had truly fallen far.

"You think I believe a word you're saying? You just want to find Sammael and attack him."

It was a bit more complicated than that . . . and he wasn't explaining his plans to the Fallen and his vamp. "Sorry, Keenan, but I have to go." And he blasted out a path with his power. Not at Keenan. A blaze of fire that charged toward the vampire.

Nicole screamed, and the sound cut into Azrael. Keenan lunged to her aid, jumping in front of her to protect her body from the flames.

Clearing Azrael's path. He let the fire circle them, but didn't let it touch Nicole's skin. After all, he didn't want to hurt the vampire. Not anymore.

Not that he expected Keenan to believe that.

Keenan pushed his power at the flames, forcing them out, and Azrael smiled as he pumped up his power and disappeared.

Sam glared down at Tomas, rage boiling in his blood like acid. *A punishment angel had been close enough to attack Seline.* She'd been alone, unprotected, and all because of this prick.

"Please," Tomas gritted, and Sam knew the angel had never begged before. Not even when the vamps had pinned him to the ground and ripped open his jugular. "Sierra's human. She doesn't—she doesn't even understand what's happening."

"And you want me to die for her?" Who the hell did Tomas think he was talking to?

Tomas stared back at him. "I'm planning to kill for her. I was hoping you'd be willing to kill, too."

Sam hesitated as he met Tomas's gaze. Despite those words, Sam didn't trust him.

"Um . . . who's Sierra?" Seline's voice was soft behind him. Her fingers seemed to burn right through Sam's shirt.

"His charge." Sam didn't drop the weapon. "Before he fell, Tomas here was a guardian angel, and he was supposed to guard *her*."

"She's psychic," Tomas whispered. "Her destiny . . . Sierra was going to see things. Change the world. I was supposed to protect her."

Yes, yes, he knew this story. "But you wanted her too badly, huh?" Guardians were always closer to falling than most angels. All that time being around humans and *seeing* the emotions.

Tempting.

"You understand want, don't you?" Tomas demanded as he slit his eyes back at Seline. "You let the enemy get fucking close."

"No, he did *not* just say that to me," Seline snapped.

Sam smiled. "You must want to die." Fair enough, he could accommodate the guy.

Sam sliced with the claw. Not deep or hard enough to kill, not yet, but just enough to cut open the skin.

"*Save her.*" Tomas wasn't fighting. Interesting. Tomas was powerful, in his way. "Kill me, fine. I probably got that coming to me. But *save* her."

"Rogziel really has her?" Seline demanded, an edge breaking the words.

Tomas nodded, and the move made the slice on his throat widen. "Don't even know . . . ah . . . jeez, ease up! How he got her, but he's keeping her at that house until I get back."

"You're telling me that Rogziel will hurt an innocent human?" Sam demanded. Not the way of the punishment angels. At least, not those who still had wings.

"No, that's not what I'm saying!" Tomas's stare glittered. "I'm saying he'll slice her up, he'll *enjoy it,* and he won't give a damn about her being innocent or not." And his eyes were still on Seline. "Isn't that right?"

Sam slowly eased his hold on Tomas. He glanced at Seline. *She was okay.* He'd gotten to her in time. So why did his chest still ache?

Seline swallowed and nodded. "I don't—I didn't think angels could do the things he's done. There was a vampire. Karen." Her lips trembled. "I did some checking on her. She hadn't killed *anyone,* but Rogziel had said Karen knew where his real prey was hiding. He said he'd make Karen talk." Her eyes squeezed shut. "By the time I got there, there wasn't a whole lot left of Karen. All I could do was hold her hand before she died."

Bastard. "That's when you decided to get away?" Sam asked.

"That's when I knew he'd be coming to kill me soon. He said Karen was an abomination. That she deserved his punishment just for existing." Her smile was broken. "I fell into that abomination category, too."

The hell she did. His back teeth clenched. Sam gritted out, "And the real prey?"

"Turned out that was you," she whispered. "But as far as I can tell, you didn't even know Karen."

An image clicked in his head then. A young blond vampire, freshly turned. Nervous hands. Wide eyes. The woman had wanted to become human again. She'd been turned by a monster in a dark alley, and she'd just wanted to get her life back.

She hadn't realized—not until Sam had broken her heart and told her the truth—*there was no going back.* Not for any of them.

She'd been an innocent, one hurt by the world. One who hadn't deserved anyone's punishment. *Rogziel, you will beg me to kill you. Beg.*

"He doesn't care about collateral damage," Tomas growled. "He'll use anyone, do anything, to get what he wants." Tomas put his hand to his throat and tried to stop the bleeding. His voice rasped when he said, "What he wants is you, Sammael. Your head on a platter for him."

An abomination. Sam cupped Seline's chin in his hand. As long as Rogziel was alive, Seline would never truly be free. Freedom was the one thing she wanted.

He'd give her anything.

Just as he'd give Rogziel what the bastard wanted. "Then take me to him."

Seline's eyes widened in horror. *"No!"*

Sam lifted the bloody claw. "It's not a mortal weapon." His lips twisted. "Made from a shifter, by a shifter. With this, I can kill Rogziel."

Her breath rushed out as Seline looked at him like he was crazy. "Or he can summon a hound to kill you! You can't just run in there and go up against him."

"I'm not afraid of Rogziel." Now he was just insulted. "He fears me." That was the heart of the matter. The true reason why Rogziel had been jonesing for his death all these years.

He'd seen the taint of madness in Rogziel's stare so long ago. Not that the powers above would listen to him. Rogziel had still been the "good" angel then.

While Sam had been the one who slaughtered humans.

"You think he's not going to be ready for you?" She grabbed his arms and actually shook him. "Look, I get it. You're the all-powerful Fallen who kicks most supernatural ass, but you can't stop hellhounds!"

"Unless you've got a punishment angel on your side," Tomas muttered, "But they aren't exactly thick on the ground."

Seline didn't look at the other Fallen, and because she was staring straight at him, Sam saw understanding fill her eyes. "You have me," she whispered.

Sonofabitch.

"I can help you." Her shoulders straightened, and she gave a firm, little nod. "I *will* help you because you're not going anyplace without me."

No, he wouldn't leave her. A smile began to curve his lips.

"Oh, no way, *no way!*" Tomas grabbed Sam's arm.

He knocked the other Fallen onto his ass.

Tomas shook his head and crawled to his feet. "He said you, *just* you. If he catches sight of anyone else, Sierra is dead."

Maybe. Maybe not. "Then I'll just have to make certain no one catches sight of her."

Lucky for him, he knew just the witch to use for a job like this. Good thing the devil wasn't the only one who spent time making deals with the *Other*.

Rogziel flew through the clouds. The world whipped by beneath him. A blur that he barely saw.

Maybe they changed the fucking locks.

His teeth snapped together as Tomas's voice rang through his mind. The Fallen was wrong. He could enter heaven, he could slide into hell, and he could walk the earth. He punished the damned, no matter where they were.

He saw the white columns up ahead. Waiting for him. His home.

Perfect. Peaceful.

Open, as it had always been.

Open . . .

"Not this time, Rogziel." Delia's cool voice stopped him.

His feet touched down on the marble floor, and she immediately appeared before him. Her wings stretched up high behind her, the way an angel's wings always did before an attack.

The way his wings were stretching now.

"This isn't the place for you," she said in her flat, slightly cool voice.

He stared at her. "I don't answer to you, child." And that's all she was to him. A child. Barely a few centuries old. He didn't care what Delia wanted. What she said. He was the one with the power.

As far as he knew, Delia had never even ventured into hell. Like many of the others, perhaps she was afraid of what she'd find waiting for her.

"No, you don't answer to me." Doors were behind her. Massive white doors that led to paradise. "Just think of me as the messenger." No expression crossed her face. "This place isn't for you," she told him again.

He wanted to rip her apart. Make her scream. Beg. Burn.

She took a step back. Ah, so she did feel his power. But she shook her head. "Good-bye, Rogziel."

He grabbed her arm. "No." Because a lick of fear had cut into his heart. "I'm an *angel*. This is where I belong."

Delia stared back at him. "You will soon be where you belong."

Those fucking Fallen. He hadn't done his job. Hadn't punished them. So now he was being punished. "I'll take them out! I'll clear the earth of the abominations . . ."

He spun away from her. He knew what to do. He still had his wings. He wasn't cast out. He was—

"Not all abominations are on earth," Delia said softly.

He stilled as her words sank in. The rage bubbled then and raked beneath his skin like claws. "You dare to judge *me?*"

"No." Her voice was still quiet. "That's not my job."

Sammael. It was the bastard's fault. He'd shifted the balance. Brought too much evil to the world.

Punish . . .

"The judgment is at hand," Delia told him. "Be ready."

Then her wings rustled, and she flew away from paradise.

The instant she vanished, Rogziel charged those heavy white doors, but they wouldn't open for him. They wouldn't *open.* He clawed. He punched. His hands broke, and he bled.

But the doors wouldn't budge.

"No!" His scream.

I bet they changed the fucking locks.

"Let me in!" he yelled.

No one answered his cry.

The doors stayed shut.

He'd served in heaven. Punished in hell and on earth.

Served . . .

"No!"

His blood stained the doors.

But they *wouldn't open.*

Sam knew where to find Mateo. He always did. Find the nearest crossroads, light a match, and whisper a quick incantation, then all he had to do was wait for Mateo to appear.

Mateo wasn't *exactly* a witch, no matter how hard he might try to claim otherwise. There was more than just witch blood flowing through his veins.

Mateo was a caller, too—one from a very long

and dark line. Summon him at the crossroads, and he had to appear. Bind him, and he had to do your bidding.

"Sam?" Seline's hand was in his. "What are we doing here?"

"Calling a friend," he told her. "Now stand back." Things were about to get even uglier than they had been, but he wouldn't block her out. She'd be there for the end game and the freedom she wanted so badly.

She stepped back. Their fingers slid apart.

Tomas paced nervously near the edge of the road. "No, man, you are *not* doing a crossroads call. Don't you know that you can't trust whatever freak comes when you do this crap? These are monsters! They slipped out of hell, they—"

Sam used a blade to slice over his wrist. Blood dropped right onto the middle of the crossroads. He whispered the summoning chant once more, then said simply, "Mateo."

The sky above them darkened. A crack of lightning slammed into the ground, and with a scream, Mateo appeared.

Mateo's shoulders hunched. His breath wheezed out. Coming to a crossroads was never easy for a caller. A caller had to slip past hell every time the crossroads beckoned. "Fuckin' asshole . . ." Mateo muttered, raising his head to glare at Sam.

"No! Not him!" Tomas snarled as he recognized Mateo. "He's working with Rogziel! I *told* you—aw, man, now we're dead!"

Sam didn't look at Tomas. "Guess Rogziel figured out how to summon you, huh?" His mixed blood was Mateo's closest secret. His mother, Aviana, had been a crossroads spirit. Summon her and she'd grant your wish. Once she granted your wish, she'd make you wish again—only this time, you'd be wishing for death.

Crossroad spirits had no remorse. No guilt. With every life they took, their strength increased.

Once upon a long time ago, a male witch had come to Aviana. He'd wanted a child. He'd gotten one.

One wish granted . . .

Mateo lifted his head. His cheeks were hollowed. His eyes flat and cold. "Rogziel didn't summon me, not at first. He called *her.*"

Sam had no doubt as to the *her* in question. There was no more powerful crossroad spirit than Mateo's mother.

"Guess I know what he wished for," Sam said.

"I don't!" Seline said, and she rushed forward. "What did he want?"

"A way to trap Fallen."

Tomas whistled. "*You're* a crossroads spirit? Oh, that is *bad.*"

"He got his wish," Sam said, studying Mateo in the sunlight. Mateo had always hated what he was. *Abomination.* Yes, that's what Rogziel would call him—and it was the way Sam knew Mateo saw himself.

Sam's teeth snapped together. Mateo wasn't evil. Not totally, anyway.

"Rogziel did," Mateo agreed. "He got what he wanted. Aviana brought me to him. Made me show him the spells." Rage bubbled in his voice. "When Rogziel got his wish, he killed her. Punishment he said, long overdue." A rough laugh. "So fucking true. The bitch deserved to burn."

"So does he." Sam held Mateo's glittering stare. "And I need you to help make sure that happens."

But Mateo laughed again. "I saw what's coming, remember? Rogziel wasn't the one choking on his own blood."

Seline gasped at that. Then she shoved right into the middle of the crossroads. Wrong move. Didn't she realize? The middle of the crossroads was always a bad spot to be standing in. "Sam's *not* dying! Do you understand? He's not——"

A growl shook the air. Sam grabbed Seline and yanked her behind him—and away from that crossroads hot spot. "I told you to stay back."

The ground buckled beneath them. The crossroads were gateways. Not a link to heaven, but a doorway to hell.

And Seline's punisher blood was like a magic key to open that door.

Cracks split the dirt.

"Seal it!" Sam ordered Mateo as he kept a tight hold on Seline.

With a wave of his hand, Mateo stilled the earth. Then, slowly, he walked toward Sam and Seline. "She can't control it." A fleeting expression of regret swept over his face. "When the time comes, she won't have the power to help you."

"I won't need help."

Mateo shook his head. "You're not immortal, no matter what you might think." Mateo's gaze darted to Tomas. "So many Fallen . . . do you honestly think you're at the top of the food chain?"

Sam didn't respond. Neither did Tomas.

But they didn't have to speak, because Mateo said, "No, to *them*," he jerked his hand back at the cracked ground, "you're just tasty prey. The hounds rip you open and drag your soul right off this earth."

And into hell.

"Then I'll make sure when they drag me . . ." Sam didn't feel even a flicker of fear. Not for himself. "That I've got one unbreakable hold on Rogziel." The bastard would go with him to hell. He pointed at Mateo. "I want my wish."

Mateo blinked. "Wh-what?"

"I summoned you, now I want a wish granted." He knew how this deal worked. Knew that even if Mateo wanted to refuse, the guy wouldn't be able to, not at a crossroads. "I want to bind an angel. I need a spell to keep him still."

"You can't—" Mateo began with a shake of his head.

"This is a bad plan," Seline said at the same instant. "*Very* bad."

Sam turned his head to meet her gaze. "Trust me."

"I do." Instant. Not what he'd expected. His gaze narrowed on her, and he realized she was staring at him with eyes that saw too much. Too deep. "I trust you, but I'm not about to let you die." She glanced back at Mateo. "If I could control the hounds, really control them, we could take Rogziel out, right?"

"You'd have to grow wings and fly first, *querida*," Mateo told her, voice rough. "The only ones with true control . . . those are the punishment angels."

"But my mother was—"

He held up his hand, stopping her. "You're a half-breed, just like me. Sometimes we get the power, hot enough to burn through the skin, but sometimes, we barely get enough to stir the wind." His stare bored into her. "When the chips are down, a hellhound won't hesitate. And if you're not in total control, the beast can even turn on you. Then you'd be the one it takes to hell."

An image of those razor-sharp teeth flashed before Sam's eyes.

"This is all fascinating, but Sierra could be freaking *dying*," Tomas spat. "Are we going to stay here, pissing the day away, or are we going to help her?"

Sam glanced at him then back at Seline. "We have to help her," she said, and the plea in her voice went right past his guard. "She's a pawn, and Rogziel stopped caring about what happens to pawns long ago."

Staring at her, Sam knew he could refuse her nothing. So he inclined his head, then focused back on Mateo. "I want the binding spell you gave to Rogziel."

"*Hombre,* I told you—"

"My wish," Sam said with a shrug. "And that's the deal, right? Whatever I want . . ."

Mateo's gaze drifted between Seline and Sam. "You'd burn for her?"

Sam knew his grin held a cruel edge. "I'd burn anyone who tried to hurt her." A much more effective approach. "Rogziel *won't* touch her." He'd make sure of it.

A muscle flexed in Mateo's jaw as he held his hand out. Sam took the offered hand, and a clap of thunder echoed overhead.

"I'll give you the spell," Mateo promised. "Damn you, I'll get it—but I need some time to get all the elements and ingredients together. It's not simple, and just so you know, it's one fucking dark spell."

To bind an angel, he would expect nothing less. "Get it fast, because we're going in."

Mateo's eyes widened. "No, just wait—"

But it was Tomas who answered. "We wait, and Sierra dies." His hands were fisted at his sides.

"I've got enough innocent blood on me." Sam let his smile stretch in anticipation. "From now on, I'm ready to balance those scales. Let's see how fast the blood of the wicked flows."

He dropped Mateo's hand. "'Cause I'm betting Rogziel is a bleeder."

CHAPTER SIXTEEN

Tomas took them to Rogziel's hideaway. There were guards walking the perimeter of the area. Three men, armed with guns. Seline had never seen them before, but Sam took one look and muttered, "Humans," and she figured if anyone could make that instant call, it would be him.

Sam's gaze swept the scene, and he inhaled deeply, then said, "Dammit."

Seline tilted her head and caught the light scent of flowers. The smell didn't come from inside the compound. No, instead, that scent seemed to be coming from . . . right behind them.

No!

Seline spun around. But Rogziel wasn't waiting with his cold eyes. Delia stood behind her. Actually, the angel floated behind her. "Time to make your move," Delia said, her gaze on Seline. "Rogziel isn't there. You can get the woman out."

Seline licked her lips and hoped this wasn't a lie. But, wait, angels couldn't lie . . . just twist the truth to suit their purposes.

"Helping me?" Sam drawled. "Delia, I thought you'd rather see me burn than ever lift a wing to help me."

"I'm not helping you." Delia shook her head. "This isn't for *you*. I just don't believe innocents should be punished." Her gaze finally slid from Seline to take in the two Fallen. "Better hurry. Someone will be coming back very, very angry."

"Coming back?" Seline repeated, voice going hoarse.

"Um, it seems . . ." and Delia's gaze cut once more to Tomas. "Rogziel finally realized the obvious. Sometimes, you just can't go home again."

Her wings spread behind her. She raced up into the air and disappeared into the clouds.

Sam laughed and glanced toward the house.

Tomas grabbed his arm. "You can't trust her. She could be setting us up *for* punishment."

The guards hadn't noticed the angel. She'd moved too fast. And they probably hadn't realized they should be watching the sky. Their mistake.

"I don't trust her," Sam said, "but I'm fucking ready to attack." Then he vanished, too. No, he didn't vanish, Seline knew that he just moved so fast he blurred—angel speed. The first guard went down, slumping back, and Seline knew Sam had subdued him.

The second guard didn't even have a chance to gasp before he hit the dirt. The third—Sam snatched his gun right out of his hand and then knocked the guy out with one punch.

Sam grabbed the front door and ripped it right off the hinges.

Seline had to admit, that was rather hot.

Then Tomas pushed her forward, and they raced inside the house. She realized immediately that those guards outside had just been the beginning. More men and women swarmed, but Sam sent them scurrying back when he let out a blast of fire.

"You don't want to fuck with me," he told them.

Two men ran away. Seline guessed they weren't in the fucking mood. Four more guards opened fire. Bullets slammed into Sam's chest. Seline screamed.

"Warned you," Sam said, and more fire burst free from his hands, flaring higher and greedily chasing Rogziel's team.

Tomas swore. "You're killin' her!" He ran away from them and hurried down the snaking hallway. *"Sierra!"*

Seline jumped forward and delivered a hard right hook to the nearest guard. She snatched away his weapon and swiveled in time to slam it against the head of the idiot who'd been grabbing for her.

But then, Sam laughed. That laughter was rather eerie. Too cold and dark. The hairs on her arms stood up. She risked a glance at him. His gaze was pitch-black. "Playtime's over," Sam muttered. He waved his hand. All the guards lifted into the air. The guards rose higher, higher. They were screaming, begging—

Sam dropped them.

They stopped screaming.

Seline's breath heaved in her chest. Her fingers touched the throat of the man closest to her. Even as she stared at Sam with wide eyes, her trembling fingers searched for a pulse. *Searched* . . .

"He's still alive, sweetheart." Sam seemed to mock her. "For now."

A light pulse beat beneath her fingertips.

Screams came from deep within the house. Sam caught her hand and pulled her to his side. "Stay with me."

His eyes were still black. The air crackled with his power. The dark edge she'd always sensed in him had never been closer to the surface. Dangerous. Evil?

Not Sam. She believed in him. "Try to keep me away," she muttered. "Try."

His lips crushed down on hers. Wild. Hungry.

Then the rooms swept by in a blur as he took her deeper into the maze of corridors. They followed the screams. Found the bodies. More guards. Some bleeding, some limp.

There was Tomas, just up ahead. He was driving his fist through a metal door and—

And Seline smelled brimstone.

"No, dammit!" Sam's roar. She knew he'd caught the acidic scent, too. *"Tomas, stop!"*

Too late.

The door caved in, and the growls spilled into the hallway, growls that were immediately followed by the hulking body of the hellhound as the beast leapt onto Tomas.

Azrael heard the screams from inside the old house. He saw the bodies of the guards outside, littering the ground. Smoke drifted into the air, a lazy beacon that had drawn him in.

The smoke . . . and the blood. Lately, the blood always seemed to draw him.

He'd known Rogziel for many centuries. Known him, watched him, wondered when the bastard would fall.

So he'd known all about this little hideaway.

His brother was inside. Already battling Rogziel? Why? To save the succubus?

Az's head throbbed as he stared at the flames. He didn't understand what was happening anymore. Sammael had never cared about saving anyone. Had he?

I ask for nothing. From now on, I take. Sam's words, when Az had asked him to seek forgiveness. But Sam had refused. He'd fallen instead of repenting.

"An angel dies today."

Az didn't turn at Mateo's words. Yes, he knew Mateo. He'd lived for too long and seen too much not to know about the crossroad spirit.

When folks wanted to cheat death, they went to the crossroads.

Foolish. No one had ever been able to cheat him. He'd been delayed before, but not stopped.

"Did you see that in your mirror?" Az demanded.

"Aren't you going to help him?" Mateo asked instead. "After all, he is your brother."

The smoke curled thicker in the air. Now, he could hear the rough sound of . . . growls coming from the house. The growls were too deep for wolves or coyotes, and they were growls that he would have preferred to never hear again. "Someone has let the hounds loose."

"Sam will trade his life for hers," Mateo said.

Now *that* made Az look at him, but Mateo's stare was on the fire. "Sammael won't trade his life for anyone's." That was a sacrifice his brother would never make.

"He'd die for her."

Impossible. Sammael couldn't—

"Even the mighty fall, sooner or later."

Az remembered screams. Women. Children. He remembered his brother, cutting a path through the dead with eyes gone pitch-black as he killed and killed and killed.

Punishing?

No, Sammael had lost his control. The beast inside his brother was too strong. "He won't sacrifice for anyone."

"You'll see. He'll burn." Mateo advanced slowly toward the rising smoke. "An angel dies . . ."

Az stared after him, watching, torn.

His heart raced too fast. His palms were sweating. His muscles locked too tight.

Sammael.

Sacrifice?

He hadn't understood the emotions he'd seen in his brother's eyes that long-ago day. But those same emotions—they'd glittered in Sammael's stare when the succubus vanished earlier.

Sammael had always felt too much, and those emotions had been the problem.

Az's hands fisted. *Now it's my problem, too.*

Because he wasn't just going to stand back while Rogziel killed his brother.

Az stared at the blaze. Heard the hungry growls, and he whispered, "Come get some, dog . . ."

This hellhound was even bigger than the one before. Bigger, darker, with a mouth at least twice the size of the last beast that had come at them. Just staring at the hound made Seline's knees shake.

This hound had sunk its teeth into Tomas's shoulder. Blood spilled beneath him. Tomas tried to grab the hound's head, and almost lost his fingers.

But Sam was there. She watched as he shoved his foot into the hound's head, giving a kick that made the beast howl.

Tomas leapt to his feet. "Get the fuck back to hell!" He roared and lifted his hands. Fire blasted out at the hound.

"No!" Seline yelled, but the fire had already reached the hound. It absorbed the flames and its eyes flashed an even brighter red. Then the hound got bigger.

Dammit.

"Help me!" A woman's scream came from inside the

room. Oh, no, that woman—Sierra—had actually been trapped in there with the hound? And the monster hadn't eaten her?

Tomas's head jerked at Sierra's cry, and he rushed forward, right into the path of the hound.

But Sam knocked the beast out of the way. Seline expected the hound to lunge for Sam, but instead, the hound's head turned, slowly. It licked its lips and focused that fiery stare on Tomas once more.

"Rogziel gave it your scent," Sam snapped. "You're its prey." The hound slammed its body into Sam's side and knocked him back.

You're its prey.

Sam had told her that a hound didn't stop until it took its prey.

Sam's shove had sent Tomas stumbling to the ground. The hound closed in on him now.

This time, Seline ran in front of Tomas. Her heart raced so fast that her chest shook. But she'd stopped a hound before. She could do it again.

Right?

"Get back," she gritted to the beast. Flames were snaking down the hallway. Great. Fabulous. Just what the hound needed—more power. "Get away from him. Go back to hell!"

The hound looked up at her with its fangs bared.

She straightened her shoulders. *"Go back to hell!"* Her words were close to a roar.

"Seline!" Sam screamed.

The hound leapt at her. Powerful paws slammed into her chest, and she hit the floor. The hound's paws shoved against her and the beast hurtled forward over her—right at Tomas.

But Tomas wasn't alone. Mateo stood beside him. "Let's see just how well you can hunt," Mateo said to the beast as he tossed a bottle into the air, a small bottle that Sam snagged with his left hand. In the next instant, Mateo and Tomas vanished.

Get-the-fuck-away spell. Seline knew the witch had used it. Talk about some nice timing . . .

The hound howled and raced down the hallway, and Seline knew the monster was chasing after Tomas's scent. Her breath choked out in a relieved gasp. That had been too close.

Sam grabbed her hand and hauled Seline to her feet. "The hound will find them."

She knew he was right. The hound wouldn't stop. Not until it had them. "I-I couldn't stop it." She'd tried, but—

"Please, God! Someone, help me!"

"You can't control them all." Sam kept hold of her hand and pulled Seline inside the room. "You can only control the one bound to you."

Knowing that little piece of trivia would have been helpful earlier. *Before* she'd jumped in front of the hellhound.

"You have to summon it, Seline. You have to control *it*. You have to get *it* to kick ass for you."

A woman with dark red hair waited in the middle of the room. Seline tried to hurry toward her.

Sam hauled her back. "No."

"Please!" The woman's fists thudded into some kind of invisible wall. Tears streamed down her cheeks. "There was some kind of wolf in here with me. I thought it was going to eat me!"

Sam pointed to the ground. "A spell has her locked in." A thin line of white powder circled the woman. "I don't think this one is too strong, but we can't take any chances on it being a trap."

"The wolf could come back!" the redhead screamed. "You have to get me *out of here!*"

"The beast has gone after Tomas." Sam frowned at the line of powder. "It won't be back till he's dead."

The redhead blinked. If possible, her face paled even more. "Dead?"

But Sam didn't answer. He pushed Seline back a bit. "I can burn through it."

Like there weren't already enough flames around them.

"Burn?" the woman whispered. "Wait, don't—"

There was no waiting. The flames were already around her, burning in a bright circle, following that trail of white powder and enclosing the woman.

Sam stalked toward the flames. "This is gonna hurt." He reached through the fire. "To get out, you have to walk through the flames."

Seline's jaw dropped. "She's human, Sam! She can't!"

He glanced back at her with one brow raised. "That's why it's gonna hurt." His arm was on fire.

The woman was sobbing.

"Take my hand," Sam ordered. "Take it now or you're dead."

Seline could barely see through the flames. But she thought the woman reached for Sam. In the next instant, the woman was flying right through the flames. No, Sam was yanking her through. When the redhead hit the ground, Seline immediately started slapping out the flames that licked around the woman. She ignored the blisters that burst onto her own skin.

I can heal. She can't.

"Now get her out of here," Sam said as the flames burning his flesh died away.

Seline looked up at him. "And leave you here alone? No way."

"Delia was right. Rogziel's long gone." His eyes still

shined black. "But when he comes back, I'll be waiting for him."

Not such a fantastic idea. "You can't! You don't—"

He lifted the bottle Mateo had tossed to him. Then, slowly, he pulled the claw from his right pocket. "I'm going to cut his fucking head off." His eyes darted to the woman. She stared at him as if he were a monster. Couldn't the woman recognize a hero when she saw one?

Seline yanked the redhead up to her feet. Time to teach this chick some hard and fast facts. "An angel risked his life for you."

Sierra swiped away the tears on her cheeks. "An . . . angel?"

"A hellhound is chasing Tomas because he came back for you. That wasn't a wolf, okay? It was a *hellhound*." She shoved Sierra toward the broken door. "Now be smart, and run. Run really, really fast."

Sierra looked back at her with dazed eyes. "Th-thank you." Then she ran, really, really fast.

Seline turned to Sam.

"You need to run, too," he told her.

Probably. "Maybe I'm just not into playing it smart." She closed the distance between them. "I'm *not* leaving you."

He shook his head. "You want freedom. This is your chance. Take it."

Didn't he see? Didn't he get it yet? "I think I want you more." The stark truth, and one that scared her to death.

Sam's eyes widened, and a burst of blue appeared around the darkness of his eyes. "Seline?"

Her lips started to lift in a trembling smile.

"You want him?" Azrael demanded from right behind her.

Aw, hell. Angels and their too-fast—

"Then just see exactly what you're getting . . ." Before she could even look over her shoulder, Azrael touched her.

And Sam roared.

Hello, Death.

She stared down at the men. She could hear the laughter, but couldn't understand their words. Their clothes were . . . different. Old. Foreign.

Another time, another place.

But Death was there.

Seline saw Sammael leap from the sky. His wings, strong, black, so powerful, thrust behind him. The men were staring with wide eyes, looking all around.

But they couldn't see him. Not yet.

Then he touched the first man.

The man with the red hair screamed, and the sound chilled Seline's blood. She'd never heard a cry filled with such terror. The redhead fell to the ground, his body frozen, his face twisted in agony. He was the first, but not the last. Far, far from the last.

Soon the men could see Sam. Seline didn't understand how or why, but they were staring at him. Pointing. Screaming.

He . . . laughed?

More men fell. He cut right through them. Killed, touched, until none were left living.

When the dead littered the ground at his feet, Sammael tilted back his head, stared up at the heavens, and smiled.

More.

"*Seline!*" Sam's roar jerked her back to the present just as he pulled her away from Azrael. She realized that only a moment had passed, barely a second.

It had felt like an eternity.

Sammael put his body between her and Az. "What the fuck did you do?"

"Relax," Az said, voice tight. "She's completely unharmed. You know the touch doesn't work on those with angel blood. Most of the demons who run on this earth have blood so diluted, it doesn't matter, but she's . . . fresh."

Her hands were shaking. Seline stared at Sam's back and saw the shadow of his wings.

And when he fired a fast glance over his shoulder, she saw his rage. Seline rose to her toes, craning to see over his strong back.

"I just wanted her to see exactly who you are," Az said as he crossed his arms over his chest. "She thinks that she wants you? Well, she needs to know just what it is that she wants."

Azrael's voice grated in her ears.

Sam must have thought the guy's voice grated, too, because he slammed his fist into Azrael's face to shut him up. "Don't fucking touch her!"

"Why?" Az hadn't moved. Blood streamed from his nose. "Because you didn't want her to know just what you were? Didn't want her to see how much you enjoy a kill?"

In a flash, Az was beside her. "Those men weren't marked for death. He decided to kill them, and he did."

Sam growled. No other word for it. He *growled.* "They had murdered a village. Slaughtered the children. Raped the women, then killed them when they were done. And you wanted—what? For me to turn the other cheek? Hell, no. Death for death. Eye for—" He broke off, seeming to finally realize just what Az had said before. "See?" he repeated quietly, and his gaze found Seline's. "He . . . showed you?"

Not just rage in his voice now. Fear.

She lifted her hand toward him. The slight edge of cruelty was still on his face. It would probably always be there, in the curl of his lip and the hardness of his eyes. But he was more than cruelty and rage. So much more. Why hadn't she seen that in the beginning?

"Can you really trust him?" Azrael murmured, like the devil whispering in her ear. "Don't you want to leave him? Now's your chance, succubus, run. I'll hold him back. Get your freedom."

Sam flinched.

Very, very slowly, Seline turned her head to meet Az's stare. "I trust him with my life. And you can just go and fuck off."

The ceiling trembled above them. Cracks raced across the sagging tiles.

"You should have run when you had the chance," Az told her with what looked to be a sad shake of his head. "Now we'll all—"

The ceiling caved in—no, fell in because Rogziel had just blasted his way through as he hurtled toward them.

"Hell's waiting," Rogziel called out, raising his bloody hands, and lightning flew across the room. One bolt slammed into Azrael's chest. Another hit Sam's back. The scent of burned flesh filled Seline's nostrils.

Burned flesh . . . and brimstone.

The hound's teeth were at his throat. Tomas shoved up, but he choked on his own blood. The witch was thrusting a knife into the beast's side, but the hound wasn't letting up.

They'd run. Used as many spells as they could, but every time they appeared, the hellhound was right on their asses.

Can't outrun a hound. Not once the beast gets your

scent. The hound would only stop by a master's command—or when it brought down its prey.

Tomas was down. No matter how hard he fought, he couldn't get up.

The thudding of Tomas's heartbeat began to slow. The sunlight dimmed. This was it.

He'd Fallen and now he'd die.

He could still hear Sierra's screams. She'd never know—

The hound's breath blew over his face, but then, the hound stiffened. The beast lifted its big, ugly head and howled.

The mournful wail shook Tomas's bones.

The hound licked his throat, drinking away the blood that poured from Tomas's gaping wounds. Tomas's hands clawed at the hound's eyes.

The hellhound leapt back. Howled again, then turned and raced toward the sun.

Tomas couldn't feel his legs anymore. Or his hands. And that thudding in his ears, so faint . . .

"Oh, fuck." Mateo stood over him. "Hold on, angel. You hear me? Your woman is out there. You have to help her. You can't go any damn place yet."

Sierra.

His lashes were trying to close.

Mateo chanted. Poured something in his wounds that burned and made him howl like the beast had.

Sierra. "Why . . ." The word came from his torn throat as a whisper. "Leave . . . ?" He couldn't manage anymore. He wasn't even sure that Mateo would understand his garbled speech.

"You're still living . . ." he thought the witch muttered *barely,* "so only its master's command would pull it back." A pause and Tomas understood, even before Mateo said, "The hellhound has new prey."

* * *

Sam rose to his feet, never taking his gaze off Rogziel. "I figured you'd be showing up soon."

Rogziel's face flushed dark red and his eyes shone black. "And I *knew* Tomas would bring you to me."

"That why you had your pit bull waiting to rip him apart? Death was the guy's finder's fee?"

Sam slipped out the small vial Mateo had tossed to him and cradled it in the palm of his hand.

"Don't worry . . ." Rogziel's eyes closed for a moment as he inhaled a deep breath. "My *pit bull* is coming home. The hound will rip you apart, too."

"Maybe next time." Sam smiled. Azrael stood in the corner, watching, waiting. *Same routine. Never acting. Always just watching.* "This time, I think I'll rip you apart." He threw the vial at Rogziel's feet. The glass shattered, and a thin layer of white smoke rose in the air. High, higher, wrapping around Rogziel.

"No!" the punishment angel screamed as he tried to lunge forward, but there was no place for him to go. He was trapped, in the cage that he'd first created. Rogziel's fists slammed into a wall he couldn't see, but it was one that Sam knew he could damn well feel. Sam smiled and pulled out his weapon. "Gotcha." Time to carve up an—

"No." Rogziel's hands dropped. His lips twisted in a grin. "I've got you."

"Sam . . ." Seline's worried voice. "I hear—"

Growls. Snarls. The scratch of claws racing over the floor. The hellhound was coming back.

Sam spun around just as the hound lunged into the room. The beast jumped right at him, teeth bared for that deadly bite.

But Az drove his body into the hound's. *"Kill . . . him!"* Az shouted as he fought to hold the beast. Teeth snapped at him. Claws ripped into his body. Blood gushed. *"Kill . . . Rogziel!"*

The scent of flowers filled the room. Flowers . . . angels. More angels were coming. No, not coming, one was already there. Sam looked to the left and saw Jeremian, his pale face stoic. He knew Jeremian. He'd worked with the Death Angel for centuries.

Jeremian's gaze was on Seline.

"No!" Sam snarled. "You're not taking her!" He stared at that thin line of white powder on the floor. Once he crossed that line, he wouldn't be able to get out, not unless Mateo freed him. He'd be bound in there with Rogziel. Neither could get loose.

If he wanted to kill the punishment angel, there was only one way . . .

Sam leapt over the line. He lifted the claw and slashed the weapon down. Rogziel's blood splattered on him as Rogziel fought back. Twisting, turning, shoving out blasts of power that just exploded in the small space.

Growls and screams surrounded them. The hellhound was fighting to break free of Az's hold. The beast's teeth were snapping, claws carving up the floor as it tried to get to Sam. Seline had clamped her arms around the beast as she tried to help Az hold back the hound.

Sam sliced the dragon shifter's claw across Rogziel's throat. Blood rained down from the wound. "You're not getting out alive," he promised.

"Seline," Rogziel whispered, and the bastard was smiling.

"You'll never touch her!" He drove the huge claw into Rogziel's heart and felt the gush of blood cover his fingers. "And you're *not* heading back to heaven."

A long drop of blood slid down from the corner of

Rogziel's mouth. "Neither . . ." He choked out, "is she."

Sam blinked.

Rogziel's body sagged. "Didn't . . . know? Some angels . . . no wings . . ."

Gritting his teeth, Sam twisted the claw. Rogziel stopped talking. A desperate gurgle rose in his throat. Sam yanked back the claw.

Rogziel fell to the ground. His blood soaked his wings. His eyes were open, staring straight up, but fear had frozen his face.

The silence hit him then. Thick. Total. He spun around and felt like he'd just had his heart carved out.

The hound wasn't at Azrael's throat anymore. Az lay on the ground, not moving, his body torn and battered.

The beast crouched over Seline, and its teeth were at her throat. And behind them, with his hand outstretched, Jeremian waited.

"No!" Sam lunged forward but slammed into the invisible wall that had been created by the holding spell. "Fuck, *no!*" He blasted the wall. He let fire rip from his hands. He shoved every inch of his power—

"Seline!"

Her head was turned toward him. Her eyes met his. The hound hadn't ripped into her throat, not yet. Maybe the beast wouldn't. Maybe it would somehow recognize her, just as the other had.

Fucking bastard Rogziel. Sam kicked the angel's limp body. He'd said *"Seline,"* at the end—because he was ordering his hound to kill her. Changing prey. Damn him. *"Get away from her!"* He yelled at the hellhound. "Come for me, hound! *Come for me!"*

But the beast wasn't moving. Jeremian wasn't touching Seline. He couldn't. His touch wouldn't stop this torment for her, Sam knew that. The Death Angel's touch wouldn't work on her because of the angel blood that flowed through her body. Jeremian's job was just to wait . . . to watch the hound kill her.

Just as Sam was watching. "No!" Sam screamed. *"Come for fucking me!"*

Jeremian looked at him. "I'm sorry," he said. Seline wouldn't be able to hear him, not yet. The closer she came to death, the more aware of the angel she'd become.

Seline—dying?

No, no, not fucking possible. He'd just found her. He'd promised her freedom.

A tear slid down Seline's cheek. Those teeth were sinking into her throat, and she was pushing against the beast and still looking at Sam . . .

"Love . . . you . . ." Her lips whispered the words as she stared at him.

Sam shook his head. No, no, she couldn't love him. He was death. He killed. He destroyed.

Pain twisted her face.

He could only watch. "Seline!" The skin of his hands split open as he battered the walls that held him.

Jeremian's fingers were inches away from her. "You don't want her to keep suffering . . ." the angel said. "It's time for her to be at peace."

At peace? Slaughtered by the hound? *"I'll kill you!"* Sam roared—the vow was for the angel who just watched and for the beast who was hurting Seline.

Jeremian shook his head. "Doubtful. Though you may try."

A red haze filled Sam's vision. He shoved his hands flat against the barrier, pushing with every ounce of his strength. Pushing, pushing, spending his energy, desperate—

Seline's eyes widened. The beast's teeth tore deeper

into her throat. Sam saw her lips try to move. Another tear leaked from her eye, and her mouth formed his name, *"Sam."*

Then a giant ball of fire exploded, and Seline, Se-line—

Everything burned.

CHAPTER SEVENTEEN

"Sam, you'd better fucking be alive in there!"

Sam heard the voice. Hollow. Distant. He lifted his eyelids, aware that every part of his body *hurt*.

"I'm gonna get you out of there, *hombre,* just hold on."

There was nothing to hold on to.

"Damn. What did you do to yourself?"

Sam managed to stare down at his chest. The claw was still embedded in his flesh. "Wanted . . . to get to her . . ." If he'd been close to dying, if he'd shed enough blood, then he'd thought that maybe the hound would come for him.

Come for me instead. He'd screamed those words as the fire erupted, and he drove the claw into his own chest. But those weren't the rules. Sam had tried to break them, but—*not the rules.*

The hellhound had taken its real prey.

Mateo chanted and threw ash in the air and Sam fell out of his prison.

He didn't look back at Rogziel's body. No fucking point. He rushed across the room, sliding in the blood that continued to pour from his body and soak the floor.

It should have been me.

"Seline!" The flames burned low now, flickering red and gold near the edges of the room.

Az lay in the corner, his skin scorched, but he was still breathing.

Seline was just . . . gone.

Nothing left. No blood—just *nothing*.

"Where's the succubus?" Mateo asked. Then his eyes narrowed. "That Fallen looks like shit."

Where are you, Seline?

If she'd died, where had she gone? Not to the fire, not her. She couldn't be in the fire. He *wouldn't* let her be. He shot to his feet and grabbed Mateo. "Our deal." Talking was hard. Too much rage and fear and pain poured through his veins, hotter than the fire.

Seline.

Mateo stared at him with wide eyes. "What are you—"

"I got my wish. We had a deal. Now send me to hell."

Mateo blinked at him. "No, you don't want to—"

"I'm not leaving Seline there." Rogziel. Fucking bastard, having his vengeance. "He sicced his hound on her. She was the prey. Now she's *gone*. And I'm not leaving her there to burn."

Mateo tried to break free of his grip. Sam didn't let him. His full power was out now, blazing. The only thing he'd ever cared about was gone.

No, I won't let her go.

"You can't bring the dead back," Mateo said, voice rumbling. "I'm sorry, but you can't—"

"Watch me." Hell couldn't have her.

"You don't know what you're messing with!"

Love . . . you . . .

He was one of the oldest angels. The strongest. He'd walked heaven and hell long before men knew to fear the monsters in the dark. "She's not dying."

She's already dead, a sly voice whispered in his mind.

"You'd burn for her?" Mateo asked, shaking his head. "Because that's what will happen. You'll get in, you'll burn, and you'll stay there forever. You don't have *wings* anymore. No one will pull your ass out."

He was the only one who could get Seline out. He could trade for her, *sacrifice*. He'd gotten out once, he could do it again.

"Send me to hell." They had a fucking deal.

"It's not that easy," Mateo snapped, trying to jump away from the flames that ate at his feet. "I have to prepare, find the right spell—"

"*Find it.*" He was shattering apart on the inside. Only fury kept him in one piece.

"Even if you get there, how do you think you'll get her out? *She* can't get out! Other than power-freaking-houses like you, only punishment angels can walk out of that prison."

Angel . . . no wings.

He shoved Mateo away and raced out of the room. He searched every inch of that place for Seline, but she wasn't there. He couldn't smell her, couldn't feel her—*nothing*.

It wasn't just like she'd died. It was more. Like she'd just . . . ceased to be entirely.

Angel . . . no wings.

"*Delia!*" The hallway shook with his bellow. "*Delia, get down here, now!*" He was desperate, so desperate he'd turn to an angel for help.

He burst outside of the old house. The dark night stared back at him. No stars glittered. Just a pitch-black sky.

"Delia!"

The angel didn't answer him. He raged, but she didn't appear.

Mateo came out with Az's unconscious body slung over his shoulder. "We need to get out of here."

No angel. No heaven for him. Hell . . . hell was *now*. Seline, gone, burning.

He stared at Az. His brother had actually tried to help him. That should matter for something.

But he couldn't feel anything right then. Just an icy numbness that suffocated him.

"I . . . saw her die, in my vision." Mateo's voice was halting. "I told you. She was covered in blood."

She had been.

"You knew the way this would end." But there was sympathy in Mateo's voice. Sadness.

Sam flinched. "I thought I could protect her." His arrogance. His shame. He'd actually thought he could change the future.

"No . . . what will be, that's what always comes." Mateo dropped Az onto the ground. "She was marked for Death. I knew it from the first moment I took her blood. She didn't belong in this world."

Without her, he didn't, either.

Sam grabbed Az. Hefted him over his shoulder. His brother, his burden. Then he began to walk into the night. One foot in front of the other.

He kept walking, walking, and he knew that he was already dead.

Seline opened her eyes to a world of white. Since the last thing she remembered was a fire so hot it scorched her breath, she hadn't quite expected . . . this.

"I was wondering when you'd wake up." The woman's voice was familiar.

Seline glanced to the left. Delia smiled at her. "Hello there."

Seline jumped up. She'd been placed in some kind of bed. Some kind of really fancy white bed. The *whole* place was fancy. With big, white columns, and wow, was that a golden floor? She paced quickly away from the bed, aware that her heart was racing far too fast. "Where am I?" The first question on her lips, but . . . *this place* . . . a twist in her gut told her just where she was.

Hair fluttered over Seline's shoulder. She shoved it back. But . . . it wasn't hair. Something softer. Smoother.

Delia inclined her head. "Welcome home."

Seline threw her hand back over her shoulder. She touched—wings. Actual, real, soft-as-down wings. "No." *This can't be happening.*

"I said you were special." Now Delia walked around her and studied Seline with an appraising eye. "It doesn't usually happen this way. Angels are born here, not on earth, and your, ah, your blood line wasn't exactly pure."

Had the woman just called her a mutt? Seline glared at her. "Where's Sam?"

"Sammael is where he should be."

Yeah, that was a big, giant answer of *nothing*.

"Do not worry." Delia's voice was so carefully modulated. No emotion slipped in at all. "It will take some time to adjust, but soon you won't miss your old life at all." A faint shrug of her shoulders sent her wings sliding into the air. "It's possible you won't even remember it."

There were sure parts she'd like to forget. Getting her throat ripped out by the hound. Rogziel. The bitter years she'd spent with him. But there were other parts . . .

Riding on a motorcycle with Sam, the wind blowing back her hair as she held him tight.

Listening to the low rumble of his voice . . . feeling his heartbeat beneath her ear as they lay in bed together.

No, no, there were parts she did *not* want to forget. *Sam.* "I didn't ask for this." The words shook.

Delia blinked. "No, this is your reward."

Her gaze flew around the room. There had to be a way out.

"Your mother loved a demon. She turned her back on her duty for him. That was a crime." Delia's footsteps tapped lightly over the floor. "But not one she had to die for. Fall, yes, but not die."

Seline stared at her. "My father . . . he didn't kill her, did he?" A lifetime of hate had hardened her heart. Yet Sam had made her doubt. "It was Rogziel." Her voice was more certain than she felt.

"From what I can tell, killing your parents was the first time Rogziel crossed the line and acted on his own."

Fury had her gut tightening. "And so what? You—" She waved her hands to indicate the fancy room, and all the *angels* that were probably behind the walls. "You gave him a free pass because it was just an incubus and a Fallen who suffered?"

Finally, some emotion showed on Delia's face. "No."

"Bull—"

The massive doors flew open. A man strode inside. No, not a man. An angel. With midnight wings, blond hair, and a lover's face.

"Leave us, Delia."

"Uriel, she's not—"

"*Leave.*"

And the chick left. Very, very quickly. Seline straightened her spine. She was aware that this Uriel had to be someone pretty damn important on the old angel hierarchy scale.

He didn't speak at first. He circled her, and his gaze swept from her head to her feet. After a few moments, he stopped in front of her and said, "You feel too much."

A choked laugh slipped from her. "What can I say? I'm a succubus . . . feeling is kinda my thing."

"No." Flat. "You *were* a succubus. You shed that coil when you left your mortality behind."

Oh, she did not like the sound of that. Seline leapt forward. No, maybe she actually flew. Weird. She grabbed his arms and glared at him. "I don't want this."

"You do not want heaven? Paradise?"

Yeah, okay, maybe saying no to that did sound kinda—

"And you do not want the chance to punish the wicked? To follow in your mother's footsteps? To show the sinners the error of their ways?"

No way. Who was she to judge sin? "I've had enough punishment and vengeance. I just want—" *Sam.*

She didn't say it, but Uriel's eyes narrowed, and she wondered if the guy had read her mind. Especially when he said, "You know what he's done."

She nodded.

"He can't be redeemed. His future has been foretold. One day, he will bring hell to earth."

"Y-you don't know that."

"Yes." Absolute certainty. "I do."

Her knees did a little jiggle, but her resolve didn't falter. "I know what he *can* be. Sammael isn't evil."

"We shall see."

She didn't like this angel too much. "Rogziel was the twisted freak. Why did he get to stay in heaven while Sam fell?"

"Because Sam was given a chance for redemption. He lost his wings, but he kept his life." His gaze actually seemed to see right through her. "No such concession was to be made to Rogziel. He would die, but not at the hand of another angel."

"So what? Sammael was your executioner?" *Let a Fallen kill him instead of an angel. Nice way around that whole not "another angel" bit.* "You used him to kill for you."

"It's what Death has always done well."

"He's more than Death!"

Uriel exhaled on what could have been a sigh. "I do not expect your transition to be easy." A faint smile curved his lips, though no emotion flickered in his eyes. "Though you are a first, angels are usually—"

"Born here, got it." She waved her hand. "*How* did I get here?"

"Delia suspected the truth about you from the first. She could feel the power in you, and then when you linked with your hound, we could all see the possibilities."

Oh, "we" could? The wings were a light weight on her back, one that felt strange. *Wings.*

"We realized that you would either die in that final battle with Rogziel or you'd evolve and become something more when your demon side ceased to be."

Wait. Back up. "What do you mean, ceased to be?" She did not like the sound of that.

Uriel just stared down at her with that pretty face of his. "The Death Angel's touch doesn't work on angels. Not winged angels and not those who possess the pure blood of angels within their—"

"I *have* angel blood." And she had a mental flash of

that fire-filled room. A man had bent near her. Pale skin. Dark eyes. The scent of flowers had filled the air all around him. Her heart thumped hard in her chest. "A Death Angel came for me?"

"He came for your demon side." Uriel's lips tightened, then he said, "The succubus you were is dead. The angel that was trapped inside you . . . well, she is free now. Jeremian's job was to watch you in your final moments, and then to ferry you back to the place you truly belong."

Her wings trembled. "I don't feel like an angel." Too much rage. Too much need. Emotions stirred and fought within her.

"Angels do not feel."

Her wings curved around her, and she had the weird impression they were trying to give her a hug. "This isn't me."

"This is what you will be." Then he turned and walked away, his steps slow and certain. "All you need is time to forget."

The doors opened instantly for him, and then they closed just as quickly in his wake.

"I don't want to forget," Seline whispered. She hurried toward the doors. They didn't open. Not even when she shoved them with all her strength. They. Wouldn't. Open.

Seline paced back to the bed. Trapped in paradise. How could that even happen? This place was supposed to be perfect. No fear. No worry. No pain.

But she wanted pain. She wanted every bit—good and bad—that came with her life.

The succubus inside you died. How long had she tried to smother that demon side?

But now, without that part of herself, Seline just felt . . . lost.

Because I can still feel. She wasn't like the angels

here. She felt, and her feelings were close to ripping her apart.

Sam, I need you!

She needed him, and she'd have him.

Breath catching, she climbed onto the bed. Seline closed her eyes and inhaled deeply. Maybe the angels were wrong. Maybe her demon side wasn't gone, not yet.

Please, not yet.

Sam . . . Sam, be there.

She let her mind drift and pushed hard for powers that didn't want to rise. She'd never been able to contact someone from this kind of distance before—she didn't even know how damn far away she was. But she'd never been this desperate before, either.

She dug into her soul, grabbed the power she could still feel, weak, but there.

Her heart ripped in two, but she pushed and pushed . . .

Sam, take a walk with me.

In dreams.

After three days, Sam slept. No, he collapsed. He'd searched nearly all of Mexico, but there'd been no sign of Seline.

Mateo hadn't carried through with his end of the deal. The witch had given him more of that containment powder, but so far that had been pretty fucking useless. There were no angels around to contain.

Don't want angels. Don't want heaven. Mateo knew exactly what he wanted.

Lying bastard. How hard was it to get a ticket to hell?

The numbness took him first, weighing down Sam's body. His chest burned even though the wound near his heart had healed.

Seline.

When Sam closed his eyes, the nightmares came. Because what more did he have but nightmares? He dreamed of fire and a fall that never ended. He dreamed of pain, agony, of wings that burned and of an unforgiving earth that broke all of his bones.

Then . . . her.

The beast was at Seline's throat. Her eyes were on Sam.

Love . . .

Why? He tried to shove the images away. He'd failed her. He'd watched while she died. Why the hell had she loved him?

The fire flared hotter. He couldn't see her anymore. Could only see the flames.

Just the fire.

Then . . .

Nothing.

Seline, come back to me.

"I can't." Her whisper.

The darkness lifted a bit, and he saw her on the bed. Shadows cloaked her.

"Seline?" Hope had him leaping toward her.

She lifted her hands to him. His mouth crashed down on hers. She tasted, oh, damn, she tasted like life. Heaven. Everything he'd ever wanted but never realized he needed. Her body trembled against his. His lips lifted, pushing against her helplessly, and he growled, "I thought you'd left me."

"I did." The pain in her voice broke the heart that was hers. Her fingers smoothed over his chest. "And I don't know how to get back." A tear slid down her cheek.

He caught the tear with his mouth. Tasted the salt. Tasted her. *Real.* "Sweetheart, you are back, and I'm not letting you go. Stay. Just . . . stay." He had to make her stay. "I'm more . . . than what you've seen. We can have a life together. We can have everything."

Because he'd give her anything.

"Stay." His hold tightened on her.

"I don't know how!" Her hand seemed cool on his chest. She eased away from him. Her head tilted back as she studied him. Her neck was smooth, unlined. No scars, no blood.

And he knew this wasn't real. Fuck, no. Just another nightmare. She'd leave him and reality would be his hell on earth. "I love you." Just a nightmare, but he'd tell her anyway. Why hadn't he told her before? Why hadn't he realized the truth? "I'd trade my life for yours in an instant."

Something whispered in the darkness, a soft rustle of sound. Wind seemed to brush over his face. He stared into the shadows around him, aware that his heart had started to thud too fast.

"I can't get back to you." Now her hands were on his face. Her fingers trailed down his cheek, over her jaw. As if memorizing him. "I don't want to forget."

"You won't." A vow. *"I won't."*

But she was fading. Her lips pressed against his once more. He tasted her breath. Life. Love.

Seline.

She vanished. The fire came back. The pain. The torture. But he wouldn't forget. His Seline had come to him.

And she'd had black angel wings.

She hadn't been dragged to hell. His angel had been sent to heaven.

He fought through the fire in his nightmares and opened his eyes. He glared at the cracking ceiling above him. "You aren't taking her!"

Sam knew he didn't have to fight his way through

hell to get Seline back. But he would have to knock down the gates of paradise.

If you wanted to see an angel, sometimes you had to raise a little hell. Sam stood in the middle of the crowded street, his gaze on the dark sky above him. Power crackled in the air around him.

"What do you think you're doing?"

Az's voice. Very slowly, Sam turned his head to the right. He'd dumped Az in a motel three days before. He hadn't wanted to deal with him. Killing him . . . well, shit, Az had tried to sacrifice himself so that Sam would be protected. Killing him after that just hadn't seemed fair. So he'd let the bastard walk away with his head still attached to his body.

Only it seemed Az was walking *back* to him now. The guy must have a death wish.

Sam sure did. Gotta be a family trait.

Sam smiled and knew the grin would flash with evil. "I'm about to call down some angels."

Az blinked. "Uh, you sure that's the best plan you've got?"

This was a much darker part of Mexico. The men and women filling the cantinas on this beaten street weren't human. Shifters. Demons. Some good, some in-between, some so vicious he could feel their taint in the air. "It's the only one I've got."

Az frowned back at him. "Look, I'm sorry about the girl, but she's dead. Sacrificing yourself won't bring her back."

A gust of Sam's power slammed into his brother and knocked him back a good ten feet. Bones popped when Az landed.

"She's not *dead*." Sam pointed to the sky and glared at the heavens. "She's just . . . there."

Az rose slowly. He snapped his shoulder back in place and adjusted his broken wrist. "You've finally gone crazy, haven't you?" Said with a bit of sadness. "I always thought the day would come."

"Maybe I have. Doesn't matter." He pulled back his hand and let a line of fire race down the street. Voices rose. Shrieks filled the air. "I'm about to make a fire so bright that heaven has to see it."

Screams filled the air. The *Other* scattered as they raced away from the flames.

But he just poured out more power. *More*. He wouldn't stop. The world didn't realize just how dangerous he could be. Time to show them.

Bring her back.

Or he'd destroy everything, and, perhaps everyone.

CHAPTER EIGHTEEN

Sam hit the dirt when he was tackled from behind. He spun around and tossed his asshole brother aside. This time, Az landed on his feet, and his bones stayed in place, mostly.

"You can't kill them!" Az shouted.

Sam's brows rose. "Since when do you care?"

"Since I fell!" Az ran a hand through his hair. "This isn't right! Dammit, you *can't!*"

The fire hadn't touched anyone. Not yet.

"He can," another voice said, this one strong and deep and coming from the shadows near him, "but he won't."

An *oh-shit* expression crossed Az's face, and Sam knew his brother recognized that voice, too.

It was a voice most heard in their nightmares because this angel, he wasn't there to comfort you. Not to give you a message. Not to guard you or protect you from the monsters in the world.

Uriel was the leader of the punishment angels. If the stories were true, he'd once been at the right hand of God, but a few centuries back, he'd been put in charge of the darker angels. He came after only the worst of the worst, and his punishments had been known to make the devil weep with envy.

His wings curled behind him as Uriel stepped from the darkness. He stared at Sam, and he shook his head. "Sammael, call back your fire."

The fire whipped through the streets, snaking long and hard, rising high, so high. It hadn't touched the flesh of anyone, but it could; all it would take was one thought and they'd ignite.

"Is this what she would want you to do?" Uriel asked.

In an instant, Sam had the bastard by his black T-shirt. And since when did Uriel wear a torn T-shirt and jeans? "You've seen her?"

Uriel nodded. "She's one of mine."

"No," Sam snarled, choking on rage. "She's *mine*."

Az closed in on them. "Are you serious? Seline's an . . . angel?"

Uriel didn't look particularly concerned about the fire or the tight grip that Sam had on him. But, what was new? Uriel was never concerned. That's why he was good at his job.

And those punishment angels who weren't so good—they wound up like Rogziel.

"Sometimes angels walk on earth. Mistakes are made. They have to be . . . called home." Uriel inclined his head toward Sam. "Thank you for taking care of Rogziel. He'd become a nuisance."

What the fuck? "Take care of your own garbage next time."

"That's not the way it works."

"How do you know?" Sam fired back. "Have you ever actually asked?"

Uriel's dark eyes narrowed. "Rogziel received his punishment."

"Yeah, no thanks to you!" Sam dropped his hold on the angel. "What? Did you want me to do your dirty work for you? And here I thought you enjoyed the punishment."

He'd hope the words would crack Uriel's icy façade. They didn't work. Because that wasn't a façade. It was just Uriel.

"You know the rules," Uriel said. "No angel can kill another. Not without earning damnation." He brushed off his T-shirt. "We didn't just want Rogziel to suffer, we wanted him destroyed."

And so he had been. "And the Fallen who got taken out along the way?"

"A Fallen was the only one who had a chance of fighting him."

Ah, right. Since they'd fallen and lost their wings, they weren't exactly angelic any longer so that whole rule about one angel not killing another wasn't technically in play. Angels hadn't just learned to twist the truth over the centuries. They'd learned to twist the entire world.

"Unfortunately," Uriel said with a sigh, "the first few Fallen he found weren't strong enough for the job."

"Very unfortunate," Az echoed, but there was emotion in his voice. Now that the guy was on earth, he was sure picking up the human ways fast.

I like him better this way. Az wasn't quite as much of an asshole.

"But the job is done now." Uriel leveled his stare back at Sam. "It's time for you to move on."

No. "I want to see Seline."

Uriel's brow furrowed. "And I do what you want because . . . ?"

"Because if you don't, I will light this whole damn town on fire." He smiled, showing lots of teeth. "I don't have anything to lose. I'll burn, I'll fight," and he pulled out the claw that was still stained with an angel's blood, "and I'll kill."

Uriel's gaze dropped to the weapon. "You're actually threatening *me?*" Now there was emotion in his voice and on his face. Shock.

"I killed one angel." Sam shrugged, then yanked out the bottle he'd gotten from Mateo. *Smart-ass witch.* The guy had no doubt seen this coming. No wonder he'd made sure Sam had a good stock on that holding powder. The bottle exploded, and the white smoke sprang up around Uriel, trapping him just as it had trapped Rogziel. "How much harder can it be to take out another?"

Uriel's jaw dropped. He slammed his hands against the invisible wall that bound him in place.

"I don't think he saw that coming," Az murmured.

"Angels . . ." Sam shook his head. "Sometimes, they're just too damn cocky. Just because they're high up on the food chain, it doesn't mean they can't still get eaten."

Uriel screamed, no, he roared, and his wings slammed into his crystal-clear prison.

"When you calm down . . ." The area was deserted now. Smart *Other* had fled. "We'll talk, and then you'll bring me Seline." Sam shrugged. "Or I'll cut off your wings."

Seline was walking through a cloud of—well, *a cloud*. Everything was beautiful. Gorgeous. But . . . there were only other angels around, and they weren't exactly chatty.

No humans. No shifters. No charmers. Delia had told her that when those beings passed, they went "far beyond the gates." Yeah, there'd been a bit of yearning in Delia's words. So when most folks died, they got some sparkly, happily-ever-after paradise. But angels had . . .

"You have to come with me!"

Seline spun around. Okay, wow, Delia's wings were all ruffled. "What's wrong?"

"Sammael."

Her heart slammed into her chest. "Has something happened to him?"

Delia glanced around, and the woman looked worried. *Not good.* Delia didn't worry. "If you don't stop him, something exceedingly bad will happen."

"Then why are we standing here?" Seline yelled as her own feathers ruffled. "Get me to—"

Delia grabbed her hand and yanked her right off the cloud. They fell fast and hard toward earth. The clouds whipped around them, and Seline could just make out a sea of blue and the thick darkness of land and—

"Use your wings!"

Oh, crap, right. Seline started flapping.

Delia didn't let go of her hand. The woman flew forward, not down, and Seline struggled to keep up with her.

The air was cold on her face. It felt like raindrops were stinging her skin. Faster, faster, they went. Their surroundings blurred. She lost track of time.

And then . . .

Darkness.

Her feet hit the ground.

"Seline?"

Broken, rough, Sam. Her eyes opened. He was there. Tall, strong, but with hollowed cheeks and wild, shadowed eyes. Pain etched deep lines on his face. She hurried toward him, and heard someone—Az?—mutter, "Wings . . ." from her side. She didn't look his way because she couldn't look away from Sam.

Her fingers trembled when she touched Sam's face.

"I dreamed about you," he whispered.

She tried to smile. Couldn't. "And I dreamed about you." Her heart beat so fast she hurt.

"I tried to save you." Gruff, torn from him.

She shoved back the memory of fear and pain and of his eyes—on hers. Afraid, angry. Desperate.

Seline stood on her toes and kissed him. This wasn't a dream, he was real now, and she needed to feel his mouth against hers.

His fingers brushed over her wings, and a shiver skated down her body.

"She's here, now let me *out,*" Uriel snarled.

Keeping Seline's fingers twined with his, Sam stepped back. He kicked away the white powder that circled Uriel.

"What is that?" Uriel demanded. "Nothing should hold us, *nothing.*"

"We can hold each other. Our own powers can lock us in. Bind us." Sam exhaled slowly. "The powder is made from angel wings. What the hell do you think happens to the wings when we fall? They burn, turn to ash and dust, but they keep a glow of our power."

Seline tightened her fingers around his.

Sam stared at her. "I wanted you to be free."

And she'd just . . . wanted him.

"Are you happy?" he asked as his gaze searched her face. "Tell me you are, and I'll just walk away."

Angels weren't supposed to lie. She was learning the rules, but not fitting in at all. "I miss you."

She saw him flinch. Then he inhaled. "Sweetheart, you smell like roses."

An angel's scent. Not her, not anymore.

"Roses and paradise." His lips flattened. "I miss the jasmine."

Such a simple, small thing. She'd used jasmine body lotion, before.

I never even realized he'd noticed.

Seline felt like she was breaking apart. She wanted to grab him and hold on as tight as she could. She just needed to know—

"I love you," he told her, the words rumbling like a growl. *That* was what she needed. He pulled her closer. "*I love you.* You got to me, Seline, and I can't—I can't let you go."

"You don't have a choice." Uriel's cool voice. The earth trembled beneath them as Uriel left his containment. "You went too far today, Sammael. *No one* dares to imprison me."

But Sam didn't look scared. He should have. He just laughed and didn't glance at the powerful punishment angel. "For Seline, I'd dare anything or anyone."

The ground ripped open. Smoke blazed forth, and the heavy scent of brimstone filled the air. Seline didn't need to hear the heavy growls to know what was coming.

"Time for *your* punishment, Sammael." Uriel strode toward the opening he'd made in the earth. "You made a deal with a crossroads spirit, a deal that I'll make sure you keep, even if he doesn't."

Seline saw the claws first, and she shuddered. Her neck seemed to throb and screams wanted to burst from her throat as she remembered death.

Sam pushed her behind him. "It's okay. I swear, I won't let him touch you. *I swear.*"

"*Sammael.*" Uriel's voice boomed. "The prey is Sammael!"

The hound leapt from the ground and hurtled right toward Sammael.

Seline screamed. Az jumped out of the shadows.

And Sam grabbed the beast and broke its neck in one quick twist.

The hound collapsed on the ground.

"Now, now . . ." Uriel shook his head. "You know it won't be that easy."

Thick black hair covered the hound's body, and a long white streak swiped across its right eye.

Seline stared at the beast and blinked, shocked. Wait, that was—

My hound.

Uriel had dared to raise her hound to come after Sam? The bastard. Her wings stiffened, then stretched out behind her.

Bones snapped, popped, and the hound slowly shook its head. Then that head tilted back, and Seline saw razor-sharp teeth glinting.

"Don't worry, Seline," Uriel told her quietly, "your hound will get your vengeance."

No, no, it wouldn't. "I don't want vengeance against Sam!" Sure, making Rogziel suffer through another very painful death was near the top of her to-do list, but Sam? No. He'd fought to save her. He shouldn't suffer.

She could still hear his tormented screams in her mind. He'd been so desperate to save her.

The hound launched. Its teeth sank into Sam's arm.

Sam didn't make a sound.

"You can't kill the hound," Uriel said, and for someone without emotions, the words sure sounded like a taunt.

"We can sure as hell slow the thing down." Now this was from Azrael. He had a knife in his hands. He jumped forward and drove that knife into the hound's side.

The beast's howl . . . *hurt* her.

Seline gasped. She saw the hound's gaze turn to her. It looked lost, confused.

"*Sammael,*" Uriel snapped.

Seline tried to push toward the hound.

Sam blocked her and turned back to face the beast. The hound slashed him. Deep slashes that cut into his chest. Slashes that came too close to his heart.

Seline shoved Sam out of her way—and, wow, Sam hurtled into the air. She guessed being a punishment angel came with a strength bonus.

The hound stared at her with its mouth open, those deadly teeth dripping blood, and it took all of Seline's willpower not to turn and run.

Claws at my throat. Teeth slicing. Digging into my flesh. Sam! Sam!

Sam was on his feet. He raced toward the hound. The hound dug its paws into the ground and prepared to leap at her Fallen.

"*Stop!*" Her bellow.

Everyone froze. Everyone, even Uriel.

The hound's head turned to her. Seline walked toward the beast, one slow step at a time. She held out her hand, and her fingers only trembled a little. "Easy." *Please don't eat me. Been there, done that, and don't want to do it again.*

The hound lowered its head and whined.

This hound was smaller than the one that had, ah, killed her. Deep scars marked its body. So many wounds. So many deaths.

Was the hound the evil one? Or was it the hound's master?

Like a pit bull. Trained to attack. But maybe, maybe, the beast could be more.

"Protect." The word came out stronger than she'd anticipated. Seline lifted her hand, and her fingers didn't shake any longer. "Protect Sammael," she ordered her hound. *Not prey.* "Protect him . . . always."

The hound's head swiveled between her and Sam. "Not prey. Not him," she said.

The hound eased forward and licked her fingers.

He's not prey, and you're more than a monster.

"Good," she whispered. Because there was good in the hound, she could feel it, struggling against the darkness that seemed to wrap so heavily around the beast.

Right then, the hound almost reminded her of . . . Sam.

Sam who stared at her with the eyes she loved. Black, not angel blue, because that darkness swirled too strong in him. Always would.

"You can't do this!" Uriel reached her side and barely glanced at the hound. "Sammael is to be punished for what he did to—"

Lightning flashed from the sky, and the bolt hit right at Uriel's feet. The scent of sulfur burned Seline's nose.

Real emotion appeared on Uriel's face then. Fear.

"I guess someone is pissing off the boss upstairs," Sam said in his mocking drawl. " 'Cause that bolt sure wasn't aimed at me."

Eyes wide, Uriel backed away. "One day, Sammael, you will be punished."

The right side of Sam's mouth hitched into a sad smile as he stared at Seline. "I already have been. I lost the only thing that made this life worth living."

But he hadn't lost her. She was standing right there.

"I can stay with you," she told him. She didn't care what Uriel might do. Sam was before her. He mattered. Her hands stroked the hound. Its fur was almost soft, once you got past the matting.

Sam's lips parted, as if he'd speak, but then he shook his head.

"Sam, *I can stay*." She knew it. Other angels had fallen. *He'd* fallen. She could do it, too. "We can be together." He'd said he loved her. They could have forever.

His jaw clenched, and after a moment, he gritted out, "You don't know what it's like. The pain . . . I won't ask you to suffer for me. I *can't*. Never for me, understand? *Never*."

"She's already died for you once," Uriel threw in, even as his wings flapped and he began to rise into the air. "What's a little trip to hell between lovers?"

"No!" Sam snarled. "She won't suffer anymore!"

Seline felt a pull then, like an energy was wrapping around her and lifting her into the sky. She fought, desperate to stay with Sam, but she couldn't break free of that strange pull.

"Don't fall for me!" he shouted up to her, his face stark. "Dammit, I'll find another way! I can get redemption! I can come to you! *Don't fall for me!*"

"He'll never get redemption . . ." Uriel's soft voice seemed to whisper right in her ear, even though he was over five feet away from her. "Some sins can't be forgiven."

Tears stung her eyes. She kept rising up, pulled by a force she couldn't stop. *Sam.*

His burning black gaze followed her. "I will find a way, Seline! Don't fall, promise me! *Don't!*"

Then she rose too high, and she couldn't see him— or hear him—any longer.

"He's going to hell."

Seline glanced up at Delia's voice. The angel walked toward her, her steps soft on the gleaming marble floor.

"Sam met with Uriel again," Delia told her. "Only this time, Sam didn't cage him."

Probably because Uriel hadn't gotten caging close. She figured the big boss had learned from his mistake.

A soft sigh eased from Delia's lips. "Sam wants to earn redemption." Delia's head tilted as she stared at Seline. "For . . . you. He wants to come back home, and it's all because of you, isn't it?"

Seline didn't speak. *Hell.* She didn't want Sam in hell.

"Uriel stripped the skin from his back." Delia whispered this. "It was the first step in Sammael's punishment."

Her breath rushed out as horror filled her. *"Why?"*

"Because that's where the wings once were, so the flesh is more sensitive to pleasure or to pain. Uriel wanted Sam to feel maximum pain."

Her stomach tightened. "No," she bit out. *Maximum pain.* "Why did Uriel want to hurt him that way?"

"They're old enemies." Delia shrugged. "And Uriel didn't exactly enjoy the fact that Sam was able to trap him. Now everyone knows that the great punisher came close to dying by a Fallen's hand."

"So he took his pound of flesh." No, Sammael had sacrificed that flesh, for her. Seline swallowed, trying to choke down the lump in her throat. "What's hell like?"

"You'll see, soon enough."

Was that a threat? She hadn't expected one from Delia. *Maybe I should have.*

Delia's shoulders bowed. "It's part of our duty. We can travel between earth, heaven, and hell. We go where the punishment takes us."

"So I'll be able to see Sam?" Yes, that was hope making her voice rise.

"See him," Delia agreed, but shook her head as she said, "not talk to him, not . . . touch him, not until his sentence is over."

"How long is his sentence?" She didn't like this plan. Not at all. Her hands fisted.

"For redemption, Sammael has to serve a thousand years in hell."

Seline leapt to her feet. "What?"

Delia stared back at her. "No angel has ever come back to heaven after choosing to fall. Sammael is to be used as an example——"

"Who decided that, Uriel? He's a——"

"You'll still be alive when Sammael's sentence is done. He can come back here to you."

After a thousand years in hell. She blinked to clear eyes gone blurry. "What will happen to him there?"

"Torture. Pain. Nightmares that won't stop."

He'd already had enough of that. "He doesn't deserve that punishment."

Delia's wings shifted a bit. "It's not really punishment. It's his choice. He's trading time in hell——and the agony that time will bring——for his wings."

Her hands clenched. *I'm sorry, Sam.* "I'm not letting him do it." She rushed for the doors that weren't barred any longer. They hadn't been barred since she'd visited the mortal realm and seen Sam. *Don't fall for me!* She could still hear his voice, but Seline was ignoring those words.

"You don't know what it's like, do you?" Delia's voice called after her. "The fall, I mean."

Seline glanced back. "No, I don't know, and I don't care——I'm going back to him. He's not going to——" *burn.* "He won't suffer for me." Not for a thousand freaking years.

"There's a reason he told you not to fall."

And how did Delia know about that? She'd thought the angel vanished after delivering her to Sam.

The angel's lips lifted, just for a moment. *Almost* a

smile. "Word spread. There were eyes watching that you didn't know about, and when Uriel got that strike from above . . . well, that was sure something folks wanted to know about up here."

"I need to be with Sam," Seline said quietly. "When I'm away from him, I just hurt."

"You'll hurt more if you fall." Delia didn't move toward her. "Your wings will burn away, and it will be a pain unlike anything you've felt before." Her lips tightened. "Or so I've been told."

"I'm not afraid of pain." A hellhound had ripped out her throat. So what was a bit of fire supposed to do? If she remembered correctly, a giant ball of flames had surrounded her right before she'd woken to heaven.

"It's not the pain you need to worry about."

Okay, now that sounded a bit scary. What was she supposed to fear if not the pain? "Look, I'm not cut out to be an angel. I can't just—"

"You feel too much. I can see it. We all can. But we truly believe that the longer you're here, the less you'll . . . suffer."

So that, what, in a thousand years, when Sam was flying with his wings again, she wouldn't even *care*?

"I'm going back home." To her real home. The only one she'd ever had. Sam. He was home to her. Love. Safety.

Hers.

Seline turned away, and her hands pushed against the doors.

But Delia was still talking. She warned, "You won't have a memory. Not of heaven. Not of Sam. Not of the life you knew before him. That all gets wiped away in the fall."

Az hadn't known who he was at first, either. "Az's memory came back. So did Sam's."

A pause, then Delia said, "Provided you can stay alive, and all those *Other* out there desperate for angel blood don't kill you and drain you, then your memory will come back. Eventually. But that eventually part is different for every angel. It could be months. Could be years. You'll walk the earth, alone, hurt, thinking that you have no one."

So she walked alone for a few years or Sam suffered for a millennia. Um . . . not such a hard choice.

"Why?" Delia's voice was ragged, and Seline knew the angel realized there would be no changing her mind.

Seline shoved with all of her strength, and the doors flew fully open. Light washed over her. "Because I love him."

A sharp breath. "That's just what Erina said."

Now she risked one final glance over her shoulder. "I guess I am like her." So much more than she'd realized. Then Seline tilted her head back and felt the light warm her flesh. "I'm ready to go home." *I'm ready to fall.*

Not for punishment. Not because she'd sinned. But because she loved.

All you have to do is ask for help.

Her eyes closed. "Please," Seline whispered, and knew that she was heard. "I want to fall."

The wind whipped in her ears. The floor beneath her feet disappeared. Her body plummeted. Fast, faster . . .

The pain would come, she knew it, yet right then, all she could think was—

Sam.

Blood dripped down his back. Sam didn't feel the pain any longer. The skin was gone. Stripped slowly away by an angel with no mercy.

It didn't matter. The flesh would grow back eventually.

"You can't do this," Az said, pacing in front of him. "This plan is just insane. You were always desperate to get off the clouds, and now you're bargaining to get back upstairs?"

Sam didn't speak.

"Insane," Az muttered again.

The light scent of roses teased Sam's nose. He spun around. "Seline!"

"No." Delia drifted down beside him. She clasped her hands in front of her body, and her gaze darted to the blood-splattered ground, then back to him. "You don't need to sacrifice. No trade should be made."

And with her words, the pain came back, only this time it was a different kind of pain. One that seemed to slice right through his heart. "Seline?"

A brief nod. "Sh-she fell."

His head sagged forward even as his hands clenched into fists.

"Well, damn." From Az.

"When?" Sam demanded. *Seline.*

"Moments ago. I tried to stop her, but she wanted you too much."

His chest ached.

"She knew the risks," Delia told him quietly. "But she still chose to fall."

A shadow drifted over the ground, and Sam felt the hard rush of wind around him.

"Are you ready, Sammael?" Uriel asked, voice low, grating. *Ready for his sacrifice?* But Seline had already sacrificed, and this bastard didn't know . . .

Sam turned toward him. "I'm afraid there's been a change in plans."

Uriel's eyes widened.

Sam braced his legs and got ready to attack. "I'm gonna have to tell you to fuck off now."

Uriel backed up a step, and Sam saw the flicker of fear in his eyes. Once an angel tasted an emotion— even fear—the feeling could sneak back inside anytime.

"Actually," Sam drawled slowly, "I think I might be gettin' my pound of flesh back, and *then* tellin' you to fuck off."

Before Uriel could escape, Az grabbed him.

Az. His brother kept surprising him.

"Uriel . . ." Sam stalked toward him. "Before you dish out more pain, I think you might need to experience a bit of it yourself."

Uriel snarled and fought against Az's hold. "Delia, Delia, help me!"

She shook her head. "Sorry, but I have my orders. And you've made someone upstairs very angry. Punishment is coming."

Delia flew into the sky.

Sam slammed his fist into Uriel's face. Bones smashed. "Punishment's here."

She hit the ground and pain was all that she knew. Her body ached, her throat burned from her screams, and bruises and blisters covered her naked form.

She pushed to her feet. Stared at her hands . . . broken hands she didn't recognize. A body she didn't recognize.

The worst pain came from her shoulders—no, her back. She tried to touch the skin, and she felt thick, hard ridges beneath her fingertips.

Tears leaked from her eyes.

She wanted to curl up. To sink back on the ground and sob.

But she stayed on her feet.

The wind brushed against her body. In the distance, she could just see the light of the sun.

Dawn.

A new day.

She began to walk toward that light. Slow steps because the rough rocks cut her bare feet and blood trickled in her wake.

She walked and wondered . . .

Who the hell am I?

And why did she feel like she had to *hurry?*

As if . . . as if someone waited.

CHAPTER NINETEEN

The crowd at Sunrise was even louder than she remembered. Seline walked slowly toward the dark red doors—the entrance. Demons were stationed at those doors, bouncers with glamour hiding their true selves.

She could see right through that glamour.

Two months ago, when she'd seen her first demon, Seline had thought she was crazy. She'd run from him, even as he shouted, *"If I go back without you, Sam's gonna kill me!"*

Sam.

A name she knew . . . now. She hadn't then, and she'd been terrified of the "Sam" who tracked her.

Seline pushed through the crowd that waited eagerly for a spot inside Sunrise, and she made her way to those red doors. The bouncers glanced her way. Their eyes widened when they saw her.

"Are you—shit, are you—" The one with the bald head and snake tattoos began.

Seline just nodded before he could finish speaking. "Is he here?"

The other bouncer yanked open the door for her. "Yes."

She let her eyes flash to black. "Good." All of her power was back now. Good, bad, and everything in between.

Guess they couldn't totally kill my dark side. Maybe that fact should scare her. It didn't.

She rather liked her dark side. Without it, she probably wouldn't have survived the last few months.

When she strolled inside Sunrise, humans muttered behind her, not understanding why she'd gotten her free pass. Too bad for them.

Bodies filled the interior of the bar. Dancers twisted and undulated on the stage. And in cages . . . ah, the cages were new. They reminded her of . . . well, a night that made her ache.

Her gaze searched the club.

There. Surrounded by his demons. Sam stood near the bar, tall, strong, but his profile looked more haggard. The lines on his face appeared deeper.

Sammael.

As she watched, his fist slammed onto the bar top and the mirrored surface shattered. "I don't want fucking excuses! I want her!"

Seline strode forward. With every step she took, her heart raced faster. So fast she thought the thing would rip out of her chest.

Then Sam looked in the mirror. He caught sight of her reflection. She saw him shake his head, as if denying what he was seeing.

She smiled. "Hello, Sam."

He spun around. *"Seline!"*

Before she could take a breath, he had her in his arms. His mouth crushed onto hers and, oh, it was what she wanted, what she remembered, from those fevered dreams that wouldn't leave her alone.

Dreams that she was sure she'd been sharing with him.

His fingers held her so tightly that Seline knew she'd bruise, but she didn't care. She was holding him just as tightly. *Won't ever let go.*

His tongue thrust into her mouth. She stood onto her toes and pressed her body against his. More, *more . . .* she needed him.

The dreams had started a month ago. The first one had scared her to death, and turned her on.

She'd seen a tall, dark man. His eyes had been pitch-black. He'd looked at her with such lust she'd trembled. He'd reached for her. Took her hand. Kissed her palm, then said, "I need more than dreams, Seline. *Come back to me.*"

Then she'd started finding her way home.

His head lifted, slowly, and she immediately missed his touch. "You're real?" he asked, voice gruff. "Not another dream."

"No, I'm real." She'd rehearsed her speech a hundred times, but now she wasn't sure what she should say to him.

Four months. It had taken her that long to find her way back to him.

What's four months compared to a thousand years?

He kissed her again. There was so much need in his touch. A desperate hunger. Her sex moistened instantly.

"You fell," he growled against her mouth. "Dammit, Seline, I wasn't worth the fall. You should have let me take the pain. I was going to come to you. I would have—"

She put her fingers over his mouth. "You were worth it." She wasn't going to regret any choice she'd made.

He grabbed her hand and led her away from the

bar. She saw Cole's shocked expression give way to a fast grin. "Fuckin' about time," the demon said.

Yes, it was.

The bouncers near the private room stumbled in their haste to open the door for them. Sam pulled her inside. The door slammed closed behind them . . .

Then he was on her. He pressed her against the wall, caged her with his hands, and his mouth took hers. Lips, tongue. Wild, consuming, the hunger burned too hot, and she could only gasp against his mouth and hold on.

His sensual power filled the room. So much desire. All for her.

"Don't ever leave me again." He hiked up her skirt. "Promise."

"Try to keep me away." Her hands were at the front of his jeans. She unhooked the snap, slid down the zipper. "Try."

He yanked her panties away and tossed them to the ground. Then he lifted her up, positioned her, and paused only long enough to say, "I can't be easy. Not this time. I've been *starving* for you."

Sammael. Her Sammael. "When did I ever want easy?"

He laughed, then froze, staring at her with eyes that saw *into* her. "I missed you."

That ragged confession stole her breath.

Then he was raising her hips higher, holding her with strong, warm hands, and the broad head of his cock pushed between her legs.

His gaze held hers as he thrust deep in one long, hard stroke.

Her legs wrapped around him, and she arched toward him.

She felt his control shatter. He began to thrust, to

pump, in a feverish drive. Too fast and wild. No, just fast and wild enough. His mouth was on hers. His hand on her breast, his cock sliding right over the sensitive flesh of her sex. It was perfect. It was—

Hard. Deep. Rough.

She came.

The explosion of pleasure rocked through her. He kept thrusting. Again and again, and a second orgasm built within her. The air crackled around them. She pulled in the energy. Took it, used it, and sent it right back to Sam.

The second time she came, he was with her.

His orgasm pumped into her, and Seline licked his neck. Licked, then bit.

Not easy.

The thunder of his heartbeat shook her chest. She didn't want to move. Finally, she was safe.

Just where she wanted to be.

Home.

Seline closed her eyes and listened to that fast pounding. "I missed you, too," she whispered.

Sam stiffened. *"Seline."*

Well, yeah, they'd covered that.

He stumbled back and adjusted his clothes. Seline shoved down her skirt, nervous once more now that the heat of their passion had cooled, and he was backing off. *Backing off? Since when did Sam back away from sex?*

The lust had always been the easy part for them. The emotions . . . those were a whole different story.

But Sam reached for her again. He held her tight, and they seemed to fall into the nearest black leather chair. "You're sure you're not a dream?"

She shook her head.

His breath rushed out on a relieved sigh. "I've got

demons and shifters searching for you . . . they're all over the world. I didn't know where to look—I didn't know where you'd fall."

"Colorado," she whispered. Good thing it had been a warm time of the year or she would have frozen her naked ass off.

He swallowed, and she saw the slow bob of his Adam's apple. "I didn't want you to suffer anymore."

"And I wanted my freedom."

He blinked and seemed surprised. Why? Didn't he understand?

"I wasn't free there, Sam. I couldn't *breathe*. The angels didn't seem to feel anything." *Seem.* She'd caught glimpses, though, that told her things might not have been quite as they appeared.

"You are free now," he told her, though the words were growled. "You can go wherever you want. Do what you want."

Rogziel wasn't after her any longer, but she had other enemies. "There are those who will always be after me." Vengeance. Over the years, she'd made plenty of enemies who would want revenge.

"No, you don't have to worry. They're dead."

Her lips parted in surprise. "What?"

"They're dead, or they know that if they don't *want* to be dead, they'll stay away from you." He brushed back her hair. "When you fell, I didn't want one of them finding you first, so I made sure that word spread—you're protected. *Always.*" His lips twisted. "Besides, that was the deal, right?"

The deal. She remembered another night. Same club. Different fear.

"I keep my deals," he told her as his gaze searched hers.

Yes, she knew he did, no matter how deadly those deals were.

"You helped me to find my brother, and now, if you want your freedom, I won't stop you."

Seline shook her head. "Do you think I went to all the trouble of falling . . . of having my wings burned off . . . just so that I could walk away from you?"

He blinked. Then his hands smoothed up her back. Through her blouse, she could feel the light pressure of his fingertips on her scars. Pleasure whispered over her.

Oh, wow.

Seline licked her lips. "I figure you owe me, Fallen."

His mouth kicked up in just the faintest smile, and she was sure his eyes lightened. "Seems you told me that before."

"Well, yeah, I did. Because every time I turn around, you're owing me." She tried to sound cocky and assured, but Seline suspected he saw right through her act.

"I'll give you anything."

"That's sure a different tune now." She'd had to fight her way to get his agreement before.

"I'm different. You made me that way." His fingers were still tracing her scars, and little shivers skirted over her body. "Say it, and it's yours. Tell me what you want."

Okay. Screw the speech she'd planned. Seline decided to just tell him what was in her heart. "I want you." Not for a day or a few weeks. "I want to stay with you forever."

His breath expelled in a rush. "You've got me." His mouth took hers, and the desire whipped through her blood. "Sweetheart, you had me from the moment you came into my dreams and stopped the nightmares."

Ah, what? She pulled back and frowned at him. "You—you thought I was trying to kill you then."

"Yes." He smiled at her. A real smile, one that made her heart feel funny.

She shook her head, still a little confused. "You thought I wanted to kill you, and you still—"

"Thought you were sexy as all sin."

He would know about sin.

A growl rumbled at the door, and then something hit the wood—hit it hard enough to send a long crack racing along the frame.

Seline tensed. That growl, oh, crap, not again . . . She knew that deep rumble that sounded like thunder from hell.

Hell.

"He's probably waited as long as he can," Sam said as he lifted her off his lap.

"He?" He could not mean—

The door was shaking now, because some*thing* was hitting it very, very hard.

"Um, yes, you got yourself a male hound." Showing no fear, Sam strolled away. "When you went back upstairs, you left me a present."

No, she hadn't. Not deliberately, anyway.

Sam opened the door.

A giant mass of black fur raced inside the room. The hellhound hurried toward her, growling and— jeez, was that some kind of really scary hellhound smile? The beast's tongue—long and black—hung out, and the hound sure seemed to be grinning at her.

Seline held out her hand. The hound bent his head and rubbed against her fingers. No attack. Just . . . warmth. Welcome. "How is he still here?"

Sam smiled at her again. Oh, damn, but that man was gorgeous. "You told him to protect me. You didn't send him back."

No, but—

"So he's been here, with me, waiting for you." Sam came closer and gave the massive hellhound a scratch behind his ears. "He's really not so bad, not once you get to know him."

Seline stared down at the beast. He looked back up at her with his blood-red eyes.

Pain. Blood. Death.

The hound whined and butted her lightly with his head.

"He doesn't want you to be afraid," Sam said quietly. "And neither do I." He squared his shoulders. "You said you loved me."

The hound lay down on the floor and stared up at them.

"I love you more than anything or anyone on this earth—or beyond it," Sam told her.

Okay, that sweet-talk was exactly what she wanted to hear. Seline eased over the hound and put her arms around Sam's shoulders. "Good . . . because that's the same way I feel about you."

She'd traded her wings for a life with her Fallen. Heaven, hell . . . everything in between . . . didn't matter. Paradise was staring right back at her.

Seline laughed, finally, *finally* free of her past, and she grabbed hold of the future before her with both hands.

Dangerous, dark . . . *yes, please*. She didn't want some kind of white knight. She wanted her lover with the wildness in his eyes and the danger at his back.

And the hellhound at his feet.

Seline kissed Sam and knew that paradise had never tasted so good.

EPILOGUE

When a woman walked into a bar with a hellhound at her side, people tended to pay attention. The smart people actually tended to run, the semi-smart folks froze, and the dumbasses kept causing trouble and picking on the innocent.

Well, they did until she let Beelzebub take a bite out of them.

Sam laughed when the hound chased a demon out of Sunrise.

Seline smiled at him. A month had passed. Her entire memory was back, now, even those parts that she would have preferred to forget.

And she was with her Fallen.

Had the pain been worth it?

Sam stalked toward her, his lips curved in that wicked grin that made her body heat.

Yes. She'd fall again, for him.

His back had scarred from the wounds delivered by Uriel. Hard, thick scars that stretched and reddened his flesh. Uriel had known just how to leave his mark.

Perhaps one day, she'd pay him back for that punishment.

Though she knew Sam had already gotten a pound of flesh from that angel. Sam always had a way of keeping sight of his enemies, even as he kept the ones he loved very close.

He hadn't killed Az yet. Those two had developed a strange sort of arrangement. As long as they didn't get too close to each other, then no one died.

Az had actually left town a few days before, heading off to track down some witch who "owed" him.

The Fallen and their deals. Seline guessed the devil wasn't the only one who liked to make trades.

"You here to dance?" Sam asked, his voice that low purr of temptation that always made her want to jump him and forget the rest of the world.

Seline didn't glance at the stage. She didn't need to steal any energy from the crowd these days. Sam kept her well stocked, thank you. But, because she liked to push him, she said, "Maybe . . ."

His eyes narrowed. Ah, jealous Fallen. He was learning to tease and lighten up—finally—but he could still miss the mark sometimes. Like now.

"No, I-I didn't mean—" he began, then broke off, shaking his head. "If that's what you want . . ."

Now she was the one who was surprised. "Sam?"

He turned away from her. "Everyone!" His bellow froze them all instantly. All eyes turned to him, and Sam ordered, "Get the fuck out."

Beelzebub leapt onto the bar and howled.

Everyone got the fuck out.

The hellhound followed them to the door, then he stopped, standing guard. The beast glanced back at her once, his ferocious teeth glinting, but his mouth spread in a happy grin.

Beelzebub was always trying to make Sam happy

these days. And to think . . . once the hound had wanted to eat the guy.

Sam crossed his arms and leaned back against the bar. "Now you can dance." His gaze raked her. "For me. Only me."

He was the only audience she wanted. Her gaze landed on the cages he'd installed—also for her. His confession.

He'd definitely been sharing those dreams with her as she struggled to find her way home. *Dream-walking*. The power to slip into his dreams had returned to her first, and she hadn't even realized it.

Seline caught his hand and slipped her fingers between his. "I think I have a better idea." She led him to the cage.

There were no worries about control breaking—her control broke all the time. So did his. Seline had no fears about taking too much—he gave her everything. Anything.

Sam's mouth touched hers, and the world fell away.

Did you miss *ANGEL OF DARKNESS*, the first in Cynthia's FALLEN series?

He Fell for Her

Nicole St. James was a nice woman. An innocent, pretty twentysomething schoolteacher with her life ahead of her. But as the angel of death, it's Keenan's job to take that life away. So when a vampire attacks Nicole, Keenan is not supposed to snap and take out the vampire instead. It cost him his wings—but she's worth it.

Except when Keenan catches up with his pretty schoolteacher, she's not so innocent anymore. Hot red lipstick, tight black shorts, and long white fangs— she's ready to kick the asses of anyone who helped turn her into a damn bloodsucker. Unless that ass is unusually shapely and attached to a certain fallen angel. Even with all of heaven and half of hell after them, someone will have to teach Keenan about the fun kinds of sin. . . .